Murder By
(and Blunt In… …nt)

An Alco-Noir

By

James Forbes Smith

ISBN-13: 978-1-0369-3209-1

Cover design by: Roderick Brydon

1

A Merry Little Christmas

Fresh snowfall. So pure, so innocent. Still the heavy stink of blood filled the alpine air. They would kill again, of course. Shoot, stab, or strangle another innocent somewhere on this mountain peak. So she ran. And would keep running, hidden for now while the blizzard raged. Maybe this wasn't quite the '*Wine Tour of a Lifetime!*'

Eight gunshots rang out. She screamed stumbling over the body—but no one came. On a mountaintop, the wind will swallow your voice. Staring down, she realised it was Christmas Eve; the holly berry earrings matching the crimson marks around their neck. No time for that tearful goodbye, she had to move. Close behind, the hulking silhouette, hunting her, hounding her every step.

Trembling, she placed two fingers onto her friend's eyelids and slid them over the glassy stare. Now they could be sleeping. *Let your heart be light.* Like a child waiting for Christmas morning. *All our troubles out of sight.* Unease slithered down her spine.

Wine tour of a lifetime? What a mistake. Come for the oak Malbec, stay for the pine coffin. What a dreadful mistake. Three people knew the killer's identity, the killer's secret; but as the saying went: three can keep a secret if two of them are dead.

Two more shots sounded. Something whistled past her face. Keep going, keep running, keep praying for no footprints. If only she could make it to the cable car. It was hard now dragging herself through the snowdrift, her muscles screaming as she reached the ragged edge. Dead end. Wrong turn. Collapsing, another shot rang out. The next one wouldn't miss. Surely, the secret shouldn't die on this clifftop.

Three people knew... The killer. Herself. And then there was him. Her eyes, darting out into the night, watched as a silver and dark snowflake landed on her chest. If she wasn't alive to keep the secret, then perhaps he was.

2

Sideways

Six days before the triple murder at the Old Elysium Vineyard, Martin Moretti was terminated with immediate effect.

Downsizing. Rightsizing. Smartsizing. However you dressed it up, Superintendent Radnor of Buxton Police Station had finally had enough. Booting the front door open, he tossed the dishevelled drunkard down the stairs.

'And stay out!' yelled Radnor. 'You're fired!'

'For how long?' the dishevelled drunkard yelled back, hands tightening around the rum bottle.

'Forever!' said Radnor, slamming the door shut.

Fired. Unbelievable! And a week before Christmas; could there be a worse aftertaste?

'Fine,' Martin shouted, 'you can stick your police station up your arse. Sideways!' He'd lived for policing. What now? Hurling the bottle against the building, it shattered to pieces, a trail of dark liquor running down the wall.

'Well, that's something,' said Radnor to the Sergeant by the window, 'at least he's thrown his rum away.'

'Er, Superintendent Radnor, sir,' said the Sergeant, 'he's now licking the wall.' Radnor turned in horror. Martin Moretti was indeed now desperately licking the rum off the wall.

'Jesus Christ!' groaned Radnor. It was hard to imagine this was the once great detective with a 93% conviction rate. Yanking open the window, he shouted down: 'Thought you might like to know, there was a tramp urinating up against that wall this morning.'

Ok, so maybe there is a worse aftertaste. 'Congratulations Martin,' he muttered to himself, 'you've just hit a new low.' How dare they forbid his drinking. Technically, of course, medicinal; to numb the night-time. It had been months now since he had dreamt of Sara Brambilla's face. In any case, he thought with a shrug, at least he couldn't get any lower.

Unfortunately, Martin Moretti was wrong. In the foothills of the alps, amongst the sleepy snowy vines, after three bizarre killings, he would sink a whole lot further.

3

The Invitation

The cheese and ham croissant Martin Moretti had snatched on the way home did absolutely nothing to wash away the taste of the police station wall. Neither had trudging through the festive glow of the German Market (mixed with drizzle and exhaust fumes) or hearing that evening's fifth rendition of "Fairytale of New York". Ugh, *Christmas* – tinsel and divorce.

Home was the top floor of The Eagle Hotel. He'd skipped the pub three floors below; the room was already spinning. Either it was vertigo or the alcohol had kicked in. He could have at least stolen something decent like Havana Club 7. Instead, he'd swiped Tesco Value Spiced Rum. And consequently, was fired. The end of Chief Inspector Martin Moretti's illustrious career. Police Bravery Award, 2017. Queen's Police Medal, 2019. The detective who had solved the Case of the Missing Astronaut, the Maserati Confusion and the Charlestown Cannibal.

But who could blame them. How many times in the last thirteen months had he climbed the courthouse stairs in vain? Six floors up and never a conviction at the top. "Case dismissed" due to the case of whisky Martin had drunk during the investigation. Infamously known as "the Defective Detective", he'd become a walking cliché as much as a walking bottle of whisky. Aspiring to expand his mind like his heroes —Sherlock and his 7% coke habit, Rebus and Morse and Harry Hole on the booze, etcetera, etcetera—he'd always hoped his superiors would protect him because of his arrest rate. And mostly, they did. But making an arrest is only half the battle, and when the courts turned against him so did the boys in blue. Followed by his wife. Hence, the hotel room; consisting of a bed, a small desk and a frosted window.

Still, at least now he had something to write about in the Moretti Christmas letter. Their annual unabashed family saga; infinitely worse than social media for self-congratulation. Pulling a piece of hotel letterhead toward him, Martin scanned the room for inspiration. His mum had been pestering him for weeks to top-up his siblings' shameless updates. Patrick had his pilot's licence. Kwami was now a surgeon. Chewing on his biro, Martin wondered what sounded better: gross misconduct or dishonourable discharge? The latter at least contained the word "honourable". How could he spin it? *Darkest before the dawn* sounded too bleak. *Light at the end of the tunnel*? Knowing his luck, it was a freight train.

He'd love to write how he'd taken revenge for being axed by Superintendent Radnor. The axe forgets, but the tree remembers. So how to take revenge? A paper cut; that's a tree's final moment of revenge. Theoretically, living well was the best revenge against Radnor. Then again, karma takes too long; Martin would rather paper-cut his balls now. What he needed was a crime to solve—a diamond heist, terrorist attack or a lost chihuahua—to prove them all wrong; that even on the grog, he was still a great detective. But in the absence of his Buxton casefiles, he'd need to find a different way, in a different place.

Still gazing around, his eyes came to rest on the sole item on his desk. An untouched bottle of wine with a golden label. Martin detested wine. Frankly, he'd rather drink bin juice. The bottle had arrived a fortnight ago, a thank you gift for solving the kidnapping of a young girl. Her father, Renzo, had become a close friend during the frenzied investigation. Even after the scandalous repercussions. But the gold label said more than it being a 12%, 2017 wine from the Savoie region of France. It was an invitation, to Renzo's vineyard "among the mystical diamonds of the Alps" and would apparently be "the Wine Tour of a Lifetime!"

Was he really about to go on a crappy wine tour just so

he had something positive to write in his Christmas letter? It was certainly better than what he'd written so far: *rock bottom is a solid foundation in which to rebuild from. Rock bottom will teach you lessons that mountain tops never will.* Rock bottom, he shuddered, might as well be his birthstone. Besides, what's the worst that could happen, and it would be nice to see Renzo again.

What's the worst that could happen.

If only he knew how much those words would come back to haunt him.

4

Delivered With A Plum

Twenty-four hours later, Martin Moretti couldn't feel his face. Maybe it was the travel (taxi, train, walk, Underground, bus, ferry, bus, walk, Metro, stumble, trip, train, taxi, crawl). Or maybe it was the extravagant tosser he'd confronted at the station. Or maybe, yes maybe, it was the weather. Snow flurries were falling thick and fast, swirling round his legs like a sugar-hyped toddler on Christmas morning. Whichever way, by 6 p.m., Martin felt like he'd been shaken up inside a snow globe.

'Let it snow, let it snow, let it snow... somewhere else!' Martin muttered to himself as the icy wind pushed and pulled him across the driveway. When snuggled up inside, he loved a crisp blanket of newly fallen snow. Less so—no matter how much Princess Elsa warbled on about it—in the middle of a bone-shaking blizzard. *Do You Want to Build a Snowman?* No, no I don't want to build a snowman. I want to build a sandcastle, on a beach, in the sun, with an extra-large mango Mai Tai. Martin's only footwear, the Nike Air Pegasus he was currently wearing, was no match for the snow, which had seeped through the mesh, his socks now drawing up the cold and numbing his toes. His chunky black coat, a faux fur hooded Everest parka jacket, might be padded enough to survive the damp drizzle of a Derbyshire shopping centre but, with only a t-shirt and thin scarf underneath, could be regarded as dumb, dumber and dumberer for the alpine mountaintops. Not that his Eagle Creek rolling duffle bag contained much else: one litre of Johnnie Walker, a toothbrush, two jumpers and a spare pair of jeans. Bloody idiot. Should've packed more whisky.

Was he an alcoholic? He was too cold to think about

that or anything else. Shunting open the huge, oak door, he stumbled into a candlelit entrance hall. The room was empty. Martin didn't care; it was shelter. Ahead was another oak door that had been left ajar, a shaft of light leading the way across the flagstone floor. From the other side, Martin could hear the merry clink of glasses, corks popping, the snap of a Christmas cracker, laughter. So, he wasn't the only one to receive an invitation. Who were they? Delicious smells of dinner wafted toward him. Stomach rumbling, Martin realised how hungry he was. But it was a different aroma that enticed him forward: the smell of a smoking fireplace. A chance of heat. He might be sheltered from the blizzard, but Martin was still shivering; his clothes sodden.

Cautiously, Martin peered through the crack in the door. Tuxedoed staff were rushing around a grand hall, offering finger food from silver trays. How many guests were there? It was hard to tell, though the Christmas cracker—not a French tradition—suggested an international flavour to the party. Eyes roving, Martin spotted one waitress in particular whizzing here there and everywhere; weaving in between the chaise lounges, baroque sofas, and gold leaf coffee tables to serve champagne. Martin wouldn't have felt comfortable sitting at any of them. And in the centre of the room, unfortunately, was the Christmas tree. Towering high above their heads, beaded with hundreds of purple lights, the freshly cut spruce sparkled and glittered with bright golden baubles shaped like roosters. Another dish zoomed by transporting the large football of a Christmas pudding, glorious flames of blue and orange rising around it to cheerful cries of "ooooooh!". Martin's stomach growled again, but there was no denying it, the air smelt... Christmassy; a heady mix of woodsmoke and wet clothes, mulled wine, pine needles and plum pudding. He could picture the people from Yankee Candle swooping in to bottle it.

And just as quick, the spirit of peace and goodwill was shattered as an enormous waiter carrying a clipboard burst through a side door, reprimanding one of the waitresses. It was the one who Martin had spotted here there and everywhere.

'*Vous êtes viré!*' hissed the man venomously. The waitress, not a day older than sixteen, looked terrified.

'What's going on?' said Martin.

'He is, he is firing me,' she said through tears.

'Yes, I am firing Mia,' he spat. 'For unprofessional conduct. Talking, gossiping, fawning over this Jimmy Stresskeller pop star.'

'I only said to one of the guests I am looking forward to meeting him,' she cried.

Martin nudged the door open for a wider glimpse. Warmth, food, alcoholic beverages. He was already late; but then, he never could stand by and do nothing.

'You can't fire her like that,' he said.

'There are strict rules, Monsieur Moretti,' the waiter said in a hushed tone, 'surely you as a policeman obey the rules?'

'Only when they're fair,' said Martin, wondering how the waiter knew so much about him. 'And it's definitely not fair when she's your best waitress.'

'You don't even know her,' scoffed the waiter.

Martin studied the waitress—now shaking like a leaf—and a flicker of annoyance, a sense of wrong, flared up inside him. After his father had died when he was eight, he'd helped his mother in the café where she waitressed. Sometimes the boss man can be harder than the customers. He'd have to be quick in applying his Sherlock scan, however; the pocket size bottle of Smirnoff he'd drank outside the Gare d'Annecy was wearing off.

With a twitch of his nose, he began: 'Mia is the only waitress I've seen facing outward tonight; not with her back to the room playing, I think I saw, Candy Crush, Tinder and Crash Bandicoot. You've recently put all your staff in shiny new shoes, but see how Mia's soles are already worn down. Probably because her section of the room is spotless. Take a look,' said Martin, fully opening the door, 'no empty glasses anywhere.

That's compared to three empty flutes on the mantelpiece, four empty plates on the window frame and one fork in the plant pot. She's sixteen and already showing signs of carpel tunnel syndrome with an overworked thumb holding overly stacked trays of Christmas pudding. If anything, you should give her a raise before she realises she's better off working at McDonald's.'

Blinking rapidly, Mia stared at Martin, while the enormous waiter sucked in a sharp breath.

'Erm, Mia…' he said to the floor, 'please return to your station straightaway.' With a half-glance of thanks to Martin, she scuttled off. '*Merci,* Monsieur Moretti, for talking me down. You are right, she is my best worker. How can I thank you?'

'I'll do you a deal,' said Martin quickly, 'we'll call it even once you've given me the lowdown on who these other guests are.'

'Deal,' said the waiter, swapping his clipboard for Martin's duffle bag. Scanning the board, Martin counted twelve members on the tour party.

Jimmy Stresskeller
Martin Moretti
Aubrey Dalton
Morton Kessler, Eve Kessler
Tate Sinclair, Holly Sinclair, Joseph Sinclair
Noel Gillespie
Pekoe Williams
Theo Oblet, Mary Oblet

'Monsieur, I swear I will give you the lowdown on these guests, but I must check on the crème brûlée in the kitchen first. Do you trust me?'

'I haven't been able to trust much lately.' Frankly, he'd struggled to trust anybody since the divorce.

'*À bientôt.*'

'Well, then, I better say hello myself,' said Martin, heading into the grand hall.

5

Le Château de Montrottier

'Welcome Monsieur Moretti. Chicken parmesan meatball or plum-glazed pork belly kebab?' asked a thin man with a thinner moustache holding out a silver tray.

Martin snaffled one of each. He deserved it. Not for saving the waitress just now, but the journey across the Channel had been gruelling, made worse by the altercation with the extravagant tosser; some bouffant-blonde flake in a fur coat cutting in line at the train station and stealing the last taxi. He'd literally headbutted Martin as they both reached for their suitcases.

The hall's surroundings were far more relaxing. Still recovering from the cold, Martin was less interested in the ornate coat-of-arms than the giant fireplace underneath; a roaring fire now bathing him in a toasty orange glow. Lovely.

Huddled around the mantel stood a family of three; the father vigilantly shielding his son from the flames while the mother jotted something onto a paper napkin.

'Room for a frozen one?' said Martin. Toes still numb, he gladly accepted the chilled champagne from a passing tray.

'Ha! Absolutely,' said the chiselled pale-pink American, his eyes twitching, his walrus moustache quivering as he slapped Martin hard on the back. 'It's colder than a penguin's pecker, am I right? I'm Tate Sinclair, and this is my wife, Holly.'

'How do you do?' she said with a strained smile. Meek and mild, with mousy brown hair to match her brown cardigan, the Hogwarts sorting hat would definitely place her in Hufflepuff. Martin could see her as a primary school teacher; though if she'd taught at his old school, the kids would have eaten her for breakfast.

'And this is our son, Joe.'

'Are you from Africa?' said the boy, looking up in amazement.

'Joseph!' his mother hissed, mortified.

'That's alright,' chuckled Martin. Out the mouths of babes or a reflection of their parents? Finishing off his champagne, he preferred to pick the former. 'I'm from England.'

'Shockingly, so are we,' said Holly. 'Relocated from New York. Although, we've been confined to a desolate farmhouse in the backwoods of nothingness for eighteen months now.'

'Surely you're not farmers?' asked Martin. Of course they weren't. His well-cut dark suit, plain tie, waxed moustache, and polished brogue shoes to match his polished bald head; definitely a lawyer, the type that had undermined his last nine cases. Her elaborate vocabulary, the scuffed sleeve, the indent on her ink-stained index finger. She was a writer. Her long sleeve dress was elegant but mismatched with an oversized handbag; no doubt containing half a library and a moleskin notepad. She was either unsuccessful or unfulfilled, given the three empty glasses her side of the mantelpiece. Takes one to spot one. Was he an alcoholic? Martin preferred to think of himself as an "almost alcoholic", one step before the darkness.

'Ha! Actually, I'm a lawyer,' said Tate Sinclair pompously.

'For your sins,' joked Martin.

'For other people's sins, to be precise,' smirked Tate.

'My Dad is law-some,' said the boy, poking the logs with a set of tongs. Joseph Sinclair. Eight years old. Spoilt brat.

His father suddenly jerked him back. 'Joseph, watch out! There should be a fireguard around that.'

'He's fine, Tate,' said Holly, anxiously twirling the gold bracelet on her wrist.

'Alright, but if we burn to death, I'm suing them.'

'Tate's very protective,' said Holly with a timid laugh. 'Every hotel bedroom, he ties a rope round the bed leg to hang out the window in case of fire.'

'And I thought the biggest peril was the minibar,' said Martin.

'Same,' said Holly, her shy smile as warm as the flickering light. It reminded Martin of someone. 'So, I'm ridding the world of this cursed stuff one glass at a time.'

Still slightly stung by the African comment, Martin politely excused himself and undertook a lap of the great hall. He was the only black person present. Surely Renzo didn't invite him just to be the "token" member of the tour party. No. Knowing Renzo, everybody was here for a reason. A call to adventure? A simple thank you? Was the wine bottle's gold label a prize or punishment? Was everybody here in Renzo's good books? Stomach squirming, it suddenly felt to Martin that both his and Renzo's fates were entwined together now... *after what we did.* A tray of champagne floated towards him through the laughter and the chatter so he lifted another glass. The way Martin figured it, if he was an alcoholic, what better place to hide than on a wine tour, flooded by fellow enthusiasts.

The snowstorm had passed. Veering away from both the Christmas tree and a large bowl of mulled wine, he headed out of the French doors and onto a wide terrace. Thankfully it was still warm out here. Peculiar, however, that instead of patio heaters, they were using multicoloured LED grow lights; the type he'd found heating cannabis plants in Barry Rutter's attic last week. It wasn't a difficult case to solve, it was the only roof without snow.

'Quite a view, isn't it, kid?' drawled a thick Boston accent behind him. Martin nearly dropped his glass at first sight of the man. Sweeping back a thread of combover grey hair, the hunched elderly gentleman had the appearance of a gothic vampire or an undertaker. Or, more precisely, the step before the undertaker—the one who put you on the slab. 'Can you settle a bet for us? I'm Morton Kessler, by the way,' he said, offering a wrinkled hand.

'Martin Moretti. Nice to meet you,' lied Martin, shaking it. The glow of the LED light onto his pale and pinched face did nothing to ease Martin's nerves.

'And I'm Eve, his better half,' she said with a twinkle in her eye. Short silver hair, flame red lipstick and a slim red dress, she must have been pushing sixty but nonetheless looked as sharp as a hunting knife.

'We're trying to guess what you do for a profession, kid,' said Morton. 'I said a teacher, my wife said a policeman.'

'Congratulations,' Martin nodded to Eve. 'Ex-policeman, actually.'

'I'll have to collect my reward later,' she replied, elevating his nerves further.

'Ex-policeman?' grimaced Morton, his teeth as yellow as the discoloured gold buttons on his mildewed jacket. 'You don't look sixty.'

'No, I'm thirty-two,' said Martin.

'I was going to say, kid,' said Morton, 'if you were sixty, you'd look like my wife.'

'Er, excuse me,' smiled Eve provocatively, 'I'm fifty-nine.'

'You said that last year.'

'Yeah, and I always stand by what I've said,' she replied defiantly.

'How about yourselves, what do you do?' asked Martin, keen to keep it light.

'Importer-Exporter,' said Morton. '*Mistletoe Atlantic Trading.* We're looking to handle Renzo's wine business for the East Coast.'

'We're collecting the most expensive wines in existence,' said Eve.

'Oh, right,' said Martin, 'here to check out the merchandise?'

Eve looked like she wanted to interject but her undertaker / vampire-husband cut across her. 'His vineyard and many others,' he leered. 'We welcome any venture that will increase our wine stock, which is abundant.'

'Well, variety is the spice of life,' said Martin.

'That's what ended my first marriage,' winked Eve. 'Like I always say: no trust... no us.'

'Tell me something I don't know,' Martin nodded.

'How about... your shoes have twenty-four lace holes.' She pointed at the eyelets of his sodden trainers.

'My wife is on the autism spectrum,' said Morton, seeing the confused look on Martin's face.

'Aren't we all,' said Martin warmly.

'I notice little things you allistic people miss; even detectives,' she said. 'It takes me a little time to connect the dots. But when I do, I'll always confront it head on.' Eve winked again, as she and her husband headed in for a drink. Presumably, a beaker of blood for him.

Martin turned away in relief. Morton Kessler was quite right about the view though. Underneath the dusky purple night sky, the valley was a patchwork of tumbling hills and twinkling farmhouses all leading towards—just as the invite had promised—the mystical diamonds of the Alps. For the first time in a long time, he felt relaxed. At peace. That is, until the Château's front door crashed open and in strolled some bouffant-blonde flake in a fur coat.

6

Jimmy Stresskeller

In sharp contrast to Martin Moretti, the rest of the Château seemed very excited by the new arrival. Swaggering amongst a gaggle of the tour party taking selfies, Martin overheard the words: *amazing, incredible, wow* and *hero*. The only words that sprang to Martin's mind were: *prat, git, clown* and *stronzo*.

Though lost on him, Martin could see the appeal. Beneath his feathered blonde hair, lay a handsome, bronzed face with piercing blue eyes. But then Martin remembered the face he'd seen from the taxi line. The expression on it then was very different. Now he was all smiles; in the taxi queue, he was more moody, ruthless. Had it been an accident? They'd both bent down for their suitcases, only for the blonde bush to whip his head up first, hitting Martin square on the nose. Eyes watering, nose throbbing, and shaking off a sharp, shooting pain to his brain, Martin had started to yell at him; only to find he'd already disappeared. Thoroughly hacked off, Martin had to wait forty-five minutes for another cab.

Clueless who this man actually was, Martin supposed he must be some kind of celebrity. A group of waitresses, including Mia, were gathered in a nervous, giggling whisper the other side of the French doors.

'Ask about *Coast Cop*.'

'No, ask for his number.'

'Sssh! Ask about *I'm A Celebrity, Get Me Out of Here*.'

'Ask if his victory was well-earned.'

'No, ask if he's well-endowed.' The giggling grew louder.

To Martin's horror, the celebrity sauntered directly towards the French doors. For an instant, they locked eyes.

Awkward. Fortunately, an explosion of screams broke out.

'Jimmy! Jimmy! Can we have your number?'

'Are you well-endowed?'

'Answer the second question first!'

Far from being terrified, he was relishing the attention. 'Ladies, ladies, how about an autograph?' Reluctantly, the waitresses handed over a set of serviettes for Jimmy to sign.

'Jimmy, I loved you on *I'm a Celebrity!*'

'Did you really eat that crocodile bollock?'

'Let's just say...' He clasped something into her hand. 'I'll see you later... alligator.' Striding onto the terrace, Jimmy winked at Martin as the waitress opened her hand, revealing his hotel door key. Kaboom. The waitresses erupted into a frenzied mania, bouncing up and down squealing. One giant, jumping shriek until the thin man with the thinner moustache furiously ushered them back into the kitchen.

Alone on the terrace, Jimmy grinned at Martin. The look of moody ruthlessness had quite disappeared. 'Groupies, you can't live with 'em....'

'You don't remember me from earlier today, do you?' Puzzled, Jimmy lit a cigarette; something Martin suspected was against his public image. 'I'm the guy you headbutted this morning.'

'I need more,' said Jimmy with a frown.

'Annecy train station. You barged in front of the taxi line.'

'Oh yeah! Nice to see you,' said Jimmy. Martin detected an Oxford accent underneath his faux-Cockney—mockney—accent. 'Sorry about that, I was a bit out of it from jet lag.'

'Where've you come from?'

'Paris,' Jimmy replied through a cloud of smoke. 'Apologies again about the queue. You won't tell the press, will you?'

'Would your feelings be shattered,' Martin asked hopefully, 'if I said... *who are you*?'

'I'm Jimmy Stresskeller,' the celebrity replied with a flick of his hair. He looked the same age as Martin; only with less late nights slouched in a Volvo, peeing in a bottle, waiting to arrest curb crawlers. 'You've probably seen me on TV. I played Matt Sunset in *Coast Cop*. Bafta winner 2022.' Martin shook his head and Jimmy's face fell. Why would Renzo even invite Jimmy here? Perhaps he didn't. Perhaps Jimmy found the golden label on an empty bottle down at the garbage dump. No. Everybody was here because of Renzo, either on account of a shared past or a promised future. Was there something Jimmy knew, something he was holding over him? Renzo had secrets, but to invite this pillock here now, it would have to be one hell of a deep dark secret. 'Lead singer of The Black Carnations? Winner of last month's *I'm a Celebrity, Get Me Out of Here*?' Jimmy listed with growing concern, much to Martin's pleasure. Although, a vague memory stirred at the back of Martin's mind, his voice did sound familiar.

'*TV Choice*'s Hairstyle of the Year?'

'I know where, that wig commercial!' said Martin.

'The Hercules Hair Serum!' Jimmy thundered gleefully. Then, taking a deep breath, and in perfect voiceover: 'Do you too have a tiger clawing out your hair? Simply one splash of Hercules Hair Serum and your flowing locks will lash that tiger away!'

Martin's mouth dropped open, curving into a grin. 'That's amazing, you sound just like that hair follicle that fights the tiger.'

'I am that hair follicle,' beamed Jimmy.

'You're not,' said Martin, annoyed at himself for grinning. Still, it was nice to meet a fellow Brit, if only to confirm the tour party didn't consist entirely of Americans.

'I am,' Jimmy said with a bow. Suddenly, at triple-speed: 'Terms and conditions apply. Consult your doctor before using. Side effects may include dry scalp, dandruff, headaches, hair loss, high blood pressure and explosive diarrhoea.' Martin couldn't help but laugh.

'What have you got there?' asked Martin. Jimmy was

fiddling with a plastic sandwich bag poking out of his jacket pocket.

'You really, really, don't wanna know,' said Jimmy.

'Fair enough,' said Martin. He could still remember the first time he'd heard that advert. Driving up to Edinburgh for a belated honeymoon. Happier times. Maybe Jimmy wasn't holding some deep dark secret over Renzo. Maybe Renzo just enjoyed Jimmy's company. Besides, for sure, Martin knew the most about Renzo Brambilla.

'I'm hoping these French surroundings inspire my music. Y'know, "Exile on Main St." vibes before the studio in LA next month.'

The echo of a loud gong brought them back to the present as the tour party began to gather around the Christmas tree. Apparently, there was to be a grand announcement. Jimmy headed inside but Martin didn't follow. He was in no great rush to officially start the tour; an epic excursion around a series of frozen fields being lectured on, *of all subjects*, wine. Ok, admittedly, he'd be lying if he said he didn't appreciate his new backdrop. Ornate alpine mansions beat watching the English rain from his boxroom window. But why did it have to be wine (a.k.a. glorified grape juice). The gong echoed again. Before he surrendered to the flock, Martin would finish his second glass of fizz; not that he was a fan of champagne either (a.k.a. wine put through a SodaStream). But as he liked to say: desperate times call for desperate measures; fifty millilitre measures minimum. He hadn't drank wine or champagne in years. Nevertheless, that still left Martin plenty of poisons to pickle his liver with during an investigation. He had solved his last case on a healthy diet of dry gin, dry vodka, pale ale and cask ale, tequila, whisky and rum, fruit beer, wheat beer, sambuca, stout, Guinness, limoncello, cider, and—as there was milk in the fridge—a White Russian.

Nestled under the warmth of the LED grow light, he gazed back out across the valley, ready to revive the inner peace of that purple night sky. Seconds later, however, the tranquillity was broken by an enraged couple thundering onto the terrace.

'No, Theo, you never understand no!'

'I've told you, Mary; I don't care about money.' The middle-aged pair were French, but arguing in perfect English.

'Because, Theo, you came from money,' Mary snapped with the smile of a loaded shotgun, 'but I've still got quarterly targets.' She couldn't have missed too many targets, judging from her Louboutin stiletto heels with dagger points to her razor-sharp business suit that probably cost more than Martin's entire education.

'Let me handle it, Mary, I know what is best,' said Theo, 'Or I might lose my commission.' He cut a handsome figure in the twilight, with glowing eyes fastened one minute on the valley and the next on her. Neither of them had noticed Martin. 'Maybe bury it, hide my misfortune among your safer investments?' There was a dishevelled, messy look about him but with a breezy charm. His tattered clothes seemed more by choice than circumstance. He reminded Martin of James Bond, had 007 ended up in art school. 'Think of it like a ratatouille tower.'

'You know I love ratatouille,' said Mary, conflicted.

Encouraged, Theo pressed: 'You have your courgettes, tomato, yellow peppers, but amongst all that… you hide the aubergine.' *Hide the aubergine.* Was Martin listening to a French recipe, financial crime or sexual innuendo? Whichever way, layering money sounded an awful lot like laundering money. Well tough luck, Superintendent Radnor of Buxton Police Station. If Martin hadn't been so unceremoniously sacked, he could have investigated this blundering fraud.

'Fine!' she snapped. 'But this is the last time. I hate it, I hate doing this. No more gambling, never.' The gong sounded again.

'*Bon*, I know what is best for us.' With a huge sigh, Theo properly drank in his surroundings for the first time.

'Oh! *Bonjour*.' The glowing eyes had spotted him.

'Evening,' said Martin.

Mary stepped in front of her husband. 'I am Mary Oblet and this is Theo,' she said. Tearing off her jacket, she threw it at Theo before pulling out her phone. 'Like most men, he is weak and stupid.' Swinging her dark copper-red hair so it whipped Theo across the face, she glared at Martin as she dialled. 'Pure vomit.'

'Mary, keep your jacket on, it is too cold out here.'

'I'm fine, Theo, I am under this giant heater.'

'Who are you calling?'

'Our London office, to fix this,' snapped Mary. *'Ah, bonjour Marie. Theo est un idiot. Theo est un imbécile incompetent.'* If Holly Sinclair was Hufflepuff, then Mary Oblet was almost certainly Slytherin. She stalked up and down the terrace, speaking far too fast for Martin's GCSE French to comprehend.

'Please forgive all this boring financial ratatouille talk,' said Theo, and he boyishly mimed falling asleep. 'My wife is an investment banker and the personal accountant to Renzo. Very clever. She has just made him five hundred thousand. Well, four hundred thousand, after my error. Please do forget all this, otherwise Renzo will be very angry with me. I may lose my commission.'

'Isn't this falsifying the books?' asked Martin.

'I suppose it depends on your truth,' said Theo with dignity. 'For me, creativity is truth. Love is truth. Art is truth. I am an artist, a painter, abstract mainly.' Martin could have guessed that from his white canvas sneakers.

Mary momentarily leaned away from her phone to add: 'He is yet to make it on the art scene, the procrastinating prick. He has never even completed a commission.'

'Because I am a perfectionist.'

'More like a control freak,' said Mary, before barking more orders down the phone.

'True, I am a control freak,' Theo grinned bashfully, extending his hand. 'Salutations—Theo Oblet, failed artist.'

'Salutations—Martin Moretti, failed detective,' he said, shaking it. Once more, the gong echoed around le Château de Montrottier, and Mary yanked her husband back into the hall without saying goodbye. An odd couple, reflected Martin, though no stranger than the Sinclairs or the Kesslers he'd met minutes earlier.

Finally, peace. Martin swallowed the last of his champagne and waited for the gong to reverberate a fifth time. But there was no gong. Instead, a scream pierced the still air. Martin recognised the sound. It was not the joyful scream of champagne being opened. Or the euphoric scream of a Jimmy Stresskeller fan. It was a scream of terror.

7

Mull It Over

'What's the matter?' said Martin. 'What happened?'

They were huddled around the large bowl of mulled wine, several of them shaking. A man who introduced himself as Noel Gillespie broke off from the group. Apparently, one of the waitresses was upset from something she'd seen inside the bowl. Probably the crappy mix of orange peel and cinnamon sticks, Martin suspected.

'Something bad, like,' Noel whispered with a strong Irish accent. 'Something that shouldn't be there.'

'Oh dear,' Martin grimaced.

'I never should have served the wine!' sobbed the waitress, Mia, her eyes reddening. 'Not after we received that letter.' Several of the waitresses tightened their arms around her, whilst all the waiters stood scowling and shaking their heads. Marshalling everybody back, Martin grabbed the ladle and stirred the contents. Inside the bowl, the spiced red wine swirled around with—sure enough—the orange peel and cinnamon sticks. But what else... chunks of apple? No, that would be unusual. Plus, the chunks were redder. Much redder. And then Martin knew what it was. Sick to his stomach, he slopped it onto the table.

'What... what is it?' the thin waiter asked.

'An organ,' said Martin, knowing exactly what it was. A large meaty organ. Human.

'A heart?' suggested Noel Gillespie.

'No, the liver,' stated Martin. Having solved the Case of the Charlestown Cannibal, he'd become quite adept at identifying body parts. The unhealthy state of this particular liver, however, would not have appealed to the cannibal. Dark-red, scarred, swollen and lumpy: its owner clearly had cirrhosis of the liver. Martin smiled grimly to himself, it was like looking at his own Ghost of Christmas Future.

With a collective shriek, the blood drained from the faces of the tour party. Eve Kessler shuddered; shell-shocked. Morton Kessler went from ghost-white to grey. Even Jimmy Stresskeller looked less tanned. Mary Oblet ended her business call, her overplucked eyebrows furrowed in concern, while her husband's impish grin had vanished. The lawyer, Tate Sinclair, shattered the mulled wine glass in his hand while backing his son into the far corner. His wife, Holly bit down on her lip so hard it drew blood. Only Noel Gillespie remained cool, calm and collected. That is, until he vomited over Martin's shoes. Followed by Tate vomiting over the Christmas tree. This at least distracted the staff, who were now deliberating how to wipe-clean the baubles.

Martin gazed back into the bowl.

'Sorry about your shoes,' said Noel. Wiping his mouth, he passed Martin the ladle.

'That's alright,' said Martin, 'I'd have done the same if I'd drank a glass of that stuff.' He scooped out a total of four blackened livers. How glamorous; his first day on the festive wine tour and he's fishing for livers.

'Where would someone even get hold of those?' asked Noel. Martin remembered the plastic sandwich bag poking out of Jimmy's jacket pocket. And then, he spied something even stranger. Peering closer, each liver had the initials "D.O.T." carved onto them.

'This is twisted,' spat Tate Sinclair, cleaning the sick from his tie. For some reason, he fixed Martin with a severe stare. 'Who did this? I'll be suing you!'

'It's obviously someone's idea of a morbid joke, like,' said Noel. For an instant, Martin's eyes flicked to Eve and Morton Kessler.

'And what's that written on those... things?' Tate

demanded, his eyes twitching.

'D.O.T.' said Martin, holding one up. Tate Sinclair suddenly lost his voice. Was that a brief flash of recognition in Tate's eyes? Or fear? But before Martin could quiz him, the doors of the Château opened.

'Ladies and gentlemen,' said a short man with an impressive blonde mullet, 'welcome to your alpine adventure.' For a small, courteous man, his voice was strikingly resonant. 'If you will all follow me outside, we depart immediately for wine country. Let's get this party started!'

8

The Guest List

Shepherding everybody outside, the man with the mullet was feverishly checking his list. All but one of the names had now been ticked.

'And you must be Martin Moretti.'

'That's the rumour,' Martin replied absently. He was loitering by the Christmas tree, hoping to catch Mia. It was she who, in-between sobs, had said: *I never should have served the wine... not after we received that letter.* What letter? Who sent it? And what did it say?

'Do hurry along now, please, Mr Moretti. The bus is waiting,' he persevered. Glancing down at his watch, he attempted a light chuckle. 'Don't make me use my tour guide voice.'

Martin studied this conundrum of a man: short and slim yet with a flabby double chin. His smart pinstripe suit looked to have been run over by an ice cream truck. His accent was also hard to place. South African? And then there was the hair. It's a strong look, the mullet; business at the front, party at the back.

'You sure are keen at scooting us along,' said Martin.

'It's a fine time to scoot, Mr Moretti.'

'Aren't you interested in who put the livers in the mulled wine?' asked Martin.

The tour guide swallowed, his steel-rimmed glasses steaming up as he peered over the bowl. 'Hell's spit! What is... what is that it says on them?'

'D.O.T.' Martin replied. Was that a glint of recollection behind the steamed glasses? The same glint as Tate Sinclair, but perhaps without the fear. 'I was hoping to speak to one of the staff. Mia. She mentioned a letter which I think might be connected.'

'Connected?' scoffed the tour guide. Reaching into his jacket pocket, he popped a gummy bear into his mouth, which seemed to fortify him. 'Connected to this bad joke? Clearly this is just a prank, a well-meaning but unfunny prank. Anyway, you're not a policeman here. Not even in the UK anymore.' He was as well-briefed as the enormous waiter. No doubt Renzo had prepared a dossier on everyone. 'The bus waits for our scooting. How about I get this letter sent onto our first resort?'

The kitchen was empty so grudgingly Martin agreed to follow their guide outside. How frustrating! Grabbing a glass of champagne, he headed into the entrance hall only to be tugged to one side by the enormous waiter.

'I must fulfil our deal, Monsieur Moretti,' he whispered, triple-checking they were alone. 'If you still want the lowdown on the other guests?'

'What? Oh, er, yes please.' The fetid scarred livers in the punchbowl had quite distracted Martin from their earlier conversation.

'Very well. I research all our guests prior to their visit, but I must warn you: I am known for my honesty Tourette's,' said the waiter, running his finger down the clipboard.

'Lay it on me,' said Martin.

'As you wish, monsieur.'

Tate Sinclair, Holly Sinclair, Joseph Sinclair

'The bald barrister is Renzo's personal lawyer. Helicopter parent but a jovial man; even more jovial when suing someone for every penny.'

'And his wife?'

'Ah, Holly,' he purred. 'She is a genius, a dreamer. Shy for such a successful novelist. Drinks too much, like most writers. In the first book of her detective series, it is the detective who is the killer, shooting the victim with an ice bullet. Devious!'

'What about the boy?'

'He seems... peculiar. Hides his light under a bushel, but probably the one who set fire to it with gasoline.'

Jimmy Stresskeller

'TV star turned failed pop star. He only won that Jungle show because of the disgusting things he ate on that bushtucker challenge...fish eyes, witchetty grubs, pig anus,' the waiter said bitterly. 'I watched that episode, personally it did not seem like much of a *challenge* for him, he was enjoying eating those animals.'

Aubrey Dalton

'Good-looking girl, but still... American. And strange hair. She seems lonely, spent half the night with her head between her knees as if in some terrible pain. Ambitious, I hear she is training to be a Sommelier; probably thinks she is above us all.'

Theo Oblet, Mary Oblet

'He is an artist's artist, but he's no artist. Amateur painter, amateur gambler. He is quite possessive of her, God knows why,' the waiter shuddered. 'Renzo's personal accountant, condescending, she has a sharp eye and a sharper tongue. She spends all day counting her collection of stocks, shares, and human souls.'

Morton Kessler, Eve Kessler

'Our sixty-something Bostonians, *oui?* Here to acquire the finest wines for their *Mistletoe Atlantic Trading* company. He gives me the creeps. He might move slow but, trust me, he has a killer instinct. *Effrayant* but has satisfied all parts of his life... except his wife's lust. I took it as a compliment when she came onto me, until I saw her eyeing up the Andouille sausage with equal affection.'

Pekoe Williams

'Ah, a true gentleman! Retired. Now hired as a Nepalese expert mountaineer, however likes to get high in more than one sense, *oui?*'

Noel Gillespie

'An ornithologist from Ireland but made his money in antiques. Very vain. Apparently, he has been given a top secret assignment by Renzo.'

Here ended the scathing summary to Martin, confirming every fear he'd ever had about what waiters really think of their customers.

'And what would you say about me?' asked Martin. The waiter hesitated. 'You can give it to me straight.'

'Washed up detective; drunk and divorced.'

'Well, that's certainly straight,' said Martin.

'You're welcome,' said the waiter. 'I hope I have fulfilled our deal?'

'One more thing, the letter Mia mentioned, our guide said that he'd get it sent onto our first resort. Will you ensure that happens?'

'Of course. And on the honour of the Château de Montrottier, I can guarantee those livers did not come from the apron pockets of my staff.'

The waiter vanished, leaving nothing but the words "washed up detective" ringing in Martin's ears. The truth hurts. Hurt him, at any rate. Superintendent Radnor was likely still laughing at Martin's termination. Laughing as loud as all those times he'd mocked Martin in front of the whole station; when his hands were shaking so much, he couldn't sign for the arrest warrants. "The Defective Detective" who couldn't solve a crossword for kids, couldn't track down the end of the Sellotape, couldn't hold onto a pen, let alone his wife. Ho-ho-ho. But if Martin was being honest with himself, he couldn't disagree. What exactly did he have left in this world? A key to the Eagle Hotel's smallest room and a P45.

So maybe he'd solve this little liver mystery. Show Radnor he wasn't completely useless. And when he'd figured out who had dropped them into the punchbowl, Martin would return to Buxton Police Station with a bottle of Tesco Value Spiced Rum in hand; to prove that even on the sauce, he was still a decent detective. And this time, Martin wouldn't smash the bottle against the wall but over Radnor's smarmy, self-righteous head.

Plus, there was another reason to solve it. A bigger reason. Because no matter how much their tour guide dismissed it, you don't send scarred livers as a prank. To Martin, this felt more sinister, more fanatical and—with a creeping sense of dread—more lethal.

9

He Who Sups With The Deville

Heading out, Martin was hit in the face with a fresh blast of alpine air.

'You're gonna need a bigger coat,' Martin muttered to himself; the stingingly icy wind resuming its bitter attack on his bones. His meagre wardrobe wasn't going to be enough. Maybe he'd steal Jimmy Stresskeller's mink coat? You know, as an anti-fur protest. At least now some shelter was offered by a large yellow coach, as Eve and Morton Kessler, the tour guide and Noel Gillespie threw everybody's luggage into the hold with scant regard for breakages.

Shuffling to the front of the coach, he was greeted by an impressive blonde mullet.

'You again?' Martin shivered.

'Scoot scoot,' beamed the tour guide.

Tightening his scarf to avoid frostbite, Martin spotted one person who was seemingly immune to the cold. Standing in front of the coach in a short pink dress was a girl hysterically waving a "MARRY ME JIMMY!" sign. Heart warming, thought Martin, if his cardiovascular system wasn't compact-ice.

As if Martin needed any further motivation to scoot, somebody pinched his bum. Spinning around, he was met with a wink from Eve Kessler. He wasn't particularly flattered. Martin had spotted her winking at all the waiters; so frequently he wondered if she was having a stroke.

Bounding up the stairs, Martin thawed into the wonderfully warm air of the coach. It was like stepping into a wood-burn pizza oven. Bliss. Not quite as warm was the monosyllabic grunt Martin received from the bus driver, his large sweaty Algerian football shirt not large enough to cover his potbelly.

Most of the tour party were already aboard, quietly brimming with excitement. Making his way down the black carpeted aisle, Martin spotted the two faces he'd yet to meet; a distinguished-looking gentlemen, who must be Pekoe Williams, and a young woman who'd wrapped a large pair of headphones around a bright-blue bob of hair. This must be Aubrey Dalton.

Tate Sinclair was lecturing his son on how to survive a bear attack. 'Brown: lie down. Black: fight back. White: say goodnight.' On the other side of the aisle, his wife, Holly, was staring nervously out into the night. Like Martin, she had brought a glass of champagne with her. Mary Oblet was barking down the phone to an office subordinate. Her sharp eyes lingered on Martin fleetingly before dismissing him. Her husband, Theo, was cheerfully sketching a melted snowman onto the back of his hand. Thankfully, Jimmy Stresskeller was distracted from making conversation, signing a large pile of autographs; or possibly restraining orders. He appeared oblivious to the pink-dressed groupie outside his window.

Martin, relieved to see the gothic vampire and his salacious wife planting themselves at the front, chose the very back row. The coach engine rumbled to life just as Noel Gillespie, the man who had vomited over Martin's shoes, crashed into the seat next to him. Before they could say more than "hello", a voice crackled over the sound system.

'Ladies and gentlemen, welcome to the Alps.' Twirling a microphone, the tour guide was grinning at the passengers, as if nothing could have delighted him more than to see them all there. 'A lot of people have been wondering about my accent. Some have said Australian… and others, slightly more offensively, South African. I am in fact, Swedish.' A collective "Aaaah!" rang out. 'My name is Sven Lindblom and I will be your guide for the wine tour of a lifetime. Why are you here and what will make it so special? All will be revealed,' Sven snickered over the tannoy. 'But for now, sit back, relax and I will say hello again when we get closer to our accommodation.'

With a great lurch, the coach pulled away from the house, nearly knocking over the groupie. The Château staff were lined up on the front steps. No waving, no smiling, just silently watching; stiff and still like a row of mannequin dolls. Where exactly had they all disappeared to when Martin searched the kitchen? And then he saw her. Mia. The waitress he'd been looking for, her reddened eyes fixed meaningfully onto him; imploringly. Was it some kind of signal? But, in an instant, she had vanished from view as the coach rounded the corner and down the driveway.

It struck Martin as odd that nobody seemed overly upset by the livers in the mulled wine. Didn't anyone believe in a sense of wrong anymore? The coach was grumble-free. And that included the man sitting next to him, Noel Gillespie. True, he was frowning, but it was more of a permanent frown line.

'Decent digs,' said Noel with an Irish lilt, 'hope the place we're staying's as nice.' Underneath a sweep of grey hair, lay a weather-beaten face which suited him.

'Your accent, Cork?' asked Martin.

'Very good, for a Brit,' said Noel. Martin smiled, more to himself; redemption for having missed the tour guide's Swedish accent. 'I hear you're a detective?' News travels fast. 'I'm an ornithologist, a birdwatcher. In a way, we're both detectives, wouldn't you say?' He didn't wait for Martin to reply. 'You are a detective of crime as I am for birds. For you, the villain. For me, the feather. I've found some of the world's rarest birds. Yellow-eared parrot. Philippine eagle. Mariah Carey. That last one was a joke.' Martin would have laughed if he'd paused. 'I've even made the front cover of *Bird Watcher's Digest*, on my thirtieth birthday.' Instantaneously, a copy of the magazine was thrust onto Martin's lap. The magazine was dated twenty years ago, placing the birdwatcher at fifty.

'Wow,' said Martin. What amazed him was that the thirty-year old Noel on the cover looked exactly the same as the fifty-year old he was now sitting next to; the same sweep of grey hair, the same weather-worn wrinkles. He hadn't aged. Or rather, he'd aged really fast and then stopped ageing; kind of like a middle-aged Peter Pan.

'I know, I'm amazing,' chuckled Noel without irony. 'Famous, like. I photographed two of the rarest species of bird in the world—the Madagascar Pochard and the New Catalonian Owlet-Nightjar—both within six months.'

'So what's your favourite bird?' asked Martin, showing polite interest.

'*Chrysolophus pictus*,' stated Noel. 'The golden pheasant, from the western forests of China. It's how I first met Renzo, he shares my passion.'

'Is that why you're here, to swap feathers with Renzo?' asked Martin.

'I've an assignment, a secret mission,' said Noel with a satisfied smile, 'to find a bearded vulture and photograph it in the wild. Preferably in the mountaintops above Renzo's vineyard.'

'A vulture?' said Martin.

'A bearded vulture. The legendary bird of the Alps, the largest, one of the rarest raptors in Europe. It only inhabits high mountainous areas, nesting on high rock ledges, like.' He rapidly raised his eyebrows up and down for dramatic effect. Did he want applause? Martin wasn't sure whether he liked Noel or not. He was pleasant in his way, but who carries around a magazine with their own face on it? For twenty years.

'You ever been to France before?' asked Noel.

'No, never.' Not that Martin was seeing much now. It was pitch-black outside, impossible to see anything beyond the trees whipping by.

Martin knocked back his champagne as the coach hurtled down another country lane. What did D.O.T. stand for? Using all of his detective-cunning, he Googled it. Over three billion answers in 0.51 seconds. Shifting into the corner, he scrolled through the results. There was DOT Foods, a North American food distribution company. Door of Time... Days of Thunder... Department of Tourism... Usefully, Wikipedia informed Martin that a dot is a small, round spot. There was the Department of Transportation, which at least referenced alcohol testing. This one looked interesting, it was the—

'Nice watch.'

'Excuse me?' said Martin, looking up from his screen.

'Your watch, the Omega De Ville,' said Noel, 'it'd be safe to say it's admired by all antique experts.'

'I just thought it was some old timepiece,' said Martin.

'No, you didn't.'

'Excuse me?' blinked Martin.

'I'm an antique expert,' said Noel.

'Of course, you are an antique, that doesn't mean you're an antique expert,' said Martin.

'No, seriously,' said Noel, 'that's how I made my money. I came across a lucky find at Elmwood & Flannery Antiquities. A mahogany duck from the seventeenth century.'

'There's money in those wooden ducks, then?' said Martin.

'If you're rich and stupid,' said Noel with another satisfied smile. Takes one to know one, Martin reasoned. 'Helps to pay for my binoculars, that's for sure.'

'Amazing, so an antique expert *and* a bird watcher,' said Martin. 'When do you sleep?'

'Never when there's free champagne, like. I'm guessing you'd agree,' said Noel, eyeing Martin's empty glass. 'I drink it more to toast the year ahead, like, and hopefully some redemption too. I've made some bad decisions over the last year... a calamitous judgement, which surprises me, I'm normally perfect. I should've taken the job into my own hands, like, and out of his liver-spotted hands.' When did this man breathe? 'I suppose my only weakness is I'm a bad judge of character but, over a glass of champagne, you seem a decent fella,' he added, confirming to Martin that he was indeed a bad judge of character.

'Well, birds of a feather drink together,' said Martin, turning back to his D.O.T. search results. Deed of Trust... Director of Technology... of course it wasn't just "some old timepiece", but he didn't need Noel Gillespie telling him that. Damage Over Time... Donald's Orange Tan... Didgeridoo or Trombone... a 1973 silver Omega De Ville is more of a formal dress watch, but Martin still wore it day to day. It was the only thing his father had left him.

Devil Or Temptress... Denver Omelette Trading... Martin gave it up as a bad job; instead, staring out of the window. Noel glanced out as well; Martin suspected, more to check his own reflection. Watching the blur of dark scenery, Martin tried convincing himself that—apart from the annoying man sitting next to him—he had a lot to be grateful for. *Every night, before you go to sleep, list five things you are thankful for in life.* That's what all of those mindfulness, well-being bullcrap books tell you. He'd read a lot of them over the last six months. Most nights, Martin found it difficult listing anything positive. Slim pickings with no wife, no friends (almost all of them had chosen "Team Stella") and now no job. But tonight felt different. Perhaps it was the fine food and drink. Or the exotic travel. Or the fact that, right now, he truly had nothing to lose. He felt reckless; devil may care. And, until the next rent was due at least, it was liberating.

So... firstly, he was grateful he'd packed a bottle of whisky in his suitcase, allowing for a proper drink before bed. Secondly, he was grateful the bullet from Barry Rutter's pistol last week had only grazed his shoulder. By and large, he was grateful he'd resisted the urge to hire ninja assassins to take out his ex-wife and new partner.

Next, his career. He'd accomplished a lot over fourteen years on the force, with only two regrets. One: not once did he get to draw up one of those country manor floor plans you always find at the start of murder mystery novels (he wasn't counting his diagram during the Trafford Centre's spate of dirty protests). Two: Martin had never fully solved the kidnapping of Sara Brambilla. Yes, he'd found her, but not what was really behind it. Aside from that, he'd been an amazing detective; right up until he was axed.

Lastly, he was grateful this wine trip had given him the D.O.T. liver mystery; something substantial to write about in the Moretti Christmas letter (and hopefully solve before the letter was sent in seven days), rather than filling it with yet another cliched t-shirt slogan, like: *the world is your oyster.* If Martin was being perfectly candid, his oyster was half empty, lying on a bed of other oysters, next to a sewage pipe.

Not now, however. Not now Martin was off on this tour of a lifetime. Renzo Brambilla, a man of excess, that charismatic millionaire, was opening the gates at last to all the secrets and magic of the Old Elysium vineyard; and Martin was one of the twelve lucky people allowed inside. The gold label on the wine bottle reminded Martin of Willy Wonka's golden ticket into the chocolate factory. Closing his eyes and settling back into his seat, Martin amused himself picturing Oompa-Lompas running around the vineyards.

Just so long as we don't all get bumped off like Augustus Gloop and Veruca Salt, he half-smiled to himself.

As If.

Moretti Christmas Newsletter

Status: **Draft - Version 1**
Date: December 17th (7 days until deadline)

Compliments of the season, dear famiglia,

You may have heard, I've left the police service. Great news - time to rethink life, time to clean up. 2023 will be my year and I'm looking forward to it already.

First step: quit drinking. Easy. I've done it a hundred times. So you'll be pleased to hear I'm off the sauce.

In sum, no more booze.
Merry Christmas and a healthy New Year,

Martin
P.S. Screw it. I'm drinking the Johnnie Walker.

10

Le Château des Allues (murder location #1)

The wine tour of a lifetime officially began the next morning. This did nothing to brighten up Martin Moretti. What did brighten him up was the view outside of the tall chilled window. It had snowed all night, covering everything as far as he could see. Springing from the four-poster bed, he bounded downstairs (one of the advantages of passing out in your clothes). No matter how many times the songs on the radio had promised it, Martin had never seen a white Christmas. A partial-cloud Christmas. An annoyingly sunny Christmas. A constant drizzle Christmas. But never a white Christmas. Barrelling outside, he nearly crashed into a woman scraping snow from the path. But what a view. A giant white quilt had blanketed the garden; now sparkling, crisp and crunchy underfoot. Fluffy pillows hung on the hedges and in the trees. Today was December 18th. They were staying in the Alps another week. Martin fancied his chances of that white Christmas.

Unsurprisingly, he was not the only tourist out here. Excellent. If Martin was going to solve this liver mystery, he must observe every guest / suspect. There were four others outside; Theo and Mary Oblet, plus an opportunity to meet the remaining two members of the party: Pekoe Williams and Aubrey Dalton. Well, one of them. Martin did at least catch a blur of blue hair as the young woman in an Adidas tracksuit went jogging by. Bright, cobalt-blue hair. Nowadays, there didn't seem as much judgement about appearance—piercings, tattoos, hair—which suited Martin just fine. Before he'd joined the police, he'd been stabbed in a pub simply for being black.

Theo and Mary Oblet were arguing again. To one side, lay a field sketching easel with a blank canvas and an unopened pot of paint. The tops of his trainers were still pristine white. *He is an artist's artist, but he's no artist.* Pacing anti-clockwise around a frozen koi pond, 180 degrees apart, circling so many times surely the fish were dizzy, Mary yelled: 'I'm sick of this, Theo. Stop gambling the account money. I wish I could summon the strength to leave you.'

'But you'd miss my charming disposition,' said Theo with puppy dog eyes. 'And, besides, you'd regret it when I'm a famous artist.' Whether it was their pile of cigarettes or the dirt from their shoe soles, the snow had been ploughed up, trudged round and round now into thick yellow mud and icy water.

Once more, the bickering couple spotted Martin too late. Exchanging a curt nod with Mary Oblet, Martin caught a steely glint in her eyes. The backbone behind Renzo's millions.

'*Bon matin*, Monsieur Moretti,' said Mary abruptly. 'I apologise for last time we met, I don't know if you remember —'

'When you called all men weak, stupid and pure vomit?' Martin had some blanks from last night, but he could at least recall that.

'I forget the detail,' she said with a thin smile. 'Anyway, that was just my Frenchness coming out.'

'Mary, Mary, quite contrary,' said Martin wryly.

'Actually, I was named Maria; changing it was my first rage against the world,' she said. 'But anyway, I didn't really mean it yesterday.' Martin gave a pacifying shrug but she'd already reared back to Theo. 'You will never be a famous artist,' she snapped, lighting a cigarette.

'I value art. I value love. Both are hard,' he said airily.

'You procrastinate too much… due tomorrow, do

tomorrow!' Martin edged away as they began circling each other again.

More static than the others was the distinguished-looking gentleman smoking on a long-stemmed cherrywood pipe (so much for the clean alpine air). The herbal scent, and content, of his pipe would have concerned Martin far more had he still been in the employ of His Majesty's Police Force. Instead, he simply stood beside him to share the vista. The sweeping views across the valley to the snow-capped Bauges mountain peaks were mesmerising. Utterly enchanting. Even the memory of his fretful search over the Southern Fells six months earlier couldn't destroy the magical charm of these mountains.

On a blistering hot day in June, Renzo's daughter disappeared from the top of Broad Crag. Swiped so swiftly, the mountain must have swallowed her whole. And with it, any hope of return. A mountain has seen all kinds of death, without a doubt unmoved by each tragic demise. But only three days later, a delivery boy rode down a quiet side street in Whitehaven and, through the brass letterbox, spotted her woollen hat.

'Hypnotic, isn't it?' puffed the man, turning to shake Martin's hand. 'Pekoe Williams.'

'Martin Moretti. Nice to meet you,' he said, delighted to have finally met another person of colour. 'Pekoe Williams,' Martin repeated, 'unusual name.'

'That's *Major* Pekoe Williams,' he said, 'when I was in the Gurkhas. Retired, now of course.' Martin should have guessed; the neat side parting, tidy clothes, rigid stance, the light moustache. 'You can blame my unique name on my Welsh father. He met my mother whilst backpacking in Nepal. Which makes me a mongrel, I suppose.'

'Aren't we all,' Martin grinned. 'My father swapped the black-man-in-Italy-experience for the black-man-in-England-experience.'

'What was the difference?' asked Pekoe.

'The weather. And the pasta,' said Martin, removing any resentment from his voice. 'Anyway, then he married a nice Jewish girl. And had me.'

'Mazel tov,' said Pekoe. 'I'm sure we can find some fizz around here to celebrate with. That's when I'm not on the clock for Renzo, of course. I seem to remember doing the majority of the work for him back in our Cambridge days, and not much has changed in thirty years.' Cambridge. That made a lot of sense to Martin. He didn't want to sound elitist, but there was no other word for it, Pekoe was... sophisticated, the exact kind of person who should be on a wine tour. Perhaps reading Martin's mind, Pekoe added: 'Though I'm not here for the wine. No, presently, I'm personal sherpa to Renzo.'

'And you don't mind that?' asked Martin, sensing some underlying bitterness.

'Do what you love and love what you do, as they say. Renzo has always indulged my passion for mountaineering, amongst other things,' said Pekoe, with another deep puff of his pipe. 'Most publicity shots of millionaires at the top of the mountain are just of themselves; all smug, gloating smiles and an expensive pair of Oakleys. The sherpa is always invisible, holding the bags in the background. But not with Renzo. Every mountaintop photo... he's pulled me right in next to him, shoulder to shoulder,' Pekoe said proudly.

'Must claim a lot of lives, rock climbing,' said Martin.

'Better to die than to be a coward.' A church bell rang out in the distance, but it couldn't break the spell as Pekoe and Martin fixed their eyes back to the snowy mountain vista. Martin could happily stay here all day.

'Wakey, wakey, eggs and bakey,' giggled a voice behind them. Sven Lindblom, officiously twiddling his fingers behind his back. 'I see you have met the number one mountaineer in the Alps. Anyway, breakfast is served so scoot-scoot yourselves to the table.' Turns out the sight of a mullet can shatter an unbreakable spell. Easily.

There were no eggs or bacon at the breakfast buffet.

Instead, there were home baked cakes and croissants and tarts, artisan bread, brioche, homemade yoghurt, jams, cheeses and smoked ham from the local area; which more than made up for it. As did the surroundings. The Château was actually a 12th century farmhouse that had been beautifully restored, filled with French chic paintings, antiques and bursting bookcases. Renzo had hired out the whole place, purely for their party, so there was no danger of disruption from the ski twits.

'Here, you've gotta try this yoghurt, it's phenomenal,' purred Eve, forcing a spoonful into Martin's mouth. Martin didn't think he'd ever hear the words *phenomenal* and *yoghurt* in the same sentence, but he had to admit it was pretty damn good.

All twelve of them sat around the table, their plates never empty as the hosts busied themselves refilling cups of coffee and bowls of granola. The woman he'd seen jogging —Aubrey Dalton— was freshly showered and buried in a book entitled "The Wine Bible". Eve was counting how many cornflakes were in her bowl. It had to be an odd number explained her deathly-pale husband with a lopsided leer. Jimmy Stresskeller was choosing the best angle to take a photo of his croissant and applying the "Ashby" filter because apparently his Instagram followers preferred the vintage look.

In contrast to the gentle warmth of their hosts, Mary Oblet unfortunately ticked the French stereotype of snootily looking down on her British, Irish and American counterparts; scrunching her nose up in disgust at Morton Kessler's multiple crimes. He was—horror of horrors—*buttering* the bread that he'd—controversially—*sliced* before placing it onto—brace yourself—his *own plate*. And when Tate Sinclair requested a bottle of ketchup for his ham, she clucked so loudly she nearly fell off her chair. Her husband Theo, at least, politely nodded along with Pekoe, Holly and Joseph Sinclair, as Noel Gillespie boasted about being the world authority on eccentrically-named birds: the yellow-bellied tit, the tufted titmouse, the dickcissel, the blue-footed booby, the Andean cock-of-the-rock and the red-rumped bush tyrant. Martin was about to interject that the last was a nickname for his ex when Sven Lindblom re-appeared, bundling them out to the coach fortunately before Noel's lecture on the fluffy-backed tit-babbler.

Outside, the bus driver, Omar, was raging. Their transportation had been defaced. In huge letters, "D.O.T." had been freshly scratched down the side of the coach. But how fresh? Martin wondered, rubbing his hand over the damaged area. Conceivably it was done last night at le Château de Montrottier, the scene of the livers; nobody would've spotted these scratches in the darkness. Or fresher, from this morning? Potentially Aubrey on her run? In truth, anyone could have slipped out. Though one thing was certain. Whoever vandalised it must have used a knife. Scratches simply remove the paint. But a cut from a knife causes the paint to split into a V-shape, the outside edges now slightly raised.

'My coach! My coach! Who has done this to my beautiful coach?' Omar shrieked, his popping eyes throwing accusatory stares as everybody quickly scuttled onboard. Sven looked a little glum as he shovelled a fistful of gummy bears into his mouth. This, at least, seemed to comfort him.

The distinguished gentleman-Gurkha, Pekoe Williams, signalled as Martin approached, playfully patting the adjoining seat. At the back, Martin spotted Noel, who was waving at him with another *Bird Watcher's Digest*. Adjusting his watch, Martin sat instead next to the sherpa.

'The D.O.T. bandit strikes again, I see,' said Pekoe grimly, watching Omar out of the window. 'The livers in the punchbowl was bizarre. Probably a good thing we scramble out of here for the day.'

'Is that true what Sven said,' asked Martin, 'that you're the number one mountaineer in the Alps?' Pekoe gave a small nod. 'Impressive.'

'Of course, I figure it helps when the Alpine Climbers AGM gets wiped out in an avalanche.' Pekoe shrugged with a smile. 'And, you know, they never count the mountain goats, but I'll take it.' Was he joking? Martin couldn't help but chuckle anyway.

Out of the window, Martin spotted the groupie from last night; still in a pink dress, still carrying her "MARRY ME JIMMY!" sign and still apparently immune to the cold. How had her legs not turned blue? Whatever hot chocolate she was drinking, Martin wanted some. The coach began to move. Half laughing, half weeping, she chased after them. Groupies. It's a fine line between dedicated and delusional. *Fanatical*, Martin considered. Maybe that's what "fan" was short for? Running until the coach gathered top speed, the groupie fell back and waved. Several seats in front, Jimmy gave her the royal wave; Tate and Morton Kessler guffawing along with him. Martin watched the girl disappear into the distance, mentally jotting down a new suspect for those scratches down the side of the coach. Jimmy's wave changed to a V sign as they turned the corner, and the girl was gone.

The overhead speakers crackled to life as the coach wheeled out of the village. 'Hey, good morning, ladies and gentlemen, welcome to Savoie. And in case anyone is wondering about the weather, today's forecast is cloudy with 100% chance of wine.' Sven was holding the microphone so close to his mouth that his cackling laugh convulsed along the whole coach and slithered down Martin's spine. 'Here among the mountains and lakes, we will find some of the world's rarest wines, with over twenty-three different types of grapes. And those grapevines will be planted on these mountain slopes, anywhere from 820ft to 1800ft high.' Several of the group gasped in amazement. Martin figured he'd give it another thirty seconds. 'Despite that elevation, Savoie vineyards enjoy a surprisingly warm and unique microclimate, mixing our southern sun exposure with the cooling effects of the rivers and lakes. So, here, you will find the grapes share the space along with apricot, fig, olive and even almond trees.'

'Now, here's where things get fascinating,' Sven said,

optimistically in Martin's opinion. 'Savoie wines are secret wines! Possibly before you received your bottle with the golden label from Renzo, you'd never even heard of, or tasted, a wine from Savoie. That is because we consider any Savoie wine which gets beyond Lyon as an export.' Sven's snigger turned into a snort. 'Fun fact: only 8% of the wine production is exported outside of the area. But please be assured, we will drink many wines today. Deep red wines with flavours of raspberry and sour plum, or cinnamon and white pepper. We will drink light, clean and fresh white wines until we are at one with the crisp mountain air.' Holly Sinclair shuffled in her seat with interest. Was it the poetic phrase or the promise of booze? 'And gone are the days— goodbye!—where Savoie wines are merely ski chalet wines, only good enough to make fondue with. On this tour, we will meet the heroes who are eliminating that rude misconception and restoring the reputation of Savoie wines. First, we will visit the village of Cruet and the legendary Monsieur Philippe Grisard.'

Everybody around him was listening avidly but Martin's mind drifted out of the window. Personally, he was more impressed with how the French dealt with the weather. At this time of year, flurries brought in over one metre of snow every day. Yet during yesterday's taxi ride, Martin had watched with astonishment their daily practice of gritting and snow ploughing; shortly before the police pulled his cab over to check for snow tyres. He could have emitted a Sven-like snort of his own when comparing it to back home. Just one inch of snow was enough to grind the UK to a halt. Not that the UK fared much better in the heat; two days of sun and people are already complaining "it's too hot". The only weather the UK can cope with is drizzle. Trusty, reliable drizzle.

Racing down a tight street of wooden-shuttered houses, the coach veered sharp left and, to Martin's surprise, pulled up outside a large stone building: "PHILIPPE GRISARD, VINS DE SAVOIE."

'That was quick,' said Martin to Sven, as everybody

excitedly piled out. 'We must have only been on the road for ten minutes.'

'Finally, you appreciate the scooting,' beamed Sven.

In spite of the bright blue skies, everyone darted into reception to escape the biting wind; everyone except Martin, who was in no rush, and Sven, who loitered for Martin while fixing his shirt collar. Through a fresh blast of snowflakes, the Swede was changing from a cornflower-blue tie into a purple one. Grinning at the bemused look on Martin's face, Sven said: 'Fun fact: I have a morning tie, afternoon tie and an evening tie.' To Martin, Sven's facts were never fun. What would the enormous waiter say about their tour guide? *Officiously giggly with a scary passion for wine,* probably.

'Why am I here, Sven?' said Martin, stuffing his hands into his coat pockets. 'And when are we actually going to find out why this is the wine tour of a lifetime?'

'All will be revealed before long, Mr Moretti,' said Sven, waggling a finger annoyingly at him.

'How long?' urged Martin.

'Before long,' said Sven firmly. 'Nevertheless, I still have a way, right now, to turn that frown upside down.'

'I seriously doubt that,' said Martin.

Confidently, Sven reached into his crumpled pinstripe suit and pulled out an envelope. 'It's your letter, the one you wanted from that waitress.'

Martin opened it immediately.

11

Loose Tongue, Wicked Hand

Typed on crinkled, yellow A4 paper, Martin Moretti read and re-read the letter.

> To the disgusting frog Renzo,
>
> Close down your vineyard now!!!!
>
> You are as mad as a box of frogs to think people love your wine. It is CRETINS like you who are damaging livers and lives. Stop selling your SWILL!!!! You know no more about making wine than a frog knows about bedsheets.
>
> End your vile Old Elysium vineyard or we will END YOU. We know your movements. We have already got rid of several of you. Like a frog in a pot, we will turn the heat up on you
> slowly until you boil to DEATH!!!! You will not even know you are dying. Until it is too late.
>
> D.O.T.

Questions exploded inside Martin's head. The fact that the word "frog", derogatory slang for a French person, was written four times was suggestive, and not only from a xenophobic perspective. For one thing, it signalled this wasn't personal against Renzo; or, certainly they knew very little about Renzo himself. Renzo Brambilla was Italian, not French. So, who or *what* was the target of this poison pen letter? The vineyard? Specifically, his Old Elysium vineyard or vineyards in general? *We have already got rid of several of you.* Was that the royal *we* or plural? How many people were behind this? And what the hell did D.O.T. stand for?

His mind was racing. He needed a beer to slow his thoughts down. Once he had a refreshing flavourful beer inside him, Martin could undertake a proper Sherlock-scan of the letter and envelope, and then the jumbled pieces of this jigsaw would fit together. Just like Asterix's magic potion, Captain America's super-soldier serum, and Popeye's Spinach, beer was his superpower; unlocking his brain's full potential. Except, there was no beer here. Only wine.

'How did the letter arrive?' asked Martin.

'By post, obviously,' said Sven, tapping the stamp on the envelope. 'Renzo said you were a good detective,' he added, shooting Martin a sceptical look.

'But why did the waitress have it and not Renzo?'

'I didn't want to bother him, just with an unfunny prank,' said Sven, glancing at his watch.

'Really? You don't think it's more sinister than that, this person?' said Martin.

'I am quite sure they are a little bit naughty,' said Sven with a shrug and glimpse at the time. 'It's a bad joke but the good intention was there, for sure.' That was the second time Sven had dismissed D.O.T. as a well-meaning prank. The road to hell is paved with good intentions, Martin reflected. Go vegan, go viral, quit Twitter, learn a language, floss, stretch, travel, lose weight. Even Martin had uttered that immortal phrase: *I'll never drink again*. Eight hundred and thirty-two hangovers later told Martin everything he needed to know about good intentions.

'Why was it sent to the Château de Montrottier?' asked Martin.

'Renzo owns the Château,' he replied with a third peek at his watch. Behind Sven, their bus driver, Omar, stretched his arms to the skies and belched. With a second burp, he started to rub at the coach scratches in the vain hope of wiping away the metallic scars.

'Yes, but why there and not to the Old Elysium vineyard?' said Martin, as he pocketed the letter.

With a final shrug and mumbling something about scooting, Sven headed into reception. Teeth chattering, and left deeply unsatisfied by his answers, Martin reluctantly followed. At least now he had something to distract him during today's outing. Sneakily concealing an assortment of yawns behind his scarf, Martin tuned in and out to what their Swedish guide was saying. There was something about destemming, pressing and pipeage, cold stabilisation, grape types and the rare opportunity at this winery to try a white Mondeuse wine. By eleven a.m. Martin was crawling up the walls with boredom. All the workers, at least, seemed jolly; jangling crates of green bottles from one room to another while whistling away (Martin pleased to pick up Jean-Michel Jarre rather than Jingle Bells).

'Mind the steps,' said Sven, as they descended into a slightly damp, slightly musty cellar. 'They are very slippy. It would be a shame to lose you before the tasting.' Weighing it up, Martin wondered if there were pubs inside French hospitals. Why did Renzo invite him out here? If he wanted to thank Martin for finding his daughter, why not a tour of the Scottish whisky distilleries? Or a ticket to space? Or an Aston Martin DB9? Or a better divorce lawyer to ensure he kept the car. Renzo knew Martin hated wine. He'd literally jumped out of his chair at Martin's violent rejection to share a Chardonnay during their first visit to The Old Sun Inn.

The tasting came earlier than expected with a tactical midpoint stop. A solitary wine bottle had been laid out on a table surrounded by "Philippe Grisard" glasses.

'A Precious Pinot gris, 2015,' said Sven, 'a patchwork of subtle and delicate nuances.' Although his priority was pouring out half-inch dollops of the golden wine, he still managed to unleash a fresh wave of puns: *Chardonay or should I go now, I heard it through the grapevine,* and *the vintner takes it all.*

They crowded around Sven like a piranha feeding frenzy; followed by—after being spicy on the nose—moans of delight. Martin strategically tied his shoelaces in the shadows. They were an effervescent group. So why did he feel so lonely? His police psychiatrist would say: *the sun is alone too, but it still shines*. Then again, his police psychiatrist had continually pushed on a door marked "pull" at Bella Italia, before ordering pineapple on his pizza.

'This wine is bold on the second sip, yes? Let me tell you why it is challenging your palate to a duel,' said Sven, the party nodding dumbly at each revelation. To break the monotony, Martin played the game he'd invented during his ex's dinner parties—who's most likely to be a serial killer?—which was both fun and practical; after all, there were currently twelve active serial killers around the world. You never know. So... Holly, the crime writer? It's always the quiet ones, plus she'd know a thing or two about murder plots. Her husband, the lawyer Tate Sinclair, could he have more than one foot in the criminal world? And then there was the son, Joesph; because, y'know, you always need a left-field choice. Eve Kessler? Indisputably a predator, but murder wasn't the purpose of her prey. As for her husband—the creepy, spooky and altogether ooky Morton Kessler—enough said. Sven's efficiency gave him the best laid plan. Pekoe? With the lethal hands of a Gurkha, he'd likely killed before. Noel, self-proclaimed to be perfect; did that stretch to the perfect murder? Nevertheless, Mary Oblet, all bitter and bile, had to be the top suspect. Unless her husband, Theo, was using his victim's fresh blood for paint? But then, he couldn't even finish a simple art commission. As for Aubrey Dalton, he still needed to make contact.

Climbing the stairs, Martin found himself at the back of the line with Holly. As thin and nervous-looking as before, her face was almost completely hidden behind her mousy-brown hair and the set of fingernails she was chewing on.

'Do you have a pen on you?' asked Holly. She'd given up her lumbering handbag, instead now carrying a moleskin notebook.

'Sure,' said Martin, handing her his Bic ballpoint.

Scribbling something illegible into the notebook, she passed it back. 'Writing a book?'

'Two books,' replied Holly, adjusting her vivid red scarf against an otherwise drab outfit. 'One for business, one for pleasure.' He'd forgotten the warmth of her shy smile. It reminded him of Sara Brambilla's smile. Specifically, the smile from her missing person poster.

'Which is for pleasure?' asked Martin.

'*The Woman and The Wasp*. It's a murder mystery.'

'No kidding? So, busy thinking of ways to bump people off?' joked Martin.

'Busy plotting,' said Holly, still twiddling the gold bracelet on her wrist. 'A good murder mystery plants the key clue before the murder's even taken place, before the reader thinks they need to pay attention.'

'Well, fair play for grinding out a living from the scribbling. Must be hard. I've got a friend, older than you, that writes Young Adult. Lucky if he sells ten books a year. Gutting, all that work and what does it get you? I mean, how many copies did you sell last year?'

'Three-hundred thousand.'

'Right. right… not too shabby,' said Martin, pencilling in to bang his head against a wall later. 'I heard in your first book the killer was the detective,' he said, remembering what the enormous waiter had told him.

'Trust no one,' she said coyly.

'Amen,' said Martin. 'What's the second book you're writing?'

'It's why I'm here,' Holly muttered. 'I'm ghost writing the official autobiography of Renzo Brambilla.' She let out a glum sigh, but by the top of the stairs she'd shaken off the gloom and said more cheerily: 'Not for nothing, I'll give props to Renzo, he's interesting enough—like he's born from Dionysus and raised by Blake—but I should be writing about one of the female-greats like Florence Nightingale, Joan of Arc, Carrie Nation, Qiu Jin, Boadicea or Beyonce. I've toured the backroom and kitchen of both establishments we've visited, and all the staff speak very highly of him. Annoyingly makes a success of everything he touches.'

Martin was about to test if she knew what nationality Renzo was, only for Sven to dramatically drum his hands on a large wooden barrel and announce that he was a "barrel of laughs". Shockingly, most of the group chuckled. Tate Sinclair, who'd become hyperactive since his glass of wine, even joined him for some double drumming.

Marching by another long line of oak barrels, it reminded Martin of *Ali Baba and the Forty Thieves*. If he hid in one now, he could get away from the group. Perhaps on the outside there was a bar in the village; with Leffe, Kronenbourg, Kwak, Despérados or Pelforth Brune? Sensing a safe audience, he whispered the idea to Holly who smiled.

Heartened, Martin continued: 'It sounds a little alcoholic, but I figure who'd spot another alcoholic in the middle of wine country.'

'Where does a wise man hide a pebble?' Holly recited. 'On the beach. And where does a wise man hide a leaf? In the forest.'

'Hey,' said Martin, excitedly grabbing her arm. She winced and he immediately removed it. Not the done thing in the twenty-first century. Or probably any century. 'That's Father Brown, isn't it?' Holly nodded, pleasantly surprised. 'My ex-wife was an English teacher, some of it must have rubbed off.'

'Crazy about the livers in the mulled wine last night, wasn't it?' Holly blurted. It must have been playing on her mind. It was probably playing on all their minds.

'A nasty little Christmas present,' said Martin. 'Still, beats last year's Secret Santa. Some grinch just gave me the leftover Bounty bars from the Celebrations tub.'

Holly laughed, but then looked quite serious. 'At any rate, I don't think any of us will plunge a cup into a punchbowl ever again.' Martin agreed with her but was kicking himself; he still hadn't discovered what was inside Jimmy's sandwich bag.

Ending on a gratuitous drum flourish, Sven scooted over to a large barrel that had been tipped onto its side and began to ramble on about the grapes being stirred and fermented and macerated.

'Now the fermented grape is pressed,' said Sven, rolling the sleeves up on his suit. 'This process is tedious.' Martin vigorously agreed until realising he was the only one. Apparently, this was something called "decuvage", which in French must have meant "digging for grapes" as Sven plunged a hand inside the barrel and pulled out a handful of dark red sludge. Martin turned away in disgust, not because this pulp became wine, but the red slop reminded him of a particularly nasty Belfast investigation involving a chainsaw.

The warring couple, Theo and Mary Oblet, had branched off from the group and were quarrelling again. Sniggering, Jimmy Stresskeller sidled over to Martin and said: 'I might write a song about this.... "Wine Not Whine". What do you think?' The pretentious pronunciation of "*h*whine" confirmed to Martin that Jimmy was secretly quite posh.

'Ok,' said Sven, now with a red-stained hand, 'let's talk about mixing.' The group strolled past six towering silver vats —Tate saluting each of them—whereupon Sven droned on about the dangers of acid imbalance and aromatic deviants. This last word caused Eve Kessler to turn and wink at Martin. Maybe she just had conjunctivitis? 'Next, the wines are left to age for up to four years, allowing the wine to develop. And then, each February or March time, the earlier vintages will come out of their barrels, ready for bottling. Fun fact: right here, they will package up to twenty thousand bottles per day.' Tate gave this fact a hearty round of applause. 'And now, ladies and gentlemen,' announced Sven, running both hands through his mullet, if you follow me, I will finally reveal why you lucky twelve are here, why you are the chosen ones exclusively invited to visit the Old Elysium Vineyard.'

Tate gave this announcement an even louder ovation.

Holly, however, rolled her eyes playfully at Martin as she drifted back to her husband. Martin enjoyed her company. Which made his next encounter all the more strange. As the rest of the party funnelled down a narrow-arched passageway, a small hand pulled Martin back. It was Joseph Sinclair.

'Come on, lad,' said Martin, 'let's catch up with the rabble.' The hand kept tugging. For eight years old, the Sinclair's son was surprisingly strong.

'H-h-help me,' the boy trembled. Behind his spectacles, Joseph's wide eyes were darting around the room, his red hair all frizzed up as he raked a hand through it. 'Are, are you, are you a policeman?' Martin didn't correct him. Instead, he nodded encouragingly for Joseph to continue. 'I'm, I'm scared.'

'What's wrong?' asked Martin.

'She, she hurts me,' said Joseph, biting his lip, the grip on Martin's wrist now urgent.

'Who does?'

'She hurt my tongue... she pulled it,' he said, swallowing. 'She's got a knife here, she says she'll cut it off.'

'Who?' Martin repeated, his eyes now darting to the archway.

'She says... she says she's going to kill me soon.' More and more questions ricocheted inside the ex-detective's head. But, dropping his hand, Joseph ran through the archway leaving Martin alone in the bottling room; shaken.

Surely not his own mother? But who else could he mean? Who else from the tour could he possibly know?

12

Aubrey Dalton

Two death threats on one tour. Suddenly wine country was much more intriguing. Was it simply make-believe, the boy's imagination running away with him? Either way, concocting that your own mother planned to kill you was pretty vivid. Was this the real murder mystery Holly Sinclair was plotting? If, indeed, Holly was the "she" Joseph was referring to. There were plenty of other possibilities among the tour party. Deeply disturbed, Martin joined the others.

'Welcome back, Mr Moretti. We're all now reunited, partners in wine,' Sven said with a titter. 'Sip, sip, hooray.'

At last, they'd reached the one place everybody had been waiting for. The tasting room. And though a set of "Philippe Grisard" glasses rested on top of a barrel, the party were drawn to the treasure displayed on the marble table; an abundance of uncorked wine bottles.

'Here we have my favourite wine of the moment... Fleur de Savoie, it offers aromatic complexity on a bed of spices. Light straw in looks...' Sven buried his nose deep into the glass and inhaled, '... and honeyed vanilla on the nose. So, the promise of the name is fulfilled!' A serious set of faces were leaning closer and closer to Sven as he waffled on about how to hold and swirl your glass; as if they weren't just waiting for Sven to pour the next drink. Sure, they might pretend they're more interested in the seven types of corkscrew or the difference between a stopper and your bunghole, but Martin didn't buy it. 'This wine is the perfect accompaniment for the most refined dishes—foie gras, scallops, fish in fresh herb sauce—that would satisfy the most sophisticated palette.' Sven inclined his head and toasted Theo and Mary Oblet. Haughtily nodding back, Mary suddenly stiffened to her husband's kiss.

'Now let's move to this very complex but very accessible red wine... the C'dhuysan. Mysterious and confidential, see the purple reflections in the light, smell the notes of maple syrup, taste the lively cherry-plum flavours.' With a new glass in hand, the party lined up like school children on their best behaviour, each enviously eyeing the glasses already poured, each hoping their furtive smile would convince Sven for an extra millilitre. 'So, be careful, because this wine will seduce you.' Privately, Martin was thinking Eve Kessler had more chance.

'And speaking of mysteries... why are you lucky twelve all here? And why is this the wine tour of a lifetime? The second question will remain unanswered for the time being. But I can satisfy you on the first point.' Sven allowed himself a small giggle. 'So, why has Renzo invited you here to the Alps? We are all here to launch his first ever wine. His debut!'

There were murmurs of excitement from the group.

'It is created purely from Mondeuse grapes; Savoie's most famous red wine grape. If Pinot Noir was the drink of the twentieth century, Mondeuse is surely the one for the twenty-first.' The murmurs of excitement were rising. 'We will drink it upon arrival at the Old Elysium Vineyard. Renzo's wine is thrillingly peppery yet nicely light. It is a masterpiece that will be called... *Vautour Barbu*!' The party stared back vacantly.

'Bearded Vulture,' Mary snapped, rolling her eyes at their ignorance.

'This will be Renzo's crowning achievement and—once Mr Sinclair has navigated us through the legal hoops, loops and red tape—we will help launch it; to coincide with the publishing of Renzo's autobiography,' said Sven, tapping his nose knowingly at Holly Sinclair. 'I will stir up the publicity, made possible when Mr Noel Gillespie, here, hopefully discovers the bird in the mountains above the vineyard. Nevertheless, I am still desperately seeking other ways to capture the imagination of the public; to hook them in...' He trailed off, lost in troubled thought. At the back, a fidgety-Joseph knocked a glass off the barrel top. It shattered on the tiled floor, jolting Sven back into the room as Tate triple-checked his son over. 'The wine label,' he continued as if there'd be no delay, 'will be designed by Monsieur Oblet's artwork.'

'Nearly there,' said Theo with a bashful grin.

'And celebrity-endorsed by our superstar Jimmy Stresskeller.'

'I live to give,' said Jimmy with a bow.

'The Kesslers, Eve and Morton, will help us distribute it to the world,' said Sven, 'and then, all that's left to do is for Madame Oblet to count the euros as they come flooding in.' He rubbed his hands in glee.

'What about me?' said Joseph, kicking the shards of glass by his feet.

'You, Master Sinclair?' beamed Sven. 'Well, you're just lucky to be here.'

'And what about me?' said Aubrey. It was the first time Martin had heard her speak. Another American. Californian. 'Am I here to taste or judge the new wine or something?'

'Definitely not,' sneered Mary derisively; and Aubrey flinched.

'Ah,' said Sven, adjusting his purple tie, 'I'm afraid, Miss Dalton—'

'Ms. Dalton,' said Aubrey firmly.

'Ms. Dalton, your reason remains a secret; even from me. Only Renzo knows the answer.' He swivelled back to the tasting table, ready to uncork another bottle.

'How about me?' said Martin.

'Secret.'

'And me?' asked Pekoe.

'Also, secret. You three are a riddle, wrapped in a mystery, inside an enigma,' tittered Sven. 'So, now our brains have been filled up with knowledge, let's fill our bellies with wine.' As everybody but Martin bounded forward for another glass, he caught a glimpse of Aubrey; looking as disgruntled as he felt. Pekoe's face, however, was inscrutable.

Once suitably lubricated, they were steered towards the wine shop; Tate Sinclair leading the charge. Now was his chance. With another strategic tying of his shoelaces, Martin whispered: 'Joseph. Joe, are you ok?' Until now, the boy had been clamped to his father's arm. For protection?

'Save me,' Joseph said in a strangled voice, nervously eyeing his parents.

'Apart from your mum and dad, who else do you know here?'

'No one,' he whispered. Did that confirm it was Holly? 'Save me,' repeated Joseph breathlessly, as his father torpedoed over to them.

'Heya Moretti, enjoying the grand tour?' said Tate.

'Absolutely,' lied Martin. 'And you?'

'I love everything about France,' said Tate. 'Beats England. Heck, might even beat my hometown of N.Y.C. We've been here about a week, so far. First half of the holiday's for the wife, the cultural part; charity gig at a French hospital and this wonderful wine tour. Next week is for the big kid and little kid,' said Tate, ruffling Joseph's red bush of hair. 'Disneyland Paris. We're doing one of those breakfasts with Snow White.'

'A Snow White breakfast, how much is that costing?'

'Two hundred euros.' Martin whistled as Tate dragged his son back towards the gift shop. 'I know, right! For that, I'd want to sleep with her.'

Surely his wife wasn't a killer? Dismissing further thought until he had a beer inside him, Martin glanced around. Not everybody had stormed the shop. Still standing by the marble table was Aubrey Dalton, pouring a dribble's worth of wine from each bottle into a new set of glasses. That was another thing that annoyed him about wine. They never pour you a proper measure. It's always one measly finger of wine, Martin reflected. *A finger. We lost a finger rescuing Sara*

Brambilla.

Perhaps just a distraction until he could unlock the mysteries of Joseph Sinclair's terror and the poison pen letter, but Martin kept drifting back to the kidnapping of Renzo's sixteen-year-old daughter. And why not. After all, that was why he was here.

It was stifling hot in Whitehaven on Wednesday 13th June. Suffocating. *Too hot.* The delivery boy, on spotting the woollen hat, had called his mother who called the hotline who called Inspector Martin Moretti. Breaking down the front door, the terraced house was empty, rented in a false name. The parched yellowing lawn led to a wooden shack, seemingly held together by a tangle of ivy that had snaked inside the shed. The interior was equally disappointing to Martin; no kidnapped girl, only a soiled picnic rug. Hope withered, his gingham shirt sticky with sweat as heat beat down on the shed. No matter how many times Martin filled his empty coffee cup from the corner sink, his throat stayed dry, his mind far cloudier than the clear warm water he knocked back. Nevertheless, among the logs, spiders, a discoloured gnome, used candles and a rusted Swingball set, they found a ticket stub for "The Rum Story" at Whitehaven harbour. Racing there, the museum was turned upside down delving through the shop, courtyards, cellars and bonded warehouses. Nothing. He and Renzo canvassed the area after hours. Still nothing. And then, Inspector Martin Moretti was somewhere around his fourth glass of Jefferson's 1785 Extra Fine Dark Rum in the Courtyard Café when the pieces fell into place. Why was the water from the shed crystal clear unless somebody else had recently used the tap? There were no flowers in the backyard, the burnt and straw-like grass clearly hadn't been watered all summer. Somebody was being kept alive in the woodshed. And so, *we lost a finger rescuing Sara Brambilla.* Constable Kendrick's little finger, to be precise. Lifting up the steel floor hatch underneath the soiled picnic rug, Constable Kendrick's sweaty hands had slipped, dropping it back down and crushing his left hand. Scurrying forward, Martin and Renzo heaved it open a second time. Bright blue strobe lights flashed behind them, illuminating—as feared—a deep rancid pit. And yet, Martin never could have imagined what he found inside of it.

A clink of wine bottles shook him back to the present. Keen to finally meet the elusive blue-haired Californian, he made a beeline to her table.

'Aubrey Dalton, I presume,' said Martin.

'Martini Moretti, I presume,' Aubrey replied.

'It's Martin, actually.'

'Super sorry.' Her tone dripped sarcasm. 'I assumed it's Martini 'cause of how much you drink.'

'I've not touched the wine today.'

'Your bones still reek of booze,' she said.

'Still a better aroma than this bin juice,' said Martin.

'Hell no! Grenache smells divine. Nebbiolo smells heavenly.'

'Why don't you just buy one of the jasmine and orange candles from the shop? It's cheaper.'

'Nope, I can't do actual citrus,' said Aubrey. 'How 'bout you, what bouquet do you prefer – antifreeze or lighter fluid; presuming you actually are an alcoholic?'

'You look pretty thirsty yourself,' said Martin, observing the line of glasses. 'So why do you pour so little?'

'Tsk, weren't you listening to Sven?' Aubrey said with a sardonic smile. 'Have you no culture? You never fill the glass more than a third of the way up. That way, it leaves space for the aromas to collect.'

'Fascinating,' yawned Martin.

'It's the same reason wine glasses are tulip-shaped, they curve inwards at the top so the scent can't escape. And swirling the glass before tasting aerates the wine to help release those aromas.' Her green eyes shone bright as she whirled a glass of vintage red. And whirled. And whirled. Martin was beginning to wonder if the wine had spent less time in the bottle. Was it a wine glass or hourglass?

At long last, she took a small sip, making one of the strangest sounds Martin had ever heard. Holding the wine in her mouth, yet still inhaling, she seemed to be sucking on the liquid; as if pulling it through an invisible straw. There was a look of intense concentration on her face now as, following this bizarre slurping, Aubrey rolled the wine around her mouth, swishing and swilling it like mouthwash.

'Are you having a stroke?' asked Martin. Pursing her lips, Aubrey spat the liquid out, a thin jet of wine landing perfectly inside the spittoon bucket.

'Woah, woah! What are you doing?' cried Martin.

'I thought you didn't like wine,' said Aubrey.

'Just hate to waste good ethanol,' shrugged Martin. 'People spend too much time tasting wine; not enough time drinking it.'

'So try some, Martini,' said Aubrey.

'What's that one called?' he asked.

'Etraire de la Dhuy.'

'See, I usually don't drink anything I can't pronounce.'

'And *I* don't have time to get drunk,' she said, tapping the spittoon, 'or a social life, or friends.' Maybe Martin wouldn't make such a beeline for her in future. 'My life begins, and ends, with wine. It puts me in a zen state of mind. I drink twenty different wines a day.'

'Really?' scoffed Martin. 'Surely you'd have to start in the morning.'

'I do,' said Aubrey. 'I taste five wines before breakfast.'

'You need to get yourself an Egg McMuffin, love, far more nutritious.'

'Wine puts me in a zen state but call me "love" again and I'll punch you in the throat,' said Aubrey with a smile that didn't quite reach her eyes.

'And just when I thought I'd left violence behind,' said Martin.

'Soldier? School teacher? Security guard at Hamleys?'

she asked.

'Detective.'

'That's cool,' said Aubrey, 'first interesting thing you've said all day. I like a Raymond Chandler paperback myself.'

'It's how I'm able to detect the sarcastic disdain in your voice,' said Martin.

'Whereas I'm able to detect a floral aroma of geraniums,' said Aubrey, burying her nose deep in the glass.

'I thought that was your perfume,' said Martin, taking a sniff.

'Nope, don't wear perfume,' said Aubrey.

'Why, because of the citrus smells?'

'Because wearing perfume or aftershave interferes with the aroma, even flavour, of the wine.'

Jimmy Streskeller barged over to them. 'You know why all American women should wear makeup and perfume? Because they're ugly and they stink.' This time it looked like Aubrey Dalton was the one punched in the throat. He swaggered off again, the only one of the three laughing.

'I'd tell you my plot to kill him if I weren't in the presence of such a globetrotting supercop,' smirked Aubrey. 'But I guess for you everybody must be a suspect, yeah? Just like everybody looks like a criminal in their passport photo. Here, I'll show you mine if you show me yours,' and she flashed her passport of a younger spaced-out geek, still with blue-bobbed hair.

'Oh, no thanks, I don't have mine on me,' said Martin, feeling it dig into his back pocket. No offence to Aubrey. He had a hard time trusting anyone.

'Anways, I guess a detective's not as glam as they make out in the movies. No actual Sherlock Holmes breakthroughs,' she added dismissively. 'Ever diffused a ticking bomb?'

'No.'

'Arrested the evil twin brother? Or a shifty butler?'

'No.'

'Left-handed killer who's pretending to be right-handed?'

'Still no.'

'Fallen in love with the femme fatale?'

'No,' he lied.

'Apprehended diamond smugglers?'

'No. Actually, yes.'

'Shut the front door!' said Aubrey, finally interested. 'And you actually discovered the diamonds? Where were they?'

'Buried in the plant pot of the tulips not leaning towards the window,' said Martin. 'How's that for Sherlock?'

'Sheer luck, more like,' said Aubrey.

'In my first week as a detective, I found a hidden panic room behind a Jackson Pollock painting hung upside down. That was after a bottle of Rolling Rock beer. Last month, I helped an assault victim too embarrassed to admit his assailant was a champagne cork. That was after a bottle of Jameson.' Aubrey couldn't help but give a quiet round of applause and Martin responded with a slight bow. 'And then I started drinking three bottles a day and got sacked.'

'You know, that last part's not as impressive as you probably think it is,' said Aubrey.

'To be honest, those cases were the exception,' said Martin. 'The majority I solved via a mix of CCTV, fingerprint, random witness, guilty confession, or—like you said—sheer dumb luck.' *Plus, what Renzo and I did.* 'What do you do?' asked Martin. He couldn't remember what the enormous waiter with honesty Tourette's had said about her.

A strikingly resonant voice chimed in: 'Chop, chop, last chance to shop!' Giggling to himself, Sven escorted them over to the wine racks. Neither Martin nor Aubrey purchased anything, but the group had more than made up for it thanks to Tate Sinclair.

'I guess a case of wine is excessive,' said Tate, eyes twitching. 'Make it two!'

'I thought you said you hated that wine?' whispered Holly.

'I do, horrible stuff. It's for when your parents visit.'

Buying a further two cases of the Fleur de Savoie, Tate capped it off with a single bottle of vintage wine worth twelve thousand pounds. Martin's eyes were watering as Tate ogled the bottle at arm's length before perusing the label. Twelve thousand pounds. For one bottle of wine. His father never made twelve thousand pounds in a whole year. Imagine drinking a year's salary in one night.

Distracted, Eve Kessler had snuck up on Martin, standing dangerously close to him.

'Afternoon,' said Martin, more to break the silence. 'I assume you're buying a bottle?'

'Never assume,' said Eve with a honeyed purr, 'unless to smash the ass out of you and me.'

'But didn't you say your company's collecting the most expensive wines in existence?' said Martin.

'Size matters,' winked Eve teasingly. 'I want bigger.'

'Well, I assume that doesn't disregard your husband?'

'I'm always overlooked,' said Morton, rolling his sunken eyes. Martin jumped out of his skin. 'It's the secret to my success, no one sees me coming,' he added; having just proved his point.

The next few wineries blurred into one. Domaine Bouvet, Domaine Jean Vullien, Domaine des Côtes Rousses. Each, aside from the Christmas decorations, the same as the last:

the cellar, the barrels, the mixing, the bottling, the tasting,

the cellar, the barrels, the mixing, the bottling, the tasting,

and always, *always*, exit via the gift shop.

Déjà vu all over again. Words like *organic*, *passion*, and *herbaceous* had lost all meaning. Did *Cru* mean growth, or village, or a superior vineyard? Equally befuddling, despite being in France, all the wine labels were emblazoned with the Swiss flag (which, as Sven quipped, was a big plus).

At six o'clock, the coach arrived back at their lodgings. Thankfully, there was no sign of the groupie loitering outside. But it had been a long, long day. Six days, three hours and thirty-two minutes to go. They'd dropped Sven in the nearby town. He was popping into the hospital to pick up some aspirin; apparently after tonight's festivities they'd definitely need it. How wonderful. More wine. How very wonderful. One faint glimmer of happiness came in the form of Omar. After much persuasion (twenty euros), their coach driver had picked him up a pack of Kronenbourg 1664. The group's dinner, apparently a lavish French feast, was scheduled for eight.

Which gave Martin just two hours to solve the mystery of the poison pen letter.

13

McMystery

Splashing two-handfuls of water over his face, Martin stared out into the large marble-tiled bathroom. He needed to wash the day off. In spite of the pleasing lack of French spoken on tour, all this winery talk was like a foreign language. He felt excluded; isolated. Well, for the next two hours there would be zero talk about which fancy-pants wine was the perfect accompaniment for which delicately dainty dish.

With a final toss of cold water, Martin headed into the bedroom, avoiding his reflection; there'd only be disappointment staring back. Carefully laying out the letter and envelope onto the bed, Martin began his Sherlock-scan. The good thing about a can of Kronenbourg is that it perfectly pairs with the other five cans. Downing the first, Martin cracked open a second can.

The letter was written on crinkled, yellow A4 paper. Paper? Slightly thicker, actually, a thin piece of cardboard. Typed. Not from a printer, but from a typewriter; given the indents on the page, as well as the consistently skewed positioning of the letter "Y". Crinkled, of course, having been rolled through the typewriter as well as residing all morning inside Sven's crumpled suit jacket. But why yellow cardboard? Simply the first thing to hand? Art shop? School project? Legal pad? Or, the backing from something else?

Opening another beer, Martin examined the envelope. Addressed to Renzo at le Château de Montrottier, the envelope was typed as well; each line unevenly spaced. The postmark over the red stamp in the top right corner confirmed—thanks to Google—it had been sent locally; only two days before the livers-in-the-punchbowl incident.

Maybe it was time to switch detectives. Sherlock Holmes was physical forensics, Hercule Poirot was psychological forensics. Besides, there was no point going down the physical-fingerprint route. Martin estimated the envelope had passed through at least ten sets of hands, including his own, *La Poste*, Mia the red-eyed waitress, Sven, but remarkably not Renzo's. Also, annoyingly, he wasn't a police officer with access to a forensic lab anymore. With a violent shudder, Martin tried to shake off his looming fears for the future. The thought of life without his police badge had hounded him ever since Superintendent Radnor had chucked him out of Buxton Police Station. Martin had lived for policing. So, what now? Live off Jobseekers Allowance and unemployment benefits? Win the lottery, then take to beekeeping or vegetable marrow growing? He didn't know how to do anything else. Frankly, he didn't much want to either. Opening another Kronenbourg, he re-read the letter.

Yes, D.O.T. was passionate... fanatical... but it would be dangerous to read too much into the exact wording of these poisonous threats. By now, Martin's police psychiatrist would have eagerly ticked the boxes: aggressive behaviour, low self-control and cognitive distortion. For Martin, the colloquial phrases were more telling, helping to pinpoint a geographic location, but even these seemed a little mixed-up. "You are as mad as a box of frogs" suggested someone British. Yet the phrase "you know no more about making wine than a frog knows about bedsheets" suggested an American. God only knows what country uses both "swill" and "cretins"? Germany, probably.

Martin rubbed his face impatiently. He could do with jump-starting his little grey cells with something stronger than beer. Arriving at le Château des Allues, they'd all been greeted—alongside a set of woolly gloves and hat—with a complimentary bottle of Cremant sparkling wine. Concluding it firmly remain his bathroom doorstop, Martin suddenly remembered he had a small slosh of Johnnie Walker left from last night. Result! He snatched it from the bedside table, spinning off the bottle cap. Perhaps it was time to merge both detectives (Shercule Polmes?). He held the letter to the light. Nothing. Sniffing it several times, there was... something distinctive. Finishing the whisky, he inhaled the letter again. Definitely distinctive. Bergamot, black pepper and lemon. *Jesus*, maybe the wine tour *had* corrupted him. He reached for another Kronenbourg. The letter had a faint smell of disinfectant; specifically, the kind of green soap you find in a hospital to clean medical instruments. And yet... sniffing again, there was a hint of smoke; which surely wouldn't be found inside a hospital. So where else would you find green soap?

He was halfway through his fifth can when it hit him. Green soap was used at tattoo parlours and piercing studios to help sanitize and clean a client's skin. Which would make sense with the yellow cardboard, used as the backing sheet of tattoo thermal transfer paper. Martin had used it himself when outlining his own design. Two years ago, as a desperate gesture to keep their marriage alive, he'd had his wife's name, Stella, tattooed onto his left arm. Following their divorce, Martin simply added the word 'Artois' underneath. He could still remember sitting in that hydraulic tattoo chair, feeling as useless as the yellow backing sheet itself. After some further research—in Google we trust—Martin discovered there was a tattoo parlour named "Blacked" only a seven-minute drive away from le Château de Montrottier.

'Easy-peasy, Barcardi breezy,' murmured Martin. Piece of cake. It should be routine from here on in: find the parlour, learn D.O.T.'s identity, solve the case, then stick it to Radnor. Congratulating himself with the sixth can, he checked his watch. Nearly dinner time. Switching from a blue jumper to a yellow jumper, he headed downstairs; still with the tattoo parlour on his mind. Admittedly, it was a pretty weak theory, however in the absence of any other facts, Martin figured

"Blacked" was definitely worth looking into; if only to escape Sven's tour for a few hours.

Sitting in an antique high-backed chair, amongst a collection of porcelain plates and other *objets d'art*, was the woman he'd nearly crashed into on the snowy path that morning.

'*Bonsoir,*' said Martin. Clearly there were no hard feelings as, gurning at him, she pushed on a wooden wall panel. A concealed door sprang open and Martin strode down a curved, darkly-lit stone staircase; emerging into the most festively decorated room he'd ever seen. Though no electrics, the cellar was illuminated by a blazing fireplace and generous scattering of candles. Most of the party, now merry and wild, were sitting at a long wooden table; sniffing and swirling their glasses of brick-red wine. A garland filled with red ribbons, candles and pinecones ran the full length of the table. Despite all the swirling, they were knocking it back pretty quick. Even Aubrey didn't have her spit bucket tonight.

A few steps behind him, the warring French couple arrived. While Theo breezed down the stairway, Mary barged past with the look of thunder slapped on her face; the revellers shrinking into their seats.

The customary Christmas tree, sparkling with gold baubles, stood in the corner next to Sven, who was playing a portable music mix of "Now That's What I Call Christmas: Volume Two". Tate Sinclair was, just like the first time they'd met, standing by the fireplace; jovially preening his walrus moustache in the mirror. This time, however, without his wife or son. Perfect. Sven and Tate were the exact pair Martin needed to speak with, the very two who'd recognised the D.O.T. reference when he was fishing out the livers.

'Room for a frozen one?' asked Martin.

'Ha! That's slightly *déjà vu,*' said Tate, 'but as it's a French phrase, I'll allow it.'

'Lost your wife?' asked Martin, pleased to hear he wasn't slurring his words. Trusty old lager, he could pound 'em all day and not be bouncing off the walls.

'Headache, putting Joseph to bed. We won't see Holly til morning.' The American lawyer seemed more interested in Jimmy Stresskeller, who was holding court at the table; an empty wine glass in one hand, a fresh cigarette in the other.

'No joke, it was like something out of a cartoon,' Jimmy chortled, and the group chortled back. 'She threw the banana peel out in front of me. I literally stepped onto it and slipped, slipped right on my derriere.' Martin noted his mockney accent starting to slip as well. Probably taught at boarding school to eat a banana off fine china with a knife and fork.

'Who is she?' asked Aubrey, amused.

'Same woman who chased down our coach this morning. Camille Duval. She's my stalker, Cammy is. She sent me this through the post last week as an early Christmas present,' said Jimmy, pulling up his shirt sleeve to reveal a chunky gold Rolex watch.

'That's got to be worth three thousand quid,' said Noel, followed by astonished-whisperings around the table. Even Pekoe removed his pipe long enough to let out an impressed whistle.

'You can't keep it?' said Aubrey. 'She's obviously seriously deranged.'

'I know, it's wrong to accept but, um... I really want it,' said Jimmy with a flick of his feathered hair. 'Anyway, back to the banana story. So, I was playing snooker down my local boozer, *The Earl of Oxford* pub...' More like, his dad was the Earl of Oxford, thought Martin; and he slunk over to the Christmas tree.

'Good evening, Mr Moretti,' said Sven, beaming with happiness. 'Everything alright?'

'Everything except your answer to my D.O.T. questions,' said Martin.

'Oh no,' groaned Sven, 'not D.O.T. again.'

'Why are you ignoring it?' urged Martin. 'You should go to the police.'

'Absolutely not! Do you think I have frickin' elves in the attic?' said Sven, tapping the side of his head. 'As well as being Renzo's tour guide, remember I am also his publicist, so I keep us far, far away from any negative energy. Now, I'd much rather talk about something else.'

'Alright,' said Martin, 'how about, why is this the wine tour of a lifetime?'

'Hell yeah!' Aubrey shouted up from the table. 'I wanna know that as well.'

'Same here,' said Morton with a lopsided leer.

'Me too,' said Pekoe. Sitting at the gloomy end of the table, only the Oblets were uninterested in the merriment.

'Ah ah ah,' said Sven, wagging a finger at the table. 'That's off the record, on the QT and very hush-hush.' He grabbed a handful of gummy bears from his inside pocket for moral support.

'Come on, Sven,' smirked Tate. 'As a lawyer, I say that golden label bottle was a binding contract obligating you to disclose such information.'

'Too much, too soon, Mr Sinclair,' sniggered Sven. 'The answer is scheduled to be revealed tomorrow night. Until then, my lips are sealed,' he added, zipping his mouth shut.

'I deserve to know now,' said Noel, playfully slamming his fist down.

'Renzo would be mad,' said Sven warningly, 'Renzo would punish us.'

'How about a bet?' The table turned to a mischievous-looking Aubrey. 'How about if the wonder detective Martini, here, can figure out something secret about you?'

'Do I get a say in this?' asked Martin, a ripple of annoyance at her use of "Martini" again. The "wonder detective" part was ok.

'What?' said Aubrey defensively. 'I wanna see you do your thing. Unless... you can't?' She smiled up at him challengingly. From the table, there was an almost panto-like "ooooooh!" Martin was unfazed. The beers and slosh of

Johnnie Walker should make this easy.

Curious, Sven rubbed his double chin. 'Maybe…'

'If Martini gets it right, you tell us tonight why this is the wine tour of a lifetime. If he can't, we stop pestering you,' said Aubrey. 'So, like… what you had for breakfast or… what's the passcode for your phone.'

'Or, like when was the last time you got any action?' chimed Eve. The entire table, even the Oblets, were now staring at Martin. A tidal wave of expectation. In truth, Martin wanted to know just as badly.

'Alright,' said Martin, glancing at Sven, 'how about if I can tell where you've been and what you've been up to the last two hours?'

'Yes, go on then, Mr Moretti,' Sven giggled. 'If you can dazzle us with your big brain, I will reveal all.' Ten pairs of beady eyes bore into him. Aubrey leapt up and switched the music off; as if Martin wasn't starting to feel enough pressure.

With a twitch of his nose, Martin begun: 'After dropping you off in town, you went straight into hospital to visit somebody close to you who's suffering from mental illness; before grabbing a McDonald's burger—specifically, a Big Mac—on your way back here to get changed. Except you didn't get changed, you crashed onto one of the sofas upstairs.'

There was a moment of quiet suspense. It was hard to read Sven's face; the firelight glazed over his steel-rimmed glasses. Clearing his throat, he said: 'In actual fact, I crashed onto my bed upstairs but, yes, that is correct and most impressive. How did you know I was visiting someone close who is suffering from mental illness?'

'Your suit,' said Martin. Sven scratched his head. The table looked equally blank. 'Your jacket confirms where you went. It has that unique hospital smell of disinfectant and death.'

'That's not impressive,' said Sven, 'I told everyone I was going to the hospital.'

'Yes, to pick up aspirin. Who goes to a hospital to buy

aspirin? Besides, we must have passed half a dozen pharmacies on the way back. So why that particular facility?'

'Yes, why?' said Tate eagerly.

'The sign where we dropped you off said *Centre Hospitalier Spécialisé de la Savoie*. Pardon my French,' he added to a pained Mary Oblet having butchered the accent, 'but I think that translates as specialist hospital centre. Which usually means: mental health. And seeing the state of your hands, how dry they are from the hospital's hand sanitiser, you must have visited regularly.' Happy to play along, Sven raised his hands; one normal, one stained red from the decuvage, both were coarse and chapped. 'Clearly somebody close, then.'

'But how did you know he had a Big Mac at McDonald's?' asked Aubrey.

Martin stared at the tour guide. 'You strike me as an emotional eater, given that you've gorged on gummy bears anytime you need comfort. Seeing a loved one in hospital is upsetting, and what better comfort food than the burger. Assuming you took the same route back home as us, once you're off the highway and past the white van and tractor stores, the first bright lights just so happens to be the golden arches.' Aubrey bestowed another of her quiet rounds of applause. 'What with drinking all that wine entertaining us lot… after all that, I don't know about you, I'd be so exhausted I'd zonk out on the sofa or bed within five minutes. Zonked, until the dinner bell rang for you to rush straight down here. No time to change, hence the same suit and same tie; still in your afternoon purple tie rather than your evening one.'

'But how did you know he had a Big Mac?' said Aubrey. 'Why not the Quarter Pounder with Cheese, or the Chicken Salad?'

'Firstly, no one goes to McDonald's for salad. Secondly, not having changed out of his suit, you can see where he slopped on his white shirt. Only the Big Mac sauce is so pink. Personally, I prefer the chicken nuggets.'

It wasn't only Aubrey's applause now; the whole table

erupted into whooping and cheering and whistling, Pekoe proudly patting Martin on the back.

'Excellent work, Moretti!' bellowed Tate, stamping his feet.

The Swede was less impressed. 'For a second, I thought you did something special there. You just got lucky looking out the coach window.'

'Yeah, I still think it could have been the Quarter Pounder with Cheese,' said Aubrey, her eyes shining.

'They don't have the Quarter Pounder in France,' said Martin. 'It's the Royale with cheese because of the metric system.' Shaking his head in mock disappointment of Aubrey, he added: 'Tsk, have you no culture?' Of *Pulp Fiction*, Martin privately thought.

The corners of Aubrey's mouth twitched. 'The wonder detective, Martini, strikes again!'

'Good work, Martin, lad,' said Jimmy, 'now we can get back to my stalker story.'

'Yes, congratulations, Mr Moretti,' said their Swedish guide, 'a bet's a bet and I'm a man of my word.'

'And listen,' whispered Martin, sidling over to Sven as he switched the music back on, 'just tell me one thing about this D.O.T. thing. Is—'

'I'm hungry, let's eat,' pleaded a voice in Martin's ear. Evidently unhappy not having everyone's attention, Jimmy had scampered over to them, only to notice he'd crashed into the middle of something. 'What are you two talking about?'

'D.O.T.' said Martin, ignoring another loud groan from Sven.

'Oh, I know all about that,' said Jimmy.

'What is it? What does it mean?'

'I'll tell you when I get my food,' said Jimmy, and Sven scurried off. 'I'm a bit of a diva, really,' said Jimmy, blowing the perfect smoke ring.

'Diva, that's Latin for numpty, isn't it?' snapped Martin. 'So what is D.O.T.?'

'Chill your boots, I'll tell you later. Don't stress the Keller,' said Jimmy, re-joining the table. Cursing inwardly, Martin squeezed in next to him. Damn. This was a new sensation for Martin; no police badge forcing Jimmy to divulge the information.

At the far end of the table, the rest of the party were avidly listening to Aubrey, who'd taken over Sven's role lecturing them about the contents of their glasses (*some sweetness in attack yet drier on the second nose*). The only ones shunning the festivities were the French couple. As Theo moodily sketched a melting ice angel, Mary attacked the keys on her laptop.

'Hey, come on, join the party, folks,' said Martin, passing his glass over to them.

'Someone's got to make the money to fund all this partying,' said Theo, not looking up from his drawing.

'Correction, I make the money,' said Mary. 'You keep trying to "help" by gambling and losing it all to the taxman.'

'Death and taxes, Mary, death and taxes,' said Theo.

'At least death only happens once!' said Mary. There was that steely glint again, the one Martin had seen as she'd circled the koi pond. The portable music mix was playing an orchestral version of "Lonely This Christmas" as Martin tried a second time to offload his glass on the Oblets but, eyes down, clearly conversation was postponed until they'd completed their tax-evading formulas and melted angels.

Another hidden entrance sprang open behind a bookcase, and their jolly hosts emerged with an artichoke and Beaufort cheese terrine. This at least cheered Martin up. The sweet-sharp mountain cheese was wonderfully nutty, everybody else washing it down with a shimmering glass of Philippe & Sylvain Ravier Chignin-Bergeron from 2016.

Aubrey was in her element. 'Entirely unoaked… tropical yet balanced… I'm picking up apple blossom, almond and honey.' What exactly was she—a waitress? A food critic? Simply another alcoholic? Sven burst into applause, beaming with pride at his child prodigy. Pursing his lips, Martin endured a small sip. Was "syrupy vinegar" the correct wine term?

'Americans...' muttered Mary, slamming her laptop shut; Theo in agreement with her. 'Americans and wine.... still the devastator.' The only person apart from Martin to overhear this comment was Aubrey herself, now looking like she'd been slapped around the face. But before she could reply, the bookcase swung open again. And, just as "Do They Know It's Christmas?" blared through the speakers, their hosts returned carrying sumptuous trays of oysters and olives, pâté, plump and juicy Boudin Blanc sausages, sweet onions marinated in a fresh tomato sauce, parsley-buttered escargots, smoked salmon and scallops; all promptly gulped down with bottles of Domaine Belluard Le Feu. Everybody tucked in. Eve and Morton voraciously attacked the oysters, while Sven—clearly not full after his Big Mac—polished off an entire tray of snails himself. Apparently only Martin had picked up on the ironic chorus of *"feed the world"* playing in the background. Just one dish remained untouched: the pan-fried calf livers.

Despite demanding the food, Jimmy hadn't touched his plate. Instead, he was eating out of a plastic sandwich bag filled with fat white jellybeans. Except, these jellybeans were wriggling.

'What have you got there?' asked Martin.

'Witchetty grubs,' said Jimmy, flicking through his iPhone.

'Witchetty grubs?' stammered Martin, his stomach turning. 'As in, the wood-eating larvae of moths, witchetty grubs?'

'Big time,' said Jimmy, happily popping one into his mouth. 'I tried them on one of those Bushtucker Trials, now I'm hooked. Taste like almonds. You want some?' Jimmy held out the bag, which was squirming in sync with Martin's gut.

'No thanks, I had cockroach for lunch,' said Martin. 'Anyway, now that you're fed and watered, what was it you were going to say about DOT?' Absorbed into his iPhone, Jimmy hadn't heard Martin. His fingers were flicking at such a speed Martin was surprised he didn't already have arthritis.

'Reviews should be out for my new album. The Black Carnations' follow-up,' he announced to the whole table. 'The difficult second album.'

'Are you nervous, Mr Stresskeller?' asked Sven.

'No way, we smashed it in the studio!'

'Well…' pressed Martin, 'while we're waiting for the reviews—'

'Hey, don't stress the Keller,' said Jimmy, swallowing another grub. 'This is make or break for me.'

By the time the main course arrived—beef *en croûte* with a foie gras crust, surrounded by dauphinois potatoes, creamed spinach, wild mushrooms and honey-glazed carrots—the party was in full flow. Noel, Pekoe and Tate Sinclair were singing along to Bob Dylan's jaunty "Must Be Santa". Aubrey was performing her signature party trick; involving a candle, an upside-down wine glass and a goggle-eyed Sven. Morton Kessler was whispering sweet nothings into Eve's ear, turning Martin's stomach faster than a witchetty grub ever could. Martin didn't quite get it. Gaunt, haggard and pale, he was wearing an eerie-black cloak with a built-in hunchback, which only added to his gothic vampire-look. Nevertheless, Eve was giggling like a schoolgirl. Moaning with pleasure as Morton kissed her neck, Martin waited for the fangs to puncture her jugular.

Ting. Ting. Ting. Ting. Ting. Tapping a teaspoon against his glass, Sven switched the music off; leaving an air of hushed anticipation.

'A lot of people have been wondering about why this is the wine tour of a lifetime. And, a bet is a bet. So now… feel free to scream the house down, because this new information will make your head explode. But, warning, what you discover is for your eyes only. A forbidden secret. Members only, for sure. Are you ready? Good, then let me begin.'

14

Passionnel

After a rhubarb sorbet and apple crumble dessert, their wonderful hosts disappeared up the stone staircase, leaving them with two crates of wine and the largest cheese platter in France (which surely made it the largest worldwide). But nobody touched it. The party were hanging on Sven's every word.

'*Du vin. El vino. Pútáojiǔ*.... Wine.' Sven polished his steel-rimmed glasses for effect. 'Wine is sunlight, held together by water. Wine is that magical mix of soil, climate and topography. I've seen the Portuguese use explosives and German vineyards on cliffs of slate but... get ready... never anything like the vintages you're about to experience.' Martin's heart sank. Of course—wine, only older. And it sounded like he wasn't the only one disappointed.

'No offence, Sven, but we've already tasted some pretty decent vintages in our lifetime,' blinked Tate, his comment met by a table of nodding frowns. 'As a matter of fact, I picked myself up a bottle worth £12,000 today.'

'True, Mr Sinclair, very true,' said Sven, waggling his eyebrows, 'but five times in human history, it's been more than a decent vintage, it has been... bottled lightning! Renzo Brambilla has gathered them all; an impossible collection of the finest and rarest wines in the world. A connoisseur's fantasy of the most famous – *infamous* – bottles known to man. Some to gaze at and most to drink.' Tate's smirk disappeared. There was now silence around the table in which every crackle and pop of the fire was magnified exponentially. 'Five ancient bottles of wine. Let me show you the first.'

Running both hands through his mullet, Sven yanked open the bookcase to reveal a cavernous passageway. The party rose together, ten silhouettes in the candlelight, tailing their Swedish tour guide down a long, thin corridor. The chilly cave at least had electricity, a string of light bulbs illuminating towering racks of dusty green bottles either side of them.

'This is Renzo's personal collection of wine,' said Sven. 'One of the five wine wonders is held here, the other four await us at the Old Elysium vineyard in two days' time.' Shuffling forwards, the group emerged into a wider chamber with a dumbwaiter lift built into the wall; explaining where their hosts had obtained the delicious food from. To their right was an oil painting of a golden apple. On their left, a carved-out hole in the wall, just large enough to fit a bottle of wine.

'Behold! Only Renzo could make this a reality,' said Sven, cradling the hand-blown amber-green bottle as if it were a new-born baby. 'Chateau Lafite Rothschild, 1787. Bought at a private auction for 220,000 euros but it is, in reality, priceless.' Martin had to restrain himself from shrugging.

'It doesn't even have a label.'

'No label, Mr Moretti, but please read the engraving on the bottle.'

1787
Lafite
Th J

In the cave's gloom, Martin was struggling to decipher the etched words; so Sven clarified: '1787... Lafite... and it has the initials T-H and J.' Martin was still none the wiser.

'Thomas Jefferson!' Aubrey gasped, clapping a hand over her mouth; and now the cave echoed with excitement.

'Correct, Ms. Dalton, this did indeed belong to Thomas Jefferson—the USA's first wine connoisseur. Jefferson picked the bottle up while serving as America's Minister to France. That, or had it shipped over to the States the following year. So, this isn't any old vintage, ladies and gentlemen, it is a piece of history.' As the lightbulbs flickered, Martin caught a wild gleam in their eyes.

'And we're going to open it up?' goggled Tate.

'Absolutely, yes,' Sven said, carefully placing the bottle back in the wall. 'Tomorrow night, for sure.' Aubrey looked speechless; gob smacked. In fact, everyone was speechless. Everyone except Eve and Morton Kessler, who were taking full advantage of the cavern's shadows to continue their amorous embrace; the two of them giggling like a pair of teenagers. As the tour party hastily returned to the dining room and Sven went to close the bookcase, Eve jammed her high heel into the door.

'Would you mind if we stayed in here for a minute?' she asked, breathlessly. Her face flushed red. 'Just to admire, you know, to look at, er, the nice bottle.' Morton flashed the room a sheepish grin. Evidently the Kessler's wanted to take things to the next level. The bookcase clicked shut and the table readily began attacking the largest cheese platter in France.

'So, what are these other four ancient bottles of wine, Sven?' asked Noel. Behind the bookcase, they could hear sporadic shrieks of laughter punctuated with silences.

'Yeah, surely you can't trump that one?' said Tate, his greedy expression mirrored on the rest of their faces.

'Merely an hors d'oeuvre,' said Sven. 'But, warning, before I reveal all, I must say something serious. I fulfil many roles for Renzo Brambilla. Tour guide. Publicist. I am also the guardian of his wine, sacred protector, sworn to defend it at all costs. So, if you are thinking of stealing any...' Sven drew his finger significantly across his own throat, which struck Martin as rather sinister. But as a follow up, Sven mimed pulling guns out of a holster and shooting them, which somewhat undermined it. Some of the group chuckled, happy to lighten the mood again as Sven raised his glass. 'So, as you English say, keep your mitts off.' He snorted into his wine. 'Now, to introduce the next vintage of bottled lightning, let me take you back to a bright spring morning in ancient Rome.'

Emulating the others at his end of the table, Martin drifted away from the history lesson; Jimmy plugging back into his phone as Theo and Mary Oblet returned to their work.

'You've made an error on Renzo's South American holdings,' Mary whispered with a tut, the flame-licked yule logs still blazing behind her, 'when you only had to transfer some files.' They were both sitting rigidly upright; clenched buttocks to match their clenched jaws.

'I know,' mumbled Theo, frantically shading the puddle around his ice angel.

'You've misfiled the Peruvian copper mine with the Peruvian guinea pig farm. So, wrong tax code again,' Mary said sharply. 'Why do keep interfering? You are an artist... allegedly.'

'Everything or nothing,' said Theo with a lazy smile. 'Right now, my efforts, I am pouring everything into the accounts.'

'Making profits of nothing.'

'I want to be close to you,' said Theo, playfully batting his eyelids. 'I want to share in your career, and to prove how easy it is, what you and Renzo do.'

'You have proved it is *not* easy, Theo, countless times!' hissed Mary. 'Stay away from my spreadsheets and stick to your scribblings.' They were both so tightly wound, like the coiled spring inside a bolt-action rifle. Martin turned away. He'd heard enough angry wife feedback to last a lifetime. Instead, Martin's eyes fell upon the fawning, gawking audience of Sven's ancient Rome lecture. Just as Sven had promised, it appeared the newly unveiled information really would make their heads explode (metaphorically, obviously).

But then something far more curious caught Martin's eye. His silver spoon, the one from his sorbet bowl, was vibrating. And so was the untouched glass in front of him; the wine now pulsing into small concentric circles. How bizarre. An earthquake in Paris? Fracking? The throbbing vein on Mary's forehead? Martin instantly zeroed in on the source of the tremors. Simple, really, now the bookcase was rattling; a full set of Encyclopaedias edging forwards on their shelf. Oblivious, Sven's audience were still applauding him. Grinning back at their amazement, Sven's smile faltered at the rhythmic judder coming from the bookcase; each thump now accompanied by a low moan. Martin chuckled. The party's awkward faces—suddenly bright red and not from the fire—didn't know where to look, but they'd certainly spotted the rattling A – Z Encyclopaedias; the letter V winning the race to the edge. If the book fell open onto the page of an erupting volcano, Martin felt people's heads *literally* would explode.

Tate, Noel, Aubrey and Pekoe jumped to join Sven opening the wine crates, clattering the bottles as loudly as they could into one another. Martin didn't care. Neither it seemed did Jimmy.

'Now, where were we about D.O.T. when—'

'Wa-hey! Reviews are in!' said Jimmy, his eyes shining as he scanned the screen. His face immediately fell. 'Outrageous, absolutely outrageous, they can't all be like this.' But the more his finger scrolled, the more prominent his frown.

'It can't be that bad,' shrugged Martin.

'Here,' said Jimmy with a scowl, 'this one's the kindest.' He thrust his phone into Martin's hand, who obligingly read it:

Jimmy Stresskeller's tasteless second album knocks another nail into the coffin of his moribund career. Distastefully nasty lyrics, and yet somehow the music is still both boring and bland. The best you could say is that it's forgettable.

Martin looked up at Jimmy.

'Hey,' he tried sounding upbeat, 'why do you care what they think?'

'I don't care, that's what's annoying,' spat Jimmy. 'This lame-brain clearly gets off on nit-picking; writing the opposite of what the punters think. Pathetic.' Snatching his phone back, he dropped it into his glass of wine. 'I don't get it. You like the singles, don't you?

'Um...' said Martin, struggling to recall even one of them.

'Mr Robson's Superior Banana? Colour Me Kubrick? Sir Reggie Kray?' Martin stared back blankly. 'Surely, you heard our first single?'

'What was it again?'

'Death of the Footsoldier Muppets?' said Jimmy, taking a chug from the nearest wine bottle.

'Yes!' said Martin, pleased he finally knew one. But then he remembered how he'd felt on hearing it. 'Actually, I, er, I thought that your target market would hate it.'

'Who's my target market?' said Jimmy.

'Anyone with ears,' said Martin. 'The lyrics were offensive.'

'No, they were a metaphor.'

'Still offensive,' said Martin. In the background, the boisterous vibrations and shrieks grew; Martin's sorbet spoon was now twitching worse than Sven's nerves, the tour guide's loud clinking of bottles not enough to drown out the noise next door.

'God, so many wines, so little time for me to taste 'em,' said Aubrey.

'A woman's work is never done, is it?' said Jimmy to her. 'That's why they get paid less!' No one laughed except him—Aubrey looking highly offended—so he turned back to Martin. 'You didn't like the song,' he said bitterly, with another huge chug from the bottle. 'Nobody liked it. I should have stuck to playing Matt Sunset in *Coast Cop*. Bafta winner 2022. Why did I idiotically quit just to be a failed rockstar? I only did *I'm a Celebrity... Get Me Out of Here* to reignite my career. But all I do now is wave on university stages at 1 AM. Prancing around with a blow-up kangaroo for row after row of ugly, ugly fan; drunken students who are only cheering me on ironically.' Martin wasn't sure what to say. Gazing at Jimmy, his bronzed handsome features all scrunched up as he chomped through the contents of a new sandwich bag, Martin couldn't help but feel sorry for him.

'Of course, like, y'know what the most exciting thing about the bearded vulture is? It can—'

'Shut up about your boring birds, Noel,' said Jimmy. The Irishman looked severely insulted. 'I'm bearing my soul here. Tragic thing is, I'm a really good musician. I know all the notes. That scream you can hear through the bookcase is a G note.'

'G-sharp, I'd say now,' said Martin. The violent banging reached crescendo, the ripples in Martin's wine glass in danger of becoming waves. And then, to the intense relief of the room, sweet silence. The bookcase swung open.

'That hit the spot,' said Eve, 'is there any more wine?' Morton let out a small, embarrassed cough, but Martin was impressed. Maybe Martin had misjudged the decrepit vampire. The man was a stud. He hadn't even removed his hunchback cloak, though his thread of grey combover hair was now twirled out of shape.

Uncannily reading Martin's mind, Morton said: 'People always underestimate me.'

'Anyone else wanna come in, to take a look at the, er, bottle?' said Eve.

'No!' yelled the group in unison, Sven slamming the door shut and mopping his brow. Coincidentally, Aubrey had finally found a bottle she liked. Acting as waitress, she poured a taste for Sven who slugged it back and smacked his lips approvingly. All wine pomp and ceremony was officially abandoned for the night. Glasses were refreshed around the table, people gaily easing back into their seats. Down Martin's end, however, there was still zero party atmosphere. His choice of conversation was either a manically depressed musician or a pair of bickering bookkeepers.

'Ooops, and you've missed another tax loophole,' Mary sneered with relish. Martin squirmed in his seat. Was this normal for French couples, simply heated Gallic passion? It didn't feel normal. Passive aggressive workplace banter, artists versus executives blowing off steam?

'I know,' snapped Theo. 'Calm down. I can fix it, trust me.'

'Trust, Theo? You have eroded it,' said Mary, stiffly, 'I can rely on you being unreliable, nothing else.' On this, Martin agreed. Trust was like the rubber on the end of a pencil; it gets smaller and smaller after every mistake. 'It is the same with your paintings, I should just do it myself.'

'It's your fault, you made the spreadsheet too complicated,' said Theo. 'But, yes, fine, I will stick to my wine label commission. The deadline's looming anyway.'

'I told you,' she said through gritted teeth, with a look that could have curdled the wine, 'to ask Renzo for extra time, if you weren't such a coward.'

'I would have the extra time if I didn't have to listen to your nagging.'

'He has the IQ of an oyster,' said Mary, turning to the whole table; most choosing to gaze into their glasses. For Martin, this was infinitely more awkward than the bookcase gymnastics. 'The fact you can't even paint by numbers shows how bad you are at two professions.'

'I'm a good accountant! And a great artist!' said Theo, his eyes glowing. 'And I never make the same mistake twice.'

'Yes, it's usually three or four times,' said Mary with a false laugh. 'A child with an abacus could do a better job than you.'

'Why are you always needling me, *boudin*?' seethed Theo.

'If you're expecting me to say sorry, it's not going to happen!' Mary sprang from her seat and Theo rose to face her. 'I can't pretend anymore with you. I've lost all interest in you.' She was glowering at him with revulsion.

'Surely not as much interest as you lost for the company in the third quarter,' sneered Theo. 'You have lost your spark.'

'I don't love you anymore,' said Mary.

'I don't love *you* anymore!' Both looked as if they could murder the other.

'Didn't you hear, I don't care!' cried Mary. 'You don't listen to me. You never listen!'

'Because you've deafened me.'

'I can't take this anymore!' raged Mary. It was as though she were seeing him clearly for the first time. 'I want a divorce.'

Theo's legs momentarily buckled. Clearly this was one step further than he was expecting. 'Don't you dare threaten to leave me or I'll kill you. If you divorce me in a dream, you better wake up and apologise.' Martin chalked this up as the third death threat he'd heard in twenty-four hours (Joseph, Renzo, now Mary).

'Ah *oui, oui,* of course, Theo.' Mary shrugged, as if shaking off a lifetime of empty threats. 'Add it to your to-do list for tomorrow along with Netflix, Mario Kart, and *Loto* tickets, before having another panic attack about your painting. It is still over.'

'But, Mary, the good times,' he stuttered, panicked, 'I treat you like an angel.'

'Yes, Theo, but sometimes I wanted to be treated like a whore.'

Aubrey spat her red wine out. Mary span around, ready to twist her anger onto anyone in sight. 'What's the matter, *la dévastateur*,' said Mary, 'is the wine not pretentious enough for you?'

'Hey, don't have a go at Aubrey just because of your marital strife,' said Eve.

'Ah, well, we can't all keep the magic alive by rutting in public; which listening to was excruciating, by the way,' snarled Mary.

'Fifty-seven ruts, if you're counting,' winked Eve.

'I'm going to bed,' said Mary. Theo grabbed her arm but she smacked it away, stomping up the stone staircase. 'You can sleep in the snow!' Ready for round two, Theo stormed after her.

Following the fireworks display both sides of the bookcase, the group took their cue from the Oblets; heading up as well. In the dwindling candlelight, only Martin, Jimmy and Sven lingered, their tour guide busy packing away his speakers, Jimmy still swirling the phone in his wine glass.

'You know,' said Jimmy morosely, 'last night, I had a dream.' Martin braced himself. He had a hunch it wouldn't rival Martin Luther King.

'I dreamt I was at The Ivy. Not dining, but on the loo. It was an amazing feeling, just to sit on The Ivy's toilet. Think of it. Mine and Justin Bieber's butt cheeks having shared the same seat. Harry Styles' bum and mine have common ground!' he said, rummaging inside a sandwich bag of what looked like pork scratchings. How many of these bags did Jimmy own? Was there one he kept exclusively for scarred livers?

'What have you got there?'

'A kangaroo anus,' said Jimmy. Martin's concern grew: where was the rest of it? 'Bush tucker's the only thing that picks me up nowadays. Although, after this review, I'll need about twenty kilos of crocodile bollock.'

Martin made one last attempt to rally him.

'What's the big deal?' said Martin. 'Celebrities are nothing but a bunch of overrated, overpaid, pompous prigs talking about their Ferraris and facials.'

'Exactly. And this review is ruining my chances of being part of that!' cried Jimmy. The wine bottle nearest him was now empty, but that look of moody ruthlessness Martin had first seen at the taxi rank had returned. 'What I need is divine inspiration, some kind of magic spark to stimulate me. Immerse myself in greatness…' he said, eyeing the bookcase. Somehow, Martin suspected Eve and Morton's public display of affection wasn't the magic he was referring to. 'Drink it in… bottled lightning.'

'Ah ah ah, remember my warning,' said Sven, wagging his finger reproachfully at Jimmy, 'keep your mitts off.' The guardian of the wine pulled out his imaginary guns and started shooting; coaxing them up from their seats and towards the staircase.

It was a hard climb, Martin lugging his stomach up behind him. Their amazing hosts had surpassed themselves tonight, which was saying something. Martin had warmed to the couple upon arrival, as soon as he'd spotted their personal bottle of cognac behind reception. Exceptional taste. It looked like a special bottle as well, probably a wedding anniversary. Bidding goodnight, he split off from the other two in the hallway. Jimmy, now a little worse for wear, staggered arm in arm with Sven over to their wing of the Château.

'Sweet dreams, Mr Moretti,' Sven called back. 'I'm absolutely positive we will all sleep safe and sound tonight.'

With a wave, Martin headed in the direction of his four-poster bed. But not before he swiped the cognac. That went without saying.

15

Crime

You are always alone at three in the morning. He hated being alone, hated it with a cold dread, but *now* was the perfect time. It had to be now.

Tired, hungry, with a leering smile on his face, he rolled out of bed and crept along the empty corridor. Towards obsession, towards greatness. A ghostly moonbeam shone through the frosted window, enticing him forwards; onwards. He felt no remorse about it, for what he was about to do.

Downstairs, the hall was alive with shadows, but nothing stirred except his own desperate craving. For that magic spark; le Chateau Lafite Rothschild, 1787.

Spotting Holly's blood-red scarf draped over the high-backed chair, he gently pressed on the wooden panel and the concealed door sprang open. In his bare feet, Jimmy Stresskeller tip-toed down the staircase. The stone floor was unpleasantly cold but would keep him awake; alert. He might need it to. The cellar's darkness was thick and black. Wood smoke from the now-dormant fireplace hung in the air. Fumbling his way over to the bookcase, Jimmy yanked it open. The passageway still smelt of sex. Just as before, flickering lightbulbs led the way past the towering wine racks. It was almost too easy. Such a priceless wine, protected not with biometric locks, rottweilers or CCTV, but merely naïve trust. Jimmy's leer grew. How pathetically sad they would all be, waking up to discover the infamous bottle had vanished, the contents hidden inside his belly. They'd probably blame it on the D.O.T. saboteur. Once uncorked, he would devour it, swallow it in one go, bottled lightening stimulating him to write the greatest album of all time. It would make Sgt. Pepper sound like the Pussycat Dolls. And then the world would love him. And then he would never be alone.

In the shadows on his right, someone silently removed a bottle from the rack, as casually as if they were picking out a wine for dinner.

Jimmy hadn't seen or heard anything, his bleary eyes searching instead for the hole in the wall. He craned his neck forward for a closer look when a crashing blow hit him on the right ear. Staggering, he glanced around. For a second time, something hard hit the side of his head. The clang of the bottle against his skull reverberated around the cave, or was that now just the ringing inside his head? Stunned, Jimmy remained upright for six or seven seconds, gently rocking. Then he clattered to the cave floor.

Dragging himself up by the wine racks, he lightly patted his face for damage. He was in no pain. In fact, he couldn't feel anything. The right side of his face was numb. From the darkest corner of the cave, the shadowy figure lifted the bottle high in the air and brought it down as hard as they could on the back of Jimmy's head. Bright flashes of light exploded behind his eyes. He felt dizzy. But not the dizzy affection how Cammy made him feel. He would treat her better. She might be the one. If he could get out of here.

'No!' Jimmy yelled, grimacing, and dropping to his knees. His bronzed face stared upwards in bewildered shock. 'Please!' Jimmy pleaded, half-hopeful, half-defiant, but his blue eyes flickered, swooning into darkness. Without hesitation, the shadow swung the bottle down on top of Jimmy's head.

Jimmy Stresskeller—once Matt Sunset in *Coast Cop*, Bafta winner 2022—was on the cave floor, gnarled, gnarling. He was dimly aware he was lying in a pool of something wet, something red, something sticky. Maybe the bottled weapon had shattered, spilling its innards? Was it the Lafite? Gently dipping his fingers into it, he touched his lips. It tasted of rusted copper. He spat it out. Not wine. With a moaning wail of dissent, he gazed upwards. If he could not taste the bottled lightning, then perhaps he could at least glimpse it one last time. Except... the Chateau Lafite Rothschild was missing. Through his blurred vision, he could see the hole in the wall was empty.

The shadow stood over him and forcefully brought the bottle down again. And again. *Boring and bland... moribund career... a fouled parody.* Shelves jangling, blood sprayed over the painting of the golden apple. And then, as Jimmy's arms went limp, his legs stopped twitching and all life went out of his body, the dark silhouette was gone. *Worst album ever... indefensibly stupid... half-arsed baloney.* Jimmy Stresskeller died right there on the floor. Alone.

16

The Snowman

Another beautiful morning, cold and white. With a big stretch, Martin opened his eyes to find flurries of snow drifting past his window, glittery icicles hanging from the lintel. Stunning, utterly stunning. Swinging it wide, he waved down as his hosts hurriedly carried logs inside. Without a doubt, this winterscape would be the highlight of his day. Before he wasted the next eight hours learning how to compare and contrast Merlot, Mondeuse and Malbec.

With a wearied sigh, Martin plucked an icicle from the window frame and dropped it into the last of the cognac. He was amazed there was any left. Though God knows what he got up to during his nightly blackouts. Downing the liquor, his stomach squirmed from the guilt of stealing it last night. But his beer buzz had long worn off watching everybody else get drunk. And as he liked to say: desperate times call for desperate measures. Martin just hoped that cognac wasn't included in Sven Lindblom's role as sacred protector, bodyguard of the booze, or whatever he'd blethered on about.

Not many people had made it down to the breakfast table. Only Pekoe, Tate (again, without his family), Theo (but not Mary), Noel and Aubrey. Theo Oblet was, after last night's blazing row, understandably quiet. Yet so were the rest of them. No doubt nursing hangovers: hunched over their plates, tentatively nibbling on the corner of a croissant. Martin half-smiled as he drained his cup of coffee. They weren't hardened like he was, but at least now the fumes oozing from their remorseful bodies concealed his own cognac breath. Determinedly, Noel lifted a red onion, gruyère and rosemary fougasse halfway to his mouth before he thought better of it. Much as Martin appreciated the freshly baked brioche, cakes and croissants, he did miss a full English breakfast. A good old-fashioned greasy fry up. England's one indisputable contribution to the Western culinary dish: cholesterol. In the end, he settled on a bowl of yoghurt before slicing open a grapefruit. At once, there was a loud squeak, like someone had stepped on a mouse. The table turned to see Aubrey in pain, her eyes squeezed shut and clutching her forehead.

'It's the grapefruit,' she said by way of explanation, 'I get these micro-migraines, shooting pains whenever I'm stressed or I smell citrus.'

Yeah right, *grapefruit*. It seemed like a classic hangover to Martin.

'It's true,' Aubrey winced, catching the look on his face. 'It started when I was eighteen. I remember I had to stop buying my kiwi, guava, and lime shampoo.' It sounded more like a fruit salad than a shampoo, thought Martin, tossing the grapefruit into the bin. What a flimsy excuse. But then, that did tally with what the enormous waiter had said—*she spent half the night with her head between her knees as if in some terrible pain*—reflected Martin, linking it back to the orange-fumed mulled wine.

With another sharp twinge of guilt as their hosts refilled his cup, Martin watched the party slope off one by one to prepare for the day. All except Pekoe, who nervously eyed Martin.

'There's probably something I should confess to you,' said Pekoe in a hushed tone. Before he could say anymore, however, an overly chirpy man with a mullet and crumpled suit marched in rattling a cowbell.

'Wakey, wakey, before heads are achy,' giggled Sven.

'Already?' moaned Martin, throwing a brioche at his head.

'You underestimated my scooting,' he beamed.

Ten minutes later, Sven was ushering everyone outside

with a violently flapping right hand, still stained red from yesterday. The snow, at least, had eased off but the icy wind persisted, flicking flakes up into Martin's numb face as the group shuffled towards the yellow coach. One man impervious to the cold was Omar, still dressed in his Algerian football shirt, and acquiring sufficient warmth from the amber glow of the cigarette hanging from his bottom lip. Gleefully greeting them all wearing a Santa hat—he'd clearly got the D.O.T. scratches out of his system somehow—he stood laughing at the collective draggle of hangovers; his pot-belly wobbling like a bowlful of jelly and resembling some kind of nightmarish *Père Noël*.

Martin was first up the stairs. Relishing that delicious first blast of heat, he immediately stripped off before he fainted from the heat of the pizza oven temperatures. This aggravating ordeal by fire and ice had simply become part of their daily routine. Surviving today's trial himself, Pekoe dropped into the next seat and gave Martin a wry look of "here we go again". Glancing around, Martin nodded to Aubrey, Noel, Eve and Morton. Arms folded, Mary Oblet had now joined Theo, a clear three inches between them, which might as well have been three miles. Tate was sitting at the back with his son, Joseph, but there was still no sign of his wife. And no Jimmy Stresskeller.

'And to think, he calls himself a *rock n roller*,' scoffed Sven, as the coach began to move. Out of the window, Martin glimpsed the "MARRY ME JIMMY" placard tossed into a bush by the side of the road. Do stalkers take a day off? He wondered. But the instant they turned a tight left corner, the sign was out of sight and out of mind.

Soon enough they were back in their old rhythm: cellars, barrels, bottlings and tastings. Back to the Sven lectures. 'Fun fact: without yeast there is no wine. Yeast converts the sugar in grapes into alcohol.' Etcetera, etcetera, etcetera.

Martin was right about one thing, however: this was the perfect place to hide his addictive tendencies, amongst a debauchery of hedonists. Brunch for most of the party was several glasses of Altesse wine served up with rich cheeses and lobster. Lunch consisted of a downpour of heavy, dark red wines presented around a succulent wild boar dish. It had occurred to Martin yesterday that being trapped in wine country posed a lot of challenges. Number one being, you're trapped in wine country. But, adapt or die, Martin was finding new cunning ways to survive. In one particularly draughty farm building, as ten sets of beady eyes compelled him to sample the Cabernet Sauvignon, he'd managed to pop a Strepsil into his mouth beforehand, successfully numbing any sense of taste. Inside an ornate conservatory, when presented with a Riesling described by Sven as a 'little prickly', Martin felt it rather appropriate to pour over the cactus. These evasive tactics had not gone unnoticed by Aubrey, who fixed Martin with a glare every time she spat into her bucket.

'So, Mr Moretti, what did you think to that last glass?' said Sven, steering them all outside.

'Made the spines tingle,' said Martin, squinting out into the bright white landscape. Figuring the easiest way to shrug him off would be with a pun, he added: 'I'm on cloud wine.' Beaming, Sven trudged over to Eve, Morton and the rest of the rabble to commence a tour of the snowy vines.

'Thought you hated to waste good ethanol?' came an angry voice from behind Martin. Aubrey was stomping up the slope looking disapprovingly at him. She could hardly talk; splashes of red on her hiking boots showed Aubrey hadn't been drinking as gracefully as she made out either. He stared back at her. Possibly mistaking his squint for a scowl, Aubrey marched away muttering to herself a variety of Californian expletives.

Martin's whole body shivered. The sun was shining hot but the wind was blowing cold, which meant he'd get sunburn and frostbite at the same bloody time. He scoured around for a distraction, eager to avoid a full-blown temperature tantrum. Stupidly, Martin had assumed on a wine tour he'd be seeing fresh, ripe clusters of green and dark-red grapes hanging from the vines. Instead, it was... desolate. The ground was frozen, the vines were clipped and dormant. Each row, acre after acre, exactly as bleak and barren as the next. Grim. The tangled shoots resembled coiled clumps of rusted barbed wire, like photos he'd seen of frontline World War One. A scattering of trees, dead and leafless, only accentuated the emptiness of this place. Or, as empty as he felt, empty as his job prospects, and as empty as his bank account after the next Eagle Hotel bar bill. Bacardi and room service is a dangerous mix. And now with no police salary or pension, how exactly was he going to pay for rent, fuel, food, TV, drink, debts and spousal maintenance? Grim indeed. Martin suddenly felt his misery plummet, plunging down with his overdraft and reputation into the realms of irreparable.

At once, the police psychiatrist's voice seemed to fill his head, smug and condescending.

'You can look back on a career of accomplishments, commendations awarded, drug dealers arrested, murderers incarcerated. You've made this county safer for the general public. And all that, whilst being ruddy half-cut.'

Yes, that would be his shrink's advice: always look on the bright side. So, Martin supposed he should be grateful now for his wider knowledge of wine, acknowledging his mistake having ever called it glorified grape juice. Unfair and inaccurate. What he should have said was: wine is grape juice with a yeast infection.

The bright side. For Martin, it depended on your worldly disposition. Some see a glass half full, some see it half empty. Martin saw it shattered on the floor; normally after breaking up a pub brawl at two in the morning. Perhaps that was it. Perhaps it was a police thing. The media coverage over the Sara Brambilla outcome had been glorifyingly positive; praising Inspector Moretti—now *Chief* Inspector Moretti—the hero policeman who had rescued the millionaire's daughter from the woodshed. Yet, Martin's anxiety had only grown over those long hot nights of disturbed sleep. Accusations that he and Sara's father had acted like crazed vigilantes were quickly swept aside in the fanfare. Officially, Inspector Moretti and Renzo Brambilla had canvassed the area after hours. Unofficially, however, the canvassing had been heatedly overzealous. Renzo, a man of extremes, had taken his role as informal deputy a little too far when interrogating a convicted paedophile named Jim Hurlan. But that wasn't what disturbed Martin. Nor was it being paraded around like a show dog at the inevitable press conference. Frankly, watching top brass hog the limelight felt more normal to him than wearing a tie. He hated wearing ties (he only ever wore a suit jacket so he didn't have to iron a shirt). Nor was it the horrific sight found underneath the floor hatch in the woodshed. A trembling Inspector Moretti, sweat dripping from his brow, blue strobe lights cutting through the putrid darkness, had been the first to see her. On top of a pile of decayed bones, lay the body of Sara Brambilla; drugged, but alive. And missing her left eye. Sara's disfigured face would forever weave into his headful of nightmares (unless numbed with vodka). Even the end of the heatwave—ending as all British heatwaves do, with a thundering electrical storm—hadn't eased his sleeplessness. But that wasn't what disturbed Martin either. What disturbed Martin, what still distressed him, was the fact that they never caught her abductor. The kidnapper was still out in the world. Somewhere.

Eyes adjusted to the light; Martin saw that the party had spread out amongst the vines, only Aubrey sticking close to Sven's official discourse. An icy chill cut through the vineyard. The annoying pair deserved each other. Pulling the collar up on his coat, Martin traipsed through the vast skeletal grid of pruned stumps. If there are ice cream trucks in summer, there should be Starbucks trucks in winter. Although in the current sub-zero climate, they'd be serving the coffee on a stick.

Tate and Joseph Sinclair were busy building a snowman next to a large sycamore tree. So, their son had actually survived the night. In truth, Martin didn't know what to make of Joseph's morbid tongue-cutting apprehensions. He seemed happy enough here and now, snapping branches off the tree for the snowman's arms. And he certainly still had his tongue, blowing a loud wet raspberry as Martin passed by. Noel was monitoring the skies through a thick pair of binoculars. Still no sign, apparently, of the bearded vulture. Veering away from the ornithologist, Martin found himself in the same row as Pekoe, happily puffing away on his long-stemmed cherrywood pipe. Perhaps it was the strong herbal contents, but Pekoe seemed to be puffing long and deep for alpine air as well. Not that Martin could blame him. The vineyard lay on a forty-five degree angle that climbed all the way up the steep mountain slopes. He did not envy the fruit pickers having to clamber skyward and snip bunches from the cliff edge.

'Hello Pekoe,' said Martin, 'chosen your favourite frozen stump from this field yet?'

'I need to tell you a secret,' Pekoe said with a shifty hangdog look.

'Go on...' said Martin warily. In his experience, good news rarely followed these words. Usually, what followed was some kind of confession. He'd heard it all; from firearms and forgery to manslaughter and murder.

'I don't like wine,' whispered Pekoe.

'You don't like wine!'

'Ssssh!' Pekoe whirled around in panic, but there was no one there.

'But you hide it so well,' said Martin.

'I don't enjoy it,' said Pekoe, meandering into another row, 'but I can stomach it. I just don't need to binge on Strepsils beforehand. Oh, don't worry, no one else saw!' he added quickly, seeing the alarm on Martin's face. 'But I figured I'd be in safe company confessing to you. What did you think of that last Merlot?' asked Pekoe, as he mimed vomiting.

'Merlot? Hell no!' said Martin vehemently. 'Cabernet Sauvignon?' He mirrored Pekoe's vomiting action. 'How about you serve us none!'

'Chardonay, nay and thrice nay,' said Pekoe, catching on. They both chuckled.

'Did we just become best friends?' said Martin.

'I think we did,' said Pekoe, turning into a new row. For a second, they froze, Pekoe in the happy act of relighting his pipe.

'Cold enough for you, kid?' drawled a thick Boston accent.

They had stumbled onto the Kesslers; Morton cutting sprigs of mistletoe from the lower part of an elm tree, Eve bending to pick up the clippings.

'Cold as a corpse,' replied Martin. 'What are you two up to?'

'Mistletoe,' purred Eve in a husky tone, pointing up to the branches. Martin had a funny feeling that Eve was bending further over since they had arrived.

'Replenishing our supply, kid,' said Morton. His voice creaked like the lid of an old coffin. 'It's for our company branding, *Mistletoe Atlantic Trading*,' he added. There was something different about his manner today. Casually leaning against the elm tree, their resident vampire of the vineyard was wearing another black cloak, this one without a hunchback. He was so fragile, he'd probably sneezed and snapped his spine back into place. That, or had it readjusted against the bookshelf last night.

'Up to standard?' Martin asked, more to break the uncomfortable silence.

'I'm positively sure,' said Morton. There was a lingering and lopsided leer etched onto his face that Martin didn't like. At least there were plenty of wooden stakes around. 'Are you sure, Eve?'

'As sure as I've counted this winery has 1036 rows of vines,' she said.

'So quite satisfactory,' said Morton. 'I guess my wife,' he added, gesturing toward her upward posterior, 'would say we've been fully satisfied since last night.'

'Maybe not *fully* satisfied, Morton,' said Eve, her eyes on Martin. Cheeks flushed, he and Pekoe politely made their goodbyes and—before Eve no doubt suggested hanging the mistletoe from her belt—ambled away as swiftly as they could without appearing conspicuous.

'So, are you hating this tour as much as I am?' said Martin.

'Honestly? So long as I've got my pipe and sight of the mountains,' Pekoe gazed beyond the vines to the peaks of Mont Blanc, 'I'm tickety-boo.' Martin glanced up at the mountains himself, pleased to see a complete absence of ski twits weaving up and down the slopes. Skiing—the only sport where you spend an arm and a leg to break an arm and a leg. 'Hopefully,' said Pekoe, 'there'll be a chance for some mountaineering on this tour.'

'Do you know why you are here, why Renzo invited you?' Martin turned to look Pekoe full in the face, desperate for the answer.

Raised voices exploded behind them. Theo and Mary Oblet, ready for round two, three and four. Artist versus accountant. Standing five feet apart, they were screaming at each other.

'I keep telling you, Theo, it's over! How many more times do you need to hear it?'

'Is this because of the crypto investment?' said Theo. 'Because that gamble made us a thousand euros.'

Mary shrieked with scornful laughter. 'You started the day with a million!' Martin winced. Though he and Pekoe were ten rows over, Martin fancied you could hear them from the top of the Matterhorn. 'You should not be allowed near money, *joueur,*' yelled Mary, 'not my money, anymore. I will take you to the cleaners!'

'Take me to the cleaners? Listen to yourself, you sound like a Yank!' Theo yelled back. Unclenching his fists, he breathed deeply, more calmly. 'Ok, ok, I'll paint my label for Renzo and then we'll talk about this when we get back to Paris.

And I tell you what, I bet you fifty euros I'll never bet again,' he joked.

'Theo, please!' she said, sounding close to tears. If the scarred livers were a glimpse of Martin's future, this was his Ghost of Christmas Past. But then, perhaps his own flashback of failures, and the painful lessons learnt, could actually help Theo win her back? 'It is not funny anymore,' Mary pleaded. 'Gambling is a sickness. It's not merely our money you're losing, it's our love.'

'So I will quit while we're ahead,' said Theo, stomping down the hill to the sycamore tree and Joseph's snowman.

To Martin's horror, instead of storming after her husband, Mary caught his eye and marched over to them; red-faced and furious.

'This'll be fun,' grimaced Martin before she reached them.

'*Quel stupide bouffon à tête de cochon!*' The light sprinkling of snowflakes from above did nothing to cool her bad temper.

'Give him a break,' said Pekoe. 'So, he's put the odd flutter on the stock market. He's not the Devil.'

'Oh, he's the Devil,' snapped Mary. 'He literally could sprout horns and turn red at any moment.'

For once, Martin was relieved to see their tour guide. 'We come in peace, Madame Oblet,' tittered Sven, both hands in the air. 'But maybe, now, it's time to take your spikes down before you cause an avalanche. We just need to find a more pleasant topic of conversation while we are all here in the great outdoors.'

'How about wine?' said Aubrey, her bob of blue hair now frosted with snow.

'Perfect! So come along now, ladies and gentlemen, breathe in the fresh air,' he said, escorting them down the slope. 'Nothing is more agreeable than a glass of Chardonnay, drunk with friends in the shade of a warm summer's afternoon,' said the Swede, gazing out across the valley.

'Yeah, but it's December 19th, and I'm freezing my butt off!' said Martin. The 19th... that Moretti Christmas letter deadline was getting closer.

'There's no such thing as bad weather, Mr Moretti, only bad clothing,' said Sven. Rounding up Noel Gillespie and the Kesslers along the way, they met Tate, Joseph and a purple-faced Theo by the snowman. A small wooden table had been set up with a glittering set of glasses and, of course, several chilled bottles of Chardonnay.

'Before we embark on the steep climb back to the winery, let's limber up with a glass of wine, courtesy of the wonderful Monsieur Daniel Boccard.'

'God no,' spluttered Tate, reading the label, 'anything but Chardonnay, please. How about a Sauvignon Blanc instead?'

'You better watch out, Mr Sinclair,' said Sven, wagging a red-stained finger, 'you're in danger of being labelled a snob.'

'Of course I'm a snob, that's why I'm on a wine tour.'

'Then it might help you to know,' said Sven, handing round the glasses, 'that Sauvignon Blanc originates from the Chardonnay grape.'

'Is that true?' frowned Aubrey, pouring generous measures into each glass. Martin's feeble request for a small serving was smilingly ignored. In fact, she'd purposely poured him the largest amount.

'Yes. Or no. Or, yes let's drink more wine,' shrugged Sven. 'The truth is, nobody knows. One of Sauvignon Blanc's parents was the ancient grape Savagnin. The other remains a mystery.'

'Maybe it was an immaculate conception,' said Martin, tilting his glass to the sky and away from his mouth.

'Well, to enjoy this one,' said Tate, looking at the bottle with disdain, 'is going to take a miracle.'

'It's Christmas, Mr Sinclair, it's the time of miracles,' said Sven. 'I appreciate some people fear Chardonnay's reputation of an overpowered buttery, oak flavour. But this one is clean,' he added, swirling around the pale gold liquid. 'It is minimal, it is citrusy, and it is so exquisite that I know your wife, at least, would enjoy it.'

'Where is she, by the way?' asked Martin, in a vain attempt to move the conversation away from wine.

'Headache. She's had it three days.'

'Three days?' said Noel wryly. 'That's a tumour!' Chortling, he elbowed Martin in the ribs, who forced a half-smile back.

'I think it's more a case of attention-itis,' muttered Tate, still eyeing his glass suspiciously.

'Here are the top ten reasons why I love Chardonnay,' said Sven. 'Number one, it is essential for making Champagne. Two, it is versatile...'

Swilling then swallowing his wine down, Noel broke off from the group and headed back out to the vines. Edging away himself, Martin trudged over to Noel. While he wasn't keen on the middle-aged Peter Pan, it trumped any wine talk. Easily.

The Irishman was back behind his binoculars, still searching for that elusive vulture.

'How ya doing?' said Noel, not looking away from the eye piece.

'Freezing, out here,' said Martin with a shiver. 'It's as cold as my mother-in-law's kiss.'

'There's no such thing as bad weather, only soft people,' said Noel, his sweep of grey hair flickering in the wind. Easy for him to say, thought Martin. Noel's navy-blue puffer jacket, woollen hat and gloves were twice as thick as his own. And clearly effective; Noel looked clammy, on the verge of getting sweaty.

'Did you see Jimmy this morning?' asked Martin.

'That melter? Who the feck cares – sorry, I mean,' he faltered, realising his tone was a little harsh, 'all I care about is finding my bird, like. Complete my assignment. No joy, so far. I've seen a lovely pair of ring ouzels, though; haven't seen any of those since the summer.'

'Or you've just forgotten you've seen 'em,' said Martin.

'I can remember every bird I've seen in every month, thank you very much.'

'From the summer? How about June?' said Martin randomly.

'Peregrine falcon, buzzard, raven, red grouse, ring ouzel and golden eagle,' said Noel with a self-satisfied air. 'What's your favourite bird?'

'I've never thought about it before,' said Martin. 'The robin, I'd say. Probably pretty pathetic compared to your eagles and vultures.'

'Not at all,' said Noel, tracking something small and feathery glide into a cloud. 'The littlest birds sing the prettiest songs. I can relate to the robin, personally. To me, those redbreast warbles sound… sad… suppressed… kind of strained… bittersweet,' he reflected.

As Martin watched a solitary snowflake drift towards him, he was sure to heed his mother's advice: *never catch a snowflake with your tongue until all the birds have flown south for winter.* 'Why did you really say who the feck cares where Jimmy is?'

Noel scrunched up his wind-battered face. 'If you're asking my opinion, I couldn't stand that man. Arrogant, like. Always slabbering on about those groupies. To look at him, he's a fine thing, but he didn't play the cards very smartly that he was dealt in life. I mean, see what he did, he quit that cracker of a TV show, only to form that absolutely rotten, tone deaf, caterwauling garage band. Wasted talent, the langer.' As if to clarify: 'I couldn't stand him.'

Sidling back to the sycamore tree, the group were finishing up. Still holding his full glass, Martin would wait until they turned to leave; then, he'd silently place his back on the table amongst the empties. The perfect crime.

'I'm getting a nutty aroma,' said Aubrey, her nose buried deep in her glass.

'I'm getting notes of butterscotch,' said Sven.

'I'm getting alimony,' said Theo bitterly.

'Alimony? Now who sounds like the *Amerloque*!' said Mary, exploding with venom, and she tramped back up the hill to the winery.

'She's still not speaking to you, then?' said Tate.

'Speaking to me is not the problem, it's the volume,' murmured Theo. 'And currently about divorce.'

'Could be just a threat, kid?' said Morton.

'No. When she says something, she means it. She commits.'

There was a painfully long silence before Sven clapped his hands decisively and said: 'Ok, ladies and gentlemen, back to the coach, let's head home'.

'Wait a minute,' said Aubrey with a raised eyebrow, 'Martini hasn't finished his drink.' With all eyes on him, and no chance to reach for the Strepsil in his pocket, he emptied the glass into his mouth. Satisfied, and Aubrey lowering her eyebrow, they turned their attention to the steep climb ahead.

The wine hit his taste buds with an acid thwack. Holding it in his mouth as long as possible, Martin rushed behind the tree and spat it out, spraying Chardonnay all over the snowman. Gasping in relief, Martin watched as the party clambered up the slope; rather pleased with himself. The perfect crime. Until a twig snapped behind him.

'Help! My snowman! My snowman!' Horror-struck, Joseph gaped from Martin to the yellow-stained snowman and back again. His father raced over to him.

'What, Joseph! What happened?' barked Tate, crouching next to him defensively.

'My, my, my snowman, look what he's done,' said Joseph. The group, which had formed a semi-circle around them, were gazing at the snowman in wide-eyed bemusement.

'And what, Moretti,' snapped Tate, 'is with the yellow snowman?'

'Yellow snowman? What, like, a Chinese snowman?' said Martin flippantly. 'I think that's probably racist, Tate.'

Rubbing the back of his neck, he forced a light chuckle, but nobody chuckled back. He could feel the blood rushing to his face.

'What did you do?' pressed Tate.

There was no point denying it; the snowman's head had started to dissolve. But who was safer to offend? Who was the lesser of two weevils: Tate Sinclair, in fully protective father mode, or Sven Lindblom, sacred defender of the wine? Swallowing hard, he said: 'I, er, I went for a pee, and some of it accidentally…' His voice trailed off.

'Did you pee on the snowman?' blinked Tate.

'Yep,' said Martin, shoes shuffling in a snow mound.

'Ew, gross!' cried Joseph.

'You peed on my snowman? It's Christmas! I oughtta sue you.'

'I'm not sure snowmen have many rights,' cracked Martin, in what he hoped was a jaunty, winning tone. The stony-faced group did not look won over. Mortified, Joseph Sinclair ran off.

'Nice, real nice, Moretti,' snarled Tate. 'What do you do in the spring—defecate on the Easter bunny?' With a bewildered shake of the head, Tate hurried after his son; leaving the rest of the party standing there in awkward silence. Clearing his throat, Martin prayed for that Mary Oblet-induced avalanche now, to crash through the valley and swallow him up whole. Rather unhelpfully, the snowman chose this moment to shed it's left arm. Only Eve Kessler looked amused as the party clumped up the hill; everybody avoiding eye contact with him. Martin let out a deep sigh. Another wonderful day in wine country.

Sheepishly boarding the coach, he wished again for some sort of distraction; anything to break the strangled silence. Discovering a corked bottle of Grenache. Red wine in the fridge. A chipped glass. Using a corkscrew on a screwcap. An overcooked steak. A cheeseboard containing no stilton. Pronouncing the 't' in Merlot.

It took just thirteen minutes for the distraction to arrive. And when it did, Martin was brutally reminded: *be careful what you wish for*.

Stepping off the coach, they were greeted by a uniformed police officer pulling something out of her blue Gendarmerie van. It was a body bag.

17

Capitaine Gallois

Under the darkening sky, the guests of le Château des Allues clamoured around the police officer. Why the body bag? What had happened? Who was dead?

'Where's my wife? Is she alright? Where is she?' demanded Tate.

The uniformed police officer raised a hand and they all fell silent. She pointed to the Château's doorway, where a tall, thin man stepped out to face them.

'Mesdames et Messieurs, my name is *Capitaine* Gallois of the *Section de Recherche.*'

'Listen, Captain—'

'Please, call me Gallois.' Behind a thick handlebar moustache, a chiselled, defiant pale face stared out at them all. 'I have been assigned because I believe many of you only speak English.' He cut an impressive figure in the headlights of the Gendarmerie van. Black shoes, black suit, black tie, and a matt of ruffled black hair; apparently this was still not enough black, leaning, as he was, on a black walking stick.

'But where—'

'Monsieur Sinclair, your wife is fine.' Gallois' slanted smile failed to reach his steel grey eyes. '*On y va*! Let's get inside, warm ourselves by the fire and reunite the Sinclairs.' Leading them in, he came to an abrupt stop in the hallway. 'Lieutenant Aimée will escort you to *le salon*. But…' he scanned his notepad, 'Martin Moretti, if you will follow me, *s'il vous plaît.*'

Nervously, the group stumbled after the uniformed officer; leaving a flummoxed Martin Moretti in the foyer with the Capitaine.

'*Pardon*, I skipped a step. Christian Gallois,' he said with a vice-like handshake.

'How can I help you, Christian?' asked Martin, readjusting the bones in his right hand.

'It's just Gallois.'

'How can I help you, Gallois?'

'If you would follow me, Monsieur Moretti,' he said, pushing on the wooden wall panel and striding through the concealed doorway. Passing Holly's scarlet scarf draped over the chair, they headed down.

'Section de Recherche?' said Martin.

'Investigation unit of the Gendarmerie,' said Gallois gruffly. 'Usually, I work in Narcotics, but... it is Christmas, and I was in the area.' He took each step of the spiral stone staircase slowly, hobbling down with the support of his cane. Gallois looked the same age as Martin, maybe slightly older. Martin supposed the limp had been picked up in the line of duty.

'And how can I help you?' repeated Martin, reaching the bottom of the stairs.

'There is no electricity down here but, then, you already know that,' said Gallois, catching his breath. The cellar was pitch black. No crackling fire or glimmering candles tonight. Switching a flashlight on, Gallois navigated them over to the bookcase whereupon he ripped the yellow tape from the door. Fluttering to the floor, Martin caught the words: GENDARMERIE NATIONALE ZONE INTERDITE. The forbidden zone. Possibilities raced through his mind—property damage, fire, theft—but the body bag removed any doubt. The question now was: who? Swinging the bookcase open, Gallois stepped back. If Holly Sinclair was accounted for, that only left one option...

The sight at the end of the passageway confirmed it. Illuminated underneath the flickering lights, lay the lifeless body of Jimmy Stresskeller. Martin hurled backwards, crashing into the very table he'd dined at with Jimmy less than twenty-four hours earlier. Head spinning in the darkness, his stomach churned violently and for an instant he felt he was going to be sick. His fumbling fingers removed his many layers of clothing and tossed them onto the stairs. Down to a t-shirt, he was still sweating. Jimmy Stresskeller was dead. The feather-blonde flake in a fur coat that Martin had actually quite liked.

Exhaling deeply, he stepped back into the cave, switching the light on from his phone. Death. Silence. Ruin. Spread-eagled on his front, lying in a pool of blood, Jimmy's head was twisted awkwardly to the side; his bouffant hair stained red, his face crushed and swollen.

'Bludgeoned,' said Martin, shaking his head in disbelief.

'*Oui.*'

Perplexed, Capitaine Gallois was watching Martin with serious concern, and Martin understood why. Gallois would have expected more grit, more professionalism, not someone at risk of vomiting over his crime scene. Martin was a little perplexed himself. Of the twenty-seven dead bodies he'd previously seen, he had never reacted like that before. Granted, Martin wasn't a police officer anymore, but surely he hadn't gone soft within a week?

'Don't touch anything,' said Gallois. 'Forensics arrive in an hour. But I doubt they will be able to tell us anything. I believe your entire party visited this chamber last night?' Martin nodded. '*Bon.* And the partying ended around midnight? *Bon,*' said Gallois, stroking his moustache thoughtfully. 'Your hosts discovered the body shortly after your wine tour left this morning at nine a.m. They phoned us immediately and look to have done a good job of leaving the area untouched. Does anything appear *différent*, out of place from last night?'

Martin peeled his eyes away from the celebrity corpse. The towering wine racks were much taller than he remembered, or perhaps it was because Jimmy looked tiny in death. Martin shuddered. His panic had eased but he still had no desire to be in here. Bright, ruby red blood was splashed over the painting, both on the frame and on the golden apple. And then he saw it. Or, rather, didn't see it.

'The bottle,' said Martin, his eyes coming to rest on the carved-out hole. 'There was an expensive bottle in there last night. Rare, apparently. Lafite Rothschild, or something.'

'*Intéressant.*' Gallois examined the empty hole, stroking his moustache again.

'Anyway, Gallois, I hope I was able to help,' said Martin, more than ready to leave the murder room. This was not his world; not anymore. He stepped around the puddle of blood and made for the bookcase.

'Stop,' barked the Capitaine.

'What are you doing?' frowned Martin. Gallois' walking stick was blocking the passageway.

'What are *you* doing?' Gallois repeated back. His steel grey eyes bore into Martin.

'Getting out of the way of your investigation,' said Martin. 'Heading upstairs.' He tried to push past Gallois, however the cane was pressed firmly against his chest.

'You are not getting out, Monsieur Moretti,' said Gallois, 'you are just getting started.'

'Come again?' said Martin.

'Investigate with me,' said Gallois.

'No,' said Martin.

'England and France together.'

'Very much no.' Striking downwards, Martin knocked the walking stick aside, but Gallois still blocked the exit with his tall frame.

'Like I said, I am usually Narcotics. And for an *affaire* like this, it would usually be investigated by a team of seven. I could do with the help. Even if it is... "the Defective Detective" from England.'

'Oh well, when you put it like that,' said Martin sarcastically, squeezing past Gallois.

'You are ordered to,' snapped Gallois. 'You do not have a choice.'

'Says who, President Macron? Sorry, Capitaine, I don't answer to him,' said Martin, striding out of the cellar.

'Far more important than him... we have a mutual Italian friend who said to give you carte blanche.'

'Renzo?' said Martin, his foot hovering above the bottom step. 'Why does he have any say?'

'This is his wine cellar. This is his wine tour, where one of his group has been murdered. Plus...' continued Gallois, with the confident air of someone about to reveal their ace card, 'we found this next to the body.' He held up an evidence bag containing several green leaves. It was a small sprig of mistletoe.

'So what?'

'Take a closer look,' said Gallois, shining his torch directly onto the bag.

Aiming his own light onto the mistletoe, Martin restrained himself from saying "so what" again. The sprig consisted of four green leaves, each with a smattering of white berries.

'*Regardez,*' Gallois pressed. 'We have wine and assassins to hunt.'

And then, straining his eyes through the murk, through the crinkled plastic and through his own scepticism, Martin saw something written onto one of the leaves in black ink.

DOT

18

The Golden Hour

'I thought that might pique your interest.' Gallois led the pair of them back into the murder room. 'Renzo says the Swede says you are obsessed with these D.O.T. *farces*, these, erm, pranks.'

'You still think they're pranks?' said Martin, sombrely eyeing Jimmy.

'So, I take it you will investigate with me?' said Gallois, staring up at the string of flickering lights. Several of the bulbs had blown; now undeniably a losing battle to pierce the cave's dank gloom.

'I always work better when not thirsty,' stated Martin.

'*Voilà*. Here, have some of this,' said Gallois, thrusting a hip flask into his hands.

Martin took a large swig. It was a warming cognac; velvety, creamy, tasting of marmalade toast and coffee beans. *Jesus*, he really had been in wine country too long.

'Oh, I like this,' murmured Martin.

'Lucky guess,' said Gallois with a knowing slanted smile; which suggested to Martin that the Capitaine had already tossed the rooms and found the empty cognac bottle under his pillow. Right now, Martin didn't care.

'Delicious.' He slugged back a second mouthful, and Martin felt the soothing warmth engulf him as though he'd sunk into a hot steaming bath.

'This missing bottle of wine, le Lafite Rothschild, I wonder how it fits into our timeline?' said the Capitaine, still gazing up at the craggy ceiling. '*Merde*!' Gallois slapped his forehead hard. 'I forgot to check, is he wearing a Fitbit?'

Flashing his light down, Martin could see there was

nothing on either wrist.

'No, nothing.' So where was the chunky gold Rolex he'd shown off at dinner last night? Surely the killer didn't steal that as well. 'Tell me,' said Martin, 'did you find a watch in his bedroom?'

'*Non*. And no Fitbit. That is a shame,' grumbled Gallois. 'Useful evidence, Fitbits, gives you an electronic footprint. Last week, we determined the precise time of death of a Madame Eleanor Calment, all from when her Fitbit recorded her heart rate fall to zero.'

'Murder?' asked Martin.

'Old age,' replied Gallois.

'I had the opposite once,' said Martin. 'After the murderer struck, he took off the victim's Fitbit and wore it for another forty-five minutes, purely to falsify the time of death.'

'How did you catch him?'

'Inconsistent pulse rates. Plus, we found fingerprints. And CCTV. He wasn't the brightest,' said Martin. 'Speaking of fingerprints, shouldn't we wait for forensics to arrive?'

'Pfft, forensics,' sniffed Gallois. 'I would take the human detective over science any day. For me, confession is key. Besides, what can they possibly tell us until we find the murder weapon.'

'So let's find the murder weapon,' said Martin, with another swig.

'We've no idea what it is.'

'Hmm, I wonder where we might find a blunt instrument in this room,' said Martin sardonically.

'A bottle?'

'Yep,' said Martin, pacing up and down the cave, his eyes roving across the wine racks.

'But surely it would shatter?'

'It's not like the movies, Gallois,' said Martin, still scanning each line of bottles. He was enjoying this game of hide and seek.

'Like I said, I am usually Narcotics,' Gallois said

defensively, now casting his own eye over the potential weapons. Their torch beams cut through row after row of emerald glass, immersing the cave in a bright greenish hue.

'This is assuming, of course,' said Martin, 'the killer put the bottle back afterwards.' *Where does a wise man hide a pebble? On the beach. And where does a wise man hide a leaf? In the forest,* thought Martin, remembering yesterday's conversation with Holly Sinclair.

'But which one? *C'est impossible,*' said Gallois. 'There are hundreds.'

'It's this one!' said Martin, peering closer. 'It's the only one without dust on it.'

'Bravo!' whooped Gallois, squeezing his shoulder in celebration. Martin would have joined in had the Vulcan nerve pinch not rendered him semi-conscious. 'A Barolo wine, 2006. And just in time,' cried Gallois over Martin's spasming shoulder. '*Bonjour, Eugene, tu as voyagé vite*!'

Eugene—overweight, with a ginger mullet and goatee—was forensics, wheezing rather strenuously with a large black case in each hand.

'*Bonjour, Gallois*,' he rasped, yanking both the Capitaine and Martin to the other side of the bookcase. Nostrils flared, Eugene was clearly displeased they dared to rubberneck—or breathe, even—on *his* crime scene. Slipping into a white jumpsuit, blue gloves and mask while Gallois updated him, he delicately placed a yellow plastic evidence marker beside the empty rack space and photographed it before bagging the murder weapon. Even in the dim light, Martin could see fragments of Jimmy on the side of the bottle. The weapon came from the wine racks on the right, at the far end of the passageway, so the murderer must have hidden in the shadows of the apple painting. Pre-meditated or caught in the act of vintage wine theft? Pre-meditated felt like a stretch, unless they had specifically invited Jimmy down here. Placing another marker by the painting, Eugene captured the moment with a dazzling flash.

'We will catch this man,' said Gallois, staring intently at Martin.

'Or woman,' said Martin. 'If there was only one blow, I'd suggest it was a man, but as there are multiple blows...' Martin counted at least three dents. 'Can you ask Eugene—this is probably a stupid question—could we calculate the number of blows by how shaken up the wine is inside the bottle?'

Gallois translated back and forth. 'You're right, says Eugene, that is a stupid question.' Eugene half-sniggered, half-snorted, and Martin wondered if this ginger mulletted man was related to Sven.

Based on the skull fractures, Martin knew forensics could determine which was the first, second and third strike, but any more than that would be too complex to interpret. And this definitely looked more than three strikes. Nevertheless, if Eugene was competent enough, he might still be able to infer the approximate height, stance, maybe weight and possibly gender of the killer. On one forensic investigation, the Case of the Naked Clown, Martin had gauged the murderer's motive and mindset purely from the ferocity of the attack.

Carefully, Eugene crouched over Jimmy's body, swabbing his neck and hands with cotton buds. Concluding the pair had sufficiently contaminated his crime scene, and nostrils now flared to the size of the Channel Tunnel, he ordered them upstairs.

'*On y va!* Come, we interrogate together,' said Gallois. Martin followed, scooping up his clothes on the way. 'We can order a scan of the brain and the skull, but only if you want to.' They made slow progress clambering back up the staircase, Gallois with one hand on the banister, the other his cane; however, the pained look on the Capitaine's face highlighted his sense of urgency.

'In France, don't you normally have some kind of magistrate who leads on such cases, a sort of investigating judge?' asked Martin, taking another nip from the hip.

'She came on the phone long enough to say she trusts

me to do a good job and is now back decorating the Christmas tree,' said Gallois with a wince. 'We've worked long enough together… she doesn't have to tell me how to do my investigation.' Halfway up, Gallois leaned for a moment against the wall, bearing all his weight on his cane. 'She knows as I know, the clock is ticking, we must go *ventre à terre*, erm, belly to the ground, erm… speed is of the essence.' Martin murmured in assent. They were in "the golden hour" as it was called in Britain. Mercifully more than sixty minutes, the golden hour is actually seventy-two hours. The first seventy-two hours of any murder investigation are critical, when the evidence and accounts of witnesses are the freshest. 'Besides, it is simple enough: examine the house, photograph the scene, take the suspects statements, *quoi*. While we waited for your tour party to arrive back, Lieutenant Aimee and I have already interviewed the owners of this Château. You can read their statements later if you like. Cooking, cleaning, tidying, sleeping. Nothing of significance. Also, we will wait for Eugene to confirm it, but I have already ruled out *le monte-plats*, the dumbwaiter elevator.'

Catching his breath at the top, Gallois declined the offer of cognac, thus Martin was obliged to drink it instead.

'I spoke to Monsieur Brambilla this morning,' panted Gallois. 'You are in the unique position of being our man on the inside. You will hear things over the dinner table that I will not, which you will report back to me.' A flicker of annoyance rose inside Martin. He did not care for the authoritarian tone. '"Operation Incognito", Renzo called it.'

'Can I speak to them as a group?' asked Martin.

'You can address them tomorrow,' said Gallois dismissively.

'Tomorrow? I'd rather tonight.'

'Impossible, but I know Renzo will be very pleased for your support on this investigation.'

'I'm sure he will,' muttered Martin.

'During his daughters kidnapping, Renzo did not only

make friends with you. He also became friends with the chief constable. If this investigation goes well, Renzo can have a word with your old boss, *peut-être...* get your job back?'

From the bottom of the stairwell, Eugene shouted up that he estimated the time of death to be between midnight and eight a.m., which didn't really progress matters; so instead, Martin asked Gallois: 'How well do you know Renzo?'

'During Sara's kidnapping, I followed up on several leads this side of *la Manche*.' With a wipe of his forehead, Gallois pushed on the concealed door and they emerged into the brightly lit hallway. 'But now the action is on this side of *la Manche*, you will follow my specific orders.'

'Obviously,' blinked Martin.

'Yes, *obviously* obviously, I was not asking, I was telling.' Again, his tone grated. Taking Martin's silence as consent, the Capitaine continued. '*Bon*, then let's commence with Operation Incognito. These last days, you have been rolling in money and foie gras and fine wine and seen everything from your golden coach. So, how many suspects do we have?'

'Nine,' Martin replied.

'*Bon*, I'd like you to round them up for me.'

'Ok, ten.'

Gallois' knuckles whitened around his cane. 'You think this is funny, Monsieur Moretti? There is a dead body downstairs and I'm asking you nicely to gather them up for questioning.'

'Fine,' said Martin, 'when do we start the interviews?' Although not a fan, Martin didn't begrudge the Capitaine's attitude. He'd faced plenty of this "juris-my-dick-tion" crap on the force and learnt long ago if you want a smooth investigation, you follow procedure, the chain of command. And amongst all Gallois' pleas for Martin's help, promoting a spirit of cooperation, it would have vexed the Frenchman to utilise an English detective.

'Start the interrogations?' said Gallois. 'Now.'

Entering the living room—a cosy, French Country

chamber full of squashy armchairs—they found the group in tears: Holly, Eve, Aubrey and Joseph clasped together on a crimson-coloured sofa; Tate, biting his lip, and Morton, a vacant look on his slackened face, awkwardly hovering behind them. As a collective wail burst from the huggle, a red-eyed Sven perched on the sofa's edge, his outstretched hand patting Aubrey on the shoulder. Martin was still astounded by the impact Jimmy had on people. Only forty-eight hours ago, he'd witnessed the waitresses erupting into a frenzied mania; one giant, jumping shriek. Here now, the room was one giant shaking sob. Astonishing. But then, there had been Martin's own violent reaction to seeing Jimmy's bludgeoned body.

Not everybody was crying. Sitting either side of the fireplace, the Oblets stared out into nothingness, seemingly in the direction of an ashen-faced Noel who was fiddling with a lampshade. Pacing back and forth in the room, Pekoe looked utterly aghast, the cherrywood pipe in his hand untouched. Standing stiffly in the centre of the room, in the eye of the emotional-hurricane, was Lieutenant Aimee. She stared over at her Capitaine imploringly, as though begging him to rescue her from the cortege of mourners.

Gallois wrinkled his nose. '*Je sors fumer une clope.*'

The frosted gravel driveway was now bustling with activity. Gallois was sucking on his second Marlboro, silently watching from the doorstep as the newly arrived Gendarmerie barricaded off the surrounding area and ushered back the onlookers. Martin wished he'd put his coat back on. The night air was nippy; his breath smoked, matching the billowing plume from Gallois' cigarette.

Eventually, the Capitaine said: 'You know them better than me, Monsieur Moretti. Who do you suggest we start with?'

But something, or someone, had caught Martin's eye.

'Actually, Gallois, you remember when I said we had ten

suspects?' said Martin.

'My sides are still splitting,' said Gallois, through another cloud of smoke.

'Make that eleven suspects,' said Martin hurriedly. 'Over there,' he pointed to the police cordon, where one of the onlookers was wearing a distinctively pink dress. 'That woman. Cammy, I think he said her name was, Cammy Duval. Apparently, she's Jimmy Stresskeller's stalker. What do you think? Worth subtly picking up when—'

'*Arrêter cette femme*!' Gallois screamed, as subtle as a sledgehammer. The Gendarmerie sprang into action fast, but she was faster; throwing a wild-eyed glance over her shoulder as she hopped a wall and disappeared into the darkness. '*Merde*.'

'Worth putting her face out to the media?' said Martin.

'*Non*, going to the press is not the Gendarmerie way.'

Looking up at Jimmy's window, Martin had an idea. 'Could you ask your Lieutenant to go up and switch the light on in Jimmy's room?'

Gallois ordered Aimee upstairs before stamping out his cigarette and turning to Martin. '*Pardon*, I must make arrangements for Cammy Duval's capture. I will see you inside.'

Martin did not need telling twice. Rushing back in before he turned blue, he crashed straight into something small. Joseph Sinclair; scared stiff. Pulling him up, the boy did not let go, his hands clamped tightly around Martin's forearm; he was freakishly strong.

'Is it true, is Jimmy Stresskeller dead? He died in the cellar?' whispered Joseph.

'Yes,' said Martin.

'She killed him, didn't she?' said Joseph, 'I heard her plotting it.' His eyes weren't red but his whole body was tremoring.

'Who?' Martin glanced left and right but they were alone in the hallway.

'I'm scared...' said Joseph, 'I'm next.'

'Who?' Martin pressed.

'My mother,' said Joseph. Martin swallowed. Holly Sinclair? Surely not. Although, where had she been the past twenty-four hours? 'I thought, I thought you'd save me,' he whimpered. 'First, she'll cut off my tongue, then she's going to kill me. She's going to kill us all.'

'Does your father know?' said Martin.

Eyes unfocussed, Joseph hadn't heard him. 'But I must be brave,' he said, trance-like. 'I will defend us all from her. Never say die.'

'You're only eight.'

'Eight and three-quarters,' he said defiantly.

The front door opened, snapping Joseph out of his daze and running back into the living room. Well, well, well. The Christmas letter just got a whole lot more interesting.

'*Pardon*, Monsieur Moretti.' Gallois' face revealed they'd been unsuccessful in the capture of Cammy Duval. 'So, our interrogations, who should we start with?'

Martin quickly replied.

'The Sinclairs.'

Moretti Christmas Newsletter

Status: **Draft - Version 2**
Date: December 19th (6 days until deadline)

Dear Liver,

This case will be rough. Stay strong.

Idea for Christmas letter – start with an inspirational quote.

TO TRAVEL IS TO LIVE! Not for Jimmy Stresskeller.
TRAVEL WITH NO REGRET! Jimmy Stresskeller's regretting it.

Who doesn't have ragrets. Where's my next paycheck? Where's Sara Brambilla's kidnapper? Where's my Agatha Christie country manor floor plan?

Plus, deadlines creeping up on me like Morton Kessler. Only 6 days to solve the D.O.T. liver killer because it's only:

- 6 days to click Send on this crappy Round-robin
- 6 days until Superintendent Radnor is back from leave and files my termination

So 6 days to trick Radnor that I'm worth it and finally maybe make my family proud. I'm not the black sheep, just tie-dye.

Seasons Greetings,

Martin Enzo Isidore Moretti
#blackgoat

19

Killer Sentence

Tossing a handful of water over his face, Martin glanced at his reflection; his dark brown skin perfectly matching his dark brown eyes. And those eyes, they confirmed everything he was feeling right now. Yes, he'd nearly vomited over the crime scene, but now there was a calm buzz about Martin, a sparkle in his eyes; like something had awoken inside him.

It was clear now, somebody was trying to sabotage their tour—the livers, the letter, the scratches down the coach. The wine had been stolen and now Jimmy Stresskeller was dead, lying next to a sprig of mistletoe inscribed with "DOT". Suddenly the previous night's conversation raced to mind. When he and Sven had been discussing those three mysterious letters, Jimmy had piped up.

Oh, I know all about that.

Who else had overheard him? It was a cliché straight out of a detective story; loudly announce to the party you know a deep dark secret, only to get bumped off before you can reveal it.

Upon seeing the body, why had he nearly been sick? Had he gone soft? What did that even mean? Surely "true grit" was nothing more than emotional detachment; routine police work disconnecting you from everyday life. For the past fourteen years, he had holidayed in the underworld, returning with the souvenirs of a straw donkey and cold indifference; numb to the most depraved things human beings can do to each other. So, why had he nearly been sick? Martin had finally figured it out. Never before had he investigated the murder of someone he knew. Usually, the first time he met the victim was in the morgue; learning about them via grieving friends, foes and family. This time, Martin had the advantage. He would catch the D.O.T. saboteur. He would pinpoint the missing Lafite Rothschild. He would bring the murderer to justice, whether they were hiding at the top of a mountain or sitting next to him on the coach. Totting that up to a sentence of forty-two years in prison; that would be plenty to shove in the face of Superintendent Radnor of Buxton Police Station.

Running a hand over his dark Caesar-cut hair, his mind started to spin. Though it wasn't the events of the past hour—dead body, stalker on the run, a child's ominous claims—that had his head whirling. It was Gallois' statement from the top of the staircase.

If this investigation goes well, Renzo can have a word with your old boss and get your job back.

Did he want his old job back? What was the alternative? Unofficial police consultancy for the Met? Carry on solving murders as a private investigator in Hawaii, or as a magician in a windmill, or in a retirement home every Thursday? Most likely, he'd become a security guard at Asda. There must still be crimes to solve there. Who knows; perhaps the thrill of his first case as a bright-eyed Southwark police sergeant —the disappearance of Viscountess Isabella—would pale in comparison with the disappearance of the Viscount mint creams? Chief Inspector Martin Moretti, the hallowed police detective, who had foiled the Arsenic Stradivarius Society in Sheffield, and the Bomber Bluesnake teens from Dundee. Now it would be a case of the missing BBQ baked beans on aisle three.

Tossing another handful of water over his face, he headed down the corridor towards the interrogation room.

'Bonjour Monsieur Moretti.'

Everything was ready in the wood-panelled, book-lined dining room. Capitaine Gallois and Lieutenant Aimee sat together on one side of a long mahogany table. Opposite, were two empty chairs; the hot seats. On the table in front of Aimee was a silver laptop; Gallois, a notepad and a small, ornately decorated tin with the word "Nancy" imprinted on it.

And in the middle, thank God, was a large pot of freshly brewed coffee. It was now midnight. Gallois insisted everyone be interviewed immediately. The golden hour waits for no man, woman or weird kid.

'Bonjour Lieutenant,' he replied to Aimee, taking a seat at the far end of the table.

'Bad news,' said Gallois curtly. It was the first time Martin had properly seen Gallois in the Château's light. Underneath his matt of ruffled black hair was a long, thin vertical scar running down his left cheek. This, no doubt, was the perils of Narcotics officers having to deal with frenetic, crazed smackheads rather than Martin's calm, motionless homicide victims. 'Eugene will not be happy. All of the clothes from yesterday have been washed. Your hosts have been annoyingly efficient at limiting our fibre transfer evidence.' He glowered at Martin as though the hosts were his responsibility. 'We might as well send Eugene home. Even if we do still find blood on the killer's clothing, any lawyer would assert it has been contaminated by everything else in the washing machine. *Merde.*'

'Send Eugene home?' said Martin 'What about DNA and fingerprints elsewhere in the cellar?'

'Let us stick to human detection and confession. We have done too much forensics already, too much time wasted in that wine cellar,' said Gallois dismissively.

'You can not dust for Beaujolais,' added Aimee.

'*Ah oui, tres bon*, Agathe,' Gallois nodded approvingly at his Lieutenant.

'Well, how about a top up, at least?' Martin slid the hip flask down the table.

'*Alcool*?' Aimee shot Gallois a concerned look.

'I'm glad you flasked,' grinned Martin. His French colleagues did not grin back.

Gallois snatched up the flask, weighed it in both hands,

observed how light it now was, and pocketed it with a pitying smile. 'We are aware, Monsieur Moretti, of your unorthodox methods… your reputation as "the Defective Detective". Look under the table, *s'il vous plaît*.'

Underneath his seat Martin found two bottles—a litre of William Peel Finest Old Blended Scotch Whisky and a 70cl Hennessy Very Special Cognac—alongside a large white mug.

'I am *vivement contre*, erm, reluctant,' said Gallois. 'But Renzo swears he has seen the results himself. These will last you the entire investigation, *comprendre*?'

'Definitely,' said Martin, happily filling the mug. It was the perfect arrangement. He could get nicely drunk in the background; Gallois, the professional face on the stand. No danger of Martin ruining their day in court.

Unimpressed, Aimee rose to fetch the first interviewee. It turned out they couldn't speak to the Sinclairs first as Joseph had run off into the grounds. Quickly caught again, his parents were currently calming him down.

Pekoe Williams entered and jabbed out a hand; a Gurkha's lethal hand. Gallois shook it, then motioned for him to take the seat opposite.

'Bonjour Monsieur Williams,' said the Capitaine soothingly, 'please make yourself comfortable.' This was a much softer Gallois than the gruff one Martin had encountered in the cellar.

'May I smoke my pipe?'

'*Mais bien sûr*, go ahead. We have invited Monsieur Moretti to sit in with us to help; in case anything is lost in translation for language and *judiciaire*.'

'Of course,' puffed Pekoe with a friendly acknowledgement to Martin. For once, he smelt pure tobacco. 'It's weird, isn't it?' Pekoe glanced down at his phone screen. 'About Jimmy, he's kind of still with us.'

'In our hearts, yes,' said Gallois with a sad smile.

'No, I mean—online,' said Pekoe. 'He's still in our tour Snapchat group. His Instagram and TikTok accounts are still open. Who switches those off?'

'His family,' said Aimee, not looking up from her laptop; feverishly tapping away, logging every word spoken while Pekoe silently scrolled social media. Martin had done it himself in the past, a final flick through Facebook after a funeral. Gave new meaning to "the Last Post".

'Did he have much family?' asked Pekoe.

'Two brothers,' said Aimee.

Pekoe's face darkened. 'No family should face this ordeal at any time. But at Christmas… a time of peace and celebration, it is always much harder to bear.'

'We will get his family the answers they need,' said Gallois.

Pekoe, pipe in mouth, stared across the table at the Capitaine. 'There was nothing untoward, was there?'

'Untoward?' Gallois turned to Martin, grasping for the word's meaning.

'Was there anything sinister,' Martin clarified.

'Ah, sinister. *Fâcheux*,' he turned back to Pekoe. 'We are still only beginning our investigation; making enquiries. What did you know, or had heard of Jimmy Stresskeller before he arrived?'

'Nothing really,' said Pekoe, shifting in his seat. 'I knew he was on TV, but I hadn't watched any of his programmes.'

'Programmes?'

'He always talked about *Coast Cop,* and that reality jungle show, and his band.'

'And what was the name of his band?'

Pekoe paused for a moment. 'Don't you know this?'

'I just wanted to know if you know,' Gallois replied pleasantly.

'Well… I believe, the Black Carnations,' said Pekoe. 'Must she tap away like that?' He stabbed in the direction of the Lieutenant with his cherrywood pipe.

'It is procedure,' replied Aimee, staring intently at her screen. 'I write everything up, for my dossier.'

Gallois cleared his throat. 'Er, when did you last see Monsieur Stresskeller?'

'At the meal last night,' said Pekoe, 'down in the cellar.'

'Ah, *oui*, the meal,' said Gallois. 'How was it?'

'We ate, we drank, we sang, some of the couples were....' Pekoe puffed thoughtfully, 'slightly boisterous.' Martin smirked into his mug, which he was pretty sure Gallois had spotted. 'Then, we went to bed.'

'What else can you tell me about the evening? Anything special?'

'Our tour guide, Sven, showed us the wine collection and the Chateau Lafite Rothschild. That was pretty special. Or, pretty expensive, at least.'

'And what time was bed?'

'Around twelve-ish, I believe, maybe slightly later.'

'Everybody went up together?' asked Gallois.

'Yes, I think so, except... I think Sven, Jimmy, and yourself, Martin, stayed down?' All eyes turned to Martin, who nodded to confirm.

'*Merci*. And your room is up the stairs between the Sinclairs and the Oblets... did you happen to hear any strange sounds in the night?' said Gallois with a laugh. Pekoe shook his head. '*Bon*. And you, no night-time wanderings? You did not pop down to the kitchen for a midnight snack?' Pekoe shook his head again. '*Bon*.'

Exasperated, Martin drained his whisky. The Capitaine's style was excruciatingly slow. They'd never get results at this glacial pace, not unless they waited a couple of decades for a death bed confession. If only Gallois would mention the actual murder. Then, they could widen the enquiry to ask such key questions as: who had reason to kill the victim? Where were you at the time of the murder? And—Martin's favourite—was it you? They needed to rattle some cages. You can get more with a kind word and a pair of thumbscrews than you can with just a kind word. Right now, Martin felt a hazy fog around motive; was the target Jimmy or was this a wider attack on Renzo himself? Pre-planned or a robber caught in the act? Maddeningly, however, Gallois hadn't even mentioned the theft of the Lafite bottle. Martin poured himself a second mug.

'Monsieur Williams, are you sure you are ok for Monsieur Moretti to sit in with us?' asked the Lieutenant, glaring at Martin.

'Of course,' said Pekoe. 'We are all on the clock for Renzo Brambilla, are we not?' Underneath his polished accent, Martin detected an edge of bitterness to Pekoe's voice.

'And what is it you do for Monsieur Brambilla?' Opening up his small decorative tin, Gallois unwrapped a golden hard boiled sweet and sucked on it thoughtfully.

'Presently, I'm personal sherpa to Renzo,' said Pekoe. 'We're hoping to get up into the mountains for the climax of the tour. He has a cabin up there. Spoiler alert,' he added to Martin.

'And how is the tour?' asked Gallois.

'In truth, I find it all quite sinister, rather disturbing,' said Pekoe with a slight frown. 'First, we find those livers in the punchbowl with D.O.T. written on them; which, honestly, still makes me feel sick.'

'*Oui*, Renzo has informed me of the livers incident,' said Gallois.

'Then, D.O.T. is carved with a kitchen knife down the side of the coach. And now Jimmy is dead. It's all feeling rather tense; enough to make anyone snap.'

'Ah!' exclaimed Gallois raising a finger. 'Did you hear that, Lieutenant? *Enough to make anyone snap.*' Aimee was militantly tapping away on her laptop. Despite the Gendarme uniform, she looked more like a secretary. 'Highlight that point will you, either put it in bold or underline it.' Gallois glanced over at her curiously. 'Which did you use?'

'Both,' said Aimee.

The Capitaine nodded approvingly. '*Très enthousiaste*, our Lieutenant here.'

'How did you know it was done with a kitchen knife?'

asked Martin. It was the first time he'd spoken.

'I beg your pardon?' replied Pekoe.

'The coach,' said Martin, 'how did you know it was a kitchen knife?'

'Er, thank you, Monsieur Williams, that is sufficient for now,' said Gallois, crossly, both hands clenched into fists. With a slow smile of relief, Pekoe headed out.

The edge of bitterness... the kitchen knife... as the door slammed shut, Martin felt the flickering flame of annoyance rising inside him again. Gallois had completely cut across him.

'What was that?' said Martin.

'I will ask the questions, thank you,' snapped Gallois, baring his teeth.

'I thought you wanted my help,' said Martin, equally outraged. 'And what's with the soft approach? Shouldn't we be leaning on them a little? Let me speak to them as a group.'

'*Non!* It is about creating the right ambience,' growled Gallois, 'so they are relaxed, easier for them to talk... to tell the truth, *quoi*. How would your people say it? Softly, softly, catch the monkey.'

His irritation rising from flicker to inferno, Martin said, as measured as he could manage: 'And when you say "your people"... you mean, you English, right?' Aimee glanced nervously from one to the other.

'*Oui*, yes, *oui*, of course,' said Gallois. Martin swallowed his anger down. Or, more accurately, swallowed it down with whisky. 'What was that smirk I saw earlier?' asked a mollified-Capitaine. 'Something the mountaineer said that made you smile?'

Martin smirked again. 'When he described the evening meal as "slightly boisterous", that was a very polite summary.' And he told them about the night's entertainment; the cellar tour, the Oblet's vicious row and—of course—the bookcase gymnastics. Both Gallois and Aimee smirked at the gymnastics part, and the tension lifted within the room.

'*On y va!* Come, let's have the next audition,' said Gallois, back to business. 'And this time, Monsieur Moretti, stay silent.' Martin poured himself a third mug.

Promptly, Sven entered the dining room and took a seat facing the Gendarmerie. He'd finally removed the decuvage red stains from his right hand. Though as the Italian proverb went: clean hands disguise dirty feet.

'How are you, Monsieur Lindblom?' asked Gallois comfortingly. His pristine black suit starkly contrasted with Sven's crumpled pinstripe effort.

'I'm not quite fine but...' Sven shrugged. For the first time ever, he was lost for words.

'Quite understandable,' said Gallois. 'You live with the party when on tour?'

'Yes, I have a room here at the Château.'

'And the coach driver as well?'

'No, he sleeps on the coach, he prefers it that way.' That ruled out Omar, thought Martin, assuming the hosts locked the front door. 'Neither of us, I think, will sleep soundly tonight.'

'How so?' asked Gallois.

'We are still, I think, a little in shock when we heard of this terrible accident.'

'Accident?' Martin chimed in. Gallois' expression hardened instantly. 'It was a little more violent than that.' Blithely, Martin mimed being bopped over the head several times.

Nervously rubbing his double chin, Sven stammered: 'One, one of the bottles fell off the top shelf?' He seemed more troubled by the circumstances than for the actual loss of Jimmy.

'Only if it bounced repeatedly against his head, causing the Lafite to vanish into thin air.' Martin returned Gallois' glower with a wide, innocent smile.

'The Lafite has gone!' Sven jumped out of his seat. 'Nobody mentioned that!'

'You think a bottle of wine more important than human

life?' said Gallois, trying to regain control of the room.

'Er, no, of course not,' said Sven. Running both hands through his mullet, he sat back down composedly, only for his right leg to start jiggling. 'But what is going on here?' His forehead was scrunched in concern. 'I'm sensing owls in the swamp.'

Aimee murmured something in French to Gallois.

'I believe you had a request?' said the Capitaine.

'Hmm? Oh yes, we need to get down to the wine racks,' said Sven.

'Nobody touches anything in the cellar,' said Gallois. 'This is a crime scene.'

'But the bottles, we must shake them all, immediately.'

'Pardon?'

'It is a wine superstition that must be upheld,' said Sven. 'When someone dies, the wine in the cellar must be shaken immediately.' The Capitaine vigorously shook his head. Between Martin's loose lips and Sven's superstitions, Gallois had clearly had enough of this interview. 'If they're not shaken at once,' implored Sven, 'then all of the wine stored there will turn sour.' With Aimee's fingers poised above her keyboard, the Swede stared pleadingly into the Capitaine's eyes for a full thirty seconds.

Wrinkling his nose, he concluded: *'Je sors fumer une clope.'*

Gallois smoked furiously, refusing to look Martin in the eye. They were standing on the doorstep again, shivering; Aimee hovering cautiously to their side. A bright full moon shone down on the 12th century alpine Château. Under different circumstances, it would have looked spectacular. Right now, everything looked bleached: grey and ghostly. The snowy driveway was deserted now. The onlookers had headed home. Silently, two officers patrolled the grounds, mostly to stay warm. The chilled air hit the back of Martin's throat and burned his lungs; or maybe that was just the second-hand smoke inhaled the past hour.

'I still need to speak to them as a group,' pressed Martin. 'Tonight.'

'We need to rethink this partnership,' the Capitaine grumbled. 'This is my case, you can not keep blurting out like a mad man.'

'I'm just excited to whip out the cuffs and catch our killer,' said Martin. He had no regrets about what he'd revealed to Sven. He knew what he was doing. And it had nothing to do with loose lips. Martin wanted the party to know it was murder. Gallois didn't understand; he was narcotics, not homicide. It was time for Martin to take charge.

'Did you ever consider, Monsieur Moretti,' he said, lighting a second cigarette, 'that probably there is a reason I am taking these interrogations gently, a good reason?'

'No.'

'That I have already cracked this case?'

'Very much no.' Martin's impatience wasn't simply about the golden hour. Right now, the whisky was beginning to kick in. He felt giddy, wonderfully lightheaded, but this drunkenness needed to be applied. Booze may open his doors of perception, but it must be channelled onto the problem with pinpoint focus. Otherwise, he was just another pretentious git getting hammered. Scientifically speaking, booze stimulates all three regions of the brain involved in self-reflection and introspection (specifically: the posterior cingulate, precuneus, and insula cortex). But it's a tightrope. Get the balance wrong, drift off aimlessly, and it stimulates the regions of the kebab shop, gutter and toilet bowl.

Gallois was still talking. '*Veuillez considerer* that I already know who did it.'

'How thrilling,' said Martin, suppressing a yawn. Attentively, Lieutenant Aimee still hovered nearby. No silver laptop to hand; instead, she clutched a small notepad with her pen ready. Martin wondered again if she might be best suited as a secretary.

'*Oui*, the culprit is known to me. Our interrogations in *la salle à manger* are procedural. *C'est tout.*'

'Most impressive,' said Martin vacantly.

'We are obtaining preliminary statements simply to put the dots on the "I".'

'So, go on, Gallois,' said Martin, 'who did it, then?'

'*Quand on parle du loup*,' said Gallois.

In a flash, Aimee ran. Bolting past the patrolmen before they or even Martin had spotted the pink-dressed woman in the bushes, Aimee flew in with a hard shoulder, knocking her face-first to the ground. Camille Duval scrambled up, only to be short-clotheslined down again. Not a secretary. Definitely not a secretary.

'*Eh voilà!*' said Gallois, popping a boiled sweet into his mouth. 'There is our killer. *De rien.*' They watched as Cammy was cuffed and bundled into the back of the Gendarmerie van. 'Caught by the great Capitaine Gallois. Jealous?'

'Well, no, we're on the same team,' said Martin.

Gallois' slanted smile widened. 'You're jealous. Because you've contributed nothing except liver damage.'

'How about I'm the one who found the murder weapon and I'm the one who suggested we switch Jimmy's light on?' said Martin, pointing upwards. 'Like a moth to the flame. Or in this case, like a stalker to an exposed window.'

'A successful arrest by the *Section de Recherche.*' Gallois blew a cloud of smoke through his nostrils. 'We will have her charged for the pop star's murder and in Fleury-Mérogis prison before Christmas Eve.' He turned to Aimee and said: '*Amenez Eugene ici.*'

'How are you so sure it's her?' asked Martin.

'I know things,' said Gallois.

Martin was less convinced. For now, the motive for murdering this C-list celebrity remained murky. Love, hate or money? Was this purely about Jimmy Stresskeller? Or was it something bigger, about hurting Renzo and his vineyard?

Gallois had it solved but Martin wasn't ruling anyone out. Sven Lindblom's insistence at disrupting the crime scene. Sven Lindblom's perennially red-stained hand. The splashes of red that Martin had spotted on Aubrey's hiking boots during the vineyard walk. Martin saw suspects everywhere. Omar, the bus driver, who'd somehow got the D.O.T. scratches out of his system; the scratches that Pekoe somehow knew were done with a kitchen knife. The gothic, sex-crazed Kesslers. The rage-filled Oblets. The Sinclairs, with their freakishly strong kid, where the only sign of Holly before tonight was her scarf outside the cellar door. And again the nagging thought. Where was the gold Rolex?

Inspired by Lieutenant Aimee's smackdown of the C-list stalker, it was definitely time for Martin Moretti to take action; to tap into his soused brainpower. Like the Capitaine had said, Martin wasn't getting out, he was just getting started. And reflecting back, over the past twenty-four hours, Martin realised he'd missed something. When trekking through the vineyards, directly before the incident of the yellow snowman, there was a conversation that suddenly struck Martin as rather telling. One killer sentence that told him precisely who the D.O.T. killer was. In fact, it was obvious.

20

The Clue of the Whispering Corridor

Yep, now was definitely the time to crank it up a smidge. If he could address them as a group, he could shake things up, put the cat amongst the pigeons, stir up a hornets nest, rattle some cages, rock the boat, push their buttons, get under their skin, yank their plank.

Martin lurched out of his daydream so violently he nearly fell off his chair. Finding himself back in the dining room, the French detectives scowled at him; their scowls deepening as he poured himself another whisky. So what. He was past the point of no return. Tilting his head, Martin toasted the pair of them; to oblivion and beyond.

They were mid-way through interviewing Noel Gillespie; the birdman, the ornithologist, the perpetual middle-aged twitcher. By some miracle, Martin made it through a further three minutes of Gallois' procedural questions (hearing the same dinner details as the previous suspects) before he decided to cut in. Yep, time to rattle some cages. Or in this case, ruffle some feathers.

'*Merci.* And *dites-moi*, Monsieur Gillespie,' said Gallois softly, 'what did you think of Monsieur Stresskeller?'

'He's sound, like,' replied Noel.

'And what did you really think to him?' interrupted Martin, receiving a dark look from Gallois.

'I… I wasn't his biggest fan,' conceded Noel. He was the first of the suspects to reach across for the coffee. Searing hot steam from his cup swirled upwards, but Noel Gillespie didn't flinch as he gulped it down in one.

'A rival for your own fame, perhaps?' said Martin.

'Fame?' said Aimee, glancing up from her screen, puzzled. Right on cue, Noel handed Gallois a copy of *Bird Watcher's Digest*, the self-satisfied grin on the cover now matching the one in the dining room.

Skimming the magazine before passing it to Aimee for noting, Gallois grudgingly asked: 'And why is it that you were not his biggest fan?'

'That melter, he was... temperamental,' said Noel, 'and by that, I mean 80% temper, 20% mental.' Chortling at his own joke, the Gendarmerie smiled obligingly. 'Thinks he is a rock n rolla.'

'*Was*,' corrected Martin. '*Was* a rock n rolla.'

'He really is dead, murdered, so?'

'Correct,' said Martin. 'His pronouns are "was" and "were".'

'Jesus,' said Noel, shaking his head in disbelief.

'Funnily enough,' said Martin, 'you used the past tense yourself earlier today, regarding Jimmy.' This was the killer sentence he had remembered from the vineyards.

'Did I?'

'You said "I couldn't stand him". Past tense. When you were looking through your binoculars, before any of us knew he was dead, you said to me "I couldn't stand him". Instead of saying "I *can't* stand him".' Martin let the statement linger.

'It's an Irish thing,' said Noel.

'I was posted to Belfast for two years. I never heard that.'

'Ah well, you see, Moretti, Belfast isn't in Ireland, is it?'

'But even when travelling to Dublin, I never heard use of the past tense like that.'

'It's a Cork thing,' said Noel, after a short pause. 'Or the slip of the tongue, like. To be honest, I wasn't paying much attention to you, no offence. I just have to find my bird.'

Martin leant forward, like a tiger pouncing. 'Did you kill Jimmy?'

'Now you're asking,' said Noel.

'I am and you're not answering,' said Martin.

Fleetingly, Noel stared at his reflection in the back of his teaspoon. 'I wasn't his biggest fan, but I didn't want him dead.'

Martin took a moment to consider their interviewee. Maybe it simply was a slip of the tongue? People often behave strangely in the presence of a police officer. 'Any idea where Jimmy's gold Rolex is?' he asked.

'I don't.'

'You do have an interest in watches, correct?' asked Martin.

Leaning back in his chair, Noel placed both hands behind his head. 'Only in antiques like my seventeenth century mahogany duck find and old watches like the Omega De Ville you're wearing.'

'How about the stolen wine? The Chateau Lafite is missing.'

'It wasn't me,' said Noel. His left eyelid fluttered.

'You know,' said Martin, 'rubbing your eye is a sign of discomfort.'

'I've got an itch.' Noel poured himself a second cup of coffee.

'And drinking is a sign of nervousness.'

'I'm thirsty.'

'And—'

'Alright, alright, who wouldn't be on edge being grilled by you lot.'

'How about the D.O.T. initials that we found on the livers, on the coach and on the mistle—'

'Thank you, Monsieur Gillespie,' said Gallois firmly. The Capitaine had clearly had enough. 'You have been most helpful.' Noel bounded out.

The room fell silent but Martin was seething. Just as he was starting to get somewhere. Martin bit back his retort, anxious he'd gone too far and ruined his chances of continuing the interviews. Bracing himself for Gallois to start yelling, instead the Capitaine said: 'Do you know why we have the coffee in here?'

'Because it's one a.m.?' said Martin, gazing at the ceiling.

'No,' said Gallois, 'because when you hand the interviewee a warm cup of coffee, they'll see you as a warmer person. It creates a more conducive environment. We are trying to reduce resistance, not increase resistance.'

If Martin had to resist rolling his eyes much longer, he'd go blind. 'I'm familiar with the good cop schtick, Gallois.'

'And what is your method, Monsieur Moretti—the blunderbuss?'

'Technically, it's called the Scharff technique,' said Martin. 'Kind of random questions... so they don't know what's important and what isn't. It works 'cause the suspect doesn't know what to hide from telling you.'

'An interesting approach, but one I would prefer you reserve for England, *s'il vous plait.*'

Theo and Mary Oblet were next summoned. Theo, however, sailed into the dining room alone.

'*Bonsoir*, Monsieur Oblet. For the benefit of Monsieur Moretti, I hope you are ok if we undertake this conversation in English?' Theo gave a small, sullen nod of the head, so Gallois continued: 'You are evidently upset by this distressing death, if you...'

'I am not upset by this death, er, by this murder with a bottle,' said Theo, the officer in charge of them obviously not as effective as Aimee at curtailing the group gossip. 'I am upset about the state of my marriage, or what is left of it.'

'Can I ask you something, Theo?' said Martin. 'Why are you so bummed about the split? Your wife, no offence is a bit of a bitch.'

'I value art. I value love. Both are hard,' said Theo with a sad smile. 'You can not help who you fall in love with. If anyone is going to be verbally abused by Mary Oblet, I want it to be me; if it makes her happy. Don't they say: happy wife, happy life.'

'I prefer: happy house, happy spouse.' Martin didn't care that Gallois was no longer sucking his sweets but crunching down on them. He had to take charge.

'What was it like for you, your divorce?' asked Theo.

'How did you know I was divorced?'

'I can tell by the way you talk about Mary,' said Theo airily, 'that you have been broken by a woman. That is something I would never allow.'

'I like to think I'm not broken, just mildly sprained.'

'Do you trust women?'

'I'm working on it. It'd help if the killer didn't turn out to be female,' said Martin, thinking about who was currently in the back of the Gendarmerie van.

'What was it like for you, your divorce?' repeated Theo.

'Mutually assured destruction. Can you think of anyone who would want to harm Jimmy?'

'I don't know, possibly... his stalker?' said Theo, a small 'ha' under the Capitaine's breath as he raised ironic eyebrows at Martin. 'She seems a little unhinged, always chasing down our coach.'

Keen to swerve Gallois' gloating, Martin asked: 'Where were you last night, after dinner?'

'I took the spare room next to Mary's.'

'So, you were alone, no alibi,' stated Martin.

'Same for you, *non?* Surely it is the same for everyone except the Kesslers and Sinclairs. And even then, husband and wife could have colluded.'

Martin cursed inwardly. He hadn't considered the marital couple angle. Thanks to the painstakingly slow questioning by Gallois, Martin's drink-to-think pacing was all wrong. 'You seem to have given this a lot of thought,' he said.

'The creative side of me,' said Theo with a gloomy sigh, 'it does make occasional appearances.'

Striving to distance himself from his remarks on Mary, Martin attempted some small talk. 'How are the ideas for the wine label coming along?'

'Great,' said Theo unconvincingly. 'I was thinking either stripes or spirals,' he added, tailing off.

'What kind of art do you do, Monsieur Oblet?' asked Aimee.

'Abstract. Last month, I did this giant painting of a bone, made up of dog pawprints. It was pretty cool, actually, until the dogs starting peeing on the canvas.'

Taking a backseat to Gallois' procedural questions to further distance himself, Martin's comment regarding Mary was, nevertheless, not forgotten when Theo departed.

'You should not have called her that in front of her husband,' Aimee said with disdain.

Gallois was looking at his English partner curiously. 'I do not quite understand you, Monsieur Moretti. What are you trying to achieve?'

'It was unprofessional,' Aimee added.

'I told you,' said Gallois, 'I like a friendly, conducive atmosphere. You could have infuriated our suspects.'

'They infuriate me,' said Martin petulantly.

'You are jeopardising my investigation,' said Gallois.

'You're jeopardising mine!' snapped Martin.

Gallois thumped his fist onto the table, causing both Aimee and the coffee pot to jump. 'You can forget about addressing them as a group tonight, or ever!' With a deep breath, he unwrapped another of his sweets and sucked on it noisily. 'You can not keep interrupting, or you may get an official ban. Does this... discourage you?'

'Just tell me who we're interviewing next,' muttered Martin.

The door opened and in strode Mary Oblet; the investment accountant and banking backbone to Renzo's fortune. She'd barely sat down before Martin dived in.

'So, a Peruvian guinea pig farm and a copper mine. That's quite eclectic,' said Martin, ignoring Gallois' coiled vexation radiating across the dining table.

'We have restaurants in Italy, nursing homes in the UK. We have a rubber kneecap factory in Stuttgart,' said Mary coolly, 'and of course the Old Elysium Vineyard here in France.'

'Any financial problems?' asked Martin.

'We urgently needed a cash injection six months ago, but that is resolved now.'

Simmering, the Capitaine slunk back into silence. He reached toward his cane and, for an instant, Martin feared Gallois wrapping it around his head. Instead, the Capitaine clenched onto it so tightly Martin was sure he heard it crack.

'*Tu as l'air perplexe...* stumped,' said Mary, relishing the awkward silence, 'I like to stump people.'

'We're not stumped,' said Martin.

'We shall see,' said Mary.

'Would you say Renzo is a savvy businessman?' said Martin.

'Savvy?' Mary frowned.

'A wise decisionmaker.'

'Renzo invested the way he saw the world going,' said Mary. 'We are getting older—false hips, false teeth, kneecaps —and angrier—tear gas, riot shields, social media. Pills, of course, are good for both. He is very... savvy at it.'

'And as an accountant, what are you savvy at—hiding money from the taxman?'

'You have a very negative view of accountants, Monsieur Moretti. Not all accountants are fraudsters, just like not all police officers are corrupt. Or maybe you are; didn't you recently get fired?

It was Martin's turn to slump back in his chair. Normally this was when Gallois took over, yet he remained silent.

'You are serious about the divorce?' asked Aimee, reasserting Gendarmerie authority.

'It has been building these last twelve months.'

'You'll just miss the sex, *oui*?' said Aimee, who smiled at her conspiratorially.

'That dried up thirteen months ago,' said Mary. 'Probably

it was doomed from the start. I wanted Jordan Belfort and got Jordan Casteel.' All three looked at her blankly. 'The painter,' she said impatiently.

'Theo dabbles on the stock exchange,' said Martin, 'surely that makes him a bit of a Wall Street bad boy?'

'He snorts more mustard than cocaine,' said Mary with a scornful laugh.

'You are saying he is tame?' said Aimee.

'Oh, he can go from nought to nuclear just like that.' She clicked her fingers. 'Everything to nothing. Mostly, to nothing these days. Fumbling tax codes, misfiling accounts, transposition errors—'

'How about the financial *ratatouille?*' said Martin, remembering back to the first time he'd met the pair.

She sighed in recognition. 'I am exhausted trying to rein in all of his crazy gambles.'

'And so, you slept apart,' said Aimee. 'Did you hear anything, any sounds in the night?'

Mary thought for a while, her overplucked eyebrows furrowed in concern. 'Yes, I think I did hear whispering in the corridor. Possibly around two a.m.'

'Who was it?' asked Aimee. 'Your room was between where Theo slept and Pekoe Williams. Was it one of them?'

'No,' said Mary slowly, 'it wasn't that close.'

'From outside Jimmy's room?'

'I can not be sure. Do you think the whispering voice was the murderer?' said Mary, looking at them inquiringly. None of the three had an answer to this question and Mary stalked out triumphantly.

With nervous trepidation, both Martin and Aimee turned to the wordless Gallois; unsure how he'd react to the last interview. Rising without his cane, he limped over to Martin's end of the table and patted him on the back. Gallois seemed to have chosen a new strategy. Towering over him, he poured Martin a mugful of whisky.

'Ne l'encouragez pas!' snapped Aimee.

'What did she say?' said Martin.

'She said "do not encourage you". But I will encourage you. Come, sit with us.' said Gallois, with one of his slanted smiles, 'let us at least appear to be a cohesive unit, *non?*' Martin dragged his chair and overflowing mug next to theirs. 'I do not mind you being the drunken buffoon. What better way to make me look like the trusting Capitaine, someone they can confide in; or, at least let their guard down with. And, crucially not to bring in the lawyers.'

'Well, this next guy is a lawyer,' said Martin, eyeing the list in front of Aimee.

'*Tu devrais te détendre*,' muttered Gallois, straightening his tie. 'Lawyers are limited compared to England. They are here more to check everyone is treated ok.'

Sensing an opportunity, Martin said: 'So can I speak to them tonight?' He desperately needed the floor, to see how they bounced off each other, how they reacted to each other's statements.

'*Désolé*, not permitted,' said Gallois, feigning remorse. 'To lead this investigation, you need composure. Nevertheless, at least you have been able to question the suspects alongside me. At least you have had access to the murder room.'

A sudden thought flashed to Martin. 'You remember when I said the entire party visited the cellar last night?'

'*Oui*.'

'Actually, that's not accurate,' said Martin, his brow creased. 'Two people were missing. Which means...' he said, putting the pieces of the puzzle together, 'if their DNA turns up in the cellar, that's pretty suspicious. Holly and Joseph.'

'Joseph? You think a child could have done this?' said Gallois, amused.

'He's freakishly strong...'

'*Trop tard pour ça*,' said Gallois, shaking his head, 'I have already put Eugene on a specific DNA task.'

'Forensic check of the dumbwaiter lift?'

'*Non*, something else.'

'When we were on the stairs earlier, why did you say you've already ruled out the dumbwaiter?'

'No one could fit in there.'

'Except a child.'

'You still like your Joseph Sinclair theory,' said Gallois with a raw bark of a laugh, though looked to be refilling Martin's mug against his better judgment. 'Ready? Perhaps the Defective Detective will solve this whole *affaire* in the next audition? *On y va*!'

Accompanied by wife and son, Tate entered the room on the attack. 'I know my rights, I'm a lawyer.'

'And a very good one, I suspect,' said Gallois cheerfully. 'To reintroduce ourselves, I am Capitaine Gallois and this is Lieutenant Aimee. And, of course, you know Monsieur Moretti.'

'Sorry again about the snowman,' said Martin.

'It wouldn't do to make a habit of peeing upon innocent snow sculptures,' said Tate, eyes flickering.

'Long story, I'll explain later,' Martin whispered to Gallois.

'It's pretty clear,' Gallois whispered back.

'I assume you both have formal ID?' Tate's bald head glistened; had he repolished or was he sweating?

Aimee slid their identification across to Tate who held it from afar before—after a shake of realisation—inspecting it up close. Satisfied, he said: 'That accounts for you two.' Then, twisting to Martin: 'How about you?'

'How about me what?'

'It doesn't seem very professional to have present at these proceedings a civilian, a disgraced police officer at that. Are you sure you're fit for this?' said Tate, stroking his walrus moustache challengingly.

'He is helping us in a consultancy capacity,' said Gallois.

Sceptical, Tate said: 'I tell you what, Moretti, you do another of your party tricks right now, tell us something secret about someone in this room to prove how sharp you are, and I'll allow you to stay. Do we have an accord?' This wasn't said in the same playful tone as Aubrey's bet last night. There was a flash of malevolence in the lawyer's eyes that reminded Martin of his ex-wife. She used to demand he perform this exact thing at dinner parties to entertain her guests. Made him feel like a prank monkey. But on this occasion, Martin welcomed the interlude. As well as burning off the ethanol fumes currently engulfing his brain, an impressive performance here could convince Gallois to let him address the group. Plus, it might finally rouse Holly; the very person he'd been anxious to interview first. She hadn't spoken or even glanced up since entering the room. Instead, she was cradling her son, gently rocking Joseph side to side as he curled up in her lap, trembling. From fright? And if so, from which side of the table?

'Yes, we have an accord.' And with a twitch of his nose, Martin began.

21

The Defective Detective

'Alright, Mr Tate Sinclair, how about I do your ocular physiology. Your eyes,' Martin added. 'You're long-sighted, have been for years. You used to wear wonky but expensive black glasses, but recently switched to contact lenses; however you're still not sure it's the right move.'

Holly and Joseph looked up in amazement.

'How!' cried Joseph.

'You may proceed,' said Tate.

'How did you know that?' said Joseph.

'Dents,' said Martin, 'behind your ear lobes, you have two deep indents in your skull, caused from years of wearing glasses that aren't properly adjusted; too tight. My brother Patrick's are the same.'

'How did you know the glasses were black?' said Holly. Her voice was croaky. Her eyes were red—new tears or the fact it was 2 a.m.?

'All lawyers glasses are black. It's like a uniform.'

'So, a guess,' said Tate. 'Much like, I suppose, you took a fifty-fifty whether I was short-sighted or long-sighted. And that I changed to contacts only recently.'

'It must be a recent switch because you haven't shaken the long-sighted habit yet: when no glasses to hand, hold whatever you're reading to arm's length. You still do it—like with the Gendarmerie IDs just now, and I saw you do it with your £12,000 bottle purchase—before you remember you don't need to, now that you're wearing contact lenses.'

'Feasibly, I had laser surgery,' suggested Tate.

'If you'd recently had laser surgery, your eyes would still

be bloodshot. Plus, given how much you've been blinking the past few days, it suggests to me you're still getting accustomed and unsure contacts are the right decision.'

'Wow!' said Joseph, sitting bolt upright. Even the Gendarmerie were impressed, as though he'd just moved up a notch in their book. Probably putting him at notch one.

'You may proceed,' repeated Tate.

'I'll use that in my detective story,' said Holly, 'if that's ok?'

'Fine,' said Martin, 'so long as you can tell us where you've been the past twenty-four hours.'

'Bed,' said Holly glumly.

'How come?'

'Headache. I've had it three days,' she replied, almost verbatim to how Tate had said it by the snowman.

'Oh dear,' grimaced Martin. 'Though if you've been in bed, how come your scarf is hung over the chair outside the cellar doorway?'

'What?' said Holly, a little flustered. 'Oh, well I was going to come down for dinner but then I took a turn for the worse. So I took another of my extra-large headache pills and crashed out til morning.'

'With only your husband to confirm your nocturnal slumber?' said Martin. And nobody to confirm Tate's nocturnal whereabouts either, he privately thought.

'Yes and, well, Joseph was sleeping in the adjoining room.'

'Fine,' said Martin, 'and that bedroom has its own door to the corridor as well?' Holly nodded. 'Fine. And Joseph, is there anything you'd like to tell me, anything at all?' The boy looked terrified but shook his head. 'Are there any worries or questions you have?' said Martin encouragingly, but Joseph shook his head again before closing his eyes and curling back up in his mother's lap.

'He said "no", Moretti,' said Tate severely.

Gallois cleared in throat. 'When I searched your room

this morning, I found a rope tied to the bed post.'

'Emergency fire escape,' said Tate, his eyes still fixed on Martin. It was the same hard stare as when they'd discovered the livers in the punchbowl. Nonetheless, when Martin had announced D.O.T. was written on them, Tate had soon lost his voice; leaving only a spark of recognition on his face. Recognition or fear?

'You know something about D.O.T., don't you?'

Tate stared at Martin for a moment, thinking. Then shook his head.

'Did you hear anyone throughout the night pass by your door?' asked Martin.

'No comment,' said Tate, eyes twitching. This time, Martin suspected, not from the contact lenses.

'Can you think who had reason to kill Jimmy?

'No comment,' said Tate.

'Any thoughts on who gains from Jimmy's death? Do you think it's linked to the Lafite theft?'

'No comment,' replied Tate.

'Have you heard anybody mention mistletoe? Think!' said Martin, with some urgency. 'Jimmy mightn't find justice without your help.'

'No comment.'

'Well, that's just as fascinating as the first thirty-two times you said that,' sighed Martin, before turning to Gallois. 'I know someone we should ask about the mistletoe.'

'Are they on the interview list?' said Gallois. Martin confirmed so as Tate murmured 'no comment'.

'Yeah, you said that,' snapped Martin.

Joseph's head lolloped forward. 'Capitaine, can we please take him up?' implored Holly.

'Yes, that is fine,' said Gallois. 'Only two auditions to go before we wrap this up for the win.'

'*Mors vincit omnia*,' Tate said quietly.

'Flip me, it does talk,' said Martin, rolling his eyes.

'*Mors vincit omnia*,' Aimee repeated curiously, staring at

Tate. 'What does that mean?'

'I'm pretty sure the answer is: no comment,' said Martin.

Next up were the Kesslers, commencing with the customary Gallois by-the-book questions before Martin interjected: 'Anything odd strike you at dinner?'

'Nothing springs to mind,' said Eve, a little too sweetly.

'Nothing from me, kid,' leered Morton, smoothing down his grey combover.

'Not about those rattling bookshelves?' asked Aimee over her laptop.

'A girl's got to eat,' said Eve with a wink to Martin. He half-smiled back. The table between them at least guaranteed no *Basic Instinct* moment.

'And after dinner, bed all night? Unless, of course, you popped downstairs sleepwalking?' said Gallois with a laugh.

'I can't risk that,' said Eve, 'I sleep naked.'

'Me too,' said the bloodless old man; Martin nearly bringing his whisky back up.

'*Bon.* And your room was between the spare bedroom, where Theo slept, and Jimmy's. Did you happen to hear any strange sounds in the night?' asked the Capitaine.

'No, nothing,' said Morton. 'But then, I sleep like a log.'

'I did, on Jimmy's side,' said Eve. 'I'm a light sleeper, I always listen out for things that go hump in the night.'

'*Pardon?*' said Gallois, confused.

'You're saying there was someone in there with Jimmy?' said Martin. This must link to the whispering in the corridor that Mary had heard.

'Aw yeah, around two a.m. There were definitely two voices I could hear through the wall. Well, for at least seventeen minutes. Jimmy's voice and a female. The bed springs squeaked thirty-seven times.'

Gallois cast Aimee a knowing look. '*Cherchez la femme.*'

'This was found next to Jimmy's body,' said Martin, sliding across the evidence bag containing the sprig of mistletoe. Both shuffled uncomfortably in their seats.

'So frickin' what?' said Eve, her honeyed purr suddenly absent.

Morton picked up the bag with a curious leer. 'Why are you showing us this?'

'It says DOT on the leaf,' said Martin.

'Congratulations, you've got eyes,' said Eve defiantly.

'We don't know anything about D.O.T.' said Morton.

'But you do know about mistletoe,' said Martin. 'I saw you picking some this morning. Didn't you say you were replenishing your supply?'

'It's for our company branding, *Mistletoe Atlantic Trading*,' said Eve to Gallois and Aimee. 'We're doing a photoshoot as part of the launch for Renzo's new wine.'

'How long does mistletoe last once picked?' asked Martin.

'Usually, two to three weeks if kept in a cool, dry place,' said Morton. 'Anyone could've packed some in their suitcase.'

'It looks pretty fresh,' said Martin.

'I've seen mistletoe everywhere on this tour,' said Eve. 'It's in the garden outside, but the branches we clipped at that vineyard were in better shape.'

'Well, you're the experts,' said Martin, 'why do you think mistletoe was left by the body?'

'Mistletoe is a potent symbol,' said Eve, 'it's why we chose it for our company name.'

'Mistletoe is very powerful... a deadly assassin. The druid's weed, kid.' said Morton. 'We all think of it as the jolly little decoration to kiss under. But mistletoe is a toxic parasite. Poisonous… it can even kill the tree it hangs on,' he said, passing the bag back.

'Or it could be that it's Christmastime,' Eve added offhand.

'Joyeux Noël,' said Gallois. He was becoming increasingly relaxed with the interviews, especially after Eugene burst into the room and muttered something into his ear before

waddling out again.

A few more questions were asked and answered and then the Kessler's departed; swiftly replaced by the final interviewee.

'Bonjour, Mademoiselle Dalton,' said Gallois.

'*Madame* Dalton,' corrected Aubrey. Martin was unacquainted with the difference, however the fierce look on Aubrey's face made clear her preference.

'You speak French?' asked Aimee.

'*Non*,' replied Aubrey. Martin noticed a small smile touching the corners of her mouth.

'*Pardon*, Madame Dalton,' said Gallois, 'I am—'

'What are you doing in here?' Aubrey asked Martin.

'Jus' detectin',' said Martin, the full effect of all the Scotch whisky he'd consumed still making itself felt. In fact, the whisky was gone now, so he poured himself a cognac. 'Solvin' the case.' Aubrey squeezed her lips tightly together to stop from giggling.

'Monsieur Moretti is helping with our enquiries,' said Gallois, eager to reassert early control of the conversation. 'Two heads are better than one.'

'Three,' corrected Aubrey. 'What's with the laptop?'

'It is procedure,' replied Aimee, furiously hitting the keys. 'I type everything up, for my dossier.'

'Is that so? Every single, tiny, little word I utter? Even tricky words like persnickety or fastidious?'

'Er, I presume it's ok if I start the questioning?' said Gallois.

'Presume away, Cap,' said Aubrey.

'You arrived in France a week ago… travelled alone?'

'Always.'

'What is it you do, Madame Dalton?'

'I am training to be a Master Sommelier.'

'What's that?' said Martin, applying huge effort into not slurring again.

'Put simply for you, I provide advice on what wine to

choose from the menu.'

'Doesn't everyone just go for the second cheapest bottle on the list? Sounds easy.'

'There are less than two-hundred and fifty Master Sommeliers in the world,' said Aubrey defensively. 'It's taken me four years to prepare for the final exam, which is by invitation only. At the blind tasting, I need to know the history, geography, soil, climate and techniques used in each region. What year it was made. The individual styles of the top producers. The best vintages from every region since 1970.'

'You are how old Madame Dalton, twenty-four?' said Gallois. 'Surely to be a Master Sommelier, you need a lifetime of knowledge.'

'I have sacrificed a lifetime to get here. It has cost me $30,000 in testing fees and travel alone.'

'Impressive,' said Martin. 'Jus' a shame that all wine sucks.'

'You should keep an open mind. What's that you've got there?' asked Aubrey, eyeing his mug with professional interest.

'Cognac.'

'Cognac is a distilled wine,' said Aubrey with glee.

'There you are, then,' said Martin placing his mug down, 'I do have an open mind. The murder weapon was a Barolo, 2006. Is there any significance to that?'

'It's an Italian wine, so I guess that gives you a Renzo connection?' said Aubrey. '2006 is an impressive vintage, all the more impressive given the droughts and scorching heat that year. Do you really think it's significant?'

'Probably not,' shrugged Martin. 'It was probably jus' the closest bottle to hand, aside from the Lafite. What did you think of Jimmy?'

Aubrey stiffened. 'I wasn't much of a fan.'

'No, it doesn't sound like anyone was,' said Martin, nodding solemnly.

'I can think of one person,' said Gallois smugly to Aimee.

'Why didn't you like him?' said Martin, ignoring the Gendarmerie.

'He'd been needling me all tour,' said Aubrey. 'You know, like when he said women only wear makeup and perfume because they're ugly and stink. And now he's dead, head bashed in, next a pile of mistletoe.'

'How do you know that?' asked Aimee. 'How do you know that mistletoe was left at the crime scene.'

'Eve just mentioned it,' replied Aubrey.

'Interestingly, did you know there's actually mistletoe here in the garden?' said Martin.

'That is a fun fact,' said Aubrey sardonically, 'you should tell Sven that one.'

'Don't you go running around the garden every morning?'

'What are you suggesting?'

'Jus' wonderin' how you got those red stains on your boots.'

Lifting her legs up onto the table, Aubrey examined the dark red splodges on her hiking boots. 'I spilt some of my glass of 2014 Améthyste cuvée from Domaine des Ardoisières,' she said. 'I remember getting annoyed at wasting such a decent vintage.'

'Let's hope for your sake it is wine,' said Aimee. 'Otherwise, you could get up to twenty-five years in some festering jail.'

'It's your touch typing that I respect,' said Aubrey, before she was briskly ushered from the room.

'Bon, c'est tout, most satisfactory,' said Gallois, banging his cane several times on the floor. 'What do you think, Monsieur Moretti?'

'I think,' said Martin, 'it'd be worth a final word with them all together, in view of what we now know.'

'And what do we now know?'

'These last few interviews,' said Martin, with maximum

effort to stop the room from spinning, 'I've learnt something—the identity of the murderer.'

'*Bien sûr*, Camille Duval.' They headed for the door.

'Actually, no,' said Martin, 'one of our party.' Granted, he'd jumped to conclusions about Noel Gillespie's turn of phrase. This time, however, he knew who it was. *Cherchez la femme*, indeed.

'Let's close this *affaire* down,' Gallois said to Aimee, 'and get some sleep. *Je suis crevé.*'

Refusing to be sidelined anymore, Martin piped up: 'Or, I tell 'em you've incompetently botched the case and arrested the wrong person?'

Lunging forwards, Gallois grabbed Martin by his jumper and shoved him against the door, slamming it shut with such force the whole Château shook.

'*Ne me poussez pas!*' Gallois hissed through gritted teeth, raising his walking cane. 'You threaten me again, Monsieur Moretti, and I will run this stick through your torso.'

'And yet,' seethed Martin, still pinned to the door, 'you're the one who said composure was necessary to lead this investigation.'

Gallois' grip loosened. 'Renzo said to give you carte blanche, so... the floor is yours.' Furiously, Martin pushed him away but the Capitaine seized his left wrist, twisting his arm up to read the Omega De Ville. 'You have ten minutes. Seeing the state of you, you'll be on the floor in five anyway.'

'Usually, I'd take an hour,' said Martin, 'to help build the case, proper.'

Corrosively glowering at one another, Gallois wasn't backing down. 'Tick, tock, Monsieur Moretti.'

22

Dictionary Challenge

All of the guests were hunkered down in the *salon*, all eyes on the man pacing up and down the room as Sven threw another log onto the fire.

'I s'pose you're all wondering...' he said, buzzing after the altercation, 'I s'pose you all know why I've gathered you here.' Somewhat sozzled, Martin was miraculously still keeping it together. But the mood was sombre, a sorry set of faces looked up at him, pale and withdrawn, as if—strangely enough—somebody had just died.

Only Aubrey shared his excitement. 'Hell yeah,' she said, rubbing her hands together, 'this is obviously your grand finale. You know, like when Hercule has got all the suspects in one room. I can't believe these actually happen!' she added.

'I am not sure they do,' said Lieutenant Aimee wearily; she and the Capitaine leaning against the far wall, arms folded. Eugene, the overweight forensics officer, had joined them, slightly bewildered by the whole proceeding.

Still pacing, and suddenly realising he had one chance not to blow this, Martin approached the solitary figure sat cross-legged in the far corner.

'Bloody hell, Martin, you're blottoed aren't you?' said Pekoe, in a hushed tone only Martin could hear.

'Be honest, Pekoe, can you tell?' he whispered back.

'This lampshade can tell,' said Pekoe, adding bracingly, 'I hope you know what you're doing.'

'So do I.' Turning back to the room at large, Martin was greeted by the hard stare of their Transatlantic lawyer.

'Yes, I'm not convinced about this summation gathering, Moretti,' grumbled Tate. Noel concurred with an unpleasant chuckle, and it suddenly occurred to Martin that his inebriated state did not elicit the respect he had hoped for. Indeed, scanning the group, their faces coming in and out of focus, the others looked far less friendly. The Kesslers were now sniggering loudly, while the Oblets stared back at him with contempt.

'May I remind you, one of your party is dead,' Gallois cut in, and the group went quiet. 'I would have expected some sensitivity given Monsieur Stresskeller's head has been caved in.' The room swallowed in unison. 'We, four, are the experts. Monsieur Moretti is, erm, a professional with fourteen years' experience; rising to the rank of Chief Inspector. He has solved more UK crimes than they serve cream teas.' Feeling his stock rise, Martin appreciated the endorsement. That is, until Gallois sternly tapped his watch, signalling Martin had seven minutes left.

'And yet… still drinking?' said Tate, observing the mug.

'He's in control,' repeated Gallois, rather less confidently than before.

'Really?' said Tate, followed by mutterings of unease. Sven, perched on the edge of his armchair devouring gummy bears, readjusted his black tie nervously.

'Taisez-vous!' yelled the Capitaine, and even the flames in the fireplace seemed to subside. Gallois took a few deep breaths and then, forcing his face into a slanted smile, said reassuringly: '*Détend-toi,* we all know, one swig is not strictly fatal but—'

'I don't know, Gallois,' said Martin, all eyes flicking to him, 'I've got some black-market Russian vodka that if you don't inhale it first before necking…' Martin mimed himself choking, as if dying from poison.

'Have you?' snapped Gallois in anger.

'Well not on me now, but I could bring it in for the next interrogations.'

Eugene mumbled something in French which Gallois translated. 'Eugene says he does not want to step on your toes but—'

'Good, 'cause he'd break em.' Appalled gasps broke out. Sensing sparks from the Capitaine, he placed his mug on the coffee table and began. 'Means, motive and opportunity,' listed Martin. 'Means is obvious; pick a bottle, any bottle. Opportunity… lots of people with the opportunity. People who could slip out of their single rooms: Sven, Noel, Pekoe, Theo, Mary and Aubrey. Even the marital pairs could be colluding together; right, Mr and Mrs Mistletoe?' he said to the Kesslers.

'Said by the skunk-drunk who looks half the bay over,' sneered Morton. Gripping her husband's hand for support, Eve shot Martin a nasty grin.

'Let him reveal the killer,' said Theo.

'That's right, I have the solution. Someone in this room… is a murderer,' said Martin melodramatically. Spinning round, he said earnestly: 'Gallois, do you want to add a *J'accuse!* at this point?' The Capitaine shook his head with a morbidly curious look, as if anticipating a car crash. Martin panicked: did he actually have the solution? Definitely… part of a solution… at least one-third of a solution. Another tap of the watch from Gallois, the clockwatch clown in the corner, just as self-righteous and patronising as Radnor. Ok, replaying it in his head, maybe one-third is not a solution. It's barely brainstorming.

'Means and opportunity are ok,' Martin continued. Was this a good strategy? Martin had never been backed into a corner like this, rushed a confession, put the murderer on the spot; usually everything was nicely slotted into place. But he was on borrowed time with the booze, and now had only six minutes left according to the clockwatch clown. Yes, this was a good strategy. This was definitely a good strategy. Gallois wouldn't let him do it otherwise, right? Besides, Martin had promised himself to crank it up a smidge.

'The motive, however, wasn't clear to me. Until now.

Wouldn't you agree, Holly?'

'Excuse me?' she spluttered.

'Just like the motive of this case, your whereabouts last night are murky.'

'I've told you,' said Holly, 'I felt headachy, popped a pill, went to bed; end of story.'

'Maybe it's the end of the story,' said Martin. 'Maybe it's just the start of Act Two. Maybe you're the murderer.'

'What?' stammered Tate.

'Is this a joke?' said Holly, her shy smile faltering.

'No way!' cried Noel in disbelief.

'How's your autobiography of Renzo coming along?' asked Martin. 'Running out of material?'

'This is ridiculous,' said Tate.

'This should make a good chapter in the memoir, right?' said Martin, still addressing Holly.

'What do you mean by that?' said Tate, his hands balled into fists. Holly's face reddened but she held her head high.

'Real life is rarely as entertaining as fiction, even Renzo's, so you jazz it up with a death.'

'You're joking, you must be?' said Holly, husband and wife were looking at each other incredulously.

'Y'know, play to your strengths. Your genre, murder mystery.' There was a collective intake of breath from the room.

'This is ridiculous,' said Tate. 'Captain, we don't have to listen to this slander, do we?' Through all the defiance, he was biting his lip so hard it was bleeding.

'You're talking nonsense, Moretti,' heckled Noel, 'your brain's banjaxed on the juice. I'd be a better detective than you.' He had the temerity to lecture him while clutching onto a large glass of whisky himself.

'What if you didn't take one of your headache pills and zonk out?' continued Martin. 'What if you waited for your husband to come up to sleep, wait for him to start snoring, then crept down to kill 'em; delighted that these DOT killings would be an effective way to spice up your autobiography.'

'These killings were not me.' Holly's fingers were digging into the arms of her chair.

'Are you the DOT killer?' Martin pressed.

'I am not a killer!' Holly cried back.

'Do you want a slap, Moretti?' raged Tate, rolling up his sleeves.

'Is it followed by a tickle?' said Martin indifferently.

'What proof do you have for this cockamamie?'

'I have a key witness.'

Noel wasn't having any of it. 'I think you should take a good look in the mirror before you open your mouth again,' he said, grabbing Martin's mug and pouring it into the nearest plant pot.

'I'm not taking advice from some boring old binoculared twitcher,' slurred Martin, 'and I'm certainly not taking advice from some soft second-hand duck seller.'

'Binoculared twitcher? Soft?' snarled Noel. 'I don't think so, pal, I've got tattoos!' Pulling up his shirt sleeve, he revealed the tattoo of an American Bald Eagle.

'That's not a real tattoo,' said Martin dismissively.

'You what?' Noel jumped out of his seat outraged.

'Please, that's a henna job all the way.'

'Rub it,' said Noel challengingly. Rising to the challenge, Martin licked his hand before starting to rub at the tattoo.

'Hey!' yelled Gallois. 'Why are you licking him?!'

Realising it's got out of hand, Martin resignedly stepped back as Noel sat down.

Clearing his throat, Gallois said to Martin: 'Go on about your witness.'

Martin swayed round to face the Sinclairs. 'Where is Joseph?'

'Up in bed,' said Holly.

'I'm afraid he's told me everything,' said Martin. 'He told me you hurt him. You pulled his tongue, threatened to cut it off.'

'Oh my god,' Holly groaned, head in hands.

Martin recited Joseph's warning: *'First, she'll cut off my tongue, then she's going to kill me. She's going to kill us all.'*

The Sinclairs stared at each other, seeming to have forgotten anybody else was in the room. 'It's from that damned movie last week,' said Holly and comprehension dawned on her husband's face.

A wave of relief washed over Tate before he said awkwardly: 'Er – yes, folks – about our Joseph. He has some compulsive lying issues that we're working through. It's hopefully just kids' stuff, a phase.' He grasped Holly's hand. 'What you're referring to... we made the mistake of showing him *The Goonies.*'

'No, *you* made the mistake of showing it to him,' corrected Holly.

'The movie has that derelict restaurant scene in it. You know, where the gangster mom grabs the kid's tongue, then threatens to slice it off.'

'Ah,' said Martin. 'I wasn't aware of that.' His stomach plummeted.

Holly asked: 'Did he shout at you *"Goonies never say die"*?'

'He may have said something along those lines,' conceded Martin.

'Yesterday,' said Tate, 'I heard him tell Sven, we have a tunnel underneath our house that leads straight to KFC.'

'Last week, Joseph told his friends that his dad owned New York,' said Holly.

'And his mum had tickled him, so she went to jail,' said Tate.

'Oh. I didn't know that,' said Martin, his world collapsing.

'Let me get this straight,' said Mary, 'you were taken in by an eight-year-old?'

'Eight and three-quarters,' said Martin.

'Candidly, kid,' said Morton, eyeing him, 'are you sure you were a detective at all?

'So, it is not Holly?' said Mary.

'Apparently not,' said Lieutenant Aimee, mildly embarrassed. Martin would have felt the crushing embarrassment himself had he not just been sick in his mouth before swallowing it.

'I apologise, *mes amis*,' said Gallois, stepping forward. 'I was reliably informed that we would see great results from Monsieur Moretti on alcohol. *Je suis très déçu*, erm, I am very disappointed,' he added insincerely. It could not have been plainer how thrilled Gallois was that Martin had imploded. 'Let me *récompense*, erm, make it up to you by revealing the real killer. It was Camille Duval.'

'His stalker?' said Sven, eyes widening.

'*Oui*. There is something you should know, Monsieur Moretti, before we started the interviews,' said Gallois, 'while you were preening yourself in *le petit coin*, erm, the bathroom, we did a little research on this Cammy Duval. We found her weekly blog that contains strong hints of homicidal tendencies. Also, there is a restraining order against her coming within two hundred metres of Monsieur Stresskeller.'

'So what?' said Martin. 'She's a stalker, that doesn't make her a murderer. We're still no clearer on motive! Why did she take the Lafite Rothschild?'

'Because she is *cinglé*! Crazy! Deranged,' said Gallois. 'She probably threw it away in a bush out there. We will find it when the snow melts.'

'How can you be so sure?' said Martin, voice shaking, legs wobbling.

'Because of the whispering in the corridor, and the sounds Eve Kessler heard through the wall... Jimmy Stresskeller invited her up to his room and they slept together.' From the couches, a breathless intake of wonder. 'That is what Eugene has been doing for me with his portable DNA kit. Not quite as accurate as a lab, but it has confirmed the hairs I found in Jimmy's bed match the ones we took from Cammy Duval upon arrest. Oh, and when we arrested her, guess what she was wearing? The gold Rolex watch.' Further impressed gasps from the sofas. 'How is that for a Narcotics officer?' said Gallois with suppressed triumph.

'I prefer a fingerprint,' declared Martin. Legs buckling, he crashed into the armchair next to Noel, hoping he'd pulled it off as dramatic dejection, rather than literally being legless. The impressed hum from moments ago was replaced with uncomfortable silence.

'You should stop drinking,' Holly said softly with a concerned look. 'The first step is to admit you have a problem.'

'What is this, Alcoholics Anonymous? Well, my name is Martin and it has been two minutes since my last drink.' He lifted his arms, challenging them to applaud.

'A.A. is no laughing matter,' said Holly. 'My brother Duncan—'

'As in, Duncan Disorderly?'

'As in Duncan Mott, my brother, he—'

'That's the weird thing,' said Martin distractedly, 'it's called "anonymous" but the first thing you say is "my name is Bob". Well, my name is Martin and it has been minus five seconds since my last drink.' Snatching the whisky from Noel's hand, he knocked it back in one.

Amidst the disquiet and head shaking, Gallois persevered: 'Perhaps we should get back to Camille—'

'No, let's get back to Holly Sinclair being our DOT culprit. And you,' Martin jumped up and pointed in the general direction of Tate, 'you're hiding something about D.O.T., I know you are. You've got to tell us.'

Tate's face had turned purple with rage. 'And how much do you ever remember past midnight? The amount you drink, you must black out every night. For all we know, Moretti, you're the killer!' he said, and everyone stared at Martin accusingly.

Scandalised, Martin staggered backwards. 'How dare he?! How dare you! I'm not a killer. Yes, I'm a bum, an alcoholic, a divorcee and a killer, but I'm not a pervert.' Martin thought for a second. 'Wait, what did you call me?'

'I think you better leave now,' said Gallois, any amused morbid curiosity wiped away; instead, he simply looked pissed off.

'Leave? Why?!'

'Because you're drunk,' said Holly.

'I'm not drunk.'

'You're the very definition of drunk!' Holly yelled.

'Oh, I'm the very definition of drunk, am I?' Stumbling over to the bookcase, he yanked a dictionary off the shelf. 'Well let's just consult the Oxford English Dictionary on that, shall we? Hah! Here we are: "the act of submerging ones head under water".'

Gallois sighed. 'Next one down.'

'"Intoxicated by alcoholic liquor". Oh. Well maybe,' said Martin, and he hung his head.

'Please stop,' implored Theo, 'give it up, Moretti.'

'No way,' he slurred, pointing his finger meaningfully at the lampshade, 'I will absolutely not stop... EVER. I'm like a bone with a dog. And I *still* think Holly is DOT because—'

CRACK! - a white light flashed behind his eyes, something hard hitting the side of his head. Legs collapsing, the world twisted and Martin fell back into nothing.

23

Blacked

BRRRRRRRINGA DING DING DING DING DING DING DING.

A half-comatose Martin slapped his alarm clock, restoring silence to the room. That was about as much movement as he could muster. Cautiously lifting the sunglasses he found himself wearing, Martin squinted around his bedroom. Ouch.

'Hungover, crap, still gotta hangover.' Returning the glasses to his face, Martin decided to go back to sleep for another eight hours.

A sudden spray of water splashed over his face. Sitting bolt upright, somebody was standing above him, happily pouring a jug over his head.

'Wakey, wakey, hands off snakey!' said Sven cheerfully.

'That's iced water!'

'Woke you up, didn't it?' shrugged Sven.

'You could've taken the ice cubes out!'

The Swedish tour guide chuckled. 'Come on, scoot scoot, it's time for breakfast. Everybody else is downstairs. I put you to bed; don't make me drag you out.'

With an agonised groan, Martin flopped back onto his pillows.

'You'll get no sympathy from me,' Sven clucked disapprovingly.

'How about an espresso?'

'No, but I can disclose today's itinerary, if you want? This morning, we are going horseback trekking near Chambéry followed by hot air ballooning over Lake Annecy.'

'Can't we just go bowling?' said Martin, pulling on

his trainers and, with rubbery legs, following Sven into the corridor.

'You don't like hot air balloons?' said Sven.

'Floating wicker, acrophobia, claustrophobia globophobia, all propelled by fire? No thanks. What's the alternative?'

'Well, Capitaine Gallois is here but I'm not sure he's keen to see you.'

'Because of last night?' winced Martin. 'Did I make a fool of myself?'

'Like my mormor would say, you have taken a crap in the blue cupboard.' A rush of horrible memories flooded into Martin's throbbing head as he shuffled down the hallway; accompanied by the creeping dread there were worse gaps to fill.

The Château's front door was open, momentarily distracting Martin from his self-pity. An Alpine A110 sports car was parked on the driveway, its engine running. Nice vehicle. With a prominent blue light on top, the car's bonnet, roof, and side panels were striped with the word "Gendarmerie". It must be the Capitaine's car; his walking stick was leaning against the front bumper. Martin could always steal the car and runaway? Listening to the excited chatter from the kitchen about pony treks and balloon rides, it made Martin's stomach churn all the more. As with the liver incident, they seemed to have moved on from Jimmy pretty quick.

Kitchen or car? A hot bowl of porridge might mend his stomach, eat away at the blurry edges. But then, he wasn't sure his frayed nerves could handle such a recriminating recap of all the bad things he'd done; retold over a plate of sanctimonious croissants.

From the kitchen doorway, he announced: 'Sorry about last night folks, minor relapse, won't happen again.' On the whole, the room smiled back forgivingly... on the whole. Gallois gazed for a moment at Martin, and there was disgust and loathing etched onto his scarred face. Tate's expression, however, was unfathomable.

Kitchen or car? It was a no brainer. Martin was in the front seat of the Alpine A110 and reversing off the driveway before the Capitaine was hobbling after him. Screaming then chasing then screaming. From the rear-view mirror, Gallois vanished in seconds; now only the bleary bloodshot eyes of disappointment stared back at him. Martin concentrated on the road ahead. After the darkness of the murder cellar and the stuffy interrogations, the bright white landscape was having a savage effect on his hangover. Fortunately, he still had his sunglasses. With a single, sweaty hand gripping the wheel, Martin set his phone navigation for the outskirts of Annecy.

What had he done last night? What had he said? Had he embarrassed himself? His skin crawled with hanxiety. What was wrong with him? He was never drinking again. No more booze. Ever. Stomach still churning, Martin was sickened by how false those words rang inside his pounding head. Pulling over, he considered a tactical chunder, but for some reason his jaw hurt too much. Instead, Martin shifted the sports car into top gear, putting as much distance from le Château des Allues as possible. He could see why Gallois drove it, the turbocharged 1.8-litre engine was built for high-speed chases, perfect for Narcotic operations. 100% adrenaline-charged. Yet as each clump of snow slid from the roof onto the windscreen before bouncing into the brown-slushed road, new shameful memories slunk to mind. The Goonie humiliation; hoodwinked by an eight-year-old. Licking somebody's arm. The dictionary failure. Plus, someone had punched him; he could remember a fist. Martin had planned to crank the case up a smidge. In retrospect, he'd possibly cranked it a smidge and a half. And so, the summation gathering had been, like pretty much everything he did nowadays, a catastrophe. He didn't want to overstate it, but there couldn't be a worse disaster than if the Titanic was shipping Chernobyl supplies to Pearl Harbor.

He'd never done anything like that on a case before. Gallois' pace had knocked him off his game. Usually, he eased off the hooch as soon as he'd found his first solid set of clues, however Martin still wasn't sure what value they'd gleaned from the interrogations. He had a niggling feeling there was something of significance. Nevertheless, oblivion being in the post, Martin had rushed his summation, desperate to shortcut the solution; prancing around like some kind of bumbling Inspector Clouseau buffoon. Idiot. From now on, he would approach the case with the standard Martin Moretti M.O.; which, right now, meant sticking to the original plan: investigate the source of the D.O.T. poison pen letter.

He pulled off the highway and zipped through the villages. French snowploughs had worked their wonders and the roads were clear yet again. Most impressive; and allowing Martin a direct route towards Blacked Tattoo Studio. The solution. Skies brightening, he opened his window for some restorative fresh air as marbled clouds sprinkled snow onto the world below, whirling down in fat feathery flakes. In Britain, the media would dub this Snowmageddon, Snowzilla, Snowpocalypse, snOMG or Kaisersnoze. Here, it was just a Tuesday.

It was his Sherlock-scan of the typewritten poison pen letter—with the residual smell of cigarettes and green soap lingering on the yellow transfer paper—that had directed him to the tattoo parlour; only a seven-minute drive away from le Château de Montrottier's liver incident. True, it was a weak theory, but it beat watching Sven's mullet bounce up and down from the back of a horse. Upon arriving at Blacked: speak to the tattooist, learn D.O.T.'s identity and solve the case. Like he'd said: easy-peasy, Bacardi breezy. Piece of cake.

Rejuvenated at the prospect of finding his first solid clue, Martin switched the radio on, untroubled by the French version of Rudolph the Red Nose Reindeer. He took a moment to admire the world whipping by. Local French folk hurrying home from the bakery with fresh baguettes clutched to the chest; their faces half-concealed by hats, scarves and upturned collars. Ski twits down from the mountains for cheaper *après-ski*. Hectic shoppers dashing in and out of the crowded shops decorated with an assortment of flowers, silver bells, Christmas lights, and endless pictures of Papa Noël, Macaulay Culkin and the Grinch.

Approaching his destination, he eased off the throttle. On the street corner was an old woman selling a dozen Christmas trees; freezing. Above her, something caught his eye: a sign for a local hospital. Struck by a curious idea, Martin checked Google Maps. It was ten minutes away but would be worth it if it led to solid clue number two.

Two hours later, handing a hot coffee to the old woman along the way, Martin arrived at his original destination—a small two-storey shopping parade, consisting of four shops and a restaurant—in a euphoric mood. The hospital visit had been a huge success. If he could connect it to his next inquiry, Martin had the D.O.T. murderer nailed.

He found Blacked Tattoo Studio on the first-floor balcony. Peering through the window, the tattoo artist was a sweaty, pale punk wearing a luminous green liberty-spiked mohawk. His leather jacket, held together with safety pins and choker chains, was peppered with as many pin badges as there were studs on his face.

'*Parlez-vous Angleterre?*' asked Martin, cautiously entering. The atmosphere of the small studio was filled with the buzz of the needle and chaos.

'Angleterre? Ah, Anglais!' said the Mohican-haired man, cigarette in mouth. 'Yeah, I speak Angleterre.' To Martin's relief, he spoke with a droll Cockney accent.

'You're English,' said Martin, delighted to find another person who spoke the Queens. Well, not exactly the Queens; more, "God Save the Queens". But still, English. If this kept up, he'd have to start holidaying in France.

'Course I'm English,' said the punk, one eye on an action

movie playing on the TV, one eye on his client. Mopping his brow, he was struggling to pin down a fidgety middle-aged Frenchman lying topless on the leather massage table. In between the customer's squirms and screams, the punk was attempting to tattoo a map of France onto his back. 'Stay down!' he yelled at the client.

'Oweee!' came the tortured reply, followed by a French expletive.

'Do you own this place?' asked Martin.

'No way, Pedro. I'm covering for Celine and Nathan while on holiday.' In contrast to the shabby unkempt punk, the parlour itself was impeccably clean; not a speck of dust on the laminate floor nor a smudge on the chrome Brabantia bin. A set of qualifications hung on the white walls, belonging to Nathan and Celine; definitely not the punk. The only other picture was the large black and white image of a warrior princess brandishing a switchblade. To the side, was a large table consisting of sketchpads, pens and pencils, paints, markers, bandages, a Union Jack ashtray and, sure enough, yellow cardboard-backed transfer paper. Even more interesting, a typewriter.

'You here to book an appointment?' Underneath an adjustable standing light, the punk squinted up at him suspiciously.

'You any good?' asked Martin.

'I did this one myself. What do you think?' Rolling his sleeve up, he revealed a ghastly tattoo of Patti Smith as a butterfly.

Martin couldn't help but grimace. 'That's hideous.'

'Yeah, early effort,' conceded the punk, 'when I was still a rookie. Do you think I should laser it off?'

'I think you should chop your arm off. Because if you see the scar, you might remember the image.'

'Arrrrgh!' yelled the Frenchman underneath them.

'Stay down, you muppet!' Behind the punk was a reception desk where a gold skull resided. And underneath that, the tattoo portfolio book. If the author of the poison pen letter did indeed receive a tattoo, the details would hopefully be in there.

'Bit rude to the customers, aren't you?' said Martin.

'Not to worry,' said the punk, leaning back in his black leather chair, 'he doesn't speak any English; not that I speak any French, either. Oh my god, this movie is so bad!' he yelled, staring up at the apocalyptic action B-movie.

'Little early in the morning for explosions and zombies, isn't it,' said Martin. His head was still thumping.

'It's never too early for zombie warfare. But, oh my god, this is so stupid!' he said, watching as the hero's sidekick was strangled to death by a mutated zombie. 'Why doesn't he pretend he's dead so the zombie stops strangling him. These movies are so bad they're good, know what I mean?' The punk had the vibe of someone who'd overdosed on films from the first safety pin on his nappy; probably switching to tattooing after Blockbuster closed down.

The buzz of his needle gun started up again. 'Anyway, if you're not here for an appointment, could you kindly bog off.'

Martin needed to choose his next words carefully. Just because the D.O.T. letter originated from inside this studio, that didn't necessarily mean the author was a customer. Conceivably, the writer was this very tattoo artist. Except, Martin seriously doubted it. From the look of it, this guy could screw up a cup a coffee; including Kenco. Even so, Martin knew the best way to play it would be as a maverick, hard-boiled, cop on the edge.

'I need some information,' said Martin, attempting a gravel-voiced tone.

'Yeah, and I need some superglue or a staple gun, know what I mean?' he said, still struggling to pin his client down. Presumably he'd used the last of the superglue on his mohawk. 'Can't you see I'm in the middle of something.'

'Well, how much longer?' said Martin, suddenly not feeling like much of a maverick.

'According to the map, a hundred and seventy miles.' The customer suddenly jerked up, causing the needle to slip.

'Great,' he said, inspecting his hand, 'and now I've got Marseille all over my fingers.'

'I need information.'

'I don't care,' said the tattooist, his manner as spiky as his hair.

'Aaaaargh! *Mon dieu!*'

'Come on, mate, we're just past Monaco.'

'I'm from Interpol,' said Martin.

'Interpol, eh?' he perked up, resting the tattoo gun on his bleach-splattered jeans. 'A Eurocop. Cream of the Continental pigs.'

Martin pressed. 'Did you have a client come in recently who asked to use the typewriter?'

'Yeah, I did, as a matter of fact,' said the punk thoughtfully, 'while I was finishing up their tattoo.'

'Did you see what they typed?'

'How should I know? I was cleaning up.'

'Who was the client?'

'I can't tell you that,' said the punk sharply.

'Owww!'

'Mate, you wriggle like that again and you'll find Normandy up your arse,' he said, leaning an elbow on his client. Martin didn't have the heart to tell either of them that he'd drawn the map of France upside down.

'Well, can I at least see the tattoo design?' asked Martin.

'No way, Pedro.'

'But I'm from Interpol.'

'Frankly my dear, I don't give a damn.'

Frustrating Martin beyond endurance, he found himself momentarily sidetracked. 'That sounds familiar, what's that from?'

'Obviously you've never seen Ghostbusters,' he said sarcastically.

'Anyway, why not show me the design?'

‘A little something called tattooist-tattooee confidentiality.’

‘You’re not a doctor,’ snapped Martin. ‘There’s no tattoo oath.’

He had said the wrong thing. ‘It’s called being professional!’ The punk bristled. ‘Let’s be honest, mate, you’re not from Interpol and you don’t have a warrant. So, bog off, Eurocop! My lips are locked.’

Evidently, this wasn’t easy-peasy, Bacardi breezy. In fact, it was turning into his first ever total mardy-mardy, Bacardi mardy. And once more, the former-Chief Inspector was not loving having been stripped of all power and authority, no badge commanding the compliance of this jobsworth simpleton. Martin was prickling to give him—to use Tate’s parlance—a slap, but he was in no condition to fight. So, if not the stick, then the carrot.

‘Maybe something from in here can liberate that information,’ said Martin, pulling out his wallet.

‘Alright fine,’ said the punk, putting the final touches to the Frenchman’s back, ‘everybody’s gotta price. You can’t keep the portfolio page, but I’ll give you a photo of the design, plus the customer’s name.’

‘How much?’

‘Two thousand euros.’

Martin casually nodded back. He’d have to haggle a bit to get it down to the twenty euros he had left. ‘Is there a sneak peek price?’

‘Sure.’

‘How much is that?’

‘Two thousand euros.’ He leaned back in his chair and grabbed the portfolio book, flicking through the pages. ‘Ah yes, here we are, nice little design, that,’ he added teasingly, holding the book close to his chest. ‘Otherwise, mate, kindly exit the premises or I’m compelled to headbutt you.’ He pressed the needle gun down with a little too much force and the client emitted their highest squeal yet. Leaping off the table, he ran over to the mirror to inspect his red and blotchy back. An upside-down *la République française*. Incandescent with rage, the client might've been French but there was no need for any subtitles, having realised that each time he showed off his tattoo he'd have to do a handstand.

'Je demande un remboursement!'

'*Non, non, non*,' replied the punk, 'no refund.' It amused Martin the punk at least knew the French for "refund".

'Je vous demande de le supprimer gratuitement!'

'Free tattoo removal service?' the punk sneered, 'I tell you what, mate, I'll lend you my cheese grater!'

Now was his chance. Lunging across the table, Martin snapped a photo of the inside of the portfolio book. He was out the door and down the parade stairs before the punk tattooist realised what had happened. A furious bellow thundered from the shop doorway.

'OI! EUROCOP!'

As quick as a flash, the punk vaulted the balcony, racing towards Martin, who was now fumbling with the ignition. Damned shakes! The tattooist dived for the car door handle as —with a squeal of burnt rubber straight out of one of his action movies—Martin floored the accelerator. Snarling, the punk sprinted after him as the Alpine A110 tore out of town; Martin roaring with laughter.

A great day! Martin's elation only grew when he remembered he'd be seeing his friend, Renzo Brambilla, tomorrow. Sharing a passion for drink, as a man of excess, Renzo was the only man to keep up with Martin at the bar. But then, everything Renzo did was to the extreme, never more so when inventing his own lethal sports. He was an adrenaline junkie as much as a wine junkie. This was the man who —for the month they'd spent together last summer—would talk passionately all evening about kite fighting, convinced Martin to play pub darts with a blindfold, snort gunpowder for breakfast and partake in UFC (the latter, thankfully, Ultimate Frisbee Club). There would, no doubt, be some outlandishly dangerous game waiting for them at the Old Elysium vineyard.

Buzzing, Martin's euphoria lasted almost all the way home, only wearing off within sight of le Château des Allues; with all its horrific drunken memories. Worse still, one final recollection seeped into his fragile mind. Last night, at the summation, a new suspect had been suggested.

For all we know, Moretti, you're the killer.

It would explain a lot. The guilt he'd felt that next morning. His uncharacteristic reaction—nearly vomiting—on seeing Jimmy's body. Was his subconscious trying to tell him something? What with all the blackouts, could he honestly account for his whereabouts? Was this all a Machiavellian scheme to keep him in the detective game? Just how badly did he want his job back; enough to kill for? Surely not. No way. This GBH, grievous bottley harm hadn't even crossed his mind.... had it?

It had, said a small and truthful voice inside his head. He did think of it and then he'd fantasised about it. After solving this D.O.T. murder with a bottle of grog, Martin had pictured smashing that bottle not against the wall but over Radnor's smarmy, self-righteous head.

Pulling onto the driveway, he switched the engine off, sweating. Ugh, what if this hangover never ends? It didn't today. Martin tried to shake the crippling paranoia, the hanxiety, knowing his mood would improve as soon as his head hit the pillow. Knowing, also, that he wasn't the one with a tattoo from Blacked. Grabbing his phone, he flicked to the last photo taken. Slightly blurred, it showed a simple yet sinister, stencil design. Surrounded by a circle of skulls, three words were written in red.

Daughters of Temperance

Moretti Christmas Newsletter

Status: **Draft - Version 3**

Date: December 20th (5 days until deadline)

Merry Christmas, you iceholes,

Yes, you're all waiting on me and yes you've all added yours above. Well let me tell you something, having read your submissions, I wouldn't be so smug.

Aunt Maria - what does "establishing an alpaca small hold" really mean? Saw a llama, bought a llama, got a llama. Big whoop.

Kwami – hearty congratulations, so very bloody proud of you, for looking up our family tree. I assume it's the one filled with nuts and bad apples that all the dogs pee on.

Patrick – are you sure narcoleptics are even allowed to fly planes? Forget Christmas, prepare for Mayday!

No, Mamma, tropical fish can't get gout. And I'm not clicking Send until I've solved this case.

Yours Sincerely,

Son of a Nutcracker
P.S. Screw you Uncle Carlo, your breath smells like Nonna's feet.

24

Mea Culpa

Midnight. Spectral. All was calm, all was bright, as moonlight shone down on the Château des Allues garden. Not a creature was stirring, not even a mouse, nor the cold lifeless body bleeding by the frozen koi pond.

Savouring a delicious violet and cherry Cabernet Sauvignon, Martin tip-toed across the ice-carpeted lawn. A row of Christmas trees, decorated with silver tobacco pipes, were blocking his way. Peeking through, he saw Theo and Mary Oblet, screaming, screeching, shrieking, husband and wife at each other's throats. But the night was doggedly quiet; soundless. Beneath their feet lay Sven Lindblom, curled in a ball and writhing in silent pain; his glass of wine spilled onto the new fallen snow.

Finishing his Cabernet Sauvignon, Martin crept forward, and now he could hear the hiss of their voices, and the agonising moans from Sven. Theo, then Mary froze; their rage tempered on the chilled air as Martin hunched over the Swede. With every strained groan, Sven vomited blood and hot chunks of his stomach, still gripping onto the glass filled with gummy bears and pale mistletoe berries.

A black glove reached down and violently tugged on Sven's evening tie; strangling out his rasping last gasp. The death rattle pulsated through the starry night. No angels would sing for him, no bells of heaven ring for him. Spluttering, choking tears dripped onto Martin's violent hands.

'Acting out another dark fantasy, Monsieur Moretti?' whispered Mary.

'You never liked his ties, did you, Monsieur Moretti?' murmured Theo.

Looking down again, it wasn't Sven in the crumpled suit anymore. It was Superintendent Radnor, his throat rattling with a derisive cackle; and so Martin pulled harder and harder and harder.

Martin's eyes snapped open, shivering in bed. Blinded by the morning light, he checked both hands. No necktie or rope. With a long sigh, he slumped back onto his pillows as a draught rattled the window shutters. What a horrible nightmare—he'd actually drank a full glass of wine. And the murdering of Sven was bad also. No more fun facts. No more wakey wakeys.

The clattering of shutters grew louder, his bedroom was vibrating, and so—braving the dazzling light—he threw open his window, checking first there really was no cadaver outstretched by the koi pond. Thank God. Skyward, Martin spotted the source of the vibrations: soaring straight for them was a large black and white helicopter, its flac-flac-flac hum dying as it landed in a field behind the Château. What was going on? The whirling blades kicked up a blizzard of snow, Martin shutting his window in the nick of time.

Wearing every layer he'd packed, Martin ventured outdoors. The delicious smell of bacon and almond croissants from the kitchen was tempting, but he still couldn't face the group. Too embarrassing. Heading out front, however, he bumped straight into the very man he'd watched die moments earlier. By his hand.

'Good morning, Mr Moretti! Another early one,' Sven twinkled apologetically. 'I was just about to come and wake you.'

Behind him, Pekoe Williams, Morton and Eve Kessler were loading their suitcases onto the yellow coach.

'What's happening?' asked Martin, a little jittery as Sven rearranged his tie.

'Today we head for the mountains and the Old Elysium

Vineyard!' Their guide beamed. 'We go by chopper, courtesy of Renzo's twin-engine multipurpose H160 Airbus helicopter. Our luggage will follow on by coach.'

Last time round, at Montrottier, the Kesslers had thrown everyone's case into the hold with reckless abandon. This time, they were delicately laying each bag in. Possibly everybody was nursing a sore head from partying again. Martin wouldn't know, he had gone straight to bed to reflect upon the Daughters of Temperance tattoo.

The baggage handlers spotted Martin, and Pekoe waved over at him. 'Normally for the mountains I'd be packing for donkeys, not helicopters.'

'Recovered, then, kid,' drawled the gothic Morton Kessler, his thin grey hair plastered to his skull, 'from the other night?' Placing into the hold a padded Protect Cell camera bag that Martin didn't recognise as Noel's, Morton sidled over with one of his trademark lopsided leers. Bizarrely, their resident vampire of the vineyard appeared more virile than ever. Two nights ago, he was so hunched he'd rivalled Quasimodo, but now his back was as straight as an arrow; as if the recent morbid events had reinvigorated him.

Martin shuddered, sick of the man's inscrutable leers. 'You alright, Morton? You look confused.'

'If I want "confused", kid, I'll try and figure how you made it to Chief Inspector.'

Feigning a phone call to escape, Martin switched his phone off "do not disturb", picking up twelve missed calls and four irate answerphone messages. All from Capitaine Gallois. Texting back *"car safely returned"*, Martin added a smiling face with halo. Instantly, Gallois replied with *"stay there! so I can kill you!"* adding an angry face with horns. Yikes.

Strolling across a fresh carpet of snow to the back garden, Martin wasn't alone on this side of the Château either. Happily curled up under a red blanket, with a steaming cup of coffee, bowl of fruit and a notepad, was Holly Sinclair. Last time he had seen her, she'd looked horror-struck while he accused her of all sorts of nasty things. Today, the shy smile was back on her face, warming the entire garden. Pulling up a chair, they exchanged morning pleasantries and she certainly seemed to bear him no ill will.

'How you doing?' he asked, peeling himself an orange.

'Still mulling the plot of my murder mystery, *The Woman and The Wasp*,' she replied.

'It must be amazing to be a writer,' said Martin, entranced.

'Bluntly? Sometimes, I want to tear my own face off,' she said. 'It means I'm always thinking about murder. Over my detective series, I've pulverised, gassed, electrocuted, decapitated, dissolved, drowned and—in my last book, impaled on the Swiss flag—a cemetery's worth of victims. Right now, I'm contemplating whether the villain injects cyanide into the contents of this fruit bowl. Not that I have!' she added quickly, seeing the panic on Martin's face; and she crunched into a green apple to prove it.

Martin let out an overly dramatic sigh of relief and she giggled. But just as suddenly, a shadow of pain flickered across Holly's face. 'To tell you the truth, death has followed me around, clung to me, the last twelve months. I... I lost my brother Duncan last year.'

'Duncan Mott?' said Martin, keen to draw a line under his "Duncan Disorderly" joke.

'Yes, he died from alcoholic complications. My mother, Elise, she—'

'Elise Mott?'

'Yes. She never recovered from the loss. In the end,' her voiced cracked and she turned her face away, 'we lost her as well. You really must stop drinking, Martin,' she implored. 'Your job, your wife, and then the other night... surely, that gathering was the lowest point of your life.'

'Lowest point of my life *so far*,' said Martin jauntily.

'Are you honestly happy with your drinking?'

'I'm super happy,' said Martin, 'I'm game show host

happy.' She jotted something down in her notepad. When he'd first arrived out back, her hands had been trembling. Two sips of the cup later, her hands were rock steady. 'Maybe you and I aren't so different,' he said, eyeing her coffee which had more than a whiff of whiskey about it.

'Alright, yes, I admit it,' Holly relented. 'The difference is, I'm desperate to stop. Clearly not even my brother's tragedy was enough of a wake-up call, so it's gotta be something even more extreme.' Though her jaw was clenched, she had tears in her eyes. 'I hate how much I drink. Why do you do it, Martin?'

'To solve cases,' he shrugged, 'and help me crack the murder of Jimmy Stresskeller.'

'Is this before or after you were drooling on the floor?' she said, and they both laughed.

'So, come on, then. You're a writer of detective stories, who do you think did it?'

'Ha! You can be Hercule Poirot, I'll be your Ariadne Oliver,' said Holly. 'I've even got the apple.'

'In fiction, isn't it always whoever finds the body?'

'Actually, my killers are usually somebody introduced quite late on in the story; makes it less contrived.'

'Apart from your first one, where it was the detective?' said Martin.

Holly nodded. 'Trust no one.' Martin would certainly never trust her son again, the Goonie lies had significantly skewed his investigation.

'So how do you hide the murderers in your plots?'

'Best way is the double-down double-bluff. Bust them early, guilty for one thing so you don't suspect them of a second,' said Holly. 'Or, similarly, they confess to a lesser crime.'

'Clever,' said Martin approvingly.

'Woooweee!' came an NYC holler as Tate Sinclair trotted over to them. 'Jeez, it's so damned cold, I just farted snowflakes.' Martin thought he'd be the one embarrassed around the Sinclairs, but it was Tate who looked shamefaced;

awkwardly rubbing a set of bruised knuckles.

'Ah, so it's your fist I have to thank,' said Martin, massaging his jaw; finally linking his assailant to the line: *do you want a slap?* Another example of the Sinclair's transatlantic mix; American accent, British threat.

'*Mea culpa*,' said Tate, his face reddening. 'You have a dozen witnesses in front of Captain Gallois; I fully expect you'll be pressing charges.'

'Don't worry, I'm British, we don't sue every time someone sneezes,' said Martin amiably. 'We tax it, but we don't sue it.'

'That's mighty decent of you.'

'I'm sorry,' said Holly pensively, 'my husband gets a little overexcited after one glass of wine.'

'No, I deserved it, we're all good,' said Martin, and they shook hands.

Underneath his waxed walrus moustache, a sheepish grin broke onto Tate's face until he suddenly remembered why he was here. 'You'd better come quick. There's a staticky Gallois getting into serious beef with Lindblom.' Springing from their seats—Martin finishing Holly's coffee—they raced round the side of the Château with Tate. 'I think he's here to arrest you.'

'Why,' said Martin, 'just because I stole a Gendarmerie car and drove off from him?'

'Facts,' said Tate. They could hear angry voices bellowing around the next corner.

At the last moment, Martin pulled Holly back; pleased she didn't wince from him touching her arm this time. 'I'm serious,' said Martin, a slight plead in his voice, 'who do you think did it?'

'Alright, if you really want to know. I think it's the birdman, Noel Gillespie.'

'Why?'

'Last night I heard Noel, by himself, rehearsing a confession to Renzo.'

'Did he mention the murder?'

Holly frowned. 'I don't know… it was more of an apology… of guilt.'

Catching up with Tate, they found Sven and Gallois yelling nose to nose on the driveway, Lieutenant Aimee struggling to hold her Capitaine back.

'Where is Moretti?' demanded Gallois.

'Leave him alone!' shrieked Sven, and Martin was so astounded, so thankful, so eager to save the Swede that, running forward, he shoved the Capitaine back with such force he slammed into the side of the coach, several suitcases spilling out.

'What do you want?' said Martin sharply.

Gallois' eyes flared. 'Ah, look who finally showed up; the Defective Detective!' By now. the whole Château had come to see what was going on. 'Come, let us rejoice at the festive return of Monsieur Moretti, on tidings of comfort and joy-ride.'

'Mr Moretti,' Sven wheezed. 'The Airbus helicopter is ready to launch so I took the courtesy of packing your bag and bringing it down, but the Capitaine refuses to—'

'You are going nowhere,' roared Gallois, shaking all the way down his cane in fury.

'Where exactly did you take our car?' seethed Aimee, handcuffs out.

'Following up on a lead. A promising lead,' Martin added in response to Aimee's derisive snort. 'For the good of the case, Operation Incognito, right?'

'*Annuler l'opération,*' Aimee hissed at Gallois, 'we must abort this operation.'

'Abort?' said Martin. 'No way! We're making good progress.' The party watched the spectacle dumbfounded.

'*Bon, alors,* you want to keep Operation Incognitio alive?' spat Gallois. 'Tell me one useful thing or I'll arrest you right now for theft against the French Republic.'

Martin was thinking fast. He absolutely did not want to give away the D.O.T. tattoo revelation yet. 'Fine, how about I return the missing Chateau Lafite Rothschild, 1787.'

'Where?' said Aimee.

'On the coach, of course.' There was a shocked murmur around the onlookers as Martin pulled a black bag out of the hold. 'A padded Protect Cell camera bag; we had one for surveillance back in Buxton.' Pushing Martin aside, Lieutenant Aimee examined the case, while Gallois stood there, seething, staring from Martin to the bag as they unzipped it. 'It was placed into the hold way too gently just now, considering it already contains foam padded cushions. Perfect for transporting—'

'Thomas Jefferson's wine!' marvelled Aubrey, high fiving Sven; the rest of the group stunned into silence.

'But who does it belong to,' said Tate, 'who stole it?'

'The Kesslers, of course.'

'Prove it,' said Eve icily, mirroring her husband's leer.

'Didn't you say, when we first met, you were here to collect the most expensive wines in existence?' said Martin, extracting their battered dusty suitcase from the coach. 'That appears to be by both legal and illicit means.'

'But how? When?' stammered Sven as Martin rummaged through the case, pulling out: strawberry lip balm, chocolate body paint, a lemon scented candle (Martin was starting to feel hungry), a leather corset, handcuffs, crotchless knickers, massage wand and (feeling less hungry) a faux fur-lined paddle.

'Careful with my candle, Moretti, it's made with real lemon oil,' said a brazen-faced Eve, defiant to the accusations.

'Those cloaks that made Morton look all crooked and bent, almost hunchback, those cloaks like... this one,' said Martin, holding up a padded black robe, 'have a jetted pocket sewn inside with enough space to conceal a bottle sideways.' Dexterously feeling beneath the collar, Martin slid his hand into the inner pocket and waggled it around to demonstrate; and this time the spectators gasped.

'So the theft wasn't Camille Duval?' asked Pekoe.

'No, and nothing to do with the D.O.T. killer. It occurred

hours before Jimmy's death; when we were all sat at the table, in fact.'

'Surely we would have seen?' said Theo.

'Those erotic sounds, that gymnastic display, was fake,' said Martin, 'to buy them time. While Eve made all those noises, Morton was concealing the wine inside his coat. Though, I don't remember you wearing any gloves that night, so I suspect it'd be worth checking for fingerprints on the bottle.' Eve and Morton Kessler exchanged a dark look; the jig was up. 'And that,' he said directly to Morton, 'is how you make Chief Inspector.'

'But what about what we heard against the bookshelf door?' said Sven to Eve. 'You on the other side, it was so, er... realistic.'

'That's not to say I didn't enjoy myself in there,' she said, unabashed. 'What can I say, I'm a method actor.'

'Where did you hide it?' said Gallois, inspecting the bottle. 'I searched the rooms on my arrival.'

'Outside the window, behind the shutters,' said Morton grudgingly, his shoulders sagging.

'Very clever, Monsieur Kessler, I did not check there,' said Gallois, less in praise of them than castigating himself.

'You dangled a 220,000-euro bottle out of a second-floor window?' stammered Sven. 'As guardian of the wine, I am very cross.'

'It was secure,' said Eve.

'It is still safe and sound,' said Morton. 'So, what happens now?' All eyes were on the Capitaine.

'Hmmmm,' mulled Gallois. 'Renzo said if it turned out to be one of you lot, he would not press charges, so long as he got the bottle back.' He shot Martin an annoyed look, as though it was all his fault the Gendarmerie weren't making an arrest this morning.

'Excellent,' said Sven, a spring back in his step, 'we are all packed; there is nothing left to do but to take to the skies.' The Kesslers led the charge, not daring to glimpse back. 'Come on,' said Sven, before adding in an admittedly decent Arnold Schwarzenegger voice, 'Scoot! Scoot! Get to the chopper!'

As the group tramped to the far end of the gardens, Gallois yanked Martin back by his hood.

'Don't you dare walk away from me!' Suddenly there was iron in the French accent, a look of demented rage now cracked across his face.

'What now?' snapped Martin, the rest of the party out of earshot.

'Too good for us now, *oui*? All because you guessed the right suitcase,' said the Capitaine. 'Check out the big brain on Moretti. Well, you're not the only one with a big brain. I have a big brain.'

'You should bring it in sometime,' said Martin, 'might speed up solving this case, instead of falsely arresting Camille.'

'You, yourself, pointed her out to me!'

'Only as a person of interest, not as the guaranteed killer.'

'And what makes you sure?' said Aimee, shaking her head in disbelief.

'It's just a hunch but—'

'I don't like hunches, they're mislaid facts,' said Gallois.

'How about the fact,' said Martin, endeavouring to keep his voice steady, 'that it was only *after* we switched Jimmy's light on that Cammy returned here. Surely she'd only do that if she thought he was alive.' The helicopter engine hummed and the blades began to whirl.

'Confident then, are you, that it is not Mademoiselle Camille Duval?' said Gallois, as he joined Aimee in the head shaking.

'Yes,' said Martin through gritted teeth, 'there's still a killer on this tour.' Their obstinance made Martin more determined than ever to solve the murder himself.

'Unfortunately for you, Monsieur Moretti,' said Gallois, popping another of his hard candies into his mouth, 'she confessed to us last night.'

Martin stopped abruptly. 'What?'

'That night, she was outside his window, he called down to her, invited her up, the front door was open, so she entered and joined him in bed before he kicked her out at three a.m. She says Monsieur Stresskeller was harping on about finding his divine inspiration. Scorned by the dismissal, she took back her gift of the gold Rolex watch,' said the Capitaine. 'When we pressed her, she then confessed the watch wasn't enough, she felt used, so she took revenge with the bottle.'

'But that can't be true,' protested Martin.

'It is over,' said Gallois. 'I told you I would have her in Fleury-Mérogis prison before Christmas Eve. *Oui,* one thing that is true, Monsieur Moretti, there will be no more murders among the vines.

25

The Old Elysium Vineyard (murder location #2)

The flight had been short, sixty minutes, gliding over a marshmallow world of whipped cream highways, silver lakes, and frosted doll houses. And yet, a hollow feeling grew inside Martin. Perhaps the fact he had no one to share this winter wonder with; his closest companion was the ragged mountaintop jutting through the bright-white clouds. Or perhaps the fact Gallois' closure of the case meant nobody would now indulge Martin investigating the minor inconvenience of first-degree murder. First-degree; total buzzkill.

It was Father Christmas who welcomed Martin to the Old Elysium vineyard. Their helicopter had landed in a large cobblestone courtyard, surrounded by a country farmhouse and circular set of converted stables. What Martin had assumed to be a flock of sheep turned out to be the white humps of a Lamborghini Miura, Ferrari Boxer, Pagani Huayra, Lancia Stratos and Maserati Bora.

'*Dolci bambini!*' boomed the man in red, full of cherry nose and ho-ho-hos. 'Welcome! *La mia famiglia!*' Each word was coated in a thick Italian accent. Stripping from the Santa suit to a black cashmere turtleneck underneath, was the man everybody had journeyed to see. Tall, powerfully built, light olive skinned, with curling black hair and honey brown eyes inviting them forwards. A true Italian family man. Arms outstretched, Renzo Brambilla hugged them all. Even out of the Santa suit, it was a warm embrace; squeezing so tight,

Morton Kessler's bones nearly compacted to dust. The only person excluded from the hug was Noel; instead, receiving a formal handshake.

'Martin!' Renzo rejoiced, flinging away the costume. 'I'm so glad you are here.' He removed the white beard but the cherry nose remained, matching his ruddy red-raw cheeks. Rosacea; drinker's nose. One advantage of being black; it was much easier to hide the alcohol-induced broken blood vessels.

'Good to see you, Renzo, great to see you,' said Martin, of a friendship forged under exceptional circumstances.

'Times are good, Martin. Happier times! Since my cash injection six months ago, everything is on the up.'

'Excellent,' said Martin, 'though, why *did* you invite me?'

'You still haven't figured it out, eh?' Renzo bellowed with laughter, brandishing a full set of wine-stained teeth. 'Shall we head for the terrace.' It wasn't a question. Renzo rarely asked questions. Instead, Renzo *insisted.* Yet, when complied with, you felt the only person the sun shined down on. 'We have much to celebrate.'

'Mr Brambilla, if we scoot over to the stables—'

'Relax yourself, Sven. We will tour the facilities tomorrow. Before then, drinks in large quantities! Let me show off the vista.'

And what a vista. The jagged mountains of the Chablais Alps rose up directly behind the farmhouse to an elevation of 4000 feet, running in deep folds each way along the valley. Martin joined Pekoe with an impressed whistle. A bar with a real brass rail had been set up on the sandstone terrace overlooking the vineyard. All around them, LED heaters—the same type as at Montrottier—bathed them in mellow multicoloured warmth.

'Have there been any sightings of the bearded vulture yet?' asked Noel.

'Champagne first, questions later,' said Renzo with a wink to the party, handing fizzing glasses round. Thankfully, other drinks were available. Martin ordered himself a Gibson martini while Mary scoured the shelves.

'*Je voudrais... un gin tonic.*'

The waiter mixed her drink. 'Lemon?'

'*Non, merci,*' she replied bluntly, 'I am bitter enough.' Twisting round to see Aubrey behind her, Mary added: 'And she will probably have a Blue Nun.'

'I'm sick of her treating me like an American,' said Aubrey, watching her leave.

'But you are an American,' said Martin.

'Yeah. An American who can tell the difference between Château Carbonnieux Blanc and Château de Fieuzal Blanc; and whether to serve it with sushi or sashimi.'

'*La famiglia è tutto!*' Renzo lifted his champagne flute to the skies in jubilation. 'Let us toast the return of my Lafite Rothschild,' he said with a glimmering eye at the Kesslers. 'Let us toast to the long imprisonment of Camille Duvall. Let us toast to good tidings for Christmas.'

'Let us toast to the memory of Jimmy Stresskeller,' said Martin gravely.

Renzo's face fell, lowering his flute. 'To Jimmy Stresskeller,' he said with a heavy chested sigh, the group staring down at the floor. Deeming twenty seconds a sufficient grieving period, he raised his glass again. 'Most importantly, let us toast the arrival of you wonderful people and the launch of Old Elysium's first ever wine—*Vautour Barbu*!'

He beamed at them all and the group beamed back. Teamwork makes the dream work. Renzo Brambilla was a distilled version of them all, as if his soul had bottled their core personalities. The mischief of Joseph, magnetism of Jimmy, vanity of Noel and the passion of Eve. As protective a father as Tate, with the nervous energy of Holly. He'd earnt the wrinkles of Morton making millions via his Sven-like organisational skills, breezy charm of Theo and inner steel of Mary. And perhaps their tour guide's description of the other three—a riddle, wrapped in a mystery, inside an enigma—added a touch of mystique about him; where the thirst of Martin met the refined air of Pekoe, sprinkling on top Aubrey's obsession with wine.

'Saluti!' boomed Renzo above the whirr of the departing-chopper. Talk inevitably drifted onto wine, so Martin was relieved when Omar's yellow coach finally arrived with their luggage, allowing for an hours break to unpack. The wine theme, however, continued inside the house, from the chandeliers made of wine glasses to the cork on the end of their room's key chain. This wine décor was double-downed with an explosion of overly-tinselled Christmas trees, fir garlands twisted around banisters, and glossy-green holly cuttings behind every picture frame. And there it hung; great bunches of mistletoe strewn above every doorway, dangling like the sword of Damocles. How soon before those three letters were written again?

By the time Martin headed back out, a roguish gleam in Renzo's eyes indicated it was time to play his latest lethal winter sport. Martin dreaded to think: ice sculpting with chainsaws, bobsleigh without breaks, polar bear wrestling or curling with landmines? Whatever it was, this was Martin's opportunity to win favour with him. As Martin had witnessed last summer, to stay on Renzo's radar, you needed to be top of the pile. Easy enough after rescuing his daughter, but now there were a dozen people vying for his attention. Win this game and Martin could keep carte blanche to "indulge" his investigation, plus potentially, at long last, discover why on earth he was invited here.

'What's with the weapon?' asked Tate. The group joined Renzo at the far end of the terrace, where the heaters couldn't quite melt the snow away. He was brandishing a wooden recurve bow with several quivers of arrows.

'My favourite game, my own invention,' announced Renzo. 'Rubber pigeon!'

'What the hell is rubber pigeon?' said Mary.

'It is like clay pigeon shooting, only more fun,' he said. 'The previous owner of this vineyard was a semi-pro tennis player. He had no trophies to show for it, but he left behind a mountain of tennis balls. Also, his tennis ball launcher. You know, one of those machines which automatically fires out balls every twelve seconds so that you can practice hitting them back by yourself. I found both in the stable before I converted it. Our challenge today... we will launch rubber tennis balls upwards and try to hit them out of the sky with my carbon fibre arrows.'

'Is it safe?' asked Holly.

'Of course!' said Renzo, master of the reassuring smile. The party were all smiles, radiating happiness back; though a little forced from the Kesslers and—for some reason—Noel. 'Bring me my balls, Sven,' said Renzo, 'and Martin, if you would be so kind as to fetch the launcher?' Pointing to their whereabouts, the crate of balls and launcher apparently always stayed outside the kitchen backdoor in a cobwebbed corner. Martin and Sven pulled them over to the group.

'Ah, the Lobster Sports Elite Two Portable Ball Machine,' said Renzo, fondly patting the contraption. 'My old friend. Capable of holding one-hundred and fifty balls.' Alcohol and archery, reflected Martin, what could possibly go wrong. If the D.O.T. murderer really was here, wouldn't this be their perfect opportunity; for their bow to simply slip? No, he concluded, the killer of Jimmy Stresskeller had enjoyed inflicting brutal blow after brutal blow.

'There's no way you make that shot unless you are Robin Hood,' said Mary, as Renzo assumed his shooting stance.

'Hit a tennis ball at twenty-two miles per hour on top of a snow mound? Ha! Robin Hood's a rookie,' said Renzo, aiming into the sky. Launching a ball thirty feet up, Martin watched as Renzo released the arrow. It perfectly skewered the ball in mid-air and dropped into the vineyard below. The whole group whooped and cheered with delight.

'Amazing!' said Theo, clapping wildly.

'Impressive,' said Aubrey.

'We have got to try that!' cried Pekoe.

'Yes, most impressive, Renzo, but I reckon I could beat that,' said Martin grabbing an arrow. The group let out an exhilarated "oooooh." Panto season had started early. But this was one game Martin might actually be good at. Aside from a post-work drink with colleagues, archery was the one extracurricular activity Martin partook in. He was part of the British Police Archery Association: *"bringing individual police archers from around the UK together to become one unstoppable force."* He had never won any medals but hopefully he'd have enough experience to place him top of Renzo's pecking order.

'How's your accuracy?' grinned Renzo, handing over his bow.

'Pinpoint,' said Martin, and with perfect balance, he took aim at the skies. Explaining the speed of the ball launcher varied from ten to eighty miles per hour, Renzo set it to the lowest speed but Martin still missed the rubber "pigeon" by several feet. Both the ball and arrow plummeted into the valley, Martin sincerely hoping there were no fruit pickers out today. Exhaling calmly, he stretched the bow string back and waited for another target. The ball fired up into the clouds. Martin released the arrow which flew through the air and hit its target with a satisfying thwack. The crowd screamed with glee and soon everyone wanted to test their archery skills.

It was a fun afternoon watching everybody try to shoot the rubber pigeons out of the sky. Martin hit several more, as well as Pekoe, Aubrey and Noel. And for a moment, on that chilled winter afternoon, Martin forgot about the murder and the dark clouds looming over the Elysium farmhouse.

Retreating to the comfort of the bar with Pekoe, it was made decidedly less comfortable by the presence of Theo Oblet, who was glowering at his estranged wife. Eek. Amidst the twang and the flight of arrows, Mary seemed determined to have a good time.

'Look at her,' said Theo sourly, 'making a fool of herself, throwing herself at anyone.' Shrieking with laughter, she playfully slapped Noel on the arm as he demonstrated how to use the bow and arrow. Theo glared, scowled, and tutted for good measure; and Martin wondered if his breezy charm would ever return.

'You sound a little jealous there, Theo,' said Pekoe.

'I am not jealous, just territorial,' frowned Theo. 'Jealousy is wanting something that is not yours. Territorial is protecting what is yours already.' No matter how Theo branded it, he still sounded desperately insecure to Martin. 'I feel like I'm losing control of my life.'

'We all go a little crazy sometimes,' said Pekoe.

'Come on, get a grip on yourself,' said Martin, 'I got divorced last Christmas and look at me now, I'm doing really well.'

'Are you?' asked Pekoe, amused, eyeing Martin's third double vodka. 'Do you know what "denial" means?'

'A river in Egypt, isn't it,' said Martin.

'Mary and I will be ok. We have our ups and downs, but we make it work,' said Theo. Now there was a man in denial, thought Martin. The Frenchman read his mind. 'I know, I know. I must find victory in letting go.' Theo's affirmation was immediately undermined by another hoot of laughter at Noel's joke. 'Regular comedian,' said Theo resentfully. 'Monsieur Moretti, I beg of you, from one jilted man to another, can you please go over there and interrupt them?'

Martin sympathised but was hesitant. 'What if she goes for me?'

'Not likely,' snorted Theo, finally relaxing. 'You are not her type.'

'Black?'

'No,' replied Theo, 'English.'

It wasn't difficult to extract Mary's suitor. Informing Noel he'd seen a bearded vulture on the farmhouse roof, Martin was instantly alone with her. Firing a rubber pigeon up into the heavens for her, Mary pierced the ball with her first arrow. Quick study.

'So how did you join this Brambilla rabble?' asked

Martin. There was too much about her to simply be counting numbers behind a desk.

'Renzo discovered me at one of his restaurants. I was the Sommelier.'

'Another one,' Martin muttered to himself.

'But what impressed Renzo was my financial excellence, I am a *mathématiques* whizz,' she said, sounding as modest as Noel.

'Out of curiosity, is this wine business insured?'

'Yes, if it fails, Renzo would actually make a tidy sum. Finance is satisfying work but now my focus is…' Mary struck down another pigeon, 'I am working on a new life. My New Year's resolutions are divorce, divorce, divorce, in that order. I will be happy again,' she said assertively. 'Live like every day it is his last.' She cast a filthy look in Theo's direction.

'That's a bit morbid, given the circumstances.' Murder was back on his mind.

'*Non*, you are wrong,' said Mary. 'Surely now, more than ever, we need to seize the day.' Though hating the conversation, it seemed only Martin was on edge. All around him: corks popped, wine sploshed, glasses clinked. As Tate, Holly and Joseph were snowball fighting (Tate sacrificing himself as a human shield), Theo jubilantly announced he finally had an idea for the wine label painting, inspired by the archery (or was it the alcohol?). Pekoe, Morton and Eve burst into hysterics watching Noel chase every feathery shadow above, while Renzo regaled the partygoers how he'd outbid Sir Alan Sugar at auction for a Pol Roger 1919 for his daughter, Sara.

THWACK! Mary skewered another tennis ball; Martin at risk of losing top spot. Having said that, surely the discovery of the Lafite gave him a boost, even if he was now receiving death stares from the Kesslers (admittedly they shot the same leer at Mary as well).

'You do not believe Capitaine Gallois has the right suspect, do you?' said Mary shrewdly. 'And you still do not know who it is.'

'I'm working on it,' said Martin.

'It takes a man as simple as you to make this case complicated,' sneered Mary. 'And so now you build rapport to catch me off guard when you suddenly accuse me of murder?'

'The thought had occurred.'

'But not this time,' said Mary, thoroughly enjoying Martin's growing frustration. 'All detectives should be women. Female intuition shows it is obviously Monsieur Gillespie... those guilty glances towards Renzo.' Sure enough, Martin caught a shifty look from Noel to their host. 'You, Monsieur Moretti, are irrelevant,' she said, as pointed as the arrow tips that skewered the next six balls. Martin hit the next seven, placing them on level pegging. Suddenly, however, the sun was setting. Martin helped Renzo pack everything away back outside the kitchen door and the guests filed in.

'C'è una tempesta di neve in arrivo, bambini.'

'What did Renzo say?' asked Holly.

Martin, of Italian heritage (via Hackney), translated. 'Snow. Lots of snow. He said there's a storm coming.'

26

Phylloxera Vastatrix

A festive mask shrouded the killer. True crime at Christmastime camouflaged in the jolly-jingle bellringing, bludgeoning, magical season. Violent death amongst Dasher, Dancer, Prancer, plum pudding, presents and Pringles. But then, wasn't murder a little like Pringles? Once you pop...

Christmas came early for Aubrey as Renzo piled bottle after bottle into her eager arms, her jaw hitting the floor as she goggled at the labels.

'Domaine du Cellier des Cray, Cuvée Albinum... Claude Quenard, Chignin-Bergeron, Savoie, France, 2015... Domaine Dupasquier, Roussette de Savoie Marestel, 2012...'

Emerging from a bustling lobster-steamed kitchen (the only way in and out of the farmhouse), they made their way down the corridor to the wine tasting room. Of course. With its open archway entrance, the room contained a wooden table and a high-backed leather chair facing out into the corridor. And next to a notepad and bowl of crackers, stood thirty gleaming bottles, thirty sparkling glasses and one waiter's friend corkscrew, ready for action.

'You will need to bone up ahead of the exam next month,' said Renzo.

'Next month?' Aubrey stammered. 'You got me an invitation?' Renzo nodded, beaming at her with pride. She ran forward and hugged him, crying with happiness.

'Wines from the region of course,' said Renzo, 'but, as we are almost as close to Geneva as we are Bonneville, I thought you could start cramming the Swiss wines. Try Thomas Studarch's 2014 Pinot Noir from Malanser, a personal favourite of mine, and this light Merlot, Riflessi d'Epoca 2012, made the old way, is so good it could be Italian.'

With no door to this room, it was easy for Martin and Pekoe to edge out and tiptoe down the corridor to the only other *chambre* on this floor: a light and airy living room which — underneath the assault of Yuletide decorations—still had all the bearings of alpine chalet chic. From the rustic exposed beams and flickering stone fireplace to the sheepskin rugs and mulberry silk sofas, everything was directed towards the large picture window overlooking the snowcapped pines and peaks of the valley. There was no sign of a storm yet. Instead, lacy flakes gently drifted out of the sky. *Bellissimo.*

The farmhouse was built into the side of a steep snow-covered slope. Plunging sharply away into the valley, it looked smooth enough to toboggan down, stretching on forever; what the ski twits would call a black run. No thanks. With a solitary farm track cutting across, Martin was surprised their host hadn't already suggested sledging down it. Propelled by flamethrowers.

'Spectacular, isn't it?' said Pekoe. Lifting a photo frame from the sideboard, he rubbed a smudge off the glass before handing it to Martin. At the top of a mountain, Renzo was grinning behind a pair of reflective blue sunglasses, Pekoe squinting in the sunlight, both crouched in front of an assortment of prayer flags.

'Makes the days in the office worthwhile,' said Renzo, sucking on a fat, gold-and-black banded cigar.

'How's business?' asked Pekoe, and there was that momentary bitterness in the gentleman's tone again.

'You're standing in it and I'm smoking it,' Renzo said proudly through a thick plume of smoke. 'Not bad for a local lad from Naples, but let me show you something really special.' Behind the far sofa, he led the group down a spiral staircase into the basement. Renzo's wine cellar was not your usual musty, dark and dank room. LED ribbon lights illuminated a modern mirrored tunnel containing zero particles of dust.

The air was clean, as fresh as the outside; a digital screen confirming it was currently twelve degrees Celsius and 70% humidity. And wine, as far as the eye could see; floor-to-ceiling metal hanging racks placing the bottles sideways to show off the labels.

'Bloody hell, Renzo,' said Martin, 'you could drown a small town if this cellar was emptied.' There must have been over ten thousand bottles.

The only thing out of place was an old protruding rusty nail, that had been used to hang an aroma wheel tapestry.

'It was here when I moved in,' said Renzo, noticing where Martin was looking. 'It's my lucky charm.'

'Maybe not for everyone,' said Martin, their Swedish guide ripping his suit jacket as he passed by. Sven apologetically gave the nail a quick polish before gawping himself at the bottles; the many, many bottles.

Laughing at their dumb-struck faces, Renzo jumped onto a steel library ladder, gliding along the entire length of the cellar.

'You can help yourself to anything in here.' Entranced, they skittered down the herringbone tiled floor after him. 'I have wines for every occasion and to match every mood. A bottle of Chardonnay with friends; Chablis Chardonnay if with seafood,' said Renzo, running his hand along a row of bottles. 'An Argentinian Malbec for a barbecue. For pasta, Italian of course, a Barbera. For date night, a traditional French Chenin Blanc.'

'Which would cure a hangover?' asked Martin.

'A Provence Rosé,' said Renzo without hesitation, 'which is also perfect for Valentines Day. Merlot for business meetings. Riesling for adventure; one of my favourites.'

'Do you have one for fresh starts?' said Mary.

'You should go for this: Château Clarke, Listrac-Médoc, 2018,' said Renzo, tapping the bottle dreamily.

'Then I shall open that at midnight.'

'No, you are not,' said Theo, 'I don't want you waking me

up.'

'I have already told you, Theo, I will sleep on the living room sofa.'

'That's alright, I was planning to paint anyway,' mumbled Theo.

Delicious smells of food tempted them back upstairs. *'L'amore si misura in piatti cucinati,'* said Renzo wistfully. 'Come now, let's eat!'

As the party headed up, the Kesslers hung back, Martin pricking his ears up on the stairwell.

'You've messed everything up,' whispered Eve.

'Relax,' said Morton, 'we got a hug from Renzo, didn't we? That's more than Noel got.'

'We're here for the finest wines, remember?' hissed Eve, her voice as sharp as a knife edge. 'I count forty-six vintages just in the Pinots. We've gotta get back in his good books, else we'll lose the whole distribution deal.'

'Relax, I—'

'The Lafite theft's ruined everything,' said Eve, slapping him hard across the face.

'Don't worry, I've got a way to fix everything,' murmured Morton, but she'd already elbowed past them both into the living room. 'Apparently our mutually agreed plan was now just my plan,' he said to Martin, still rubbing his face.

In the short time they had toured the cellar, the sideboards had been cleared, replaced with a Christmas banquet of oysters and crayfish and pheasant, salmon souffle with fresh herbs, braised beef in a Barolo wine sauce, salted cod, lentil ragout with smoked bacon, a three-cheese lasagna, foie gras with rustic breads and onion jam, spaghetti bolognaise, and a grilled goat's cheese salad. And for dessert, next to the Christmas tree with a star on top, a gigantic panettone pudding served with Alba white-truffle ice cream. Merrily whistling Jingle Bells, Sven undertook the role of waiter, topping up everybody's drinks.

Piling lasagna onto his plate, Martin found himself next

to their host. 'So, why did you invite me?'

'Can't it be enough for a father to thank you for rescuing his beautiful daughter,' said Renzo.

'Where is she, by the way; Sara?'

'Just arrived home and unpacking before bed,' he said, 'we will see her in the morning.'

The last sideboard was the highlight. It was loaded with crystal carafes, Martin proudly identifying them all by appearance: the dark brown rum, ruby red port, crystal-clear vodka (Renzo hated gin), the pale amber of the tequila compared to the golden whisky (the amaretto option eliminated since Renzo didn't do things by halves). Martin picked the carafe at the far end. In contrast to the other clear liquids, this one looked slightly cloudy. He sniffed to confirm it was a non-chill filtered whisky. Martin's favourite, he worshipped the cloudiness, indicating the whisky was as close as possible to what came from the original cask. A splash of water, or to have it with ice, produced the haze; caused by the natural aromatic compounds, esters. When he'd solved this case, Martin was demanding that Highland distillery tour from Renzo.

Sitting on the sofas, feasting on the wintery grandeur outside as much as the sumptuous food, the merriment was only mired by a torrent of ill-tempered tuts from Mary. Clearly, her happy new life was on hold as she swore loudly, recoiling at Aubrey's plate.

'What now, Mary?' said Aubrey bluntly. 'Why don't you go ahead and charge me with my latest gastronomic crime.'

'First of all,' said Mary, with the blanched face of disgust she normally reserved for Theo, 'never eat your salad before the main course. In France, you have your salad to finish a meal, not to start it! And then, you have the nerve to cut your lettuce with a knife. The chef has spent time preparing it exactly as it should be, it doesn't need you interfering.' Aubrey's hand momentarily shook, spilling her wine. Steadying herself, she sliced her bread; which only further incensed Mary. To Martin, it was simply a salad, but Mary looked like she wanted to grab the Christmas star and stab Aubrey through the eye with it.

'Aaaah, *cara* Mary,' cooed Renzo, 'she is more cultured than you think. Why don't you tell her, Aubrey.'

'I'm training to be a Master Sommelier,' said Aubrey, her green eyes shining with pride.

'So what,' sniffed Mary, 'when I was a Sommelier I earnt 30,000 a year, but now as an investment banker I can add two zeroes to that of a Sommelier.' She wrinkled her nose on the final word.

'I said I want to be Master Sommelier, not a Sommelier. A Master Sommelier earns 150,000,' said Aubrey stiffly.

'You will fail,' said Mary.

'Watch me,' said Aubrey.

It was Theo's turn to sniff. 'We do not need another American woman ruining wine country with—'

'It was women who invented wine,' said Aubrey.

'Yes, but centuries before your country was even discovered,' said Theo. Martin was fairly certain the Native Americans were already there, but there's no way he was stepping into this conversation. Nobody else dared speak or breathe; instead, taking a long sip of their drinks. Out of the snow-flecked window, thick, swirling flakes were falling heavily over the estate now.

'Actually, my ancestors have been traced back to Bordeaux,' said Aubrey.

'That must have been the swamp area,' snapped Mary. 'You should have stayed over there. You Americans destroyed our vines. Our vineyards were happy until you stepped onto French soil, *la dévastateur.*'

'What is that, you keep saying to Aubrey?' asked Martin, forcibly light. He'd heard them mutter that phrase twice during dinner the other night. Last time it was mentioned, Aubrey resembled someone who'd been slapped around the face. This time, there were tears in her eyes, but she blinked them back.

'The devastator: phylloxera vastatrix. A microscopic insect from the Mississippi valley,' said Theo, 'hopped on a bundle of vines, made its way across the Atlantic and arrived in Europe in 1870.'

'1860,' said Mary irritably. 'The female phylloxera—the more deadly, of course—will feed on the roots and leaves of grapevines, sucking the sap from the plants.'

'Destroyed 90% of Europe's vineyards. God bless the USA,' taunted Theo. 'Wine wages were cut in half, bankrupted businesses; it cost France over ten billion francs.'

Martin, disliking the bullying tone, was eager to step in but was clueless about wine history. Aubrey glanced around, perhaps for backup from her fellow Americans—the Sinclairs and Kesslers—but both pairs were sitting rigidly silent, eyes averted. Sven played with his pink tie.

'We suffered as well,' said Aubrey. '85% of the Napa Valley plantations were wiped out.'

'How tragic,' said Mary with ironic scorn. 'I'm sure the world will weep without any Ernest and Julio.' Theo sniggered and Martin wondered if he was piling on in one last attempt to reunite with his estranged wife. In response, she shifted on the sofa, her back now to him. Drawing a deep breath, Mary raged on: 'The grape growers tried everything to fix it, from prayer and flooding to garlic and urine. So, *merci beaucoup* to the Yanks.'

'Yanks? Well, you Frogs should be thanking us you've got any wine left at all,' said Aubrey, and Martin was glad that she was fighting back. 'Surely you know the only successful way they controlled the bug was by grafting our stronger, phylloxera-resistant, American rootstock to your more vulnerable European vinifera vine. By 1900, two-thirds of French vines were bound to American roots.' Eyes ablaze, Aubrey smiled at Mary. 'You skipped the part where pretty much every vine today now grows on American vines.'

Seizing an opportunity to restore the spirit of peace

and goodwill, Renzo said: 'A joyful ending! Let us toast to the saviour of wine!'

'No, thank you,' said Aubrey, with forced politeness, 'too much venom on the aftertaste.'

Mary's lip curled. '*Trop de poison autour de cette table*,' she muttered to herself. Snow was filling up the window now, the outside world completely obscured. 'Did you know, one of the ways they tried to fix it in France was to bury a live toad under each vine to draw out the "poison"?' Aubrey nodded. 'The Yanks saved us before, perhaps you can save us now. What do you say, Aubrey, it is better if you were buried underground?'

Livid, Aubrey threw the contents of her glass in Mary's face. Rising, she spoke in an oddly formal tone: 'If I'm going to pull an all-nighter in the tasting room, I'd better get started.' With red wine still trickling down Mary's cheeks, Aubrey calmly exited the room. It was only eleven o'clock but the party hastily headed up as well, leaving a stunned Mary to choose a non-soggy sofa for her bed.

Propped up in his own bed, Martin was brooding over the argument and the tempestuous Mary Oblet. Could a killer instinct in business transfer to actual killing? Absolutely. The unceasing caustic bile that spewed from her mouth definitely placed Mary as D.O.T. suspect number one. Then again, she had accused Noel Gillespie. As had Holly, the crime writer, this very morning. But if Holly's books were any guide, it was usually somebody introduced late on in the story.

Arguably, he should stay up drinking to reflect on the whole affair, yet Holly's words from this morning had struck a chord. Undoubtedly his life on the lash was starting to take a toll. Time for a new chapter: his recovery era. Give up the one thing for everything. Mrs Sinclair was a wise woman.

Sometimes Martin fancied himself as a crime writer like Holly, in the same way everyone told him they'd make a great detective. Even so, he'd always loved hangman, Boggle,

Scrabble, Wordle and cryptic crosswords; playing anagram games with everyone's names. Reaching for his pocket notebook, he tried it now with every name he'd heard on tour, even Holly's relatives Duncan Mott and Elise Mott. Snapping his pencil in surprise, the last name shook Martin to his core.

27

The Second Body

Martin woke early, lumbering downstairs to a silent world. He seemed to be the first one down. No wonder; checking his watch it was 7 a.m. The corridor had the faint smell of lemons. He checked the kitchen but it was empty, the rear windows glazed with ice.

Heading down the hall, a sleepy voice greeted him. 'Hey, morning.' Aubrey was still sitting at the tasting room table, thirty bottles uncorked, piles and piles of paper scribbled on. 'Sleep well, Martini?' She yawned widely.

'You stayed up all night swilling wine?' asked Martin, impressed.

'Just finished, finally.' In spite of tiredness, her bleary eyes still shined. 'I'm desperate for sleep, and a pee.'

'Maybe switch that order round,' said Martin. 'No one else up?'

'No one's come by,' said Aubrey, rising with a stretch.

Tiptoeing into the living room, Martin switched his phone on to Google the name "Elise Mott." One random coincidence doesn't make a killer, does it? The room was quiet, the fireplace now powdery ash. Bright frost swirls coated the giant picture window. If Mary was awake, he'd offer to make them both coffee to quickly escape from her. But he couldn't find her, she wasn't there. Martin's pulse quickened. Unlike Capitaine Gallois, he trusted his hunches.

Venturing into the cellar, Martin found her. She wasn't alive. D.O.T. had struck again. Skin tingling, Martin sunk weak-kneed onto the steps, grasping the banister to stop from sliding into darkness. How could he let this happen?

Another of Martin's calm, motionless homicide victims. "The undemanding dead," as Adam Dalgleish would say. Sadly, Martin had never found that so. The dead always cried out, screamed out, to Martin for answers, for justice. Somewhere in the background, Martin was vaguely aware of someone shouting. At the top of the stairs; Aubrey, shrieking for help but the sound was muffled. Anyway, nothing could help Mary now. His head felt both sharp and fuzzy, alert yet confused. Crawling forwards, Martin forced himself to look.

Lying on her back, arms and legs splayed apart on the tiled floor, Mary's skin was pale, her eyes wide with fright. Scarlet bruising indicated three or four blows to the head; for starters. The killer had shattered her teeth as a wine bottle had been rammed halfway down her throat, dislocating her jaw in the process. And there, on top of her twisted body lay the mistletoe leaf with DOT written on it. Last night, he'd gone to bed thinking she was the prime suspect, not the next victim. How the wonder detective had fallen.

Above her, still on the rack, was the bottle she had come for—Château Clarke, Listrac-Médoc, 2018—the one for fresh starts. On the wall opposite, one bottle was missing, the one now lodged in her windpipe. Rising thoughtfully, Martin almost hooked himself on the protruding sharp nail. Genius move, given this was the wall her blood was splattered.

As the entire party came thundering down the staircase led by Renzo, former Chief Inspector Moretti's muscle memory kicked in. Stretching his arms out wide to block the passage, he couldn't hold them back as they jostled forwards, straining their necks, gaping at the sight of her body, until Theo barged past him. Breathlessly, the group watched as Theo slid silently down the mirrored wall beside her. Sobbing into his knees, a shaky hand outstretched towards his dead wife. Out of reach.

'What has happened?' gulped Renzo.

'Murder,' said Martin. The whole staircase seemed to quake as Joseph, with panicked eyes, ran back up to the living room, Tate racing after him.

‘But Camille Duval is in prison,’ spluttered Sven. ‘What does this mean?’

‘We have a serial killer among the vines,’ said Holly, now clasping the banister herself.

Martin shook his head. ‘A serial killer is three or more kills,’ he said, trying to bring some practicality back to proceedings, ‘this is a spree killer.’

‘Camille must have broken out of jail,’ said the Swede.

‘This isn’t Arkham Asylum, Sven.’

‘But, but this is impossible,’ said Aubrey, ‘nobody went by me. Until… you, just now.’ She glanced nervously at Martin.

‘She’s been dead several hours,’ he said sharply, keen to stamp out that theory immediately.

A hoarse voice came from the hunched-up ball of pain. ‘*Je ne m'en remettrai jamais.* My wife. This… this… should never have happened, the DOT killer should never have got this far.’

Swallowing hard, Martin turned away from their helpless faces, but he couldn’t escape his own reflection in the mirrored walls, glowering back in bitter failure. Another cellar, another dead body. Martin felt crushed. Radnor was right to sack him. And worse was to come. No matter what he’d said, this had all the traits of being a serial killer. Mary’s murder was more vicious than Jimmy’s. Unfortunately, Martin had seen it before. Serial killers escalating their behaviour, shifting the type of victims selected, increasing both the violence and frequency of their killings. The next victim would probably have their eyes plucked out with a corkscrew.

No. There must not be a “next victim”. There was still hope. He was their best hope. Martin was, after all, the only one to call out the wrongful arrest of Camille Duvall. Swiftly, Martin made the well-reasoned, strategic, logical decision to start drinking again as soon as possible. Drink to think; to solve the case. This wasn’t about petty revenge over Radnor anymore or something to put in the Christmas letter. Any one of them could be next. Solve the case to save their lives.

28

The French Conundrum

Ushering them upstairs with the strict instruction no one go near the body until Capitaine Gallois arrived, Martin received the bad news the Gendarmerie would not reach Elysium until tomorrow. No surprise; last night's storm had built a six-foot high snow wall around the house, as well as over all of the Auvergne Rhône-Alpes.

'But I could take over,' said Renzo, leading them into the kitchen for a fortifying breakfast. 'I am an auxiliary volunteer officer for the local town, sworn in when the mayor panicked during last year's riots.'

'Ever called into action?' asked Pekoe.

'No, but I kept my handgun, here.' The gun cabinet was next to the spice rack (turn left at oregano). Typing in the three-digit code that every single one of them must have spied over his shoulder (0-0-7), Renzo unveiled a SIG Sauer SP 2022: a no-nonsense, polymer-frame handgun; standard issue for the French police, .45 calibre, eight round magazine. Martin might have completed his firearms training, but he hated guns. The violent recoil at the back was nothing to the damage it did upon exiting the barrel.

'Keep that cabinet locked and do not open it again until this investigation is over,' said Martin. 'But since you are deputised, you can be the official photographer. I need you to take photos of every room in this house from every conceivable angle right now; while we eat these delicious pastries.' And then, thought Martin, interrogations.

Slightly startled, Renzo saluted spiritedly. 'Sir, yes, sir.'

They ate in silence around the kitchen island, laid out

with an Italian breakfast so sugary-sweet it would dissolve the Tooth Fairy: petite horn-shaped croissants filled with marmalade, light and fluffy fried doughnuts dusted with icing sugar, sweet brioche buns split down the middle with whipped cream, chocolate chip cookies, and sticky sponge fingers soaked in rum; all washed down with latte macchiatos, double espressos and frothy cappuccinos. Martin was back to seven years old in the snug family kitchen, his mother frantically packing him and his brothers up for school, waiting for their father to return from the night shift; exhausted but holding warm paper bags from the Rozzano bakery. Everybody managed to eat something, except for Theo, who sat silently in the corner staring into his coffee.

By the time they'd finished breakfast, the ice had melted from the windows; the LED heaters cutting a pathway through to the courtyard. And so, this is where Martin chose to conduct his interviews. Though tragic, Mary's death significantly helped the investigation. The first murder was tricky: the higgledy-piggledy rooms of le Château des Allues, the erratic drinking, Gallois breathing down his neck, everybody's opportunity to sneak attack Jimmy. Whereas last night's logistics—Elysium's straight corridors, Mary's midnight wine trip, Aubrey's nocturnal vigil—would make it easier to pin down everyone's movements. Martin didn't have the solution yet, but he was certain the key to the D.O.T. mistletoe killings was murder two.

Nevertheless, after everybody had provided their statements, Martin had zero new leads. Aubrey drank through the early hours, taking notes, looking out into the corridor but had seen nobody. In fact, no one had seen any of the party sneaking down the halls. All was quiet. Despite the early bedtime, however, it had still been a night of disturbed sleep. Tate and Holly spent half the evening calming Joseph down from a nightmare; eventually giving him a sedative. Eve and Morton had gone straight to bed but were kept awake by Theo's non-stop thumping against their wall as he'd spent all night throwing paint at his new canvas; an artwork he called "Land of a Thousand Spots." This was backed up by the splatter of red paint on his hands, as well as green, yellow and blue paint splodges over his white trainers. Noel had been watching the night skies for his bird, with no joy. Sven tossed and turned, restless after the phylloxera vastatrix argument. Renzo, still very protective of his daughter, woke several times to check that Sara was sound asleep. Only Pekoe had slept peacefully through until morning. Highly disappointing. On the plus side, Martin finally got his Agatha Christie diagram, drawing up a plan of the house for the night in question:

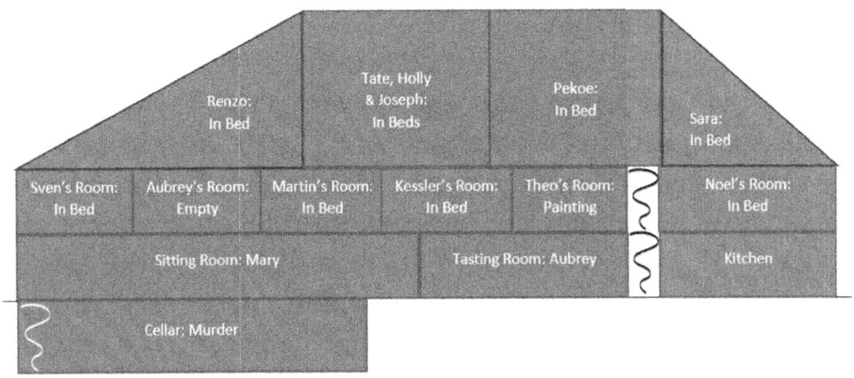

Somebody must be lying. Shockingly, nobody had locked their bedroom doors. Disheartened already, Renzo's next announcement did nothing to rally Martin.

'Good news, Martin, we are starting the tour of my vineyard. Onward and upward.'

'Is this really an appropriate time?' said Martin, shoving his hands deep into his pockets and turning away from the biting wind.

'What do you want—us all trembling? Biting our nails? We will not be cowed.'

'But these killings...' said Martin, 'aren't you worried?'

'Would it help?' said Renzo.

'What about Sara? And where is Sara? She's the last I

need to interview.'

Renzo's face darkened. 'She was about to come down, but when she heard of the murder... she will be down for dinner. You must solve this, Martin. This is your hero's journey, my friend. Promise me you will solve this.'

'Everything I can do,' said Martin.

'*Bene*.' His face brightened. 'Then I will gather the others.'

The first face out was just as bright, but forcibly so. 'Who is for another round of Rubber Pigeon?' asked Theo, carrying the ball launcher out of the house with a stapled grin. 'Do you mind if we do something to try and take my mind off things? I am not ready to process... this...'

'Renzo was about to start a tour,' said Martin. He had seen such acts of bravado before. The shock would hit Theo soon enough.

'*Oui*, R-Renzo is right,' stuttered Theo, 'we might as well distract ourselves while we wait for the police.' Martin was about to mention that firing sharp arrows into the air might not be the wisest plan with the police arriving when the group burst out of the kitchen ready for the winery outing.

Again, heaters had carved a path through the white wall of snow, wide enough to march two-by two to the stable. Leading the way with Renzo, Martin made another attempt. 'Why am I here, Renzo? Haven't you got a beach house in the Bahamas?'

'*Coraggio!* I adore the snowy weather for the same reason I adore Christmastime. It brings us all together, one happy family frozen in time.' Off Martin's hard look, Renzo relented. 'Alright, Martin. Tonight, I will tell you. Meet me after dinner on the terrace and I will reveal my real reason for you being here.'

'But, it's a strange time of year for a wine tour, isn't it?'

'This is business,' said Renzo. 'I need the right people at the right time, so we can launch my wine in the spring. Nothing must get in the way of the launch. Nothing! We will sample it together now; although, the one inside here is a younger version. We will drink the official one for market at dinner, when Aubrey can give us her official verdict,' he said, uncharacteristically nervous. Moments later, however, Renzo smiled back at the troop clustered near the entrance and, spinning through the doorway, called out: 'Welcome, my dear family, welcome to my humble factory!'

Christ, thought Martin, he really was going full Willy Wonka. Sadly no Oompa-Lompas, however as glasses of the prototype *Vautour Barbu* wine were passed round, Martin couldn't help thinking the converted stables resembled something out of a 1950s sci-fi comic. A line of giant, egg-shaped concrete fermenters, each standing ten-feet tall, dominated the rubber-floored warehouse. It looked like Godzilla had laid five eggs. Or, standing on metallic legs—with a variety of wheels and dials and taps—like a set of bulbous taupe space rockets.

'Each one of these,' said Renzo, devotedly rubbing one, 'contains five hundred gallons of the finest wine. The grapes are crushed, trodden on, in fact, over here…' Their jolly vinter bounded over to a large stone trough which, at waist height, was filled with a viscous, lumpy-looking red wine, grapes and stalks still floating within. '… my granite tank; made from a solid slab of volcanic rock. It is capable of holding one hundred and fifty litres of wine. We climb in barefoot; it is a fun process. We put on Rossini's "La Danza" and then a ring of five or six of us dance around stomping on the grapes. This vat is actually our leftovers. Ah, and here is our chief stomper!'

Motioning to the far corner, they found their coach driver, Omar; snoring violently, mouth wide open. If Martin was hesitant about wine before, the image of Omar's sweaty feet clumping down on the grapes failed to further entice him.

'When he is not driving the coach,' said Renzo, 'Omar helps out here.' He didn't seem to be helping much, unless the job title was "catching flies." Snoring; reflected Martin, the reason for duct tape. Laugh and the world laughs with you;

snore and you sleep alone. As Renzo spoke passionately about the vineyard, Martin swirled his wine. Wondering whether these particular grapes had been between Omar's grimy toes, Martin tipped his glass into the coach driver's open mouth. With a momentary gargle, Omar slept on.

'Here, it is about hard work,' continued Renzo, arm in arm with Aubrey. 'It's about family. We are a small winery, but we will compete against the world-famous brands. Our secret weapon is the Mondeuse grapes, native to Savoie, the grape variety that ripens amidst the snow!'

Ambling through the stables, Martin scanned the rest of the group: Holly and Tate swinging Joseph back and forth; a dispirited Theo looking bewildered and lost; Eve, Morton, Pekoe and Noel playing with a forklift truck. He suddenly noticed somebody was missing. Sven. Where was their usurped tour guide?

Sidling up to Martin, and locking arms so he couldn't escape, Eve's warm breath poured over him. 'Hey, Moretti, if you want a chance at redeeming yourself as a policeman then —'

'I did track down the Lafite Rothschild that you stole,' said Martin fairly.

'I meant from the night you gathered us all up but were too skunk-drunk to crack the case,' she said more loudly. 'If you wanna redeem yourself, somebody's stolen my candle. If you could solve that too, I'll make it worth your while.'

'Definitely,' said Martin, 'I'll add it to my to-do list, right after we solve the first-degree murder.'

Noting the sarcasm, Eve added defensively: 'It's my fancy candle with essential oils. I hadn't even used it yet. Last time I saw it was on my bed before dinner. Anyway, Moretti, let me know if you have any promising leads?'

'Leads, sure,' Martin chuckled. 'I'll check with both the Avengers and the Justice League. See if we can assign Batman and Robin to the case, working in shifts with Superman.'

'Trying to steal my wife, kid?' said a slow Boston drawl.

Once more, Morton Kessler had crept up on Martin without detection; the pale skin, hollow eyes and lopsided leer as consistently creepy as ever. His ski jacket looked so old, he must've lifted it from Captain Oates' body. 'She always flirts with other men to punish me. This time for the Lafite failure.'

'Humiliating,' fumed Eve. 'We've gotta get back in his good books, you igit, we need the import contract for this *Vautour Barbu* wine. Don't forget, we're here for the finest wines, and down in that cellar I counted twenty-one vintage Chiantis.'

'How do you remember all that?' asked Martin.

'I told you, my wife is on the spectrum,' said Morton, smoothing his weak combover. 'That, or finicky.'

'Or you're just grouchy?' suggested Martin. 'Kept awake by Theo's thumping against your wall, chucking paint at his new artwork; at what time?'

'Enough to give you a headache,' Morton nodded. 'Every twelve seconds Eve counted a thump. She's fussy like that,' he said, pleased to snipe back at his wife. 'If this is another of your stealth interviews, I'd say Theo was making his racket from eleven-ish until two a.m. Eve popped out for a few minutes, maybe five, to tell him to be quiet but in the end she decided to leave him alone.' So, Eve had left her room during the crucial midnight murder window. Martin made a mental note.

'I ended up just texting our tour group with a complaint.'

'After that, I had her restrained in handcuffs.'

'How's this helping us with Renzo?' hissed Eve. 'Sven told us he's got more of those bottled lightnings here.'

'Ah! Speaking of Sven,' said Morton, '*that* is how we can get back in Renzo's good books, by revealing the key clue to these murders. Tell the policeman what you observed about Sven this morning.'

Comprehension spread across her face. 'You have your genius flashes,' Eve purred, 'not many, but you have them.'

'At least I have them.'

'Cheeky.'

'You love my rascal ways.'

'I wish I did.' She bumped shoulders with her husband and he smiled coyly back. Martin could plainly see it. For all their fussing, feuding, and Eve's flirting with others, they were in love. Deeply; in a way that his marriage hadn't.

'So, what is this key clue to the murders?' said Martin, wondering how this linked to the conundrum of a man named Sven Lindblom. Now missing.

'He was wearing the same pink tie at breakfast that he wore last night,' said Eve.

'How is that relevant?'

'You're the detective,' shrugged Morton. 'But at least strike us from your list of suspects.'

'I haven't ruled anyone out,' said Martin. 'No matter how ancient.'

'You wanna watch out then, kid,' leered Morton. 'The older we get, the less life in prison is a deterrent.'

A glass shattered behind them. Theo had slumped against the forklift. Dizzy from the fragrant stench of mashed grapes? Martin knew better. His beloved wife. And after all those words of anger between them. A love-hate, love to hate, relationship.

'I'll take Theo for some fresh air.'

Traipsing back down the chilled white corridor, they re-entered the farmhouse. 'Actually, I can not do this yet,' said Theo, as if to justify the disappearance of his constricted smile. 'I will lie down. *J'ai besoin de repos.*'

Martin made sure Theo went up before checking with the staff that no one had accessed the cellar. Then, grabbing the carafe of vodka from the sideboard, he searched for the Swedish tour guide.

Sven. Svend. Svein. Please, don't be dead. He must be on the estate. Beyond the Elysium gates, the outside world was still buried in snow. But there was no sign of him, nor Renzo's daughter. Martin added it to his To-Do list: *déjà vu* hunting her down again. Was Sara Brambilla's kidnapper here among the vines? Was that why Renzo had brought them all here? In truth, Martin was seeking the answer as well. For Martin, she hung over the whole case. It was, after all, why he had merited the invite in the first place.

With a shaky laugh, Martin found Sven on the now-melted terrace overlooking the vineyard and woodland below. Tapping away on his laptop, he was sitting on a wooden bench underneath the heater with a flight of wines (four white, one red); his steel-rim glasses reflecting in the pale sun, like two silver obols.

Making room on the bench for Martin, Sven picked up the first glass in the flight and drained it in one. From his crumpled suit and pristine pink tie, nothing quite connected. Perhaps that was his charm; like the eclectic décor of a blind grandmother.

'Tell me, how did a Swede end up amongst the French vineyards? I thought Sweden is part of the vodka belt, isn't it?' said Martin, shaking his carafe.

'Fun fact, wine is now starting to be grown successfully in several parts of Sweden. There's strong growth in a number of vineyards in the southernmost region of Skåne.'

'Sven, your facts are never fun,' said Martin amiably. A falcon was now circling above them.

'They are to the tour party,' said Sven.

'That's because they're cork dorks,' said Martin. 'Why does Noel Gillespie seem so cagey around Renzo?'

'What is with all the snooping?' said Sven.

'It's a fine time to snoop, Mr Lindblom,' said Martin. 'You disapprove of my detective work?'

'Not at all, Mr Moretti, I am a big fan. When Renzo returned with his daughter, I looked you up. Your record is impressive. Well, it was. What I loved was the case names—the Case of the Missing Astronaut, Death of a Lollipop Lady, the Maserati Confusion—wow!'

'The tabloids love a catchy headline,' said Martin. 'They're going to have a field day with these two killings, especially with Jimmy being a celebrity.' The falcon divebombed out of the sky and vanished amongst the vines. A small squeak later and it emerged with half a mouse. What you might call a wine flight of the more deadly kind. 'In a twisted way, wouldn't this be the best PR ever for your Mondeuse wine launch? I mean, they're still doing Jack the Ripper tours around Whitechapel a hundred and thirty years later.'

'Mary Oblet is lying dead, spreadeagled on the cold cellar floor, Mr Moretti!' Sven protested, closing his laptop. But before shutting his screen, Martin caught the draft headlines: "Gold, Frankincense and Murder!" and "Grievous Bottley Harm". To be fair, the latter had popped into Martin's head the other day.

Martin pressed. 'You did say you wanted to drum up publicity.'

'Did I?' said Sven with a puzzled frown.

'When you first mentioned the launch of Renzo's wine, you said you were desperately seeking other ways to capture the imagination of the public, to hook them in.'

'Since you bring it up,' said Sven curiously, 'how about the "The Mondeuse Murders"?'

'Wouldn't work,' said Martin. 'Nobody's heard of Mondeuse wine in Britain. Merlot, maybe, or Malbec.'

Eagerly, Sven played them over. 'The Malbec Murders... The Merlot Murders...' Realising a little late he'd failed to hide his enthusiasm, Sven dipped his double chin to his chest and said: '*Okej*, it's true. As head of PR, I am thinking we should get out in front of this thing, control the story.'

'What other headlines have you got?'

'Plenty of them: It's the Most Wonderful Crime of the Year, Deadcember, Violent Night, You Better Watch Out.'

'The French Conundrum, that's what you should name this case.'

'The investigation still perplexes you?' said Sven anxiously. Martin nodded gravely. 'I believe in you, Mr Moretti,' said the Swede, more to convince himself.

'You're still wearing the tie from yesterday. Unusual for

you,' said Martin, offhand.

'*Vad? Åh ja,* I think we have all had bigger things on our mind.'

'Yeah, I was wondering if the breakfast cookies were homemade as well.'

'So long as they're chocolate not mockolate,' Sven laughed. Though why did the laugh carry so much relief?

'When we first met,' said Martin, now with some urgency, 'when I showed you those livers in the punchbowl with D.OT. on them, I saw the recognition on your face.'

'I'd seen the poison pen letters, of course,' said Sven. 'There have been several sent over the past twelve months, but I don't know who writes them.'

'Where are the other letters?'

'I shredded them.'

'Where were they from? What postmark?'

'All over; France, America, England.'

'Was anybody else on tour aware of them?'

'No.'

'How would you feel if I told you the T of D.O.T. stood for temperance?' Sven didn't reply so Martin continued. 'Aren't you Swedes quite militant on alcohol controls?'

'So are the Americans,' said Sven.

'Straight edge ...Systembolaget...' listed Martin. Off Sven's astonished look, he added: 'Snoop snoop.'

'You asked me how did a Swede end up here? It is because of wine,' said Sven. 'France is the home of wine. I love Sweden, but not so much the strict drinking laws. The British, Irish and Russians all drink for necessity. America, alcohol is a dirty pastime. But the French, they drink for love. In France, wine is religion.' He made a good case. If D.O.T. was an anti-wine serial killer, then, by definition, it ruled out their sacred protector of wine.

'You never answered me just now,' said Martin, 'why does Noel Gillespie seem so cagey around Renzo?'

'You must ask Renzo that. It might be the missing piece

of this French conundrum,' said Sven, rising from the bench. His took his time polishing his glasses, and then, with a desperate plea in his voice: 'You really haven't solved it?'

'Just about to,' said Martin with a resolute sip of the carafe. And he meant it. The moment to squarely outline the facts of the case—the facts of death—had come; before things could possibly get any worse.

29

The Third Body

Alone on the terrace in the frosty twilight, Martin took a big swig from the carafe. Drink, detective, drink; fill this jigsaw with the missing pieces. The clean-cut vodka tasted of house parties, festivals and bygone freedom. It burned his lips, burned the edges of his mind down to the core facts. Perfect. Less perfect was what the facts suggested: the beginnings of a serial killer. An anti-wine serial killer, which probably placed him as prime suspect.

A message buzzed on his phone. Mamma; chasing up the Christmas letter. He really needed more of an update than he'd shortly be sleeping in a Post Office doorway. With a thumbs-up emoji, Martin promised to send the Round-robin by midnight Christmas Eve. Three days and counting. Yes, to the whole Moretti family. Yes, the entire D-list. Their small Italian family; just the forty cousins.

Martin took another swig. Within the valley below, there was an eerie red glow emanating from the Elysium wood, like a UFO landing zone. Something else to ask Renzo about. But first, time to resolve the murders by mistletoe.

Three unusual points would help Martin uncover the killer: Aubrey Dalton, daughters and D.O.T.

Martin scanned his sketch of the house for the night in question. No matter which way he looked at it, Mary's murderer had to pass by Aubrey's tasting room twice, and yet she'd seen nobody. Of course, there was an alternative explanation. All these mullings of who snuck past Aubrey's archway ignored the fact it could simply have been Aubrey. She didn't have to get past herself because she was herself; quickly slink out of her tasting room into the living room, bop Mary over the head, then return to her chilled bottle of Chablis.

But why? She seemed the least likely to have a grudge against wine. She did however have noticeable beef with both victims. And hell hath no fury like a woman scorned. Both Jimmy's sexist jokes and Mary's *dévastateur* bug had insulted Aubrey, but surely these were purely jibes. Just how sensitive was Aubrey? She'd certainly looked mortally offended.

Was anything enough to warrant what happened to Mary? Martin gave a small shudder picturing those final moments. They'd left her at eleven, Martin had found her at seven, presenting an eight-hour window. The time of murder, however, was obvious. Everybody knew where Mary would be at midnight, she'd announced it to the whole group: fetching the Château Clarke, Listrac-Médoc, 2018, from the cellar. The killer had crept down behind her, grabbed a bottle off the rack, struck her several times and—when Mary dropped to her knees—forced the bottle down her throat. Nasty. Martin would have to wait for Eugene to confirm whether she'd suffocated to death—the bottle blocking her airway—or whether the blunt trauma of multiple blows to the head had caused massive haemorrhaging. And then they'd left their calling card, the mistletoe leaf, for added dread.

At least Martin now knew what D.O.T stood for. But he still wasn't ready to reveal to Gallois or the group what he knew about the Daughters of Temperance tattoo. Experience dictated not to show your cards too early on a serial killer case. Plus, he didn't want to go off half-cocked like the last summation gathering. Nevertheless, Daughters of Temperance was easy enough to find online, a late nineteenth-century women's organisation supporting abstention from alcohol; one of many American groups pushing for prohibition. As the movement waged on, their activists became more and more extreme, personified in Carrie Nation—a.k.a. "Hatchet Granny"—who, for ten years, used rocks, hammers and axes to smash up drinking saloons.

Illuminating. It certainly fit the bill of anti-wine. As did the detour to the hospital enroute to the tattoo studio, specifically the Hepatology department. So, who did the tattoo belong to? And was it exclusively the one tattoo? Thinking back to the poison pen letter—*we have already got rid of several of you*—how big was this particular temperance cell? Sven had said there'd been several letters from multiple countries. One thing was certain, Martin was unlikely to see it on the suspect's skin anytime soon; everyone's flesh being buried under three thick layers of wool and polyester. Perhaps he should crank the heat up on the thermostat, forcing everybody to strip off? If only he could trust Gallois, they could obtain a warrant for the Blacked tattoo parlour, demanding the identity of the Daughters of Temperance image.

Daughters… there were two daughters of note on this tour. Firstly, Holly Sinclair. The name of Holly's mother—Elise Mott—was an anagram of "mistletoe". Surely coincidence, right? In a criminal investigation, there's always the possibility of coincidences. But then there was Duncan Mott; her brother. Holly had said he'd died from alcoholic complications; which, in Martin's opinion, skirted around the facts. An online news article from 2021 reported he'd been out walking his dog in Santa Barbara when he'd tragically been hit by a drunk driver leaving a vineyard. As motives go, that was a pretty good reason to hold a grudge against wine.

Secondly, there was Renzo's daughter, the lesser-spotted Sara Brambilla. Heading in for dinner, to Martin's intense frustration, she remained elusive. Was she even alive?

Greeted in the living room by a cheery Renzo, Martin got straight to the point. 'Renzo, where's Sara and when can I speak to her?'

'Relax yourself, Martin,' said Renzo, slapping him on the back, his hand resting upon Martin's shoulder. 'I promise you will meet her later, I promise. Right now, I need to pep up the group.'

'I'm not sure they're capable of being pepped up,' said

Martin, eyeing the room. The entire party were silently hunched around the sofas; a low-slung table of food in front of them. They'd eaten well on this tour, but this was another level. Surrounding a giant bowl of salted chips and hors d'oeuvres were the richest dishes Martin had ever seen: sweet roasted scallops with Colonnata bacon foam and black sarrasin blinis; sauteed guinea fowl with cinnamon jus and pomegranate, roasted figs and rosemary; and—the *pièce de resistance*—a plump breast of Ardennes chicken with salty crisp chicken skin, Albufera sauce, and bolete mushrooms. No one touched any of it. Small wonder, they were one staircase away from a day-old corpse. Theo Oblet was sitting with his back to the room, gazing out of the window into the night.

'Where there's a wine, there's a way,' said Renzo, unperturbed; and as a sign of normality, Renzo removed the pastry chef guarding the cellar entrance. Arm around Martin, he guided him over to the sofas. There were other points to probe—the Noel Gillespie caginess, the relevance of the candle—but otherwise Martin had all he needed to know. Perched beside Pekoe, he crammed one of the hors d'oeuvres, a cheese puff pastry, into his mouth; more to soak up the vodka.

Brightly, Renzo bounced on his toes and, with a clap of his hands, announced: '*Figli e figlie*, before the official opening of my wine,' Renzo's nervous glance at Aubrey nearly as awkward as the one at Noel, 'Sven promised you bottled lightning, and I deliver!' Sven, again, undertook the role of waiter, wheeling over a drinks trolley containing three musty bottles. 'God made only water, but man made wine. You have seen the Chateau Lafite Rothschild, 1787; some a little too closely,' and now it was the Kessler's turn to look awkward, but Renzo's tone was playful; he was enjoying himself. 'Behold, the most expensive bottle of sherry in the world.'

The party leapt up, none faster than Aubrey, and scoured the black and white label. 'A bottle of the Massandra Sherry de la Frontera, 1775,' she gasped.

'*Corretto!*' said Renzo, overjoyed at the sight of them

gazing at it, transfixed. 'Smuggled out of the Crimea before the winery was nationalised in 1922. In 2015, Vladamir Putin and Silvio Berlusconi allegedly drank a bottle worth $90,000.' Martin wasn't keen on the company it kept, but the others were impressed. 'Let us also drink a cheeky tipple of it on Christmas Eve.'

'Each drop's worth hundreds of dollars,' said Morton, mesmerised.

'I'll never wash my liver again,' said Eve.

'*Ecco*, Apostelwein 1727, what do you know of this wine, Aubrey?' asked Renzo, cradling the second; a long thin bottle with a faded orange label and ingrained layer of dust.

'It comes from the 12 Apostles' cellar in Bremen, Germany,' replied Aubrey, gobsmacked, and a reverential silence descended over the party.

'*Corretto!* From twelve barrels of wines in vintages of 1683, 1717 and 1727, reduced in number due to evaporation until—when one barrel remained—the wine was bottled in the 1960s. Discovered in a bricked-up cellar in Hamburg, stolen in Salzburg, and bought in Budapest at a private auction last year for a... notable amount of money. Thanks to its high sugar content, the wine is still drinkable, so let us drink it on Christmas Eve.'

'Three sips of this and you're officially an aristocrat,' murmured Tate.

'What's in this one?' asked Eve, holding up the third; a more modern, flat shoulder-shaped bottle that could fit through a letterbox. There was no label but, to Martin, the liquid inside—apparently a white wine—bore striking resemblance to a urine sample.

'I have managed to scoop a bottle's worth from the Strasbourg Wine Barrel of 1472.'

'Shut the front door!' Aubrey cried.

'It is true,' said Renzo. 'Underneath the Strasbourg city hospital is the oldest barrel-stored wine in the world, and this particular wine has been tasted only three times in history:

to celebrate the 1576 alliance between Strasbourg and Zurich; when the hospital burned down in 1716; and in 1944 when Strasbourg was liberated in World War II. The fourth time will be here at the Old Elysium vineyard. Well, more specifically, at my mountaintop chalet. We will take all three up—under the guidance of our master mountaineer, Pekoe—to join the final and most infamous bottle of lightning awaiting us there.'

'But how did you obtain this Strasbourg one?' asked Tate. Aubrey was now speechless, gripping Sven for support.

'The wine had to be transferred to a new barrel in 2014 after the original barrel started leaking. At that time, I had an artful envoy sneak in and scoop a bottle of it for me. It was too good an opportunity, so let's ease out the cork and taste history.'

'Well, I decant miss that,' joked Sven. Renzo roared with laughter. Martin, however, did not share his host's good humour. To dangle these wines in front of them seemed nothing more than a cynical hook to keep them all here. The snow was starting to melt and soon the roads would be clear to drive far away from this murder spot. But no one was leaving now. Sadly, the fact Renzo kept them here for his launch didn't surprise Martin; he'd found most captains of industry to be psychopaths. Admittedly, it helped Martin's investigation that they didn't all run off. But then, it facilitated D.O.T. also.

'*Figli e figlie*, it is time for the main event, a brand-new bottled lightning, hopefully,' said Renzo, 'the unveiling of my *Vautour Barbu*.' Still sniggering from his decant joke, Sven handed round generously poured glasses of a wine deep purple in colour. 'All the other vineyards... everybody around me is growing Gringet, dry white or sparkling wine. We will produce the region's first exceptional red wine. And though we drink this wine in difficult circumstances, Theo, it will taste all the more sweet. Extreme times heighten our senses.' A frazzled-looking Theo finally turned to face them. He clearly hadn't slept, nor showered or changed; his hands were still splattered in red paint, with the accompanying green, yellow and blue splodges over his shoes. 'Holly, remind me of that quote I love from the Iliad.'

'Any moment might be our last,' recited Holly uncomfortably, Joseph's head cradled into her bosom. 'Everything is more beautiful because we are doomed. You will never be lovelier than you are now. We will never be here again.'

Carafe now empty, Martin felt woozy and weak, but his mind was sharp. He must stay alert to these conversations. Somebody would give themselves away.

'*Salute!*' said Renzo. The party toasted avidly back between long greedy swallows. Pivoting nervously to the blue-haired Californian, he asked: 'Well, Aubrey, what do you think?'

'Good sugar levels... limited acidity... a strong personality....' She took another sip. 'The balance is interesting: freshness, black fruits, spices, tender tannins. Dances more on my palate than a Pinot.' Placing down her glass, Aubrey had reached her decision. 'As Luigi Veronelli put it: drinking this wine is like listening to the earth singing to the sky. In conclusion, I love it!' The weight lifted from Renzo's shoulders and, as Sven topped up their glasses, everybody finally relaxed. Everybody, except Theo, who was beyond tears, looking borderline catatonic.

'What do you think, Martini?' All eyes flickered to him to answer Aubrey's question. Where was Omar's snoring mouth when you needed it? Holding the last of the vodka at the back of his throat, Martin took a sip of the wine, creating a makeshift Red, White & Night cocktail in his mouth.

'Spherical yet cubic,' said Martin. 'A masculine wine, but with an almost feminine aftertaste; indeed, one might call this the ladyboy of wines.'

Everyone laughed, even Aubrey. 'Ok, ok, no more pretentiousness,' she smiled, though Martin noted it was through gritted teeth. Theo gave Martin an appreciative nod.

'*Bene,*' said Renzo, 'we have the wine, so now the label

design.' Sven, levelling up from waiter to butler, dashed to grab a large canvas from the corner. 'Theo, would you like to introduce it? Only painted last night, yes?'

'*Oui*, this is my "Land of a Thousand Spots" painting,' said Theo slowly, one hand gesturing to the artwork Sven held up. Perhaps it was still the aftertaste, but Martin was slightly sickened Renzo was making Theo parade his painting around.

There were impressed "ooohs" among the admiring chatter, but Theo swatted them away dismissively. Through a vacant set of eyes, he stared out at Martin. 'I want someone who will tell it like it is. Do you like art, Moretti?'

'I know what I hate,' said Martin, 'but, actually, I quite like it.'

'Tell me what you see,' said the artist, every word an effort, yet there was a sense of longing in his voice. Hesitant, Martin called out what he saw: the canvas' background was entirely bright yellow and peppered with at least twenty-five big blue and green dots.

'Twenty-six, to be precise,' said Theo, correcting Martin's description. 'It symbolises the wine's perspective, looking up from the bottom of the glass, observing us, the drinker.' Personally, Martin preferred a melted clock, but it was decent enough.

'*Complimenti, molto ben fatto*,' said their host, '*bravo*, Theo!' But the approval only saddened Theo.

'If only I'd spent my time with Mary instead of dilly dallying around with art,' said Theo, turning back to his window. 'Ironically, my painting gives me the perfect alibi.'

'I'd be careful saying you've got a perfect alibi,' said Aubrey. 'In detective stories, the murderer is always the one who says they've got a perfect alibi.'

'For the love of God, Aubrey!' said Holly.

Still eyeing the bottles, Eve simpered: 'Well, nobody kill me until I've drank all those wines.'

'Can you stop saying we're in a detective story.' Holly was twisting her gold bracelet.

‘Oh please, Holly, look around you,’ said Aubrey, amused, ‘we’re in a detective story, don’t try and pretend otherwise. You, of all people, should know that. The mansion out in the country. Us—as the willing victims—just sitting around, waiting to get rich off Renzo, and being murdered one by one. Then, there’s the washed-up, alcoholic detective, the brilliant but quirky Sherlock sleuth, accompanied by the bumbling cops arresting the wrong suspect.’

‘Well, if this is a detective story,’ slurred Martin, happy to switch the subject from wine, ‘we’d better follow the rules. That is, for anybody who wants to survive the night.’ Most of the group shifted uneasily but Martin was happy to needle them. He was still upset how they’d reacted to both incidents. Mary with a broken head. Jimmy with his cracked skull. Yet the party went on. One of the people in this room was the killer, for Christ’s sake.

‘This is preposterous,’ muttered Tate.

‘The first rule of a murder mystery is to never, ever, say,’ and Martin adopted a theatrical voice, ‘*I have something very important to tell you… but it can wait until the morning.* Because you will be killed in the night,’ he added; though his smile faltered for a moment, remembering Jimmy had said something similar.

Noel, Pekoe and the Kessler’s cackled with laughter but Holly’s face flushed. ‘I think this is highly insensitive.’

‘Rule two: watch out for Little-Miss Meek and Mild,’ continued Martin, pointing an accusatory finger at Holly. ‘It’s always the quiet ones.’

‘Settle down, Moretti,’ said Tate.

But Martin was on a roll. ‘Rule three: never trust the couple who appear to have fallen out,’ he said, eyeing Eve and Morton, ‘their very public bust-up is usually fake, all an act while they secretly conspire to commit murder.’ Plus, thought Martin, the fact Eve was out of her room around the time frame. ‘And then, what about you, Theo?’

The French artist spilt his wine whirling round.

'Rule four: it's always the one you least suspect—mourning his wife, no opportunity to commit the murder, painting all night—so it must be you, surely?'

'What about you?' said Theo, now drying his trousers. 'Rule five: undertake a half-arsed investigation to cover your own tracks. Have you even interrogated Omar or Sara yet? And, if it's detective stories, I always thought it was the butler that did it.' Everybody turned to Sven, currently loosening his pink tie. Why hadn't he changed out of that tie? If he'd worn it while murdering Mary, was he now hiding in plain sight, hoping for sufficient wear and tear to cross-contaminate the evidence? Martin had ruled out Sven as the anti-wine serial killer because he was the "sacred guardian" of Renzo's collection. But there was a flip side to that coin. Exactly how protective was he of the wine—enraged at Jimmy eyeing the Lafite? Maddened by Mary's audacity taking what she wanted? The Swede continued to be a conundrum to Martin.

'So, why don't we break there,' said Renzo, and then addressing Martin, 'you can interview Omar and I'll fetch Sara.'

'Where is he?'

'Probably where we left him.'

Staggering into the cold night, Martin was kicking himself he hadn't targeted Omar sooner. During the Château des Allues interrogations, on hearing Omar always slept on the coach, Martin had ruled him out on the assumption the hosts locked the front door. But before boarding the helicopter, Gallois—while gloating over Camille's arrest—had said the front door was unlocked. And just now, as everybody dispersed for bed, Renzo confirmed his kitchen backdoor was never locked either.

The winery warehouse was empty. So where was Omar? The coach, Martin suspected. Probably built up enough energy for his main evening's sleep following his afternoon nap. A snors d'oeuvre, if you will.

In the shadowy moonlight, the warehouse looked more 1950s horror than sci-fi now. A spooky, eerie scene; as if the five giant eggs were about to hatch a monster. Would he have needled the group if sober? Was Aubrey offended by his mock tasting notes? Who cared. Vodka told him it'd be fine.

Something stirred. Maybe Omar *was* here, curled up in a corner? Still searching, Martin stumbled over to the large granite trough, the blood red sludge as unwelcoming as ever. And then he saw it. On the far edge of the trough lay a mistletoe leaf. Dropped from the killer's collection? He flipped the leaf over to see "DOT" already penned. Odd, thought Martin, that there were no periods between each letter. On reflection, neither had the ones left atop Jimmy and Mary. DOT rather than D.O.T. And yet, the perpetrator had taken their time to add periods when carving each letter on the livers and coach. Granted, a mistletoe leaf doesn't allow much space. But still...

Lost in thought, Martin heard a swift, single movement behind him, and was suddenly smacked between the shoulders. *Help!* Toppling into the vat, Martin's head plunged under, dark wine surrounding him, filling his vision. *Murder!* He'd taken a deep breath but the shock almost jolted his mouth open. Martin clamped it shut, holding in as much air as he could. He tried twisting round, to pull his head out, but the hand firmly held him underneath. Helplessly, his arms pinned behind his back, Martin thrashed and thrashed with his legs; kicking his way to oblivion. Not like this, he can't die like this. Not to wine. Now the grapes mocked him, floating serenely by in the shadows. He must fight back. Stamping down on the foot behind him, several precious bubbles escaped his mouth. His lungs were feeling the strain. His breath was running out. Dizzy, Martin stamped down again and his head surfaced; only inches above the gloop, but time enough for the panicked sucking of air.

Was D.O.T. running out of strength? Or was the killer playing with him, like a cat with their wounded prey?

'Stop!' Martin spat. The deathly force pressed further down, his nose touching the wine. 'Stop, please!' Martin yelled. Neither the killer nor their powerful hands listened. The crimson muck glistened beneath Martin, waiting for him. 'Don't kill me, please, don't.'

With a desperate gasp he was plunged back into the depths, among the wine and the grapes and the stalks destined to be his watery tomb. He wrestled his right arm free, then his left. But where could they go? Hands flailing, he fumbled for the bottom of the red abyss. What exactly was he searching for—a plug? Bloody idiot. He was out of time, his lungs on fire, he longed to breathe. No. Must keep lips closed. Still the vice-like hand pushed down. He was going to drown. Expire. It wasn't fair. It could at least have been a vat of whisky or rum. With no air left, the Mondeuse grapes in front of him were fading away. Surely Renzo would come. Surely somebody would save him. Wasn't this supposed to be his hero's journey? A senseless heroic sacrifice, obviously. Martin was the third victim, the third body. But if this was to be a hero's death, why couldn't he die in a samurai sword fight against his ex-wife's lovers? Or robot-ninjas. Or strangled by a mutated zombie, like that movie in the tattoo parlour. Eyes bulging, Martin gave a convulsive judder, a final bubble, and suddenly his body slumped; lifeless and still.

30

The Wolf In The Fairytale

In death, it was Sara Brambilla that flashed before Martin. Swiped from the mountaintop, found in the woodshed, missing an eye, Inspector Moretti was the one who had lifted her to safety six months ago. Rescued her into a life of night terrors, paranoid rage and bone-trembling shame. The heatwave only added to the strain on the hospital ward; so hot and humid, the wax in the lava lamp melted even switched off.

Martin and Renzo lived by her bedside, Inspector Moretti only ever leaving for another futile lead on her abductor. It vexed Martin they never found him. Their best break was an elderly taxi driver named Finbar Elmwood—a chance witness —but he'd died of heatstroke in his cab before the police could interview him. Yet, where Martin floundered, Sara flourished. In rehabilitation, she grew stronger, bolder, more resilient.

And so, Sara survived; and, instead, it was Martin who was dead. But if this was death, why could he feel the sticky rubber floor underneath, and smell the pungent stench of fermented grapes? Was this heaven, or must this surely be hell? Something, or someone, hovered over him; an innocent golden face, a halo of champagne blonde hair, she looked like an angel. An angel from heaven, or angel of death? No; if he was with the angels, his iPhone wouldn't be poking into his backside.

Martin gulped in cold, clear oxygen—sweet, sweet air!— before throwing up a bellyful of wine. Finally, he croaked: 'So I'm not dead then?'

'Apparently not. *Buon Natale!*' The sixteen-year-old Sara Brambilla grinned down at him. She was wearing the same black, heart-shaped patch over her left eye as on the day he'd departed; reassigned to an urgent spate of burglaries in Ilkeston. No proper goodbye, no closure for either of them.

Nostrils stinging, eyes watering, lungs burning, it hurt to prop himself up on the warehouse floor. Sara must have dredged Martin out of the trough. The top half of him soaked in red sludge, he wanted to cry, but not in front of her.

'Are you ok?' he panted.

'Am *I* ok?' said Sara incredulously. 'Look at you now. Are you sure Clifford the Big Red Dog hasn't sneezed over you?' She tossed a wet rag into his face. 'I found you floating on your back, I thought you were dead,' she swallowed, watching as he cleaned up. 'Then I saw your chest moving so pulled you out.'

'I meant, are you ok since the... summer.'

'Bless you, Martin, still trying to save me when I just saved you.' He wiped his swollen red eyes. 'What d'you want from me? I still go to therapy, if that's what you mean. Without Papà, though. He is too busy for that,' she said sadly.

'No disturbed sleep?'

'Only when Papà wakes me opening my door every two hours.'

'I still feel so guilty about what happened, what the kidnapper did to you.'

'Martin, I lost this,' said Sara, tapping her patch, 'the day before you were assigned to the case. Relax yourself. If it wasn't for you, I would still be in that pit, part of that pile of decayed bones.' This element, at least, was true. Sara's statement revealed her captor had dropped bread and water down the hatch every morning. But on the fourth day, nobody arrived. Or the fifth. Starvation loomed. On the outside world, Renzo had paid the ransom. One million pounds. However, his daughter was not returned, nor was there any further word from the kidnapper. His mask of calm dropped. Renzo became crazed, rabid, for Martin to find her, and wept for days once he had.

'Nothing else has come to you about him?' asked Martin.

At the top of Broad Crag, Sara never saw her assailant coming, no memory beyond the sharp stab of the needle into her neck (toxicology confirmed scopolamine in her blood stream).

'I told you, I didn't see his face. And like I said, he wore a balaclava. All I remember is his wrinkled hands, the liver spots. He was so frail,' Sara giggled, 'I swear I heard his hip pop out when he dragged me into the shed. After he didn't turn up that next day… I wondered if he'd died of old age. Or, choked on a Werther's Original.' Was that pity Martin detected in her voice? She seemed unaware she was rubbing her arm up and down. 'He was so kind, bandaging up my eye, it must have been a mistake. At least the drugs numbed my pain.' Stockholm syndrome aside, there was something to what Sara said. Her damaged eye did appear to be by accident, facial bruising indicating she'd fallen onto the sharp edge of something. The bones in the pit turned out to be small animal bones. The hatch itself, originally a bomb shelter. 'On the plus side, just before I was kidnapped, I saw a golden eagle in the sky. The only place in England apparently, so that was pretty special.' *Optimism feels better*, his shrink would say.

As she helped Martin to his feet, he caught a sudden waft of her zesty lemon perfume. Overpowering the stink of the winery, it helped to reinvigorate him. *Optimism beats pessimism.* With a wheezing cough, Martin spied the mistletoe leaf at the end of the trough and pocketed it. Direct evidence. Proof. He played with the leaf between his fingers. So, it hadn't simply dropped out of the killer's collection; it was meant for Martin. Him specifically? Everybody had heard he was heading for the warehouse to look for Omar. Given his inebriated state, he was certainly the easiest to pick off. *Pessimism prepares you. Pessimism keeps you alive.*

Senses returning, Martin realised he'd mislaid his Omega watch. No doubt now resting at the bottom of Davy Jones's liquor. Regardless, with a final glance at the unforgiving scarlet surface, Martin wasn't going anywhere near it. Those fancy bottles of wine could just enjoy the aromas of metallic watch strap.

Arms linked, the pair scuttled outside underneath a glowing moon and peppering of stars. 'And now we face death again with Jimmy Stresskeller and Mary Oblet,' said Martin, walking Sara into the moonlight to read her face. Thank goodness somebody else here was saddened by events. She truly was an angel. So sweet. So innocent. He'd interrogate her properly tomorrow.

'*Orrendo!* Do you know who did it?'

The ground, a slippery grey slush, was at least lit by several bedroom windows. And there, from a square of yellow light on the first floor, stood the hunched, watchful figure of Morton Kessler.

'Almost.' Martin let out a shudder which had nothing to do with the night air. The vampire of the vineyard always said people underestimate him. But would he have the strength to submerge Martin underwater? Truthfully, the surprise attack —tipping his vodka-induced spindly body off-balance—could have been done by any man, woman or freakishly strong kid.

Martin couldn't think straight, his mind was twisted in suspicion. Three other windows were illuminated, three little boxes of unusual suspects, lit up like an advent calendar of killers: Pekoe with his pipe, folding clothes; Noel back with his birdwatching binoculars; and Aubrey Dalton, with a glass of red in hand, obviously. How much offence had she taken against his pretentious impression of her wine tasting earlier? And what about Pekoe? Not many folk have the confidence to kill with their bare hands. A Gurkha might, however. Hadn't he confessed to hating wine also? He hated it as much as Martin but was better at hiding it. What else was he good at hiding?

Another set of curtains opened, light spilling onto the iced ground, helping guide them to the terrace. Up on the top floor, Joseph was staring blankly across the valley until his mother, armed with pyjamas, pulled him away. Where was Tate Sinclair right now? Martin had been so quick to accuse Holly the other night, he shouldn't be so hasty dismissing her husband. The lawyer; the criminal lawyer. On the night of Jimmy's death, Holly said she'd taken her headache pill and zonked out until morning. Time enough for Tate to slip out...

Trust no one, as Holly kept warning him. Unfortunately, right now, that included Renzo; their gregarious business-psycho host. At dinner tonight, Renzo kept placing his arm around Martin, like a pet python sizing its owner up before eating them.

And what about the girl standing next to him; was it her skin emblazoned with 'Daughters of Temperance' from the punk tattooist? It had been the memory of watching that movie in the tattoo studio that saved him tonight. Specifically, the hero's sidekick being strangled by the mutated zombie. Like the punk had said: *why doesn't he pretend he's dead so the zombie stops strangling him.* And so, why not fake being drowned? Somehow, he'd held on long enough to convince the killer to leave. Or perhaps Sara scared them off? Or perhaps it was Sara? Martin shook his head. Granted, he'd found the strength to flip onto his back, but Sara could have easily finished him off if she so desired. She'd saved his life, unless she was just waiting for the right time.

'Martin! What has happened?' Renzo, sitting at the same bench Martin and Sven had hours earlier, sprang up in alarm. 'Are you ok?'

Eventually easing her father's nerves, Sara blew them both a kiss goodnight. '*Buona notte*, Martin. *Sogni d'oro*, Papà.'

Dazed, Martin slumped heavily onto the bench next to his friend. What a night. As soon as he thought he had all he needed; this tipped (literally) the case upside down.

'Next time you should hyperventilate before you go under,' said Renzo, 'better than a single deep breath. It reduces the carbon dioxide in the blood, gives you more survival time to remain conscious.'

'Hey,' said Martin, 'don't tell me how to breathe my own breath.' He rubbed his eyes in frustration. 'My throat's sore, my pride's hurt, and my eyes are itchy.'

'Red wine is good for the sight.'

'Tell these peepers that,' said Martin.

'Relax yourself, I have the cure,' said Renzo, and he plucked two bottles of beer from a snow mound, passing one to Martin. '*Vieni*, let's sit here and drink the chill out of this fine and frosty night.' Was it weird to drink beer after his deadly alcoholic dip? No. Just like the survivor of a burning building escaping with a lungful of smoke and immediately sparking up a cigarette, it's precisely what's needed.

'I appear to have lost my watch in the grapes also,' said Martin, still catching his breath.

Renzo shrugged. 'If it's had Omar's feet on them, they can survive you.'

'Still, seems like a waste.'

'Then, I'll sell this batch to the Germans.' Renzo drained his bottle with a satisfied sigh and plucked another from the snow. 'I am so pleased I could show you the heart of my operation. My whole estate...le Château de Montrottier, even when I rent le Château des Allues, I consider all my properties part of the Old Elysium vineyard. Even the mountain above us is mine. It is all for the Elysium vineyard. The nerve centre. I adore this place.'

'That's good, Renzo.'

'The soil, the terrain, the climate, the... *terroir!*'

'Nice.'

'The whole lot. The soil, the terrain, the climate, the... *terroir!*'

'The terror of you repeating that phrase,' said Martin.

'Do you know what I love about my winery, about any winery? There is always life. Even now, in the heart of winter, our vineyard is very much alive. There is still much to do. We prune, we trim, we repair the trellising, repair the roads. And underground, the vines are growing.'

'Are you sure it's not all... dead?'

'Our Holly could pick a better quote, but as Tolkien said: deep roots are not reached by the frost,' Renzo recited. 'Nature takes care of it, Martin. I use the heaters for other purposes.'

'You mean for your cannabis farm?'

Renzo dropped his bottle, the colour draining from his face. 'How did you know?'

'The excess of multi-coloured LED grow lights, the red glow from the forest. Don't worry, I'm not on the force anymore,' said Martin, a savage glee thinking of Superintendent Radnor.

Renzo blew a sigh of relief as he retrieved his beer. 'It's the new gold rush. There is legalised recreational use in Canada, Georgia, Luxembourg, Malta, half the United States. I will be ready to fulfil France's demand when needed.'

Shoulders hunched against the cold, Martin shivered. 'Wouldn't it be easier to do it in a warehouse?'

'But the soil, the terrain, the—'

'Ok, yes, yes, I get it,' Martin laughed. Renzo might be ruthless at business but that didn't make him a murderer. 'Is that the reason Pekoe is here, as your weed sommelier?'

'I need his hiking experience for when we head up to the chalet. But, yes, that helps.'

'And is that why you invited me here,' said Martin, crossing his arms, 'you need my police and border contacts?' Turning a blind eye to spite Radnor was one thing, anything more made him uncomfortable.

'Oh, *per tutti i cieli,* no! You are here to fall in love again,' said Renzo. 'It is time to jump back on the horse.'

'No,' said Martin, suddenly wishing they were back to discussing marijuana.

'To get back in the saddle.'

'Very much no.'

'Like the roots of my vines, I refuse to let your heart wither away. You need a good woman in your life.'

'What about you?' said Martin.

'It is different,' said Renzo earnestly, 'I still love my wife, and I would tell her that every single day if I could, my Maria, *buonanima.*'

'You want to set me up with someone?' said Martin in disbelief. 'Who?'

'Aubrey, of course.'

Martin doubled up in hysterics. 'Renzo, a good businessman you might be, but a poor matchmaker—'

'I am an excellent matchmaker. In Philadelphia, I once set up a Democrat dentist with a Republican confectioner.'

'Sounds like a bad sitcom,' said Martin. 'Does she know anything about this?' Renzo shook his head. 'Because I'd describe her feelings towards me as disgust.'

'Surface deep, wine differences. Plus, you both like crime fiction. And it's rare for a real policeman to read Rebus and Harry Hole, isn't it?'

'My father used to read them to me when I was five.'

'Trust me, Martin, I will reunite you with your father's watch. And trust me, you and Aubrey are meant to be together; like a shooting star split in two, rejoining.' A broken meteor burning up in the atmosphere didn't sound the most flattering but Renzo was on a role. 'I'll do anything to make you look good. Anything. Why do you think I picked archery for our sport? I remembered you'd played for the police.' Renzo handed them fresh bottles. 'Do you trust me?'

'Maybe.'

'And after Stella, do you trust women?'

'I'm resolutely working on it.'

'It is the same between Sara and I these days. There is a blockage between us that I don't know how to unblock.'

'Perhaps the healthiest way is to confront it,' said Martin. They silently drank their beers.

'Are you happy, Martin?'

'I'm super happy, I'm game show host happy; y'know, when I'm not drowned in wine.'

'Aubrey is lonely,' said Renzo. 'She does not realise it, but I know she is. She needs to take time out to smell... well, anything other than the wine bouquet.'

'So you brought her here to play matchmaker?'

'No,' said Renzo, 'I brought you here to play matchmaker.'

'So why is she here—just to taste the wine?'

'No. I'm hoping, if she passes her Master Sommelier exam, she will run my brand-new New York restaurant for me. That is what I purchased with my cash injection six months ago.'

'You're crazy, Renzo.'

'There's no length I wouldn't go to find happiness for you both. If sparks should fly, then *ottimo*,' bunching ten fingers together, Renzo lovingly lifted his hands to his lips, 'but there is no pressure, absolutely no pressure... Perhaps you could impress her with your deductive reasoning. Have you solved the case yet?' Martin remained silent. 'Well, no pressure, no pressure.'

'That reminds me, how are the photos you took after we found Mary?'

'Take a look yourself,' said Renzo, passing his phone. 'I kept snapping.' He'd done a good job documenting every unmade bed, coat-strewn chair, toiletry bag, wine textbook, smouldering pipe, even the Sinclair's fire-escape rope around the bed post. 'Do they help?'

'Yes.'

'*Bene.* What a fairytale romance this could be; wowing Aubrey with the solution. You are on a hero's journey, my friend. This is your call to adventure.'

'This is my refusal of the call.'

'We are both Italians.'

'Renzo, I grew up in Hackney.'

'Latin blood flows through us. You can not deny she is beautiful.'

'Don't you think we have more pressing issues,' said Martin, 'down in the cellar?'

'*Lupus in fabula*,' murmured Renzo, tilting his head up to the heavens with a heavy sigh, 'the wolf in the fairytale. You never know if the devil is hiding around the next corner, so find love when you can. The wolf is cruel; tearing us, ripping us, killing us before our time.'

The graphic savagery jolted something inside Martin's half-drowned mind, and it was his turn to jump from the bench in panic.

'We're in danger. Even if the killer does think I'm dead, they won't be satisfied by this. We're all in danger,' said Martin, now running back to the house. 'D.O.T. needs more brutality.'

'What are you saying?' said Renzo, hurrying to keep up.

'There's going to be another murder. Right now!

31

Confessions and Croquet

The ambulance arrived at two in the morning. Theo had been stabbed in the night. Staunchly, Renzo rushed to hospital with him, ordering everyone to sleep and he'd call if there was an update. In terms of witnesses to the stabbing and drowning, unfortunately it was back to the higgledy-piggledy whereabouts, observing everybody and nobody, memories clouded by the Mondeuse before bed. The party returned to their rooms; this time, locking their doors.

Martin couldn't sleep. Every time he closed his eyes, he was back in the wine tank, drowning again in gloopy red gravy. It did at least give him a chance to grill Omar and Sara regarding the night Mary was murdered. Sixty minutes of the truth, the half-truth or anything but the truth. Maddeningly, there was nothing of note; each had remained in their quarters. Deep down, he knew Sara had more to reveal; but how to extract this information? For now, innocent until proven guilty. In such cases, does Santa tick the naughty or nice box? In the old days, Martin and SCO19 knocked on innocent doors with a hardened-steel battering ram.

Miserably, Martin hunkered down underneath the heater on the terrace in a state of hypervigilance. DEFCON 1. The lookout point worked both ways; the bench giving a good view of any assailant approaching. Still Martin fretted. Would Theo Oblet survive, or had he lost another one on his watch? A kitchen carving knife and DOT mistletoe leaf lay next to his body. Insanely, even after these events, no one chose to leave; the hook of bottled lightning too enticing.

A weak silver sun finally broke through. Was this the

heavens opening up, angels descending to collect another soul? The roads were clear so Capitaine Gallois would be arriving imminently, and no doubt resurrecting Operation Incognito. What exactly did Martin have to report? Nothing except questions. Who was Sara's kidnapper? Who wore the Daughters of Temperance tattoo? What was the significance of the stolen candle and where was it now? Why leave behind mistletoe? What was behind Noel's awkwardness? How had the murderer passed by Aubrey? Shoulders sagging, Martin stared out aimlessly. A mist hung over the vineyard as if to shield its secrets, as a new message buzzed from his mum about the Christmas letter. Two days and counting.

At 05:42, Renzo arrived back with Theo. Alive. The weight rocketed off Martin's shoulders.

'What have I missed?' said Theo with a bittersweet smile, shuffling painfully over to join Martin on the bench. Renzo raced back in to check on Sara.

'How you doing, Theo?' said Martin, his dirty jeans and wine-stained jumper somehow still smarter than Theo's multi-coloured shoes and red paint splattered hands; with worse blemishes underneath.

He pulled his jumper up, revealing a large bandage. 'Famished, I demand filet mignon.'

Martin ordered them both steak and chips from the kitchen; Theo, an accompanying glass of Mondeuse. While they waited, Theo insisted on bringing a blank canvas and set of paints down from his room; apparently to paint "outside in the elements", but clearly he was scared to be alone. Declaring his intention to paint five large red diamond shapes "delicately and carefully", within minutes there was more paint on his trembling hands and face than on the canvas; but he looked slightly happier by the time his filet mignon arrived.

'How's your stomach?' asked Martin, through a mouthful of fries.

'They stapled it shut and injected me with something. Actually, the staples probably hurt more than the knife stab.

Plus, I have to take these,' said Theo, washing a chunky blue pill down with his wine.

'I can't believe you got stabbed,' said Martin, wiping his mouth.

'It is fine, all the best people get stabbed,' Theo smiled grimly. 'Sid Vicious, Martina Hingis, Julius Caesar.'

'Obi-Wan Kenobi,' added Martin.

Theo chuckled appreciatively. 'Ow! Don't make me laugh,' he said with a wince. 'Luckily it didn't go too deep, just through my fat and a little way into the muscle. I think I must have stepped back as he lunged.'

'He?' repeated Martin.

Theo thought for a moment. 'I suppose it could have been one of the women. It all happened so fast. I was listening to music trying to get to sleep when there was a knock on the door. I assumed it would be Eve, demanding I turn it down.' He swallowed painfully. 'I opened the door... it was so dark in the corridor; I think they were wearing a hoodie… maybe there was a flash of gold around the wrist, and… then it happened.' Theo took another long swig of wine, then returned to his painting of the red diamonds.

Eve and Morton were the first out the farmhouse. Still arguing.

Spotting Martin, she redirected her anger. 'You found my candle yet?' He shook his head. 'Another failure, then, Moretti. Frickin' useless.'

'At least he is trying,' said Theo, 'more than we have seen from the Gendarmerie.'

'Oh, and you can talk, Theo. Blaring out your music last night, no wonder somebody stabbed you,' said Eve. 'And the night before, chucking your paints against our wall—one hundred and fifty times I counted!'

'Fussy,' Morton muttered, rolling his eyes.

'And you, Mr Not-So-Smooth Criminal,' said Eve in a high-pitched voice, 'do you really want to make the mistake of annoying me a second time today? We're gonna lose our distribution deal.'

'Don't argue, please,' said Theo sadly, 'don't make my mistake. I said a lot of things in the heat of the moment I regret.'

Noel and Pekoe were next to emerge, kitted out with helmets, harnesses, ropes and climbing clips.

'Where are you two off?' asked Eve. Not the local Lidl, Martin suspected.

Packing then repacking his rucksack on the bench, Pekoe pointed up at the craggy white mountains, towards the highest one, the peak stubbornly shrouded in cloud. 'It hasn't shown its face yet.'

'Hopefully, though, it shows us the bearded vulture. That's the target,' said Noel, lifting his camera bag a little stiffly. 'If anybody can find one, it's me.'

'Expecting trouble?' said Martin, eyeing the orange Barracuda folding knife in a side pocket.

'You never know when the mountain will turn on you,' said Pekoe.

'Hey, Moretti, you can join us, if you're quick, like?'

Martin politely declined their offer. In the current climate, he absolutely did not fancy a stroll among the pickaxes, cliff edges, ropes, knives and crampons of the Alps. In actual fact, however, they looked relatively light on gear. 'So only packing the essentials?' said Martin, as Pekoe added his cherrywood pipe.

'There's nothing better than getting high up high,' said Pekoe. 'First part's by cable car. After that, it's quite flat at the top. We could drive, but it's the long way round.'

'Don't you need oxygen tanks or something?' asked Eve.

'This mountain is only four-thousand metres, the death zone starts at eight.' Seeing their reaction to the words "death zone", Pekoe added reassuringly: 'The world's going to pot, but not up there. Pure tranquillity... it's hard to know where your soul ends and the mountain begins.'

'I'll find my serenity hopefully down the end of my

camera lens,' said Noel, rubbing the back of his neck.

'You alright, Noel?' frowned Martin.

'Just a bit of warbler neck, like,' said Noel, rolling his shoulders as they bid farewell to the group. Warbler neck, or from the wine vat tussle? Martin accompanied the pair to the cobbled courtyard where an Uber driver was impatiently revving their engine. Noel dashed on with the bags.

'Pure tranquillity, eh?' Martin said to Pekoe. 'And there was I thinking you might miss Renzo's worldly goods down here.' Martin hovered by their host's collection of supercars, remembering that resentment he'd occasionally heard in Pekoe's voice. 'I suppose not all Cambridge graduates end up with a Ferrari.'

'No, I suppose not,' Pekoe replied amiably.

The taxi driver honked, but Martin wasn't finished. 'Well, if you want to key one of his cars, I won't tell,' he said with a wink. 'Incidentally, how did you know the D.O.T. scratches down the side of the coach were done with a kitchen knife?'

'It was the only knife around,' shrugged Pekoe. Another honk. 'Look, Renzo and I are both doing what we love; only, what he loves pays a whole lot more.'

'A weed sommelier for that hemp forest over there should bring in some extra bucks.'

'So I hoped, but the conditions aren't good enough. I only made one batch and ironically it was too potent. I'm currently thinking of North-East India.' Did that sound like a job offer? Following a double-honk, Pekoe jumped into the taxi; as Renzo arrived to see them off.

'Think they'll make it alright?'

'Pekoe is more mountain goat than man,' said Renzo.

Eagerly, Noel waved goodbye to the pair: Martin lifted his left arm (remembering he no longer had a watch) but Renzo didn't respond.

'What's going on between you and Noel,' said Martin, 'what's with all the caginess?'

'He has disappointed me,' said Renzo, as the taxi snaked down the driveway. 'I confess, I need him to find my bearded vulture for our marketing, but I can never forgive him.'

'Something he did?'

'Not directly, but a calamitous judgement was made,' said Renzo, draping a muscular arm across Martin's shoulders. In his other hand, he was holding a long, thin, green canvas bag.

'*Vieni*, the four of us will take a walk.' Steering him around, Martin was met by the beaming faces of Sara and Aubrey. If this was a romantic date, Martin promised to place the mistletoe on Renzo's body himself. Still, it would at least give Martin another opportunity to question Sara.

After morning pleasantries, they descended into the vinery, heading down towards the lake. Cheerily, Renzo and Sara took the lead, hand in hand, leaving Martin and Aubrey to walk side by side in silence. Potentially awkward, Martin was unfazed. The news of Theo's survival had put a spring in his step. And finally appreciating his own near-death experience, he breathed in the fresh, glittering air as a falcon soared high above the vineyard. Granted, Old Elysium's clipped vines were as dormant as elsewhere, but a new, lighter layer of snow sparkled from the stumps. *Vive la France!*

While Aubrey mirrored his joy, she was shivering. Remembering Sven's maxim that there's no such thing as bad weather, Martin offered her his scarf, saying: 'I see you went for bad clothing as well.'

'I'm from Monterey,' her teeth chattered, 'if you're not barefoot, then you're overdressed. Good times and tan lines, yeah?' Ironically, her shivering was the first warmth she'd shown him.

Halfway to the lake, they came across the statue of a bearded man in robes, his arms aloft to the skies above.

'Who's that whacko?' asked Martin.

'I built this statue among the vines for good luck,' said Renzo. 'It is St. Vincent: patron saint of winemakers.'

Martin should have guessed. One of Renzo's tamer passions – hagiography, the study of saints. 'Legend has it, Vincent was sent down to earth to visit the vineyards of France because of the lack of good wine in heaven. The wine on earth so entranced him that he forgot to return to heaven, so God punished him by turning him to stone.'

'Is there a St. Martin?'

'There is,' replied Renzo, a wry smile at the corners of his mouth.

'What is he the patron saint of?'

'Drunkards.' All four burst into laughter. '*Vieni*, our game awaits on the frozen lake.'

Wonderful, thought Martin, another of Renzo's hazardously invented games. 'Let me guess, ice hockey with live grenades?'

Renzo roared even louder. 'No, no, no! Croquet, with regular balls, regular mallets. There is enough danger around. Best of three hoops.'

'Sounds easy enough,' said Martin.

'Oh, sorry, Lord Double-eye,' said Sara, in mock outrage, 'Us cyclops can't do 3-D. Check your privilege. I'll never watch Avatar again.'

'There's a 2-D version,' suggested Martin.

'No, I just didn't like it,' she grinned at him. In such playful surroundings, it was going to be difficult to extract the necessary information.

'This game is good for Sara,' said Renzo, 'practice her periphery. Though as I have told her, a whole-eye transplant is now possible.'

'I like my eye patch,' said Sara, 'I own it, makes me feel like a pirate. Anyway, I am getting better at this whole depth and distance thing. I can pour the wine into my own glass now.'

'God,' said Martin, 'as if you haven't suffered enough.' Something hard, wet and white hit Martin between the eyes. He withdrew his head sharply, his face covered in snow but still clocking the wicked delight on Aubrey's face; a second snowball in hand. Stumbling sideways, Martin tossed one back, grazing her shoulder.

'You throw like a girl,' giggled Aubrey.

'So do you,' said Martin defensively.

'Well, I've had quite a lot of practice.'

Firing a volley in her direction, Martin braced himself for Aubrey's retaliation. Instead, she emitted a loud squeak, clamping her eyes shut in pain. Martin and Renzo span around in concern to see Sara spraying herself with a bottle of perfume, releasing a strong lemon-scented mist.

'I take it that perfume contains real lemon?' said Martin, explaining Aubrey's previous micro-migraine reactions to both citrus and stress.

'Rosa Salas, *sì*,' said Sara apologetically, swiftly pocketing it.

'Thank you,' said Aubrey, pressing her forehead, her eyes still closed.

'*Si,* Sara, do not damage our precious asset,' said Renzo, turning to the Californian. 'Aubrey, I have told you of my new restaurant in New York. I want you to run it for me if you pass your Master Sommelier exam.'

'What?' said Aubrey, eyes now wide.

'I plan it to be an Italian restaurant with a psychiatrist theme,' said Renzo. 'You know, pictures of Sigmund Freud, Eugen Bleuler, Nathan S. Kline.'

'I suppose New York is the shrink capital of the world…' said Aubrey slowly, playing for time.

'Exactly! And we'll get Kelsey Grammar to open it,' said Renzo. 'It'll be easy: throw in some therapy couches, get some pasta on the boil, uncork some bottles of my *Vautour Barbu*.'

'Tell her your name for it,' said Sara, dramatically bracing herself.

'This is the best bit. We call it—Penne For Your Thoughts.'

'Dad joke,' groaned Sara, but Martin was chuckling.

‘Papà, have you literally spent a million opening a restaurant just to make that terrible pun?’

‘It will work,’ insisted Renzo, ‘with Aubrey at the helm. Promise me, you’ll think about it.’ Aubrey gave a hesitant nod. ‘*Squisito!* And now to the game.’

They had reached the lakeside, Martin’s confidence evaporating on seeing the playing surface: the size of a football pitch and theoretically frozen solid, each hoop lay forty yards apart. ‘Er, is this safe?’ He’d heard enough horror stories of people falling through ice.

‘It’s really thick this time of year,’ said Sara.

‘But do you want to head back, in case it breaks?’ asked Martin, a yearning look at the farmhouse.

‘It’s fine, I smacked the hoops in myself this morning,’ said Renzo, failing to reassure Martin. Unzipping the green bag, a set of wooden mallets and multi-coloured balls spilled out. Renzo handed Aubrey the first ball. ‘Blue.’

‘To match your hair,’ said Martin. She rolled her eyes as Renzo handed him the second.

‘Red.’

‘Rhymes with dead,’ said Aubrey, pleasantly.

‘I’ll take Black. Which leaves you yellow,’ said Renzo, handing his daughter the final ball.

‘Girls versus boys,’ said Aubrey ‘seeing as Martini finds it “so easy”.’

‘It’s Martin,’ he corrected.

‘Super sorry.’

‘I tell you what,’ said Martin. ‘I’ll make you a bet. If we beat you, you stop calling me Martini.’

‘And if we beat you?’

‘I’ll drink a glass of any wine you put in front of me.’

‘First through each hoop, best of three, yeah? Deal!’ she said, firmly shaking hands.

Renzo hit his ball onto the ice and ran after it. ‘Come on, Martin. Grab a stick,’ he called. The falcon began to spiral, descending toward the vines below, as three figures followed the first across the silver surface.

'Woah, I don't know,' said Martin, taking a tentative step on the ice and nearly landing on his back. 'Did you hear that crack? Shall we just do the first hoop?'

'It's not going to crack or break or... it's rock solid,' said Sara, arm in arm with Aubrey, singing Joni Mitchell in unison. '*I wish I had a river, I could skate away on...*'

With his best impression of a penguin, Martin waddled over to the painted baulk-line as Aubrey took up a side-style stance.

'This is going to be fun,' said Sara.

'A Brambilla bash is always fun,' boasted Renzo.

'Yes, almost spoils things there's a wine serial killer up at the farmhouse,' said Martin. 'Shame we don't know who's behind it.'

'Oh please, who hates wine more than you do, Martini?' said Aubrey. She took one or two careful, concentrated practice swings and then, with her eyes glued to the ball, thwacked it hard; a pulsating blast of lasers reverberating across the lake. Her blue ball rolled halfway to the hoop.

'Hey,' said Martin, swinging the mallet between his feet, 'in my favour, I figure you cork dorks still owe me for retrieving the Lafite.' As soon as Martin struck, he knew he'd mis-hit it, his red ball scuttling so far to the right he was back on land.

'It was rather ingenious,' said Renzo proudly, 'Eve and Morton faking that they— what is the word you say in England—shagged?' With a smooth unhurried swing, like the pendulum of a clock, Renzo hit his ball perfectly. It rolled straight and true thirty yards across the white plateau, edging just in front of Aubrey. Any advantage to the men, however, was immediately wiped out by Sara. An attacking thwack, that looked more at home in a mine shaft, knocked both her and her father's balls over to Martin's edge of the lake.

'Don't avoid my point,' said Aubrey, her second shot gaining another ten yards. 'Why are you so anti-wine?'

'It's overpriced, pretentious, and gives the worst

hangovers,' said Martin, striking the ball at least in the direction of the hoop this time. 'I can drink a litre of gin and feel fine the next day. In my opinion, a bottle of red plonk would make an Alka-Seltzer vomit.'

'So drink in moderation,' said Aubrey. 'I love wine but hate getting drunk.'

'No word in that sentence made sense,' said Martin.

'I can't wait,' said Aubrey resentfully, 'to pour you the largest glass in the world.' Clack! Behind them, another well-practiced hit from Renzo; but, again, Sara targeted his ball, ricocheting them both off in the wrong direction. 'And if you hate wine so much, why are you even here?' With a gentle tap, her ball stopped three yards from the iron ring.

'Nothing else to do. I've just been sacked by the esteemed Superintendent Radnor,' said Martin bitterly, 'basically for liberating one bottle of cheap rum.' With a hard wooden whack, his ball whizzed off on the trajectory desired, stopping one yard short and surely blocking Aubrey from any line at the hoop.

'Weren't you about to get suspended by Radnor before we met in the summer?' asked Renzo with an amused look. 'So you were already on—'

'Don't say thin ice,' said Martin.

'What were you getting suspended for?' asked Aubrey.

'He's kinda always had it in for me ever since I smiled at his wife.'

'Change "smiled" to "shagged", and change "wife" to "daughter",' said Renzo. They howled with laughter; in between hoots, Martin clarifying the daughter was twenty-eight. A forceful smack from Renzo sent his and Sara's balls skittling across the lake. 'Revenge!' he said, before the flat wooden clunk of Sara's mallet sent them flying back the other way. Evidently, the battle of girls versus boys depended very much on Aubrey and Martin, a ferocious grin of concentration now on her face as she took aim.

With a beautiful tap, her blue ball squeezed by Martin's

red and through the metal u-shaped gate. 'One-nil!' cried Aubrey jubilantly. Clearly, Martin needed to level up on his croquet. And on the Sara Brambilla interrogation. But it was hard to switch subject while Aubrey, waiting on the second baulk-line for the Italians, pressed on. 'You realise wine is good for you.'

'It's not good for my tongue,' said Martin.

'One glass of wine contains the juice of one hundred and fifty grapes.' Her green eyes grew happier the more she rambled on. 'You'd need to drink seven glasses of orange juice to get the same amount of antioxidants. Cannonau di Sardegna is even more powerful.'

'That's another thing,' said Martin, as the Brambillas rejoined them, 'there's a thousand different labels for it. How am I supposed to know my White Zinfandel from a rosé, or a Bordeaux from a claret?'

Aubrey looked up from the ball with a pitying expression on her face. 'Ok, listen— Chardonnay, Merlot and Sauvignon Blanc are just names of grapes. Those varieties, like apples in a supermarket, have different characteristics. You like apples, yeah?' Martin nodded as she struck her ball. 'But not all of them, yeah? What's your favourite?'

'Granny Smith.'

'It's the same with wine. We just need to fine the right grape for you.'

'Never gonna happen,' said Martin with a powerful whack that scuttled past Aubrey's ball by ten yards.

'We'll see,' said Aubrey.

'Such perseverance!' Renzo chuckled. A slow, unhurried backswing then smooth forward swing knocked his ball into the lead; Sara's following close behind. 'You see, Martin, with such expertise, these mistletoe murders are the perfect case for Aubrey to help on. She can list you the suspect's temperament simply by their choice of drink. And now bottles are the weapon, if the killer spills their wine, she can taste the drops to identify them.'

In spite of Renzo's clumsy matchmaking, Martin finally felt relaxed around him and Sara again. Maybe there was no need to re-question his daughter. Last night's suspicions of the Brambillas were clearly unfounded; Renzo was the one he'd ran in with to discover Theo injured. And as for Sara, periphery vision aside, she couldn't risk sneaking down to murder Mary if her father was checking on her every two hours. Plus, neither of them were at le Château des Allues when Jimmy was killed.

'Couldn't you do that, Renzo, detect the wine drops?' asked Martin.

Confirming Renzo's vigorous head shake, Aubrey added: 'Women make better wine tasters. Pregnant women are the best, more sensitive to smell, but actually women are more adept at describing what they taste.'

'You see, Martin,' said Renzo, 'you two could be partners in crime.'

'Or "partners in wine" as Sven would say,' said Aubrey. She went through the long rigmarole of sizing up her shot.

'Wine,' muttered Martin, 'you treat it like it's art.'

'Fun fact,' said Aubrey in such a good imitation of Sven that Martin looked around in shock and then laughed, 'Leonardo Da Vinci swapped one of his paintings for a vineyard.'

'Which painting?'

'The Last Supper.' Firing straight, the blue ball hit the iron ring with a tink and rolled backwards. Undoubtedly, she'd win the hoop next hit. 'But, you know what, Renzo? I don't think Martini needs a partner. You should've seen him do his detective thing on Sven a couple nights ago,' said Aubrey, her face shining with excitement. 'He worked out where Sven had been all afternoon simply by looking at his tie. Remember where?'

'Before McDonald's…' said Martin, frowning, 'I think, the *Centre Hospitalier Spécialisé de la Savoie.*'

'That was with us!' Sara beamed; Renzo less so. 'I was checking out of hospital. Sven came to help me pack before

Papà picked me up.'

Martin nearly dropped his mallet. So they *were* both in the area when Jimmy died. 'That must have been a long drive back to here,' he said conversationally.

'We stayed at a hotel nearby.' Renzo fixed Martin with cautionary look, undeceived. 'Well, I did…'

'I went out dancing,' she said proudly to Aubrey. 'Life's too short now. I have, I have been recovering.' Sara swung her mallet nervously from side to side.

'I can't imagine there are many nightclubs in wine country?' said Martin, lining up his shot.

'*Le Madison Club* is ok, it kept us dancing until dawn,' she happily shrugged. Martin's ball bounced off Aubrey's and through the hoop.

'You knocked my ball out the way!' said Aubrey, advancing on him.

'Super-sorry,' said Martin.

'One to Aubrey, one to Martin,' said Renzo, happy to refocus on the croquet. Sara was still swinging her mallet, a weapon of pure bludgeoning power, and Martin wondered if the killers in Holly's novels had ever disposed of someone this way. Perhaps Martin shouldn't be feeling so relaxed around the Brambillas. Granted, on the night of Mary's death, Renzo had checked on Sara every two hours; but then, it doesn't take one hundred and twenty minutes to murder somebody. And now he knew; they were both nearby on the night Jimmy was killed.

'Next hole wins!' cried Sara.

Despite his new suspicions, Martin still couldn't figure how anyone could pass by Aubrey's tasting room. He raised the subject with her. 'You definitely saw no one?'

She shook her head. 'No one. I was facing the corridor the whole night.'

'Eyes wide the whole night?'

Scowling fiercely, her hands tightened on the mallet. 'Yeah. Well, I mean, it's possible I closed them briefly. I did get a couple of my stress migraines, but you try telling the difference between the Sopranceneri and Sottoceneri regions of Ticino.' Her blue ball rocketed forwards, closely followed by blurs of red, black and yellow. 'So I guess it makes this case pretty difficult, yeah?'

'Good thing I'm here, then.'

'So long as you solve it,' she said, twisting a long strand of blue hair. 'You really need the booze?'

'Yep,' he proudly replied. 'Booze makes my synapses fire faster.'

'I don't know,' said Aubrey, unconvinced, 'it sounds pretty convenient.'

'Works for me. I indulge in everything but restraint,' Martin grinned. 'Drinking too much of the Christmas spirit, y'know, in the local hometown pub. 'Tis the season of giving, myself a hangover.'

'Ho-ho hammered, said Aubrey, unimpressed. 'I wish you didn't, it's like watching a slow suicide.' Crack! Her ball whizzed off, a beautiful shot, as good as she'd struck, reaching halfway towards the final hoop. 'You know what I'm missing from home—reindeer corn. It's this red, white and green candy you only get over the holidays. Might be a good substitute for you.'

'We will go into town tomorrow for some last minute shopping,' said Renzo. 'There is an American candy store there. I think it's probably a money laundering front, but they sell that kinda *ciarpame.*'

'Here,' said Aubrey, 'let me give you my personal deets.' Passing his phone to her, Martin's shot skidded ten yards short of the lead as she typed away.

Keeping her talking had served as a useful distraction on the previous hoop, so Martin tried the tactic again. 'Is it true what you said the other night, that women invented wine?'

'Hell yeah! According to the Persian legend, she was a Princess who'd fallen out of favour with the King, so tried killing herself by drinking the table grapes that had spoiled in their storage jar. Instead of dying, she got giddy, giggly, at ease, and eventually fell asleep, waking up cured; all the troubles of her life had vanished.'

'Did she regain favour with the King?' asked Martin.

'Who cares? She had wine!'

'*Esattamente*!' chimed Sara, her whack knocking all four balls in different directions; Aubrey using her next hit simply to get back on the ice.

With the Brambilla's pirouetting away, the former Chief Inspector lined up his shot but kept his mind on the case. 'Seems a lot of pressure Renzo's placing on you for this Master Sommelier gig. Although, I suppose if his wine business folds, there'll likely be no money for your exam or his new restaurant?'

'Pressure is a privilege,' she said.

Martin avoided looking at Aubrey who was standing in his eyeline swishing her mallet impatiently. Stand still… head down… smack it for plenty of zip. Clack! His red ball skittered across the ice straight for the hoop, just ahead of Aubrey and way in front of Renzo and Sara, who continued to wallop each other out of contention. Aubrey nudged hers forward, coming to a halt five yards out, slightly to the right of the hoop. With a direct shot, it was Martin's for the victory. Renzo and Sara gave up. Instead, coming to watch the finale. Martin took aim. No more wine… no more 'Martini'… it was an easy hit.

'This to win,' said Aubrey, 'no pressure…' Something moved at the corner of his right eye. Aubrey was tapping her foot, apparently playing her own mind games.

'*Buona fortuna*, Martin,' said Renzo.

'Did anybody else hear a crack?' teased Sara.

'Peril at hoop three,' added Aubrey.

With a deft tap, they all gawped as Martin's ball, rolling over the crystal-crunchy surface, rebounded off the iron ring with a painful ping. The pressure had got to him. It would get to her. Defiantly, she punched her ball straight through the hoop.

'And that's game, Martini!'

Martin's valley-echoing groan roused the falcon above as all four exited the silver surface; the surface with a giant crack splintered down the middle.

'So, go on then,' said Martin, climbing back up to the courtyard, 'what wine will it be? There's an opened Mondeuse on the terrace.'

'No, not that,' said Aubrey thoughtfully.

'Why not?' asked the condemned man, resigned to his fate.

'You'll keep,' she said with relish, and the trio cackled.

Suddenly, however, the cackle was caught in their throats with the shrill whine of the front gates; an Alpine A110 sports car prowling up the lane towards the farmhouse, as if driving a hearse. Two pairs of beady eyes, Capitaine Gallois and Lieutenant Aimee, were staring directly into Martin's soul.

Automatically, Martin took a few steps back into the shadows of the stable doorway. The car crept closer as the other croqueteers fled. Cowards. Swallowing hard, Martin walked out to greet them. Time to end Operation Incognito. Time to end all of this.

32

The Defective Detective Strikes Back

After any catastrophe, it's far easier to shift the blame; so as the Capitaine came limping hurriedly towards him, leaning on his walking stick, Martin felt a wild fury stir in his gut. If Gallois hadn't prematurely closed the case, then Mary might still be alive.

Nevertheless, another—much smaller—part of Martin rejoiced at their presence. With the return of the Gendarmerie, and forensics, things could move rapidly.

'*Bonjour* Capitaine, *bonjour* Lieutenant.'

Gallois did not speak immediately, lighting a cigarette instead, and only after several long, hateful drags, announce: 'It turns out Monsieur Stresskeller's stalker, Camille Duval, lied to us about being the murderer.' Martin had to bite down on his tongue. 'She's admitted she only said it to add meaning to her life. Confessing kept her close to Jimmy or some *absurdité*. They did sleep together,' declared Gallois, as if justifying previous suppositions, 'and she did take back her Rolex watch. *Mais*, Monsieur Stresskeller kicked her out of the château an hour before his murder.' Martin's tongue had scars.

'So, our assassin is still on the loose,' said Aimee, impassively, 'and has killed again.'

'And you, Monsieur Moretti,' Gallois said with stiff formality, 'what have you got to show for Operation Incognito?' Martin looked across through the smoke clouds into the steel grey eyes. They were judging him, so he updated them on all the events of the Old Elysium vineyard, including Aubrey's argument with Mary, Renzo photographing the rooms, and his own close call into the baptism of red wine.

Seeing the slanted smile on Gallois' face at his near-fatal dip, Martin moved on. 'Did you know both Renzo and Sara were in the area for Jimmy's death?'

'*Bien sur*, of course,' said the Capitaine, gruffly, 'I told you, I spoke to Renzo personally that next morning. *Souviens-toi*, he could get your job back if this investigation goes well.'

'Pffft,' Aimee scoffed.

'Speaking of doing it well,' said Martin, 'there's a few points I'd like checking on.'

The Capitaine barged past him. 'From now on, stay away from my investigation. Speak to Agathe, if you must,' seethed Gallois, stalking away with six uniformed officers into the farmhouse.

'*Quoi?*' said Lieutenant Aimee, lips pursed, notepad out.

'Three things,' said Martin. 'Can you check the CCTV for the Madison nightclub on the night of Jimmy's murder? Sara Brambilla says she was there until dawn, so...' He couldn't finish the sentence. Googling the place, it was only a ten-minute drive from the Château des Allues. 'Also, in the cellar here, you'll find an annoyingly protruding nail sticking out. Can you test it for blood and DNA.'

'*Oui*, and lastly?' Any burning curiosity was well-hidden.

'There's a tattoo parlour named Blacked in Chavanod. We need to know who got inked with the words: Daughters of Temperance. It should be in the portfolio book.'

To Martin's surprise, she nodded briskly. '*Oui*, I will move fast. The chief magistrate is fighting to keep this case out of the tabloids. Sick, sick people salivate over celebrity death.'

Jammed with important meetings all afternoon, the farmhouse was filled with so much hot air no log fires were necessary. Renzo held court in the tasting room, covering: Sven's marketing strategy, mass production of the wine label, Holly's autobiography, Tate securing liquor permits, plus the recruitment plan for a new accountant and new celebrity endorsement (Jason Statham was available). Meanwhile, Gallois interrogated them one-by-one in the living room. Even Martin; which would have been far more tense without the copious yawns and eyerolls.

Back outside, the bar with the brass rail was set up again just as a game of Rubber Pigeon commenced. Ordering a Heineken, Martin watched from afar. Sip, detective, sip. Though Theo suggested the game, he'd opted only to launch the tennis balls; hurting too much to pull back on the bowstring. It made sense why Theo wanted to play it. It was the last spot Mary had been happy.

'New balls please!' said Eve in her honeyed voice.

The Sinclairs and Kesslers unleashed a volley of arrows up, but the first pigeon of the day was yet to be struck. Their son, Joseph, ran over for refreshment, yawning as he ordered a Pepsi.

'Keeping you up?' said Martin.

'Definitely. I had another nightmare last night,' said Joseph. 'I dreamt I was the one who killed Mary.'

'Is that another lie?'

'I haven't lied in forty-eight hours,' said Joesph, indignantly.

'Is that true?'

'No,' he conceded, adding, 'sorry about the Goonies stuff with the tongue, and my mom. It was only a joke.' Martin wasn't laughing. What was it they say? Many a truth is said in jest. So, could it really be Holly?

'You're not interrogating my kid, are you, Moretti?' said Tate, marching over.

'No more interrogations,' Martin reassured them. There was no need.

Gallois and Aimee emerged to fetch Holly, interrupting half-way through a recounting of last night's stabbing. 'You must have felt scared,' she said, 'in the back of the ambulance.' She was no longer wearing her gold bracelet.

‘Honestly, I felt… guilty,’ said Theo inspecting his wound, ‘how relieved I was that I had at least finished my wine label masterpiece; the Land of a Thousand Spots. I know I should have been thinking of something more noble, of Mary.’

Gallois cleared his throat irritably. His suit jacket had a rip in it; another victim of the cellar’s annoyingly protruding sharp nail. ‘Well, if you don’t mind, we have a murderer on the loose who still hasn’t completed their masterpiece yet. And we are wasting time, we need to stop them before they add any more… finishing touches.’ Frogmarching Holly inside with a frustrated scowl, clearly Gallois’ questioning was as effective as before. As in, utterly ineffective.

His Lieutenant, at least, had been more successful. ‘I have some updates on your request,’ said Aimee to an astonished-looking Martin. The magistrate really mustn’t want this hanging over their roast turkey. ‘We have checked the video surveillance. Sara was in there with friends, but not until dawn. She left at 2 a.m. So, that is that on the Madison club,’ she said, ‘but the *salon de tatouage*, erm, Blacked, I can not access the tattoo parlour. They have already closed for Christmas.’

‘Don’t worry,’ said Martin, ‘there’s a simpler way we can find out.’

Illuminating developments from Lieutenant Aimee. Nevertheless, her voice had changed, now as hard and emotionless as the granite mountains behind them. She was glowering back at Martin like *he* was the criminal. Very odd. Good vibes returned immediately, however, with Renzo and Aubrey skipping over to the courtyard.

‘A bearded vulture? A bearded vulture?’ asked Renzo excitably.

Pekoe slung his rucksack off as Noel bounded over. ‘We found one! The rarest raptor in Europe! Some great snaps in the nest, perched on the ledge, flying over the valley.’ He raised his camera bag in victory. ‘Best shots I’ve ever taken!’

‘Majestic,’ said Pekoe.

Renzo hollered to the skies above and, just for an instant, life felt great. Like everything was going to be ok. The whole group rushed over as Renzo sprayed champagne into glasses, even toasting and hugging Noel. The four females burst into a chorus of "Have Yourself a Merry Little Christmas" while Eve showed off her festive holly berry earrings, promising to buy a set for them all. Man of the moment, Noel, treated them to a bizarre jig resembling a drunken monkey practicing taekwondo.

'Is he alright?' asked Martin.

'Up high enough, many minds warp. Mostly, they return to normal when they descend. Mostly,' said Pekoe quietly, his voice lost among the merriment.

Almost as swiftly, the mood swung the other way again with Aimee ordering the two climbers in for interrogation and Capitaine Gallois escorting Mary's body bag out. Horrendous. The crowd sombrely dispersed except for Martin, Renzo and Aubrey.

'*Une tragédie.*' The Capitaine lit a cigarette as Theo shook by the van. 'We have extracted the murder bottle which will now, of course, remain in our evidence locker.'

'Which wine was it?' asked Aubrey.

'The Vecchio Maniero, 1969.'

'What a waste,' cursed Renzo, adding off Martin's look, 'of life, of precious life.' Martin believed him; nearly.

'The bottle, I was thinking,' said Martin, 'I'm sure the killer wore gloves, but the fibres on the wine label or the top of the cork, we could—'

'No more of your party tricks, like with Monsieur Sinclair's eyesight, *s'il vous plait!*' growled Gallois, as angry as Martin had seen him. 'No wonder you were fired. You are an insult to real police officers! It is Agathe and I doing the hard work around here. You play your croquet, making clever observations about, erm, I don't know, just because someone has got grey chalk marks on their sleeve, they must be a snooker player.'

'Wrong colour chalk for a snooker player,' said Martin.

'Or a teacher,' said Gallois sternly.

'Teachers don't use chalk anymore,' he said, Aubrey disguising her giggle with a cough.

'The point is, we are the ones doing the proper policework,' finished Gallois.

'Mountaineer, if you're interested,' said Martin. 'White chalk stains the rocks, so mountaineers use rock-coloured chalk.'

Escaping Gallois' fierce stare by collecting the arrows from the slope, Martin trudged through the vineyard with a satisfied stride. No need for any more interrogations. Everything was solved, properly this time. No Gendarmerie rush job.

Yanking an arrow out of St Vincent's head, several more projectiles lay in newly-formed puddles, the sun melting away the fresh frost; soon to freeze again when night fell. Procuring the last arrow, something else caught his eye. Directly beneath the terrace, on top of a holly bush, rested Eve's candle. Clearly dropped from above, it looked to have been burnt on at least one occasion.

'You can cancel that call to Superman, Eve,' said Martin, tossing the candle to her once back on the terrace. 'Just need to find my watch now.'

'I went fishing for it in the trough, but it wasn't there,' said Renzo. 'Usually I only fish with wine to catch a buzz.'

'Dad joke,' groaned Sara. Martin could now connect her kidnapping to their wine tour. The question was—did Sara know as well?

Rubber pigeon resumed all afternoon. Back at the bar, Sven sidled up to Martin, having been freshly questioned by the Gendarmerie. He didn't appear very flustered. But then, who did under the mild interrogations of Gallois.

'Hello Sven, dreamed up any more headlines yet?'

'How about: It's The Most Murderous Wine of the Year?' The Swede stared across at the archers with the same look on his face as when Martin had caught him watching Mary shoot arrows. They headed over to join the party.

'I'd stick with The French Conundrum, if it was up to me,' said Martin, observing he'd finally changed out of his pink tie.

'The case still perplexes you?'

'Actually, no,' said Martin, 'it's solved. Could you gather everyone in the lounge at seven o'clock tonight?' The tour guide happily began to round everyone up, arousing the interest of Gallois and Aimee. 'If that's ok, Capitaine?'

His handlebar moustache twitched. 'I was hoping you would say that. Do not be surprised if I interject with my own thoughts again, *oui*?' said Gallois; no doubt anticipating another car crash, and he wasn't alone.

'This isn't going to be like last time, is it, Moretti?' said Morton, trademark leer on display.

'We all like a glass of wine, but that was crazy,' agreed Eve. The ball launcher fired a target up for her. Missing by inches, her arrow came plummeting back down into St Vincent's groin. Amen.

'If I wanted to, I could control myself, if I wanted to.'

'You're not gonna get very far if you won't even admit there's a problem,' said Holly. 'Do you even admit you're an alcoholic?'

'Well, someone's got to keep the NHS in a job, right?'

'There's four simple questions which answers this. It's called the Cage Questionnaire. If you answer yes to two or more of these four questions, then—yes, it's very likely you are an alcoholic,' said Holly. She fixed Martin with a pained stare while Aubrey fidgeted with an arrow quiver.

'Shoot,' said Martin, intrigued.

'Have you ever felt you needed to cut down on your drinking?'

'No.'

'Have you ever felt guilty about drinking?'

'Very much no.'

‘Have people annoyed you by criticising your drinking?’

‘Do lawyers count as “people”?’ said Martin, ducking as Tate aimed the bow at him.

Holly persevered. ‘Have you ever felt you needed a drink first thing in the morning to steady your nerves or to get rid of a hangover?’

‘A Bloody Mary is a nutritious breakfast of tomato juice and celery.’ Tate pulled back on the bow string.

‘What you need is a role model,’ suggested Holly.

‘You? asked Martin, eyeing her white wine.

‘At least I’m trying, by any means,’ she added solemnly.

‘So what is it, Moretti, you like pickling your brain?’ said Tate.

‘Maybe I love it. Or maybe it helps solve the case,’ said Martin insolently. ‘Maybe it freed me from the shackles of Superintendent Radnor of Buxton Police Station; helped me escape my evil ex-wife; or if we’re going full-Freud, maybe it helps me sleep, numbing the faces of all those horrible crooks I see when closing my eyes. But before you start playing the violins,’ he said, finishing his beer, ‘let me tell you—I drink ‘cause I like it. It makes me feel good.’

The group gasped, their sanctimonious judgy-eyebrows rising. No need for Pekoe’s nylon-ropes to climb this moral high ground.

‘You still like to drink?’ said Sven. ‘After everything?’

‘Yeah, I love alcohol,’ said Martin. They were onto his favourite subject. ‘Wasn’t it Dean Martin who said: I pity people who don't drink. When they wake up in the morning, that's as good as they're going to feel all day.’

‘No, it was Frank Sinatra,’ said Aubrey.

‘Well, one of the Rat Pack anyway.’

‘But alcohol is the enemy,’ said Holly earnestly.

‘For you, *de toute façon,*’ said Theo with a queer glance.

Martin countered. ‘Alcohol may be man's worst enemy, but the Bible says: love your enemy.’

‘What, have you been reading a book of Frank Sinatra

quotes or something?!' said Aubrey.

But Martin was bullet proof to their barbs. He was nowhere near drunk. He'd been nursing the same bottle of Heineken all day. Because, funnily enough—after the disastrous first summation and his legless defence in the wine vat—perhaps, just perhaps, Holly (hell, even Superintendent Radnor) really did have a point. After all, this one drink was sufficient to recall his working theory right before the wine trough attack. Quite revealing... and no poison pen letters since the one Sven showed him.

Soon, the sun was setting over the valley and the final few arrows of the day were fired up. Martin helped Theo put the ball launcher back into its usual cobwebbed corner outside the kitchen door, just as a solitary figure sparked up a cigar on the terrace parapet.

'Renzo,' said Martin, 'I'm afraid it must all come out. All.' The Italian nodded gravely to the valley, as if drinking in his final sunset.

Last time, Martin had rushed to judgement; the cardinal sin for a detective. At last, he had it all: the solution, witnesses, evidence. Nothing could stop him. A chance to redeem himself. The Defective Detective strikes back. And this time, sober.

33

Three Red Herrings

Well, sober-ish. Martin had promised himself one drink. One victory drink, just to keep his throat lubricated while revealing all.

The room wasn't empty when he entered. The murderer was already sitting in one of the two high-backed chairs; silhouetted by the fire.

'It took me longer than it should have,' said Martin, taking the other seat. Between the pair, a coffee table with two lowball glasses, a whisky carafe and bucket of ice. The killer's hand reached out from the shadows and poured them both a large glass, then dropped three ice cubes in, splashing the table. It was all done so formally, it felt impolite to sniff for poison. Was it safe? Reading his mind, the dark figure took a huge glug and swallowed for reassurance. Martin matched their movements.

Very nice. It was the non-chill filtered whisky Martin had admired when perusing the line of carafes the other day. How closely had the killer been watching him? And how appropriate to have chosen this cloudy liquid. Admiring his drink, like many elements of the D.O.T. case, it was exceedingly murky. But, as with Martin's protracted progress, when the ice cubes melted bringing the whisky up to room temperature, all the cloudiness would disappear.

'Yep, much longer than it should. You played a good game,' said Martin begrudgingly and they clinked glasses. The hearth blazed between them, flames licking round the ash logs. At least his one drink was a strong one. 50% strength. Enjoying a second sip, more like 55%. Unpeated style, ex-

Bordeaux wine casks, the snobs on tour wouldn't approve of his notes, but Martin smelt salted caramel on the nose and, on the palate, chocolate orange. If he had to guess, it was the Glen Scotia 10 Year Old Campbeltown Malts Festival 2021 Whisky. Once he'd solved this affair, Martin was absolutely demanding that Highland distillery tour.

'You played it well; what with there being two red herrings.' Across the table, from the gloom of their armchair was a shake of the head; instead, holding up three fingers. More mind games.

Nerves buzzing, the clock on the mantelpiece struck seven. Martin rose and paced the living room, staring out of the large picture window to compose his thoughts. Reflecting over the past week—hell, the last year—he needed this win.

The guests, suspects, poured in with the Capitaine and Lieutenant, switching on the main lights. Please don't muck it up again. By the time he turned to see their freshened-faces staring up from the sofas, the murderer had of course mingled back amongst them; the Gendarmerie taking custody of the roaring fireplace. Please, please, don't muck it up again.

Sven, Renzo, Sara, Aubrey, Pekoe, Theo, Noel, Eve, Morton, Tate, Holly and Joseph; Martin had also invited Omar, citing the more the merrier.

'Ok, let's do this one last time,' said Martin, butterflies in the stomach but his head was clear. 'No more random guesses. I know who it is and I can prove it.' If he'd hoped for a big Hercule Poirot moment—the suspects sitting upright, eagerly listening to his earth-shattering conclusion—he was sorely disappointed. Slumped on the sofas, all three Sinclairs were lazily flicking through their phones, while Noel was sharing his best shots of the bearded vulture to Theo and the Kesslers.

'If you already know who the murderer is,' said Eve impatiently, 'can't you just skip to the end and arrest them, instead of boring the rest of us with how clever you are.' Sniggers rippled their side of the room, except for Sara, who remained strangely quiet.

'And if you do know who the murderer is,' said Theo, 'wouldn't it be better to take them by *surprise,* rather than listing all the reasons you suspect them. Otherwise they might run away before you have even reached for the handcuffs.' Several more titters. Sara seemed unaware she was rubbing her arm again.

'Tais-toi!' Gallois swept a fearsome glance around the room. The poor Capitaine, thought Martin. Dear, simple, Gallois, so desperate he needed the solution spoon-fed to him. His partner looked less enthused. As did the Sinclairs.

'Captain, why do you indulge this?' said Tate. Beside him, Holly's face flushed.

'Come on, you know my record,' said Martin.

'Your *past* record,' said Aimee.

'I was right about Cammy,' pressed Martin, 'I got this.'

Gallois glared across at Martin, tapping his fingers on the mantlepiece. 'I will let you have your moment, before I interject.'

'I think it will be a spectacular flop again,' said Aimee. 'No offence.'

'Lots taken.'

'Come on, Martini, you've got this,' Aubrey shouted.

'Coraggio!' said Renzo, lighting one of his cigars.

Bolstered, Martin began: 'Before we come to the D.O.T. mistletoe murders, there's something else to clear up. Too many other crimes getting in the way, distracting me.'

'Like my missing candle!' cried Eve.

'Right. And the Lafite theft is solved, so let's crack the last other mystery before we focus on D.O.T.'

'What could be more important than the identity of the murderer?' puffed Renzo.

'How about the abduction of your daughter from the top of Broad Crag,' replied Martin. The cigar fell to the floor.

'The sinister snatching of Sara Brambilla,' murmured Sven, shovelling a new pack of gummy bears into his mouth.

'But that case is solved, you found her,' said Renzo,

gripping Sara's hand, 'she is sitting here beside me.'

'Yes, but not who was her actual kidnapper. What was behind it? And why did we never hear back from the kidnapper once he was paid?'

'Because he was greedy, got what he wanted?' said Sven.

'Who?' Sara whispered to the now-smouldering sheepskin rug.

'Finbar Elmwood.'

'The witness who died before he could give a statement?' frowned Sven.

'The chance elderly witness, died of heatstroke in his cab before I could interview him.' Swirling round his translucent drink, Martin swallowed the remainder of his Scotch. 'Finbar Elmwood's name always stuck in my head. Why would an elderly cab driver be hanging round the fifth-highest mountain in England? You don't get many mountaineers taking taxis to base camp. He didn't live nearby either, so what was he doing up there? We checked with the taxi rank and there'd been no jobs in the area. There was zero connection between him and Sara. Quite the conundrum. But then, I like solving conundrums. Best guess, he'd been hired by somebody to undertake the kidnapping. But who?'

Screw it, he poured himself a second glass of the whisky; now amber clear. Not to drink, just to hold, the comfort of knowing it was there for him. Always.

Martin continued: 'So who hired Elmwood? Elmwood… Elmwood, where've I heard that name on tour? Care to answer, Noel?'

'Why me?' asked Noel shiftily.

'When we first met on the coach, you said you'd made your fortune in antiques. Specifically, a mahogany duck from *Elmwood* & Flannery Antiquities.'

'Elmwood must be a pretty common name, kid,' leered Morton.

'Elmwood put me on alert,' Martin's eyes bored into a shamefaced Noel, 'so when you asked me to randomly test your memory on which birds you'd seen each month, it wasn't so much random as me precisely picking the same month as the kidnapping. June.'

'June? Peregrine falcon, buzzard, raven, red grouse, ring ouzel and golden eagle. So what?' said Noel defiantly. 'A lot of those birds are scattered throughout the world all year.'

'But not the golden eagle. Sara said she saw one just before she was kidnapped. The only place in England apparently. I searched online and she's right. The Haweswater valley is the only English location of the golden eagle. And, correct me if I'm wrong, but Broad Crag is pretty close to Haweswater. All those birds you listed live there. So, last June you were in the same location as the Brambillas.'

The room stiffened.

'You've looked spectacularly awkward around Renzo since we arrived here. When I asked Renzo why, he said you'd made a "calamitous decision"; the exact phrase you had said to me on the coach. And, incidentally, in the same breath as that phrase, how you were wishing you'd taken "the job into your own hands and out of his liver-spotted hands". Would those be the same liver-spotted hands that Sara recalled?'

'Wait, so, Renzo knew?' asked Aubrey.

'I'm afraid Renzo orchestrated it,' said Martin, turning miserably to his friend. 'When I asked Mary if you'd any financial problems, she told us how you urgently needed a cash injection six months ago, but that it's resolved now.'

'I told you the same,' said Renzo, 'when you first arrived.'

'But not where that cash injection came from. Tell me, does kidnap insurance cover ransom reimbursement?' Renzo nodded at the burnt rug. 'One million. Used to prop up your business and fund your New York restaurant.' A smaller nod to the floor, and the group stared between them in amazement.

'Renzo hired Noel to fake a kidnapping for the insurance money. Noel recruited that old geezer. Next time you pick a kidnapper, Noel, choose one that's not a ninety-year-old man.'

'Hey look, my bench is limited,' protested Noel, his face

creased in anguish, 'I don't know a lot of dodgy blokes. Renzo asked me for a favour, so I set him up.'

'Sounds a simple plan, Renzo. You two distanced yourself from the details, plausible deniability, gave the kidnapper instructions not to harm her, got your money, so now Sara can safely return. The perfect crime. Only, suddenly Finbar's gone missing, there's no word from him. Worse still, we find him, died of old age, heart attack, too much exertion in the heat. That's why you were so relaxed at the start, Renzo, and so frenzied after you heard of his death. Because now nobody knows where Sara's hidden.'

'Papà? How, how could you do that?' breathed Sara, dropping his hand, tears sparkling.

Reddening, Renzo attempted to speak but the words were stuck in his throat. 'Sara... I'm... sorry.' But it was too late. The veil lifted, Sara stared at Renzo, seeing her father clearly for the first time.

'Your daughter lost an eye. She could have died of starvation if we hadn't found her.'

'But we did find her! Noel searched every corner of Broad Crag and the *polizia* searched the towns. I got the police chief to put their best man on it, and he gave me you, and you found her, I knew you would.'

Martin was far from reassured. Neither were the guests nor a heartbroken Sara, who clutched the sofa for support. Something had broken between father and daughter.

'I didn't know what would happen,' he implored. 'Noel vouched for him. She was supposed to be in safe hands. How was I supposed to know... I hoped we could move on, that nobody need know.'

Martin gazed intently at Sara. 'I wondered if you must suspect already, on some subconscious level, given your aggression playing croquet?'

'So, that is why she did it?' said Theo, leaning forward.

'What?' said Martin, startled.

'The mistletoe killings?' said Theo.

'Of course, revenge!' cried Aubrey. 'She already knows and is lashing out against her father's empire!' Suddenly realising what she'd blurted, the insensitivity, Aubrey said quickly: 'Oh, I'm sorry, Sara.'

'That's ok,' she said with a sad smile. 'You, I forgive.'

'Perhaps we should come onto the murders, Moretti,' said Gallois, gripping the back of an armchair. The main event.

'Yep, yep,' agreed Martin, glancing down at his Scotch and pleased to see he'd abstained from drinking any of it. 'The key to solving these mistletoe murders is the second death. Mary Oblet, killed with a blunt and alcoholic instrument. She informed us all where she'd be at midnight. Somebody crept down behind her into the cellar, where she was murdered; battered by the Vecchio Maniero, 1969.'

As well as Gallois and Aimee, two burly officers were positioned by the living room door. There'd be no escape for the guilty. 'Any one of us could have done it,' said Martin, turning to the Algerian coach driver. 'Omar, did you take advantage of France's apparent open-door policy? Simply to use the facilities.' Omar shook his head at the rhetorical question. '*Non*, so you say.'

'How about Joseph?' said Martin, turning to the boy sitting nervously between his parents. 'Our sneaky little liar.'

'Careful, Moretti,' his father said warningly.

'Then there is Tate and Holly. The D.O.T. poison pen letter is potentially suggestive with its transatlantic comments.'

'Noel, have you seen how suspect, how awkward, how guilty you've looked the longer the tour goes on? And it'd be dangerous to dismiss you purely because you've already been busted tonight. What Holly calls the "double-down double-bluff"; confessing to a lesser crime. After all, where there's smoke, there's fire,' said Martin, eyeing the singed rug.

'Same for the Kesslers. Eve left her room at the crucial time on the night of Mary's murder. And after the Lafite deception, how can we trust her? What else are you capable of? As for her partner in crime—if Eve left her room, maybe Morton slipped out also? Owner of Mistletoe Atlantic Trading, he's the master of sneaking up on people. And, well, y'know, generally being a creepy, freaky guy.'

Now Martin had his Hercule Poirot moment, the party raptly sat on the edge of their sofas. 'And I'm sure, Theo, with your painting, you were not thumping that whole time.'

'No, he was,' said Eve ruefully. 'Much as I'd like to shift the focus from me, his frickin' thumps were constant all night! I still have the bags under my eyes as evidence.'

'Ok, but making death threats against his own wife—'

'Yes, but not Jimmy,' said Theo.

'True,' conceded Martin. Swivelling round, his hand knocked into Aubrey's glass, spilling her red wine over the table.

'Are you ok?' asked Holly, as Aubrey quickly mopped up.

'I'm fine.' Martin felt light-headed, the moment apparently more overwhelming than he'd anticipated. Shaking away the wooziness, he pressed on.

'Aubrey, where were you during the livers in the punchbowl incident? And the coach scratches? Then there's Sven, with your pink tie and your suspect glances at Mary during archery.' Out of gummy bears, the Swede's hands were twisting in his lap. 'But again, no such glances at Jimmy. Nevertheless, both deaths would help drum up your required publicity for the wine launch. And Renzo—if Sven wouldn't do it for the publicity—you would because, no offence, you're are a bit of a psychopath. And how far does the apple fall, Sara? Maybe it's like Aubrey says: revenge on your father's vineyard to punish him for the botched kidnap?'

Just one suspect left to call out. Pekoe had positioned himself in the far corner again, half-hidden in pipe smoke. 'Pekoe, I can not rule you out, your bitterness when talking about Renzo's business... and if anyone has the mettle, it's an ex-Gurkha.'

'But how could anybody get past Aubrey in the tasting

room?' asked Sven.

'Why don't we let the killer tell us,' said Martin. 'It had to be one of you twelve, so which one?'

'I have a thirteenth suspect,' said Gallois.

'I would agree with you but then we'd both be wrong,' said Martin. 'Call it a hunch but—'

'I told you, I don't like hunches,' said Gallois. 'The thirteenth—'

'It's not Joseph,' said Martin, 'despite his strength.'

'No, not Joseph,' said Gallois smugly.

'And this is based on another confession, is it? Because once again, you've completely ignored forensics.'

'There's no need for forensics when there is clear evidence of the murderer.'

'Who?'

'You.'

'Good joke,' said Martin, turning his back firmly on Gallois. 'I can now reveal that D.O.T. stood for... Daughters of Temperance!'

'What is that to do with anything?' said Gallois. 'I don't care about D.O.T or your daughters of reverence.'

'It's temperance. And you should care because Sara is not the only daughter of note on this tour.'

'What I care about is how, when we lifted the body of Mary Oblet, we found this.' Gallois dangled a 1973 silver Omega De Ville dress watch. 'No wonder you didn't want anyone to move the body,'

'Give me back my watch, Gallois.'

'*Non*, it is evidence.'

'It's the only thing my father—'

'How did your watch get underneath her?' said Aimee.

'I don't know,' said Martin, feeling another wave of wooziness.

'You obviously lost it in the struggle with her,' said Gallois, 'but we can discuss this further when you are behind bars.'

'You're not seriously going to arrest me?' said Martin incredulously. Suddenly swaying, his eyes closed but he forced them open.

'Your blackouts are more extreme than you realise, Monsieur Moretti,' said Gallois, insincerely tender. 'You were desperate for your old job back, so you create a case only you can solve.'

'But I know who it really is and I can prove it.' Martin's eyes span around the room for the murderer, but the room kept spinning, faster and faster, his power of speech rapidly fading. So sleepy. Gallois' face blurred in and out of focus. So very sleepy.

'He's sloshed again!' said someone, possibly Tate.

'Beurré,' said Theo.

'I'm not as think as you drunk I am,' slurred Martin. Stumbling over to the blazing fireplace was a struggle, his head propped heavily against the wall. What was happening? Had he drunk more than he had meant to? No, he'd only had the one whisky tonight; the second glass in hand still full. He urgently needed fresh air.

'You believe me, don't you?' Martin begged the party. There were just five steps between him and the picture window, but it was an acre away; his concrete feet no longer under his command. 'You gotta believe me.' Martin could still win over the room, a jury of his peers. He had important things to tell them. Before discovering Mary, the smell in the corridor… that citrus blast. And then there was the rope.

But he caught the same disappointment on their faces as the first summation, more than a few sharing Pekoe's pained look of disbelief. 'From now on,' said the Ghurka. 'I shall call you *ghadhaa.*'

'Sounds noble,' slurred Martin.

'It means donkey.'

Sven shook his head. 'In Swedish, you're a *rövhatt.*'

'That sounds better.'

'It means asshat.'

'How about in English we all just call me a hero.'

'Hero!' spat Aimee. 'What the hell for?'

'Sacrificing my liver to solve this case.'

'Ach, you've been tit-faced even before the murders,' said Noel, miming him drink from a bottle.

'I'm a visionary,' said Martin.

'Vous avez le droit de vous taire,' snapped Aimee. *'Tout ce que vous direz pourra être retenu contre vous devant la justice.'*

'Ooh la la!' slurred Martin angrily. *'Excusez-moi, où est la bibliothèque?'*

'It translates as: you have the right to remain silent. Anything you say may be used against you in court.' The Capitaine grabbed hold of him with a vice-like grip, almost snapping his forearm. Martin had to escape. How? Where? The cellar was a dead end, and he was in no state to barge past the burly officers.

Suddenly, without thinking, Martin tossed his whisky into the fire. A roaring whoosh of flame leapt out at them, Gallois loosening his grip. Dragging his feet over to the window, Martin slid it open, the cold, black-oil night failing to revive him.

'Vous êtes en état d'arrestation!'

Lifting one foot onto the frame took all his effort. It was a ten-foot drop onto the white slide. If the snow directly beneath him wasn't soft, he'd break his legs on impact. If he hit the slope at a bad angle, he'd snap his neck.

Lieutenant Aimee strode forward with handcuffs. 'Wrists out,' she ordered.

'Vous êtes en état d'arrestation!'

Looking down at the long, lethal slalom, running a kilometre into the veil of mist below, Martin recoiled in terror. He could not die. For Jimmy and Mary's sake, he could not die.

'Vous allez crever en taule!'

Hearing footsteps behind him, Martin leant forward, staring into the dark, and jumped.

'Merde.'

Moretti Christmas Newsletter

Status: **Draft - Version 4**

Date: December 24th (1 day until deadline)

Happy Holidays!

One empty soul up for rent. Amazing views of Hades. Non-smoker.

I tell people I'm happy, super happy, game-show host happy, but I'm not.

In text speak - I may LOL, but actually I'm COTI. Crying on the inside. I've cried every night from November 2020, and haven't eaten properly since. My stomach's too jangled up in nerves.

Sod all those well-being bullcrap books.

"Darkest before the dawn" is just advice on when's best to steal a car.

"You want the rainbow, put up with the rain," laughed Noah, watching them all drown.

"The world is a fine place and worth fighting for." Wrong and wrong.

"Happiness can be found even in the darkest of times if only one remembers to turn on the light." Until next month's leccy bill.

Just keep swimming. Just keep swimming. Just keep swimming into the propellor, Dory.

You can't fire me God. I quit. Don't judge me, I've won this battle many times; just lost the war.

FML, Martin.
p.s. consider this my note

34

If The World Perished Twice

Martin was somewhere cold. A crypt, mausoleum, or the mortuary slab? He didn't have the strength to open his eyes. That, or his eyeballs were frozen shut. A nauseating, twisting, feeling in the pit of Martin's stomach was growing; something catastrophic had recently occurred, but he didn't want to remember what it was just yet.

Prizing his frosted lashes open, he found himself in a large dilapidated barn. That explained the sickly-sweet stink of hay and manure. Yet there were no pigs or cows or horses around. The closest thing to life were the icy strands of an empty cobweb in the rafters above. It was beyond freezing. With no gloves, hat or coat, he'd never felt so cold. Snowflakes whistled through the cracks in the wooden walls, building him a shoebox-tall snow pillow and, ironically, offering some form of shelter from the gnawing wind.

What had happened? Martin's whole body ached; one dull, constant throb. He must have cracked at least two ribs. Had Tate hit him again? Sprawled across a dirty-clumped bed of straw, his right ankle hurt to move. A bad sprain or broken? Martin feared worse—torn ligaments—which, from experience, took longer to recover than a break. Tugging his trousers up, his legs were covered in puffed-up, dark purple bruises, too tender to touch. What the hell happened? How had he ended up here?

The window! He'd climbed onto the window ledge! With excruciating effort, Martin lifted his leg onto an old milking stool, packing a fistful of snow around the swelling. He'd jumped from the Elysium window! Hazy images flashed to mind: torpedoing down an icy mountain, buffeted from snowbank to snowbank, crashing through bracken, his kidneys cushioning the blow. Also, mumbling and drooling on the pink plastic seat of a car. Possibly, a taxi? Though it didn't explain how he'd ended up here, let alone string two words together for the driver. But then, this wasn't his first rodeo as a fully-functioning alcoholic. Yep, that was what he was.

He scanned the room for a first aid kit; finding nothing but rusted shovels, brooms and pitchforks. Martin must look terrible. If he saw a mirror, he'd smash it; surely eighteen months into a seven-year term already. He'd jumped from the window. But why? And then the full horror hit him. The humiliation, recrimination, the abject failure of delivering his summation. The murderer was running rings around him. For all his bumps and cuts, Martin felt more bruised on the inside. Jesus. If he had the energy, he'd slap himself for being so bloody melodramatic. But the killer was right. It wasn't two red herrings, it was three. And it turns out Martin was the third. Very clever. Cleverer than Martin anyway.

Would there be a manhunt for him? Definitely. The Gendarmerie had everything they needed. As well as Martin fleeing the scene, Gallois had his timepiece "evidence". The murderer must've removed it during the wine vat struggle, placing it under Mary later that night. Devious. His father's Omega De Ville, gone. Another disconnection from the world. And now in the grasp of the moronic Gallois, whose entire basis for arresting someone was whether their watch was in the vicinity. And of course the Capitaine, allergic to intelligence, had swallowed it hook line and sinker. In the land of idiots, Gallois would be king; proof it's possible to live without a brain. Some drink from the fountain of knowledge; Gallois gargled.

Renzo's words— *trust me, Martin, I will reunite you with your father's watch*—sounded a little sinister now. Renzo Brambilla... yet another reason for Martin to be jubilant: his only friend in the world was most probably psycho.

More words tumbled to mind; concerning his insured wine business: *yes, if it fails, Renzo would actually make a tidy sum.*

Where had it all gone wrong? Maybe Martin should have taken a different approach with the interviews, or gathered more evidence, or reconstructed the sequence of events, instead of wasting time firing arrows, whacking croquet balls and drinking Gibson martinis. Maybe he should've followed the methods of the *Section de Recherche*; to gently draw out the truth. Well, he was pretty sure he'd get a chance to discuss it with Gallois as soon as he battered down the barn door. It wouldn't be long now. The Gendarmerie might not have gone to the press, but Gallois would have made sure Martin's face found its way into every police station and hospital within the Auvergne-Rhône-Alpes region.

The first cars of the day were starting up; the whine of an engine, the rasp of a scraper across a frosted windshield. Martin looked through the crack but all he could see were skeletal tree branches bending under the weight of snow. Did he also hear the crunch of footsteps outside the barn?

Seven days ago, Martin thought he'd hit rock bottom at the Eagle Hotel after being fired. Apparently, rock bottom has a basement. Having died by the roaring fireplace last night, he might as well really die here as a giant ice cube. It was all over now anyway. Tomorrow, Radnor would return from leave and file his termination. Tomorrow, the Moretti family would sit down for their Christmas morning pancakes and read out the Round-robin; the Round-robin still missing his update. Having nothing worthwhile to write, he was unlikely to hit tonight's 24th December 11:59 p.m. deadline. Another failure.

Cold to his bones, Martin calmly watched the ice forming on the sleeve of his torn jumper. What would his ex-wife make of him now? When she'd first left him, he'd been so lonely, but at least he had his job. Now he didn't even have that. No job, no family letter, and he could kiss goodbye to a life of detecting after last night's fiasco. A new low. Was this a taste of his future, sleeping rough, another anonymous sleeping bag in a doorway? Nah, he'd be dead before then. Good.

His subconscious attempted to rally him. *Find things to be grateful for.* Well, hypothermia was one of the best ways to die; his body being so cold he'd feel a toasty warm glow as his blood retreated to the central organs. He would drift off in a snowy doze, never to wake up. Tempting. Then again, hunger was just as likely; his gut was churning, his stomach eating itself. All those groaning buffets and loaded sideboards; he should have guzzled more. Closing his eyes, Martin fantasised about the Christmas roast he'd be missing back home. As a Jewish-Italian family, Christmas day was always an interfaith feast of seven fishes, a juicy beef brisket, fried chicken, cassola, as well as the glistening dark-golden turkey. Behind a bucket, Martin found a stale packet of Canistrelli biscuits; less a crispy hazelnut flavour, more soggy and tasting like nail varnish. Wolfing them down, his stomach still gurgled. Probably the drugs in him.

Outside, the brittle crunching of footsteps came closer. So, the Gendarmerie had found him. No amount of sway from Renzo could save him this time.

What had he been given last night? Some sort of sedative or sleeping pill would be Martin's guess; crushed into a powder at the bottom of his glass and camouflaged within the cloudy Scotch. Who did he know on tour with sleeping pills? After that, he never stood a chance; his feeble mind defenceless to the Capitaine's accusations. So now he was on the lam. Public enemy number one. A rogue fugitive on the run. Notorious. What a way to spend Christmas Eve. Some small consolation —Martin wasn't the only infamous character to come from a humble stable. But at least Black Beauty had a happy ending.

Through the stillness and silence, he heard the soft crunch of snow by the barn door. Here comes the fuzz, Capitaine Gallois undoubtedly leading the charge.

The tall double doors swung open. But it wasn't Gallois. It wasn't even Renzo.

35

If The Cap Fits

It was Aubrey Dalton.

There she stood, his faux fur hooded Everest parka jacket in one hand, a shopping bag in the other.

'What are you doing here?'

'Helping you out,' she said, throwing his coat at him; hat and gloves in the pocket. 'Baiting a serial killer. Bringing the homicidal maniac to us.'

'What! Why?' Martin craned his neck in alarm, but she was alone.

'They're bound to kill again, yeah?'

'Yes!' Martin nodded, panic rising.

'If we walk the streets, it might draw 'em out. With any luck, they might try and exterminate you again.'

'This is helping me out?'

'You're welcome,' said Aubrey, brushing chicken feathers from his jumper. Currently, hypothermia sounded the best option. 'Come on, put your coat on. Snow kinda freaks me out, seeing you shivering like that.' Martin remained motionless.

'How'd you find me?' he asked.

'During croquet, when I typed my number into your phone, I also switched your Snapchat live location on.'

'Stalk much, Little Miss Nosy?!'

'Not nosy; interested, in catching the killer with you,' said Aubrey. 'And I'm also the one who ordered you an Uber last night, so let's call it even shall we, Martin.' It was the first time she had ever called him Martin, and it was this, more than anything else, that made him sit up. Aubrey stared down at him, struggling with his coat and hat. 'Wow, jumping from that window was wild! The human bobsleigh! It was so dark out, nobody could see where you were after thirty yards, but my Snapchat showed me you landed on a farm track.'

'Did Gallois say anything after I left?'

'He just stared out the window and then looked at Aimee and said "*le* chase begins".'

'Don't do the accent. And if he catches me, I'll thank him for it,' said Martin miserably. Even jacketed up, getting thrown in jail seemed a better, warmer, prospect.

'But he'll arrest you.'

'So?'

'So, you'd be in jail.'

'What's not to like—free food, free board, free bed.'

'Free anal rape.'

'Gallois will figure out the real killer, eventually,' said Martin, rubbing his ankle.

'Well, we need to hurry up because after they left, there's been another development. The gun's gone missing, the one from the kitchen cabinet. I think that's why Renzo took us to town so early; safety in shoppers.'

'No surprise,' said Martin. You didn't need Eve's brain to remember the code: 0-0-7.

'I picked you up some sleuth-tonic,' she said, jangling her bag, 'in case you're still figuring whodunnit.'

'I know who it is,' said Martin, nettled. 'The same person I was gonna say last night, until I ballsed it up.' He'd need more than a grand announcement now. Any chance the Gendarmerie would listen to him was long gone. Besides, knowing was one thing, proving it was quite another.

Aubrey raised two bottles. 'You wanna drink? I've got absinthe—'

'An 80% proof hallucinogenic might be a little damaging at eight a.m.'

'The vodka then, much more healthy,' she said, tossing him the bottle.

Martin read the label. 'Kiskilla Kek Bitchen?'

'I think it's Russian for "lost liver". It's actually quite drinkable,' said Aubrey. Playing with the bottle, Martin stared at it thoughtfully. 'What's wrong?'

'Hmmm, one's too many and a thousand's not enough, if you know what I mean?'

'No. What do you mean?'

'It's like at the police Christmas party last year, Radnor's handing out these vodka lime-jelly shots. Amongst the top brass, I know I shouldn't indulge in a jelly shot. But I do. And I get that happy, giddy euphoria. But that euphoria only lasts for, like, a minute. So I knocked back another jelly shot. And I want more, like a jello-chugging machine. It's my whole dinner. Starter, main and dessert, jelly shot, jelly shot, jelly shot, jelly shot, jelly shot, jelly shot.'

'How many jelly shots is that?' said Aubrey.

'A lot. Anyway, one vomit into the Superintendent's wife's handbag and I'm doing Bikeability at primary schools for a month.' His hand wavered over the lid. 'Anyway, I thought you didn't want me drinking?'

'I don't but I do,' said Aubrey. 'Just until we solve this case. You're rubbish sober.'

'You believe me?' Martin tried lifting himself up, but the ache of his battered body was too much. 'You believe I wasn't drunk last night?'

'I saw that you weren't twenty minutes before,' said Aubrey. 'Did you get spiked?'

'Yeah,' said Martin, 'I'm lucky it wasn't something more lethal like Châteauneuf-du-Pape.'

She pulled him up. A sharp pain seared through his leg. 'Come on, there's a tap outside you can wash from.' As Aubrey walked out, something fell from her pocket onto the floor. Martin picked it up. It was a mistletoe leaf.

Events were escalating. If the gun really was gone, things were about to get a lot worse. So how to finally expose the killer? Unscrewing the cap, he knew exactly what to do.

36

Arrête-Moi Si Tu Peux

'Worst. Case. Ever,' declared Martin. 'I'm gonna write a letter of complaint to the French tourist board.'

Hoods up, they had limped briskly from the rural outskirts into Bonneville town centre.

'Cheer up,' said Aubrey, 'you know who it is and said you can prove it.'

'Yeah, but they keep outfoxing me,' muttered Martin. 'I don't wanna be outfoxed, I wanna be in-foxed.' Aubrey glanced nervously at his bottle of vodka.

'Oh please,' she said, 'you've got the element of surprise. You've got me helping you, for some goddamn reason. We should be celebrating our upcoming triumph.'

'Worst. Case. Ever.'

Arms linked, they crossed over a bridge festooned with a brunt of European flags; none of them fluttering on account of being frozen solid. Hark back six days, Martin's biggest problem was enduring Sven's jokes about the Swiss flag being a big plus. Simpler times.

'Why did you order the Uber driver to drop me so far away,' grumbled Martin, a stabbing pain with each step. He could do with Gallois' walking stick.

'I kinda figured you might want somewhere remote,' said Aubrey defensively.

The compacted snow on the pavement was hard and slippery where last-minute shoppers had stomped across it all morning. Everything was sore, and not solely from his cresta run. His skin was chapped and numb from the same alpine air that stung his nostrils. But for the first time in what felt forever, Martin was away from the vineyards. He was out in the real world with real people; as if he'd just exited Disney World. On their way into town, they'd hobbled past overloaded postal workers, delivery drivers, sprout pickers, kids sledging down the long white hills, and snowmen in the front yards of cottages, clouds of hot air swirling from their chimneys.

'Does anyone know you went looking for me?'

Aubrey shook her head. 'Nobody else went to the candy store.'

'Did you get your reindeer corn?' asked Martin, stomach still growling.

She shook her head again. 'Ran outta money.' A police car sped by. Lowering their hoods, they slipped down an empty side street, the shutters on the houses thankfully shut. Christmas Eve wouldn't stop their manhunt, but hopefully there'd be slightly less officers on the roads.

'Tate, Noel and Theo are helping the cops patrol the area. Noel's insisting he take the lead, saying his eagle eyes make him a better detective than you. I think they just wanted an excuse to drive one of Renzo's supercars. I took one myself,' Aubrey grinned.

'Where is it?'

'Not far now. I parked outside a realtor's office to stay covertly stealth.'

'Once we get back to the car, I'll jump in the boot, and you drive me to the British embassy. I'll sort this whole mess out from there.'

'The boot?'

'The trunk,' said Martin. 'After I'm dropped off, you head back to the shops so we don't tip them off.' A chestnut seller on the corner was giving him the evil eye. Did he know something? Was a wanted poster out already?

'So who is it, the murderer?' asked Aubrey.

'If you're going back to the group, I don't want to put you in danger. Any facial tell might alert the killer, and then you'll be next.' The sun vanished behind a dark cloud as another police car drove by, so they ducked into a narrow alley. His ankle was agony. 'Worst case—'

'Don't say it. You think I'm not cold and scared? I'm terrified and freezing,' trembled Aubrey. 'I want to go home to California. I'm a solar-powered person.'

'Nice earrings,' said Martin of the holly berry earrings gleaming each side of her flushed cheeks.

'Thanks. Eve bought 'em for all us gals for tonight's party. That's where we're heading later,' she pointed across to where—amongst the rolling grey clouds—spikes of ancient granite thrust upwards, 'to Renzo's cabin, for the grand unveiling of the most infamous bottled lightning ever, apparently. We're travelling there in another of Renzo's own investments.' Aubrey gestured to where a rattling cable car was creeping up into the mist.

Leaning on Aubrey, Martin rummaged through his pockets as they limped through the streets. His newly-cracked phone was on 1% battery before immediately dying on him. 'Can you phone Renzo for me?' Calling, she handed him the phone.

'*Ciao,* Aubrey! Where are you? I'm in Boutique Campistron.'

'Renzo, it's me.'

'Martin! *È un miracolo!*' cried Renzo, piercing both the phone's speaker and his eardrum. Then, in a hushed tone: 'What's going on? Where are you? Are you ok?'

'Don't worry, I'm fine, but I need you to pick something up for me from Elysium.' Martin gave instructions as he and Aubrey shuffled past a chorus of carol singers outside the Catholic church, emerging into the town square car park. Could he trust Renzo?

Reaching the realtor's, Martin immediately stepped back. A dozen admirers were gawking around Aubrey's vehicle. Her choice of a Silver Bentley Continental GT wasn't quite "covertly stealth". In fact, it's a wonder how James Bond successfully tailed anybody in his Aston Martin. Picking up a honey-baked ham baguette from the local boulangerie, Martin tore into it while they waited for the crowds to disperse. How long before someone recognised him? Aubrey watched from the window as he warmed his hands by their oven. The heat didn't reach his fingers. Assuming he still had fingers. Anxious, Martin checked his wrist for the time, then remembered Gallois had requisitioned it. Even if Martin did clear his name, it'd probably be years of red tape to obtain back. What a mess.

Eventually the pack moved on, and Martin climbed into the boot. So far so good. 'Am I going to need a sick bag?' he teased.

'Says the punk in the trunk,' chuckled Aubrey, leaning in to inspect how much of his sleuth-tonic he'd actually finished. 'Shouldn't you drink up before we reach the embassy?'

'It's two hours away, I think I've got plenty...' What was that movement? It couldn't be. 'Aubrey! Look out!' Too late; Aubrey was violently shoved inside with him. The boot slammed shut, the solid thud of the lock sealing them into darkness. Total darkness.

'Ok,' said Aubrey, panic-stricken, 'worst case ever.'

37

Red Light

'I'm having a heart attack! I'm going to die!'

'Aubrey, you're not having a heart attack.' Martin couldn't assure her on the second part. For the hundredth time, he smacked the lid for help. He knew, however, they'd already be on the outskirts; the only sound above the engine was their clattering of snow-chains.

'I'm not gonna make it! I can't breathe!'

Incarcerated. No way out. How could he tell her to "relax" in such circumstances? 'You're ok, you're doing good, Aubrey,' said Martin as calmly as he could. Their biggest enemy wasn't brain damage from a sharp turn or the mad driver's intentions; it was panic. 'I'm here with you, we'll make it out.' Her breathing became more frenzied. They mustn't hyperventilate. They mustn't pass out.

Wedged between the wall of the boot and his body pressed against her back, Martin could feel her shaking and noticed he was not. Understandable. Civilians didn't need to armour-plate their minds on a daily basis. 'Breathe from here.' Martin placed a hand on her stomach. 'Not your chest.' Aubrey slapped his hand away. Brushing past her pocket, it was filled with mistletoe. 'Breathe deeply.' No easy task. With space for four large suitcases—or two terrified humans—the air was stuffy, pungent with petrol and aluminium. Yet while they were moving, Martin felt safe. It was only when their crazed chauffeur stopped the vehicle...

Gasping for oxygen in the dark, Aubrey said: 'Where the hell are we going? Why've they taken us?'

'Maybe just wants to use the carpool lane?'

'Don't joke.'

'Fine,' said Martin, 'they're probably driving round to find somewhere quiet to.... talk with us.'

She wasn't fooled. Soaked with perspiration, her whole body stiffened. 'And until then, we make our peace with God from in this trunk?'

'You mean boot.'

'Let me get this straight,' Aubrey flared, 'we're captive in the back of a serial killer's car, who's racing somewhere secluded to murder us, and you're worried if it's a boot or trunk?!'

'Sorry.' Bumping along in their metal coffin, Renzo had got his wish: Martin and Aubrey forced together, partners in crime. *There's no length I wouldn't go to find happiness for you both.* How long was this "happiness" to last?

'Please, Martin, take my mind off it. Test me on my Master Sommelier exam.'

'I don't know what to ask.'

'Anything. Please.'

'Alright... what colour is Beaujolais?'

'Something harder.'

'I don't know what to ask. I'm not an expert on all this aromatic appellation stuff.'

'I need distracting.'

'Alright.' Martin was thinking fast. Though calm, Martin's muscles were twitching. A promising sign his body was healing? Unlikely. 'Tell me another of those mythical wine tales.'

'Ok, ok, ok, er... did you know, it's said that the world's original wine glasses were moulded on the shape of Helen of Troy's breasts.' Martin felt her shifting, wriggling around to get comfortable.

'So, she was an A-cup.'

'Seems you're an expert on some things.' said Aubrey, her breathing slowing. 'It's 'cause the ancient Greeks wanted to shape it on the most beautiful woman in the world.

However, when Marie Antoinette came along, she created a new champagne coupe glass moulded on her own breasts. Being, y'know, more voluptuous, the wine glass went from an A-cup to a D-cup, changing the shape of the glass entirely and, basically, how much wine a glass could hold.'

'History's first girl fight!' smirked Martin.

'Based on the boobs *du jour*,' snickered Aubrey. 'It's definitely a myth, but it's a nice story.'

The conversation ending, the silence inside their casket was deafening; and Aubrey's breathing became rapid again.

'Hey, I thought you're supposed to be pinpointing the perfect wine for me?'

'OK, yes, yes, let's find your wine tribe.' Her whole body relaxed. 'Favourite spice?'

'Oregano.'

'Favourite dessert.'

'Cheesecake.'

'Favourite beer?'

'Belgian. A Kwak beer in a Kwak glass or Duvel in any glass.' Tipping towards her, the Bentley was climbing upwards. The mountain pass. Great. Let's add high altitude into the mix.

Aubrey's shoulders tensed again. 'I don't know, maybe it's all pointless. At the end of the day, it's just a liquid in a glass.'

'It brings a lot of people joy,' said Martin.

'I was never good at anything before wine. Since my first Sonoma County Zinfandel, I've neglected family, lost friends, and all for nothing when I fail my exam.' Nonsense, thought Martin, they'd be dead long before she stepped into that exam hall. Dead within the hour. 'Anyway, how 'bout you, Chief Inspector Moretti?'

'How about me what?'

'Well, are you a nice person?'

'I'd get off my seat for a pensioner, but I wouldn't go so far as to call myself nice.'

'Come on, open up. I need the chit chat distraction.'

'Like what?'

'Ok... why'd you become a cop? What's your favourite season? How about music? If you had a time machine, where'd you go back to?' Was she still quizzing him purely about his taste buds?

'What was the first question?'

'Why'd you become a cop?'

'I was between misdemeanours,' said Martin evasively.

'What's your favourite season?'

'Maybe... Spring, maybe.'

'How about music?'

'I hate Ed Sheeran. And AirPods. And especially AirPods playing Ed Sheeran.'

'If you had a time machine, where'd you go back to?'

'Easy. Ryder Cup, 2012. Rory McIlroy and Poulter's comeback.'

'Weren't you alive then?'

'Yeah, I just can't remember it.'

'Favourite country?'

'Australia.'

'Have you ever been?'

'No, but it looks like a good place to survive an ice age.'

Careering around another corner, they bumped heads. 'How about we survive this trunk first? This is supposed to be your job,' cried Aubrey, 'can't you get us out of here?'

'We're trapped,' grimaced Martin. 'Try Renzo again.'

'There's no signal.' But she kept the glow of her phone screen on. 'How did I let 'em creep up on me like that?" cursed Aubrey.

'At least you didn't accept the drink they offered,' said Martin, grinding his teeth. He knew the killer would be sneaky, but never anticipated *this* sneaky. So how to catch them? To quote Gallois, confession is key. But it wouldn't be the simple admission Renzo and Noel had offered up. Somehow, Martin must wheedle it out; *if* they ever escaped this death box. 'Hey, I've got a question for you. How come you're helping me?

Surely you didn't want to end up like this?'

'I didn't think it would end like *this!* I thought I'd get to act out one of those crime thrillers I love.'

'Come on.'

'Yeah, ok,' said Aubrey. 'Straight up, I didn't like what happened to you last night. It was just so… unfair. I felt, these deaths… they deserve justice. So, we've gotta get out of this!'

'Sure,' said Martin, 'got a screwdriver or a blowtorch on you?'

'I've got my waiter's friend corkscrew.'

'I'll put it on the reserve list. What you said just now, though… that's how I feel, when I see the victim, even as a kid I could never just stand by and do nothing; wouldn't be fair. It'd be unfair to let them get away with it. But this situation, I'm not smart enough,' fretted Martin, 'killer's outwitted me at every turn.'

'You were pretty smart with the botched kidnap,' said Aubrey. 'I can't believe that of Renzo. Poor Sara. When did you piece it together?'

'Croquet,' said Martin. 'How are they both?'

'I don't think they've spoken since. She didn't come shopping with us,' said Aubrey. 'What will happen to him and Noel?'

'They've broke a ton of laws. But, if I know Renzo —and I'm not sure I want to anymore— with his finances and connections, he'll escape prison. The hardest thing is the damage done to Sara,' lamented Martin. She said she'd danced until dawn. Two a.m. is not dawn.

'At least clears them out the field for murder.'

'It proves who snatched her, nothing else. You can't rule out any of them.'

'Have you suspected me of murder?' asked Aubrey.

'Have I suspected you of murder? Yes and no. Actually, just yes.'

'Why?' she demanded.

'Everyone who needles you,' said Martin, 'seems to come

undone.'

'That's not true!'

'So you weren't angry at Jimmys sexist comments?'

'No! Well...'

'How about Mary's sap-sucking bug lecture?'

'The glass of wine in her face was satisfaction enough,' said Aubrey. 'Do you trust me?'

'Well, you didn't tell me about the Snapchat snooping.'

'Of course I wasn't gonna say. You wouldn't even let me look at your passport photo. What is it, you've got a dodgy moustache?'

'Massive pornstache, but you ain't gonna see it.'

'I can't believe you thought D.O.T. was me.'

'Then what's with all the mistletoe in your pocket?'

'I didn't want the murderer having any more resources, so I went round the farmhouse and yanked it off every ceiling. Kinda obvious, yeah?'

'It's an interesting point,' conceded Martin.

'So, did the murderer really walk right past me? How?'

'Actually, that part was pretty clever. Eve—' With a jolt, Aubrey lurched towards Martin. The Bentley had stopped.

'What's happening?' gulped Aubrey. The driver's door opened and Martin swallowed too; his worst fears confirmed. There were no sounds of life above the howling wind. When to warn her? Now or at the last moment? The captives weren't bound or handcuffed. When the boot was unlocked, Martin could spring up.

But deep down he knew the lid wouldn't lift on this boot, this trunk, this dead man's chest. And now he heard a different sound. The cock of a gun. This was the end. Would his phone call from town be enough?

Two gunshots rang out with a sickening sliced sound into metal. Metal and more.

38

High Flying Birds

More bullets would punch through. Penetrate and perforate and puncture their riddled corpses. Another pair of lives lost to the mountains.

Two holes of light shined through but the light was blue, flashing, and now there were sirens. The Bentley started back up; the acceleration pulling the prisoners to the rear.

'Terwilligers,' cursed Aubrey.

'Sssh, no more wine talk,' whispered Martin. 'If they think we're dead, it gives us half a second to spring an attack when the lid opens.' But any hope of a stealth assault was wrecked by their loud groans tossed around the back, the driving becoming more erratic, reckless, speeding away from the police. Crazy maniac; they'd plummet off the cliff edge!

'We've gotta escape 'em,' hissed Aubrey.

Praying their car hugged the mountainside, it was a miracle the pair had made it this far. They were nothing more than fish in a barrel. At the cock of the gun, Martin had pushed Aubrey away before flattening himself against the boot wall, leaving a gap in the middle where the metal slugs had landed. And now, they'd been saved by a siren.

Straining his eyes through the peep hole, Martin whispered: 'Can you see anything out of yours?'

'Not much. You?'

'Not much.'

'I think it might be Noel's car, the Lamborghini,' said Aubrey. 'But with one of those portable police lights on top.' So, Deputy Noel Gillespie had joined the hunt, acting like one of his birds of prey. 'How much air have we got in here? It's getting stuffy.'

'Stay positive,' said Martin, 'we just got extra air supply.'

'Positive, yeah?' said Aubrey sarcastically. 'The killer's risking a car crash so he can murder us somewhere isolated, our source of light's from the police car here to arrest us, but— hey— at least we got bullet holes for oxygen.'

'Try Renzo again,' snapped Martin.

'Battery's dead.' Worse still, the siren was fading, the blue lights dimming. The killer was pulling away; inevitably bringing forward the time of their execution. Aubrey sensed it as well. 'I don't wanna die, Martin. I haven't lived my life. I've wasted it on wine.'

'A life on the lash is never trash,' said Martin. 'Trust me, the mouth of the happiest person on earth is filled with alcohol.' Their vehicle jerked to a stop and Aubrey tumbled on top of him. Biting his lip, Martin rolled underneath so he was closest the exit. The car boot opened, and Martin felt a SIG Sauer pistol shoved into his face; pressed so forcefully against his forehead it drew blood. Clenching his eyes, he braced for the gunshot.

Reopening them, however, the killer was gone. A distraction somewhere? Martin didn't wait to find out. Dropping onto the snowy road, a spike of cold raw air hit his lungs. They'd emerged into a swirling blizzard. Between wild flurries, Martin saw they were at the jagged roof of the world, sharp furious gusts threatening to rip them from the clifftop. So much for Pekoe's state of pure tranquillity. Promptly, Aubrey fell out of the boot and vomited over the snow tyres. No time to joke about feeling peaky.

The Bentley was parked immediately after a hairpin bend on the rim of the mountain. It was impossible to squint fifteen feet in front, but in the far distance Martin heard the blessed sirens. Thank God. Noel and the police were back on their trail. And now Martin saw the killer in the flickery blue light, saw what had distracted them. The crazed maniac was twisting a "Sharp Turn" road sign round the wrong way, so the arrow pointed from the left to the right, to the cliff edge!

The shriek of the Lamborghini brakes came too late, flying over the precipice and out into the night. Vodka bottle in hand, Martin tore off in the other direction, pulling Aubrey to her feet and along the road ahead. They didn't have time to watch the car plunge below, but they heard a horrific clang. Then a second clang and a third. Martin grimaced. Where's your feathers now, Noel?

Any second now the killer would return their attention to them. So they sprinted. Up and up, they made it round the next corner. Somehow his ankle kept up with Aubrey; adrenaline overriding any agony or fatigue. Run, goddamnit. Behind them, the engine began to rev. Run for your life. The Bentley roared closer. Chasing. Stalking. Gunning for them.

'Look, over there!' cried Aubrey. A crack in the mountain wall. Following her lead, Martin squeezed into the tight crevice. Shelter. Sanctuary. His fingertips and toes tingled in pain. Catching their first breath since the car boot, plumes of fogged breath threatened to give them away. Martin snatched a fistful of snow and shoved it into his mouth. Aubrey copied him. Pressing themselves against the cave wall, the Bentley zoomed by, the wheels churning up earth, ice and gravel as it sped past their narrow opening.

Martin waited for a few seconds, then peeked out. The ridge was silent. Above, he spotted the cable car station, a log cabin, and—more disturbingly—the Bentley racing towards the cabin. Surely the murderer's lust would be satisfied by the Lamborghini's dive into the valley? No. Of course they'd kill again. It's all they had left.

Exhausted, the duo started to climb. They'd no choice but to go on; up the long, rocky, winding road. If not, they would freeze to death; the relentless fury of the snowstorm engulfing them. Seek help. Save the cabin. Stop the killer.

Around the next corner, the blinding headlights of a parked car. But it wasn't the Silver Bentley Continental GT. It was the Alpine A110. Capitaine Gallois stepped out. He was ugly. He was rage. He was hate.

Steadied by Aubrey, Martin hobbled forwards. Seek help. Save the cabin. Stop the killer. Could he finally put his faith in the Gendarmerie? Desperate times call for desperate measures; fifty millilitre measures as minimum. Taking a giant swig of the vodka (no ice required), Martin recited his mantra.

Seek help. Save the cabin. Stop the killer.

39

Once There Was A Wine

'Confession is good for the soul, Monsieur Moretti,' yelled Gallois, his black tie flapping wildly in the blizzard, 'so confess!'

'Capitaine,' shivered Aubrey, 'where's your back up?'

'Arriving right now.' Gallois' eyes seemed to glow the same colour as the end of his cigarette. 'In a Lamborghini Miura.'

Martin's heart sank. 'No, Gallois, that just flew off the mountain with Noel inside.'

'Liar!' snarled the Capitaine. 'You have told me nothing but lies from the start.' Martin endeavoured to stay calm. Seek help. Save the cabin. Stop the—

THUMP. Gallois swung a powerful fist into Martin's stomach, knocking all the wind out of him. It wasn't far to fall, the snow was past their knees. And now Lieutenant Aimee leapt from the Alpine A110. Fighting the impulse to throw up, Martin was jostled into handcuffs. Plastic ones, from the pinch of it. And to his horror, so was Aubrey.

'What the hell you doin'?' cried Aubrey.

'Arresting you as an accessory,' said Aimee.

'Alright, alright, go easy! I promise I'll reveal all if you let me keep my vodka,' wheezed Martin, cradling the half-empty bottle.

'Pathétique.'

'Agathe, it is worth it for a confession,' said Gallois in glee. With a pitying look at Martin, he added: 'It will be your last drink for a while, apart from the prison wine made in your cell toilet.' Suddenly, a peppery Mondeuse didn't sound too bad.

Half-marched, half-dragged to the cabin, Martin caught a glance of something horribly evil, and the other three, seemingly, had not. A mound of snow. The size of a human being.

'Welcome! *Entra, entra!*' beamed Renzo. 'There you all are. Everybody's trickled in all afternoon but we've been worried sick.' In contrast to their own bedraggled outfits, the cabin was strictly black tie; single-breasted tuxedoes and chiffon evening gowns. Sven, Omar (looking very uncomfortable in a dinner jacket), Renzo, Sara, Pekoe, Theo (painted hands present), Noel, Morton, Tate, Holly and Joseph. His smile faltering on seeing the handcuffs, Renzo rearranged his face into a relaxed, unfazed expression. The others, however, were far less welcoming to Martin.

'I see you've got your man, then, Captain,' said Tate approvingly.

'And his accomplice,' said Aimee. The entire cabin gasped as Martin and Aubrey collapsed in front of a stone hearth, their hands reaching towards the warm, orange, crackling flames. Squirming, the party didn't know where to look. The rustic lodge comprised of a living room and kitchen nook. Beyond that, several sleeping alcoves. Personally, Martin could just curl up here on the bearskin rug and sleep for a hundred years. The murderer, of course, had blended back in with everyone else sitting around a hand-carved wooden coffee table. Everyone? No. Someone was missing and somebody else looked troubled. But, again, apparently it was only Martin who caught it; the agitation on their face.

'Noel! You're alive!' It was Aubrey who'd spoken first. Martin—incapable of speech, teeth chattering like crazy—stretched his hands closer to the fire. And closer. Still digging into his wrists, could he melt the plastic cuffs off?

'Alive, alive, oh,' replied Noel playfully, slightly puzzled at her relief.

'I thought you were in the Lamborghini,' cried Aubrey.

'Ach, no, the guards commandeered it from me, so I came up with Gallois and Aimee.' Despite their posh suits, they were all still wearing their normal shoes. Wind howling, the creak of the cabin timbers groaned as the patter of snow and ice beat harder against the roof. A line of the *Vautour Barbu* Mondeuse jangled from the kitchen counter. 'But I'm sorry to see you've been corrupted by this eejit. Moretti, can't you leave us all alone, like?'

'We will remove the fugitives very soon,' said Gallois, 'they will be in prison before *notre dîner.*' Glancing at the clock, Martin was shocked to see it was only three in the afternoon; outside was as black as midnight.

'Stay for one drink, *per piacere*,' said Renzo, hands pressed together. 'We were just about to open the vintage Apostelwein 1727.' Aimee raised her eyebrows; curious. 'There's a storm outside and they are both secured in handcuffs.'

Enamoured, the Capitaine grudgingly nodded. 'Until our reinforcements arrive. Also,' said Gallois, watching Martin carefully, 'we have a room of witnesses waiting to hear Monsieur Moretti's confession.'

'You've brought all the bottled lightning wines up here?' rasped Aubrey.

'*Si*, all of them, among other things,' Renzo winked knowingly at Martin.

Only in France could this happen. A raging blizzard outside. A serial killer inside. A missing pistol. A missing person. And they all stop for wine tasting. Very delicately, very devoutly, five ancient bottles of wine were placed on the table. The Massandra Sherry de la Frontera, 1775. The Chateau Lafite Rothschild, 1787; with it's presidential initials T-H and J. The aforementioned Apostelwein, 1727, with its faded orange label and ingrained layer of dust. And the flat shoulder-shaped bottle filled from the Strasbourg Wine Barrel of 1472. Martin was more interested in the location of the SIG Sauer SP 2022, .45 calibre; no doubt hiding in a flannel blanket or plant pot. Tread lightly, Martin. Whatever happens, tread lightly.

The awestruck cabin didn't dare touch or even directly glance at the fifth. 'That can't be...' breathed Aubrey, 'it can't be...'

'The Speyer wine bottle; our wine tour of a lifetime's *pièce de resistance*!' boomed Renzo. 'The world's oldest bottle of wine, from Rome of old. Buried in the tomb of a Roman nobleman near the city of Speyer, experts date it to 325 B.C. When the tomb was excavated in 1867, most of the bottles found were empty, or long since shattered, but two remained. One lives in Germany's Historical Museum of the Palatinate. The other was smuggled out of the site by the excavator and bought by me on the black market; legitimately,' Renzo added with a glance at the Gendarmerie.

Holding aloft a 1.5 litre glass jug with dolphin-shaped handles, Sven looked terrified of dropping the Speyer wine, but Martin was more concerned about drinking it. The oily-brown sludge resembled a science experiment gone wrong.

'Is it still drinkable?' asked Theo.

Renzo fervently nodded. 'We can absolutely still drink it.' But it won't taste good, thought Martin. Whilst his spiked-whisky from the previous night had looked murky, this was positively bog-like; as if the result of a milk spillage into a Florida swamp. 'Made from local grapes planted during Roman rule, and secret herbs added as a preservative, this bottle has remained undisturbed and airtight for over a millennia, the wax seal preserving the wine from evaporating. So, no stealing this one, Morton,' said Renzo, in good humour. Morton Kessler, however, was distracted. Biting the inside of his cheek, he kept staring out of the window. *'Che cavolo! Facciamolo!* Let's start with the Speyer.'

A hallowed hush fell as Sven eased out the cork, followed by a round of applause as the wine was poured. 'We are truly tasting history in a bottle,' said the Swede, handing glasses round.

'Drink in those ancient sun-kissed vines!' said Renzo. He

went to place a hand on Sara's shoulder but thought better of it. 'Let us taste empire, valour, virtue; civilisation with a hint of vanilla.' As always, Renzo's ability to compartmentalise crime from wine remained remarkable, and his carefully groomed business associates were no different.

'If God bottled his piss, this would be it,' said Noel with a reverential murmur.

'Infamy,' puffed Pekoe.

'Irresistible,' whispered Holly, her lap-bound son twirling her hair. Bewitched, the Gendarmes even offered a pair of flutes to the outlaws. Where was the SIG Sauer? While the rest of the party sniffed and swirled their glasses, Aubrey gulped it down in one. Wrapped in a scarf or hat? Among the moans of ecstasy, Martin, of course, refused. If this was to be his last drink before jail, it certainly wasn't going to be wine. Zero chance. As everybody was inhaling an aroma of cinnamon and old apples, Martin smelt the burnt hairs on the back of his hand and melted plastic.

'Here's to life in prison,' said Gallois, a mad gleam in those steel grey eyes as he lifted his glass to Martin.

'We always catch our target,' said Aimee, toasting him.

'Any chance you could catch my wife for me, kid?' Morton asked the Lieutenant. 'She went out for logs. Probably now searching for the lumberjack, to be his lumberjill.' It was said in a cheery voice, but Martin caught again the agitated look on his lined face.

Prizing his jaw open, Martin croaked: 'She's dead. Outside. Beneath a snow mound.'

'You all heard it,' said Gallois, 'another confession! Or another lie; it is impossible to tell with this *homme dérangé*.'

'Eve? She can't be,' stammered Morton.

'I will fetch her.' Yanking her hood up, Aimee slipped out; the blast of ice crystals, a stark reminder they were all trapped.

'Eve… you really think so?' said Morton, his sunken eyes filled with water.

‘I’m sorry,’ said Martin, solemnly.

‘Too late for apologies,’ growled Gallois. ‘Continue your confession, *s'il vous plait*.’

‘Is this what you said to Camille Duvall after the first victim?’ Putting his weight onto the vodka bottle, Martin heaved himself onto his knees.

‘The noose tightens. We have a witness who saw your altercation with Monsieur Stresskeller at Annecy train station,’ announced Gallois, the cabin very much on his side. ‘And, do not forget, we found your watch under Madame Oblet’s body.’

‘It was planted! Ask anyone here; I lost my watch two days ago,’ said Martin, defiantly meeting their watchful, unwelcoming eyes.

‘How handy for you; and the watch,’ jeered Gallois.

‘Alright, you want to know how the murders were done?’ Necking a quarter of his bottle, Martin began: ‘Like I said last time, the key to solving these killings is murder number two. Too many higgledy-piggledy rooms and too much drinking the night Jimmy was killed. Murder two is key. So how did it happen? Aubrey saw no one go by... but is that really true? At first, I wondered if Tate had used his emergency bedroom rope to climb out of his window, but there were no snowprints outside. So, yes, the murderer crept through the house.’ Swaying round to their host, Martin slurred: ‘Renzo, please could you bring out the item I asked for?’

Gallois was as bewildered as everybody else when he returned from the bedroom and placed a familiar-looking object on the table; the fat yellow candle.

‘Eve’s posh new candle!’ cried Morton, glancing out of the window again.

‘Yep, although, not-so new now. It’s been burnt on at least one occasion.’ With a twitch of his nose, he lit the candle.

‘*Zut*! What is this—a séance?’ sneered Gallois. ‘Are you going to summon the spirits of Jimmy and Mary to tell us who killed them? Shall we all hold hands, Moretti?’

'We know the candle was stolen the first day we arrived at the Old Elysium vineyard,' said Martin, staring at the small flicker of light. 'But when was it burnt?' Soon the cabin was filled with an overpowering lemon fragrance. 'I suggest it was used during murder two to help the killer.'

'How can a candle help the killer?' asked Theo. There was a loud squeak to his side. The group twisted round to Aubrey, her eyes clamped shut in pain. Martin quickly blew the candle out.

'Sorry Aubrey,' said Martin, 'I needed to prove the citrus scent would trigger one of your micro-migraines.'

'That's ok,' she said, rubbing her forehead, eyes still closed. 'I do remember getting a couple of those pains that night. I thought it was just the stress of my Master Sommelier revision and the goddamn regions of Ticino.'

'That is how our killer used the candle—to blind Aubrey,' said Martin. 'In the corridor, they lit it once to slip by Aubrey and into the wine cellar. After killing Mary, they lit it a second time to sneak past Aubrey again and return to their own room.' The group gazed at the groggy Martin with increased respect; but, inside, he was kicking himself. The morning he discovered Mary, he'd detected a lemon scent in the corridor. For too long, Martin suspected Sara's citrus perfume, before realising it wasn't present in the lounge or cellar. 'Most of us were there during my grapefruit breakfast,' he continued, 'so most of us saw Aubrey's reaction to citrus. Frankly, anybody could have got by her, and everybody is a suspect.'

The roar of the terrible blizzard signalled Aimee's return. She was alone.

'Any sign of my wife?' said Morton.

'I can not find her,' shivered Aimee, before murmuring to Gallois, '*la voiture est enneigée et le téléphérique s'est arrêté.*' And now Morton fell to his knees, weeping; Holly and Sara helping him back onto the sofa.

'*Ne perds pas espoir,*' said Gallois, 'erm, do not lose hope, Monsieur Kessler. She may have taken shelter in the woodshed or our car.'

'And if the worst is true, at least there will be an *incarcération.*' The Lieutenant glowered at Martin, as Morton Kessler wept harder.

'If she's dead,' said Martin, 'and I was in cuffs, how could I be the murderer?'

'Obviously, you killed her earlier,' hissed Aimee, crossing her arms, 'and then doubled back.'

'That's not true, I've been with him all day!' blurted Aubrey 'And how can you accuse Martin after what he's revealed about the candle.' The Lieutenant's face became stonier with the lemon-scented recap.

'Tu sais quoi?' said Aimee, her arms still folded. 'Just because the candle may or may not have been used like that—'

'It was,' said Martin.

'May or may not have been used like that, it does not necessarily rule you out for Mary,' said Aimee.

'Or Jimmy,' added Gallois. 'If anything, this candle revelation only compounds you are the murderer.'

'Alright, you want more? How 'bout I give you D.O.T.?'

'Who is it?' Renzo, as well as Aubrey, leaned forward. But not everyone was as eager.

'Please, *non,*' groaned Aimee. '*Tu plaisantes?*'

'Come on then, Moretti, is it time for round three of your festive fiasco?' said Tate. 'I can't wait to hear your solution.'

'Neither can he,' said Aimee.

'Last speech of the condemned man,' said Gallois zealously.

'Thank you, thank you for the morale boost,' said Martin.

Again, Pekoe had stationed himself in the far corner, surveying the room. 'I hope you know what you're doing this time.'

'So do I,' winked Martin. 'Ok, let's do this one last time. Capitaine, I'll speak slowly, try and keep up. If the killer is anti-wine... who hates it? Does Theo Oblet?'

'*Non*,' said Theo.

'Agreed,' said Martin, 'you've savoured many a wine. So, how about Pekoe Williams, does he enjoy a glass?'

'Yes, no, well, it's not my top choice,' said Pekoe, still nursing his Speyer.

'So, who is D.O.T.?' said Aubrey.

'Same person I accused first time round.' Tottering up and clutching a large set of mounted antlers for support, Martin turned to face the accused. Holly Sinclair.

As Holly's face reddened, her husband's turned purple. 'Oh, here we go again, Moretti, playing the same record as last time, slandering my wife, my family. Lest we forget, you were found guilty yesterday, remember?' Clearly, Tate had the support of the room.

'As we say in Sweden,' Sven stared at Martin, crushed, 'you have planted your last potato.'

'He's a useless scut!' said Noel. 'What class of an eejit are you, Moretti? Leave it to the real detectives, like.'

'Martin, please stop,' said Holly herself. But Martin was sick of it. No more lies. No more deception. Batting away a tirade of legal threats —police harassment, wrongful prosecution, negligence, mental assault, breach of human rights—Martin staggered over to her. In one swift movement, he eased Holly's sleeve up; revealing a fresh tattoo emblazoned with a circle of skulls. And in the centre, were three words written in red.

40

Daughters of Temperance

Tate's purple face went green. But the Sinclair boys were on the attack.

'Leave my mom alone, you big bully!'

'I will counter-sue you, Moretti, for being a sexist, misogynistic xenophobe.'

Martin poured the remaining contents of his bottle into a wine glass. One litre of vodka in two hours. Not bad. Right now, he felt fine, but intoxication was in the post; imminently. For the briefest of moments, Martin and the murderer locked eyes. He could feel the growing arrogance and knew why. The gun must be close. Surely the Gendarmerie held weapons? Surely! But one glance confirmed they were armed with nothing but Gallois' walking cane and Aimee's formidable contempt.

'How did you know Holly had the tattoo?' asked Aubrey.

'Our first day on tour, I touched your arm and you winced. Apologies,' Martin spoke intently to Holly. 'Second time, two days later, you didn't wince. Because you'd warmed to me, or because your new tattoo was no longer sore? D.O.T.... Daughters of Temperance—the anti-wine, anti-alcohol, nineteenth-century women's organisation personified in the extreme physical attacks of "Hatchet Granny" Carrie Nation. Where've I heard that name before? When you listed the female-greats that you should be writing about, in between Florence Nightingale and Joan of Arc, you named Carrie Nation.'

'A coincidence!' heckled Tate.

'And speaking of writing, that poison pen letter

demanding Renzo close down his vineyard, the turns of phrase, had a transatlantic quality. Hands up here any New Yorkers who live in England,' said Martin sardonically.

'Objection,' countered Tate.

'Overruled. But,' conceded Martin, 'it's difficult to prove the author of a malicious letter among the thousands sent each year. A much easier way to identify D.O.T. would be to find who acquired a bagful of cirrhosis livers.' Glancing at his cuffs, Martin's hope plummeted. His time at the fireplace had done nothing to weaken his shackles. Idiot. What did he expect, the simple snapping of a rubber band? 'The first time we met, Holly, the night we discovered the livers in the bowl of mulled wine, I was struck by your oversized handbag; incidentally, the only time I've seen you wearing it. I assumed it was stuffed with half a library. Turns out, that's actually where you hid the human organs.'

'Speculation.'

'The second time we met, you told me you'd toured the kitchens of both places we'd visited. Why—for Renzo's biography or to plop the livers in the punchbowl?'

'Badgering.'

'By the way,' said Martin, finally facing Tate and drunkenly knocking a table lamp over, 'enroute to the Blacked tattoo parlour—y'know, with the poison pen typewriter and a stencil design identical to the one on your wife's forearm —I took a detour.' Picking the lamp up, Martin took the opportunity to stretch and twist his brittle cuffs. But Houdini, he wasn't. And an overcooked spaghetto, this was not. 'Y'know, follow in the footsteps of the Sinclair's Euro trip. How did you describe your holiday itinerary to me, Tate? *First half of the holiday's for the wife, the cultural part; charity gig at a French hospital and this wonderful wine tour.* So I stopped off at the local hospital; specifically, the Hepatology department.'

'What is hepatology?' frowned Theo.

'That's a good question. Hepatology focusses on diseases that affect the pancreas, gall bladder and… liver,' said Martin.

'And they remembered the Sinclair's visit very well. Charitable donation aside, it's not often they get a request for the souvenir of four scarred samples. Quite the goody bag.'

'Well done, Martin,' said Holly, quietly.

'Holly, don't say—'

'Tate, please,' she said firmly. 'I'm not ashamed. You know, Martin, the temperance movement allied with many other noble causes, like the suffragettes.'

'Yes, and the KKK!' spat Martin, and her head dropped. 'But our Holly is so meek and mild, so innocent, so shy. And who would ever suspect an alcoholic.'

'I really wish I could resist,' she said bitterly. 'It sounds stupid, I think I hoped if I could get it banned, it would force me to abstain. Pitiful, really.' Pouring her wine on the floor, nobody stopped her.

'I understand your reasons,' said Martin, his wobbling nothing to do with his ankle. 'Your brother, Duncan, he was hit by a drunk driver leaving a vineyard, wasn't he?'

'Yes. Yes. I should've driven him, then he wouldn't have been walking by the side of that road. I'm not naive to think I can stop all alcohol.' Holly forced herself to meet Renzo's eyeline. 'I am so sorry, Renzo, but I couldn't stand by and observe first-hand this winery grow. And I'm sorry, Martin, that it's clouded things. What tipped you off?'

'The fact you never denied you were D.O.T.'

'Oh.'

'At that first gathering, I mentioned the D.O.T. killings, and you say: "these *killings* weren't me". I asked: are you the D.O.T. killer? And you replied: "I am not a *killer*". You disputed the killer element, but not D.O.T. It got me thinking—what if they're two separate things?'

Holly implored: 'As soon as I saw the murderer had used my initials, I stopped my protests. I didn't want to confuse the investigation. My campaign will continue but I'll wait until they're caught.'

'I believe you,' said Martin, 'there've been no poison pen

notes of D.OT. carvings since Jimmy's death. Illuminating, however, that while the letter, livers and our coach all had D.O.T. written, the mistletoe left on Jimmy and Mary had no periods between each letter. DOT rather than D.O.T.'

'Maybe mistletoe leaves are too tiny to write on?' said Sven.

'Maybe,' said Martin with a shrug of his shoulders, transferring the motion to his bound hands, 'but it was enough for me to look at this case differently.'

'Wait a minute,' said Aubrey, confused, 'so Holly isn't the murderer?'

'I could ramble about how—on the night of Jimmy's murder—Sara Brambilla says she was at the Madison Club until dawn but CCTV shows her leaving at two a.m. And I'll choose to ignore that Elise Mott is an anagram of mistletoe. I always allow one coincidence. But why don't I just skip to the end? Let's get on with the real murderer, shall we, Theo?'

'Pardon?' said Theo, looking up from his glass.

'I wonder why you did it, Theo Oblet, our friendly mistletoe murderer.'

'Don't be ridiculous, I love wine and have just lost my wife!'

'Your wife, that's kinda, that's kinda the whole point, isn't it? What it's been for,' said Martin. 'This whole thing was about Mary and her plan to divorce you. And if you can't have her, no one can, right?' The air was electric now, the group sitting a little straighter in their seats. 'In our conversation yesterday, you talked how you regretted things you'd said in the heat of the moment. And how I bet you did; openly announcing your motive in front of us all, that big argument down in the Château des Allues cellar. *Don't you dare threaten to leave me or I'll kill you.*'

'So he killed for jealousy?' said Aubrey incredulously.

'Who's to say what anybody would do, if what they loved was threatened,' said Martin. Love or money; what it always boiled down to. 'She'd threatened to take 'em to the cleaners financially, but I think it was for love. Possessive, jealous, love. The first time I met Theo, he admitted he was a control freak. Do you know what happens when a control freak loses control? They freak! Couldn't handle the rejection. He resolved right then and there to kill Mary. But now his intentions are too obvious, so he hid his motive. *Where does a wise man hide a pebble? On the beach. And where does a wise man hide a leaf? In the forest.* Theo Oblet concealed the real murder amongst a group of murders. He only wanted to kill one person, Mary. The other two deaths, Jimmy and now Eve, were just to distract us.'

'Theo?' said Renzo, gaping at him. But Theo was still smiling at Martin in disbelief.

'Ok! Yes, alright, I admit it,' said Theo. Despite the accusations, he maintained his casual manner. 'I argued with my wife in the heat of the moment and said some aggressive things; empty threats.' He glowered back at Martin. 'That doesn't mean I murdered my wife, or the rest of them. But please, carry on,' sneered Theo, 'the recollections of a drunkard won't stand up in court.'

Tread lightly, Martin. Tread lightly, else you'll end up one more mounted head on the wall (minus the antlers). 'You used two red herrings. One, this whole thing was the work of an anti-wine serial killer. Two, it was connected to D.O.T. Or DOT, as you wrote on the mistletoe. So what that you never added periods?' said Martin with a blasé shrug. 'You didn't care what D.O.T. meant, you simply seized upon it for the perfect cover. Fabrications; layered and layered like a ratatouille.'

'This is crazy!' Theo burst out in laughter, but no one else was laughing. 'So how exactly am I supposed to have killed these three?'

'Murder one,' said Martin drowsily. 'Mary's plan for divorce has been declared. As soon as the house was asleep, Theo got to work; he slipped down into the cellar and waited.'

'That is false, actually,' said Theo, shaking his head.

'You knew someone would come for the Lafite Rothschild,' Martin continued. 'Which means you saw the same wild gleam on the party's faces that I saw. What sharp little eyes you have. It didn't matter who came; anybody would do.'

'False, false, absolutely chock-full of falseness,' needled Theo.

'So, at three a.m. Jimmy arrived and you killed him,' said Martin with a hiccup.

'Getting falser all the time,' snarled Theo. 'Capitaine, you can not honestly believe this rubbish, can you? *C'est naze!*' Theo snarled.

'But how could he do the second murder?' said Gallois, tugging reflectively at his moustache.

'Ok, *continuez, s'il vous plaît*,' said Theo, 'the more we listen to these drunken ravings, the more your case disappears.'

'I'm not drunk; I'm just more fun to be around!' Rolling his shoulders and shaking his arms, Martin pushed his palms apart and finally felt some stretch. Some. Not enough.

'Ivrogne.'

'Murder number two, Mary Oblet,' said Martin, signalling Renzo to bring the second item out. 'Even during Jimmy's final moments, you were already plotting the real murder in your mind; waiting for an opportunity. At Elysium, you knew where Mary would be at midnight. But then—disaster!—you knew Aubrey was pulling an all-nighter in the tasting room. Quite the dilemma. Fortunately, those sharp little eyes of yours had spotted Eve's candle when I'd rummaged through the Kessler's bag for the Lafite. So you steal it from their room, ready to use later that night to help kill your wife.'

'Don't be ridiculous,' said Theo, 'I was painting the night of Mary's murder.'

'How do we know?' said Martin, with another hiccup. Hiccup; morse code for inebriation.

'See for yourself,' said Theo proudly, 'the Land of a Thousand Spots.' Carting out the canvas, Renzo enjoyed a full thirty-second rest before Martin whispered something else in his ear and he dashed out again. It was as Martin remembered it: a bright yellow background, peppered with twenty-six blue and green dots. 'Lieutenant Aimee told us Mary's murder was at midnight,' Theo persisted, 'Eve and Morton said they heard me clattering about with my artwork, thumping through the wall between eleven p.m. and two a.m. so I couldn't have killed my wife. Bursts of artistic creativity can't be stopped, even by you, Moretti.'

'Yep, your masterpiece propped up against their wall,' said Martin, admiring the painting. 'You, chucking on your blue and green paints to create the spots. Although, there's not exactly a thousand spots, are there? In fact, I would've expected a few more than twenty-six dots for three hours' worth of thumping. What was it Eve said, one hundred and fifty thumps she counted?'

'Exactly that,' a broken, desolate Morton Kessler nodded. 'Every twelve seconds she counted a thump.'

'One hundred and fifty thumps, every twelve seconds,' repeated Martin. 'Does that frequency ring a bell with anybody? Gallois?' Scowling, the Capitaine looked as confused as the rest of them. Right on cue, Renzo returned, this time wheeling in a contraption. It was the tennis ball launcher.

'My Lobster Sports Elite Two Portable Ball Machine,' said Renzo, as if re-introducing an old friend, 'automatically fires a ball out every twelve seconds. Capable of holding one-hundred and fifty balls.' The party burst into horrified wonder, every eye fixed upon Martin.

'Exactly,' he said. 'And where do you always keep the ball launcher?'

'Cobwebbed corner outside the kitchen,' Renzo and Sara said in unison. They shared a gentle smile.

'Exactly!' cried Martin. 'It never stayed inside. And yet, it occurred to me, that the morning after Mary's murder... I'd seen Theo lugging the launcher out from the house.' Both police officers were leaning forward, impressed. Internally,

Martin chastised himself; another point he should've picked up on earlier. 'So, now Theo has the launcher and the candle. Everything is ready. Theo knows the exact time Mary will be in the cellar. Down there, he'll have his choice of ten thousand blunt instruments. What next, Theo? With the balls automatically hitting Eve and Morton's wall, and lighting your candle in the corridor to blind Aubrey, into the cellar you crept and bashed in the brains of your wife. Mission accomplished! Pop back upstairs and return to your room to paint the actual spots yourself.' Theo remained silent but was shooting daggers at Martin.

'I can't believe this, Theo!' cried Holly.

'Don't be too upset, Holly,' said Martin. 'He tried to pin one of the false trails on you; saying he'd seen a flash of gold round the wrist of his knife attacker, like your bracelet, I suspect to fool us into thinking it was you who'd stabbed him. Theo, you've caused so much suffering, I do hope it was at least agonisingly painful when you sliced your own belly.' While the rest of the room was grasping this latest statement, Martin stumbled over to Renzo who, anticipating another errand, hadn't even attempted to sit down. Rushing into the kitchen, he returned with a soapy wet cloth.

'It is a fascinating theory, Moretti, but I'd like to see you prove it. Lots of proof, please,' smirked Theo. 'I hope you weren't expecting me to simply breakdown and confess? I deny everything!'

'What I love most about this painting,' said Martin, gazing at the artwork, 'is the vivid use of colour. Blue, yellow and green; strewn all over the canvas, as well as your shoes.' Backing up Martin's point, Theo waggled his legs in the air, showing off his paint-splattered trainers. 'Though I notice there's no red on your shoes. Nor any red in the painting. And yet, every single day since Mary's murder, your hands have been covered in red paint.'

'Why?' said Tate.

'Anybody who's been into the Elysium cellar knows it

contains a particularly annoying sharp nail. It sticks out of the wall and seems to scratch anybody that's not paying attention. On the night of Mary's murder, Theo caught his left hand on that nail. A deep cut, I imagine,' said Martin, nodding to Renzo. Armed with his dripping cloth, their host began to scrub the left hand of an extremely reluctant-looking Theo. 'After that, like I said, you returned to your room, no doubt, for a good night's sleep. In the morning, amongst all the chaos, you simply wheeled the launcher outside again. The perfect crime, you might have got away with it if you didn't scratch yourself on that pesky nail.'

'That is, assuming you're correct about the nail?' said Aimee. Inquisitively, Martin looked over to Renzo, who had finished removing the red paint. The Lieutenant forced up Theo's left arm, revealing a deep gash on the back of his hand.

'There you go,' said Martin, 'caught red handed.' The room was filled with a deathly silence. Pekoe was puffing on his pipe without realizing it had gone out. 'Lieutenant Aimee's forensics on the nail will confirm your blood on it. But if you want *lots of* proof… Renzo's photographs taken of everybody's room the morning after Mary's murder, shows the Lobster Sports Elite Two Portable Ball Machine still in your bedroom. Plus, when the DNA report comes back from—'

'ENOUGH!' screamed Theo. 'It's true. Just… can the vodka freak stop babbling.'

'A-ha!' said Gallois, triumphantly.

'*You're* not allowed to say a-ha!' said Martin. 'You thought it was me.'

'A team effort,' Gallois replied.

'So, he used our tennis ball launcher,' said Sara, still processing the last few minutes.

'And I bet that's what Eve put together,' Martin nodded gravely, eyes unfocussed, 'the frequency of the thumps.'

'Eve…' Clutching his chest, Morton Kessler rocked back and forth. 'Once she puts two and two together, she always confronts it head on.'

Martin didn't correct his statement to the past tense. Instead, Martin braced for a sudden strike. Nostrils flaring, face reddening, hands curling into fists, Theo launched himself at Martin. Handcuffed, he was powerless to defend himself. The wild, thrusting, arm was caught by Gallois; his vice-like grip clamping down on Theo's wrist.

'How did you know?' asked Martin.

'A hunch,' said Gallois.

Snatching Martin's glass, Theo tossed the contents into the fire. But no roaring whoosh of flame leapt out at them. '*Je ne comprends pas!* If… not vodka… then…'

'Water.' Rock steady, eyes focussed, Martin's swinging two-handed punch landed square on the bridge of his nose. Theo flew back into his armchair, blood spurting. The plan had worked. It was over. Finally, Martin hadn't been outfoxed, he'd in-foxed Theo. 'D'you think I'm dumb or something?'

But they'd all missed it. The group, too thunderstruck to speak. The Gendarmes, releasing Aubrey from her cuffs. Martin, too busy congratulating himself to see Theo's hand slip under the plaid scatter cushion.

Clasping the SIG Sauer in one hand and several clips in the other, Theo wiped the blood from his chin, his face full of suppressed glee. 'Quite dumb, yes.' Martin held his ground. Gallois stepped back, arms wide, as if somehow he could catch the bullet. 'I warned you before, you should take the murderer by *surprise*, rather than showing off how clever you are. Well, now you're going to see exactly how clever I can be.' There was a crazed glint in his eyes that Martin had never seen before as he pulled the hammer back on the pistol.

41

The Return of the Defective Detective

'I am afraid there will be a tragic log fire tonight.' Theo's eyes darted around the room for a rush attack, but no one dared move. 'I, alone, will bravely make it down this mountain to tell of the unforgiving flames that melted the flesh off your backs. I might even brush up a painting about this, maybe.'

Horrifying, utterly horrifying. Martin had drunk a litre of water, but his mouth was still dry. He was going to die. Through his own ignorance—reckless, deadly, ignorance. And deadly for the cabin dwellers. All those plans for the future. Little Joseph, sweet Sara, both starting out in the world. Renzo's winery, Holly's book, Pekoe's cannabis farm, Aubrey's Sommelier exam, Sven growing out his mullet (hopefully). Just another set of unfulfilled dreams. And what about himself? Even without the badge, Martin had nearly made a go of it.

'I have always understood people, Moretti. Of course I caught the gleam in their eyes, the greed for the Lafite. I knew someone would come for it. The theft was inevitable. All I had to do was wait. I am very empathetic.'

'You killed your own wife!' yelled Martin.

'And that made me very sad,' said Theo, waving the pistol around, 'but I could not live knowing she'd be out there with someone else. And like Mary said, she'll take me *to the cleaners.* I always knew she would. I heard her the next morning, instead of calling the stock exchange, she was talking to our lawyers. Mary wanted a fast separation? Ok, *très bien*, I gave her an instant divorce.' A contorted smile twisted at the edges of his mouth. 'You were right, Moretti, I could not kill her first; everybody had witnessed my threats. And you are right, Eve did confront me; told me she'd worked it out,' said Theo, breathing fast. 'Fortunately, we were the last two in the woodshed. I threatened her with the gun outside, but she kept needling me.'

'She wouldn't be scared of a scumbag like you,' said Morton.

'She should've been, Kessler, she really should have. And now she is dead. Even in the blizzard, I took my time squeezing the life out of her,' said Theo, amused as Morton crumpled in on himself. Damn him, cursed Martin. Damn the evil, vile, depraved Theo Oblet, still swerving justice. Jimmy. Mary. Eve. Those poor police officers driving over the cliff edge. And now, everyone here, burnt to death. God, Martin needed to fix this screw up! But how? Didn't they say, always rush a gun? Not with Theo so jumpy, it was too dangerous. For now, keep him talking.

'Before you no doubt added a mistletoe leaf on top of Eve? Why d'you do that?' Martin knew the answer but needed others to hear it firsthand.

'To look like a serial killer,' said Theo, glowing eyes fastened to Martin. 'All serial killers leave a calling card, don't they? Plus, I needed some way to link all this to the DOT saboteur. You gave me that idea, Moretti, constantly babbling on about it at dinner. An effective distraction. Just as I said, I've always understood people. *Par exemple*, how you like to drink— even one of my crushed Zolpidems into your glass— and how you love an audience; babbling on long enough for the pill to take effect.'

'And, of course,' added Martin, 'planting my Omega De Ville.' With an exaggerated mime of wearing a watch, he flexed his wrists outward. There was only one way to fix this mess. Draw the killer out of the cabin. Everything Martin knew about Theo, he would give chase. Martin was his primary target. But how to escape? He had no idea if there was a back exit. And, given the distance from the front door, Martin estimated he'd make it across the room as far as the first bullet. In sum, another undignified window departure was required. Edging over, the lock looked fiddly. He had to break out of his cuffs.

'Ah, Moretti, my third red herring. How funny watching you flounder when Gallois revealed your watch. I'd slipped it under Mary's body straight after I tried to drown you.' Desperate to draw Theo's attention away from the window, Martin attempted to signal Aubrey. 'And then you dodged my bullets inside *le coffre de la Bentley*. I suppose it will be third time lucky for killing you. I must kill you all to hide my secret. Capitaine... Lieutenant... assuming you have more handcuffs, if you could manacle everyone to the furniture, I will prepare our relaxing inferno.' Reluctant at first, the Gendarmes were coaxed along by the pistol pointed directly into Gallois' face.

'I'd suggest we toast marshmallows,' said Martin, 'but maybe something soft and squishy was the real reason Mary left you.'

'I have a gun pointed at Capitaine Gallois' brain,' said Theo.

'You'll miss,' said Martin. This time, Aubrey picked up on his facial signal.

'Or maybe I'll overpower you,' she said.

'A woman?' Theo shrieked; a sharp, callous shriek that jarred against his breezy exterior. 'You can't.'

'Watch me,' said Aubrey. Charging over, Theo screamed so forcefully in her face it could have triggered an avalanche. That was all Martin needed. Yanking his cuffs down on the mounted antlers, the ties finally snapped. Martin was out of the window before the gunshot hit the frame.

'I hit you! I think I hit you!'

If he was going, she was going too. Aubrey dived out of the door into the swirling white; the thunderclap of Theo's pistol spurring her forwards. Keep going, don't look back. Was that the blur of somebody else jumping out? Keep going, don't look back. Had Theo executed everyone left in the cabin, or was he firing just at her? Or at Martin, if he wasn't dead already the other side of the window. Just the three of them left at the top of the world. How many more murders would there be this sub-zero night?

42

A Merry Little Christmas (Again)

Fresh snowfall. So pure, so innocent. Still the heavy stink of blood filled the alpine air. They would kill again, of course. Shoot, stab, or strangle another innocent somewhere on this mountain peak. So Aubrey ran. And would keep running, hidden for now while the blizzard raged. Maybe this wasn't quite the '*Wine Tour of a Lifetime!*'

Eight gunshots rang out. She screamed stumbling over the body—but no one came. On a mountaintop, the wind will swallow your voice. Staring down, she realised it was Christmas Eve; the holly berry earrings matched the crimson marks around their neck. No time for that tearful goodbye, Aubrey had to move. Close behind, the hulking silhouette, hunting her, hounding her every step.

Trembling, she placed two fingers onto Eve's eyelids and slid them over the glassy stare. Now they could be sleeping. Let your heart be light. Like a child waiting for Christmas morning. All our troubles out of sight. Unease slithered down her spine.

Wine tour of a lifetime? What a mistake. Come for the oak Malbec, stay for the pine coffin. What a dreadful mistake. Three people knew the killer's identity, the killer's secret; but as the saying went: three can keep a secret if two of them are dead.

Two more shots sounded. Something whistled past her face. Keep going, keep running, keep praying for no footprints. If only she could make it to the cable car, but it was hard now dragging herself through the snowdrift, her muscles screaming as she reached the ragged edge. Dead end. Wrong turn. Collapsing, another shot rang out. The next one wouldn't miss. Surely, the secret shouldn't die on this mountain.

Three people knew... The killer. Herself. And then there was Martin. Her eyes, darting out into the night, watched as a silver and dark snowflake landed on her chest. If she wasn't alive to keep the secret, then perhaps he was.

43

The Riddle, The Mystery & The Enigma

What was it that would kill her? The cold? If only the gnawing frost numbed her fear as well as her face. The killer's gun? His crushing hands? A fatal fall? Avalanche? Altitude asphyxiation? The rasping dagger of frozen vapour burning a hole straight through her lungs until her heart exploded? Death and all his friends edged nearer.

Shivering, Aubrey curled behind a rock as the blizzard roared. And roared. The shapeless thing didn't care. It stalked right towards her; above her. She had no strength to fight back. And then his hands were on her, wrenching her up. It was Martin.

'Get down!' screamed Aubrey. 'He's coming for us, he's right behind us!'

'No, it's alright, Aubrey, it's alright, he went the other way,' yelled Martin. 'Come on, before he doubles back, let's head for the cable car.'

'Leave me,' groaned Aubrey, 'I can't go on.'

'Let's not split off like that again,' said Martin, ignoring her pleas. 'Stay together.' Like Sara dredging him from the wine vat, and Aubrey rescuing him inside the barn, Martin would save her now. He would save them all. He should never have let things get this far. His obsession for a confession had endangered the lives of everyone in the cabin. Martin had to make this right. Exhausted, he tugged her into the whiteout, the snow swirling round and round and round until he felt the one spinning.

'Just leave me.'

'If we stay together, we'll survive.' It was impossible to see three steps in front. Nostrils stinging, Martin inhaled —aftershave, sweat, gun powder—anything to alert him. But there was only the cold crisp tang of the ozone. Under the cover of the storm, Martin tacked away from the dark shadowy figure ahead, as fast as he dared with a four-thousand-foot drop one misstep away. The figure loomed closer, and closer still. Speeding up, they crashed into a rock. But the rock was moving. And shouting. Pekoe Williams; crouched beside Eve, shaking her body.

'Pekoe, there's nothing more you can do for her. We have to leave,' said Martin, 'and get to the cable car. Now.'

'The cable car's not working,' cried Pekoe. 'As soon as I jumped out after you, I went straight there, but it's snowed in. There's nothing out here but a derelict cable pylon.' All three collapsed around Eve's corpse; huddled, catching their breath, praying for shared bodily warmth. Pekoe shook Eve's body again. A state of denial? Not with the tears frozen down his cheeks. This wasn't going to have a happy ending. How long could they last before the inevitable bullet?

'Let's go back in the cabin,' said Aubrey.

Ankle throbbing, Martin shook his head. 'We have to lead him away from the party.'

'It's minus ten degrees,' said Pekoe, 'we'll be dead in under an hour.'

'Gotta weapon?'

'I grabbed the only thing to hand,' said Pekoe, brandishing a bottle of the *Vautour Barbu*. It had proved a deadly instrument, Martin considered, maybe it was time for a taste of his own medicine…

The blizzard dropped. The flurries ceased leaving the world silent and still; until the first gunshot. They'd lost their camouflage! Fully exposed, their sniper was half a football field away and gaining. Even in the dying twilight, moonbeams betrayed their position. The crack of a second shot punctured the air, kicking up the snow in front of Eve. And now it was Aubrey's turn to heave Martin up, Pekoe propped under his other arm; three targets lumbering painfully away from a serial killer. Too painfully. Ten thousand volts seared through his leg with every hobble. The snow was up to their waist now. Any second, he'd pass out in agony. Surely Pekoe knew as well there'd be no happy ending. How about Aubrey, did the detective-novel nut, know? Outside of fiction, evil wins.

An icy mist rolled in; clouding the killer's vision if his next shot was anything to go by. A brief reprieve. A stay of execution.

'I can't go on. I'm slowing you down,' said Martin, beckoning them on.

'We stay together, we survive,' trembled Aubrey.

Stupid sentiment. 'Still have your waiter's friend?'

'Always.' Aubrey handed it to him.

'Here, give me that bottle, I've got an idea.' Uncorking it, Martin poured some out.

'Ok, we get it,' snapped Aubrey, 'you don't like wine.'

'Theo thinks he's shot me, right? Let's see if he'll follow the blood trail.'

'To where?' said Pekoe.

'The cable pylon,' said Martin, dripping more wine as they tugged him up. 'Use me as bait, before you use the bottle against him.'

'That's a terrible plan,' said Aubrey.

'Do you have a better one?'

Pekoe led the way, dark scarlet drops behind him, laying out the red carpet to the peak. Somehow, Martin powered through the pain. The end of his hero's journey.

At last, the bleak and black tower jutted out from the cliff edge. Would he come? Before they froze? Theo's SIG Sauer versus their surprise bottle. Concealed in the fog, Aubrey and Pekoe crouched behind the titanium structure as Martin stood on the precipice. The riddle, wrapped in a mystery, inside an enigma. Twenty feet below, a small ledge on an otherwise vertical cliff face. Climb down? Jump down? There was fresh snow amongst the jagged rocks.... but they were out of time. Through the gloom, a brooding Theo Oblet emerged, pistol aloft.

'Au revoir, Monsieur Moretti, tu me saoules!' No clever quip sprang to mind; no closing words for his gravestone. The mistletoe murderer crept closer, his teeth gnashing for the final strike. 'Tell me now, Moretti, where are they?'

The Ghurka and Californian tiptoed forward but Martin fixed his eyes on Theo, not wanting to giveaway their assault. It was the clink of the bottle against the pylon which did that. Leaping backward, now Theo had them both in his line of fire. The inevitable bullet. With a nasty grin, Theo cocked the hammer and fired, precisely as Martin shoved him off the cliff. Arms flailing, Theo wildly grasped at the only thing within reach—Martin—jerking them both over the rock face.

A sheer drop of frozen air, frozen abyss, frozen darkness, frozen regret. Plummeting down, his life didn't flash before his eyes. All he felt was a hard, dull thump. After several moments —or long lifetimes—Martin pulled himself up, ready for combat. There was no need. Both had landed on the cliff ledge, but where Martin woke spreadeagled in a snow mound, Theo had smashed onto the rocks; the fall only cushioned by his vital organs.

'Hey, Moretti… Moretti… *j'ai peur.*'

Ears ringing, Martin dragged himself over. Spilling from Theo's jacket, mistletoe fluttered out into the night. Evidence no longer necessary. 'Hey, Moretti,' rasped Theo, through a mouthful of blood, 'did you really like my painting?'

Martin swallowed down his acrid loathing. 'Salutations, Theo Oblet, successful artist.'

'Salutations,' croaked Theo, 'Martin Moretti, successful detective.' With a pained smile, he closed his eyes; his smoky breath vanishing on the alpine wind.

Moretti Christmas Newsletter

Status: **SENT**

Date: December 24th (11:59pm)

Joyeux Noël!

Well, what a year it's been. Conquering the lows and riding the highs (literally writing this from a helicopter above the Alps). In fact, during my sabbatical I've embraced the whole winter sport scene – snow sculpting, archery, bobsleigh and cliff jumping.

Met some decent folks over here in France. Even offering for me to stay with them in New York, North India and Kattstjärten (which apparently translates as Cat's Arse).

New Year's Resolution: heal the spirit. Not that you'll find me wearing leopard print yoga pants anytime soon. But I have signed up for The Chakra Lounge juice programme. You know the drill: Gulp down your Zen Zinger. Gulp down your Mango Splash (once they've unclogged the carrot from the NutriBullet's lunch rush). Detox. Recharge. Cleanse. Lose a pound, gain a pound. Grasp that "Drink Responsibly" means more than not spilling your beer. Gulp down your existential Kumquat Quencher. If you're gulping down a change in minerals and a change in vitality; can you also change your leopard print spots?

Merry Christmas and a Happy New Year,

Martin

44

Auld Lang Wine

Christmas morning dawned, fresh and white; the golden glow of the mountaintops shining like children's cheeks the world over. It was the most magical day of the year, yet the occupants of the Elysium farmhouse were working; a board meeting for the wine launch. To cash in on the celebrity murder headlines or not?

Two taxis waited out front. Martin threw his duffle bag into the first.

'*Buon Natale,* Martin!' said Sara, kissing him on both cheeks. 'Are you coming for breakfast?'

'No, I'm gonna catch the early flight.'

'We're going to McDonald's,' said Sara enticingly.

'Another time,' said Martin politely.

'Eager to get your job back, yes?' said Renzo, a warm slap on his shoulder. 'I put a good word into your boss first thing. You single-handedly solved the case!'

'I'm sure Gallois will claim it this side of the Channel.' It wasn't said in spite. It was said in pity. Right now, the Capitaine was probably at the bottom of that valley digging out the frozen bodies of his friends.

'He left you a gift.' Renzo handed him a small, ornately decorated tin.

'Christmas miracle.' Opening it up, the tin contained his father's watch. Martin couldn't speak as he fastened it around his wrist.

'Papà, sbrigati per il McDonald's.'

'What about the wine launch?' asked Martin.

'We have family therapy,' said Renzo, bouncing slightly.

‘Together this time,’ beamed Sara.

‘Sorry I had to drag it all out,’ said Martin.

‘Confronting it has helped us move on,’ said Renzo.

‘Still, calling out the insurance fraud.’

‘I wasn’t particularly thrilled myself, but your distraction, jumping out of my window, the police running around, it gave me time to make a charitable donation to “Friends of Notre-Dame de Paris”, so we will see.’

‘What about that Madison nightclub, then, Sara? What were you up to instead of dancing til dawn?’

‘I will tell if you come for a Bacon and Egg McMuffin.’

‘Another time, then,’ said Martin, as Sara pulled *Papà* into the taxi with her. ‘What, you didn’t get me a present, Renzo?’

‘I already have,’ he replied, glancing over Martin’s shoulder as the cab sped off.

‘Hey, what d’you know? We lived long enough to say happy holidays.’ Aubrey Dalton was wearing three coats and every pair of socks she owned. Shiftily, she had her hands behind her back.

‘Happy holidays.’ Martin held out the bag of reindeer corn that Renzo’s staff had obtained for him.

‘Thanks. Your gift was the bottle of vodka you poured away; which was really expensive, incidentally.’

‘So why are you grinning?’

‘I’ve chosen the wine for you,’ said Aubrey, revealing a full-bodied glass of red. The croquet bet. Damn, she’d remembered.

‘Which French beauty have you picked?’ shuddered Martin.

‘Nope, I’m going home advantage; California. This is a 2017 Merlot from the Buttonwood winery in Santa Barbara that I was saving for today.’

Jimmy Stresskeller. Mary Oblet. Neither of them obtained the bottle they’d sought, nor Eve Kessler her collection of fine wines. It was for them that Martin grabbed his glass and knocked it back. Final drink of the holiday. Of the year? Of his life?

'You should be getting a bouquet of red plum, baking spice and warm earth, and flavours of currant and raspberry; layered with crab-apple-acidity and cacao-ish tannins on a lasting finish.'

It tasted like sugar-free Dr Pepper to Martin. 'It's not undrinkable.'

'I'll take it,' she smiled in relief. 'All packed?'

'Still wanna see that massive pornstache?' said Martin, waving his passport from the back of the cab.

'Next time.'

'Good luck with the exam. Reckon you'll blow them away?'

'Watch me,' said Aubrey. 'Hey Martin, just remember, I'm only a Pinot Noir away.'

45

Cold Turkey

Six days after the triple murder at the Old Elysium Vineyard, Martin Moretti was back at Buxton Police Station. December 30th. Crimbo limbo, perfectly summed up by the dull drizzle. When nobody knows what day of the week it is. Too soon to diet, too sick of turkey sandwiches, turkey curry, turkey fajitas, turkey sushi, and turkey tiramisu.

And there on the steps outside stood Superintendent Radnor, with his lovely smashable face. A cardboard box under one arm, he was dressed in full riot gear. Must be off to the bingo hall. The Superintendent looked frazzled and Martin knew why. The headlines were filled with the football hooliganism from Boxing Day. Local derby too; the spirit of peace and goodwill was definitely over.

'Moretti, what are you doing here?' said Radnor, his spare hand momentarily twitched toward his pepper spray.

'Replace your rum, sir,' said Martin, presenting him with the bottle.

'Er, this isn't going in anywhere sideways, is it?' said Radnor. His cardboard box contained vodka lime-jelly shots. Of course, the festive morale-boosting police party before the madness of New Year's Eve. 'Looks better rum than my Tesco Value.'

'I don't think they sell that anymore.'

'There's still a job for you here, y'know.'

'Got the call from Renzo Brambilla, then?'

'A Captain Gallois, actually. Plus, saw it on the news. "The French Conundrum." Very impressive policework, Chief

Inspector. What were your conclusions?'

'Started deducting. Got alcohol poisoning. Case closed,' Martin said with nonchalant finality. 'But, actually, I thought I might try and make a go of it myself, sir. New year, new me, and all that.'

The Superintendent gave an understanding nod. 'Good luck out there, Moretti. And don't forget, even in the midst of winter, you can still find—within you—an invincible summer. Believe you can and you're halfway there.' Certainly, Martin wouldn't miss these morning pep talks. They shook hands and, for old time's sake, Radnor handed him a jelly shot. Cordially accepting the plastic pot, he'd bin it later. 'Happy New Year, Moretti.'

Sitting by the river, lazily playing with the pot, Martin felt revitalised. Seven days sober. Sleeping better. His mood was better. His skin looked better (though, maybe that was just away from the mountain windburn). The Derbyshire weather was wet and miserable, diesel-choked cars grunting down Bakewell Road, but Martin was feeling good. It had been simple to quit the booze, simpler than expected. And now with good friends around, Martin had a sneaky feeling there were many ways, in fact, to catch a healthy giddy euphoria.

He tossed and caught the jelly shot. For the final time, he was holding alcohol in his hand; the wobbly wonder of the lime green pot reminiscent of celebrations, good times, jelly and ice cream of old. 2023 was going to be his year. Martin was proud, also, of how calmly he'd handled Superintendent Radnor. He would reward himself with just one nibble on the corner of the lime jelly. Perhaps, actually, just this once, the whole thing. Especially as he had missed breakfast that morning. Yes, just the one shot. After all, one jelly shot couldn't hurt. Right?

MARTIN MORETTI WILL RETURN

Printed in Dunstable, United Kingdom

67334283R00201